SLEEPER

ALSO BY GENE RIEHL

Quantico Rules

SLEEPER

GENE RIEHL

ST. MARTIN'S PRESS
NEW YORK

This is a work of fiction. All the characters, places, and events protrayed in this novel either are products of the author's imagination or are used fictitiously.

www.stmartins.com

Library of Congress Cataloging-in-Publication Data

Riehl, Gene.
    Sleeper / Gene Riehl.—1st ed.
      p. cm.
    ISBN 0-312-31053-6
    EAN 978-0312-31053-0
     1. Government investigators—Fiction. 2. Espionage, North Korean—Fiction. 3. Undercover operations—Fiction. 4. Women spies—Fiction. I. Title.
PS3618.I3924S59 2005
813'.6—dc22

2004051413

First Edition: March 2005

10 9 8 7 6 5 4 3 2 1

In memory of the Honorable Judith N. Keep, Judge,
United States District Court for the
Southern District of California—
so much courage, so much grace

SLEEPER

PROLOGUE

Samantha Williamson wasn't born to be an assassin.

She was never meant to be a whore either, or an art thief, or a terrorist.

And she wasn't any of those things until the day Pyongyang decided it was time to begin her training. The occasion was American-born Samantha's sixteenth birthday. For all but the first forty-eight hours of her life she'd been called Sung Kim, and she had no awareness of ever having been anyone else.

Paris was unusually warm that day, especially for so early in spring. Tourists jammed the Rive Gauche, the sidewalks of the Quai des Grands Augustins a crawling throng of visitors from all over the world. Sitting with her adoptive parents at a table in the Salon de Thé—one of the most popular of the outdoor cafes along the street—Sung Kim reached across and touched her mother's hand.

"How's your tea, Mom?" she asked, in the flawless English they'd taught her before she'd ever heard a word of Korean.

"Fine, sweetheart," her mother answered, but her eyes stayed every bit as sad as they'd been all day. She squeezed Sung Kim's hand hard enough to make her wince. "You're so special, my darling," she told her daughter. "You will always be special to me."

Sung Kim looked more closely at her mother, puzzled by the somber tone of her voice, but she had no problem with the words themselves. Her parents had been telling her how special she was since she was old enough to understand the word, and by the time she was twelve she'd decided to believe it. Now, as a full-blown teenager, she was tall, leggy, model-slim, and utterly convinced her life would never be anything but perfect.

Like this trip to Paris, for example, and this flawless day.

Across the street the Pont Saint-Michel seemed almost alive, as the bridge bore its burden of noisy traffic across the Seine. Even the tea was somehow sweeter today, almost as satisfying as the crunch of her teeth into the Brie-slathered hard rolls brought by an overattentive waiter who didn't bother to hide the longing in his gaze at every part of Sung Kim's body.

She'd been to Paris before, of course. Her adoptive parents had made sure she would grow up knowing all about the world outside North Korea. It was an important part of her education, an invaluable preparation for the college years she would spend in America. And it was pretty much the same for her classmates back home, as well. All ten of the *ipyangban*, the "adopted children," spent their school holidays in the most glamorous cities in the world. Like Sung Kim, they'd all been told the same lie: that they'd been abandoned by Americans too obsessed with wealth to be bothered by unwanted children. Like Sung Kim, they would never know the truth about the kidnappings. She took her eyes off the crowded sidewalk and looked at her mother again. "What's the matter, Mom? Are you feeling okay?"

Her mother nodded. "Just tired, honey." Her smile was even smaller this time. "I think the trip's beginning to catch up to me."

Her mom's pretty face, with her strong chin and dark brown eyes, looked so morose Sung Kim wanted to stretch out and hug her.

She turned to her father. She was lucky to have been adopted by someone so kind and generous. Sure he was strict, but all fathers were. She wasn't the only one of the *ipyangban* who hardly ever got to leave the compound in which they all lived back home, the two-square-mile walled enclosure near the palace that set the elite apart from the rest of Pyongyang. Her dad's vigilance was just another sign of his love for her. Even here, in the safety of Paris, he couldn't seem to relax. Across the table his strong square features were frowning, his eyes scanning back and forth, up and down the street, as though he were waiting for someone to join them. Sung Kim couldn't see his feet but she could hear the nervous tapping of one of his shoes against the pavement.

"Having a good time, Dad?" she asked him.

He nodded but said nothing. Her father had a great sense of humor, but she couldn't remember him smiling since the day they'd arrived.

"Hey," she said. "I'm a big girl now, and I'm perfectly safe here." She glanced over her shoulder toward the kitchen, then made a mock-serious face at her dad. "The waiter's the only one you've got to look out for."

This time he did manage to smile, but his eyes never left the street.

Sung Kim followed his gaze but couldn't tell what he was looking at. The street was busy, clogged with the Mercedes taxicabs that flooded Paris. From the sidewalk she heard a number of languages. French, of course, but German, too, in addition to Italian, Japanese, and English.

It wasn't hard to pick out the Americans.

All you had to do was listen.

It wasn't only their distinctive English—the same English Sung Kim spoke—it was the way they talked. Overly loud, aggressive, obnoxious. We own the world, their manner shouted, and we'll act any damned way we want to.

Sung Kim turned back to her mom, but a sudden commotion over her right shoulder brought her eyes back around to the sidewalk. Two men had pushed their way right up to their table and stood staring at the three of them. Short men in American clothing, tan slacks, and flowered shirts not tucked in. The heavier of the two was carrying a newspaper.

"No!" Sung Kim's dad shouted as the man raised the hand carrying the newspaper. She heard what sounded like a sharp cough. Her father's hands flew toward his throat as he fell back into his chair.

"Dad!" she screamed, as she started for him.

Before she got there Sung Kim heard a second cough. She swung back toward her mother just in time to see her mom's body slump sideways.

Now the man with the newspaper turned to Sung Kim.

"Please," she heard herself saying, her voice distant in her ears. "Dear God, please."

He lifted the paper. "God? This hasn't got anything to do with God."

Sung Kim stared at him, frozen as she waited to die.

But suddenly a third man darted from the crowd and crashed headlong into the shooter, knocking him sideways, slamming the newspaper and gun out of his hand. Sung Kim saw the black steel pistol clatter along the sidewalk. The shooter's partner pulled the gunman to his feet and they raced off into the mob.

Sung Kim couldn't make herself move. Or look at her parents. She tried to form a thought, but it was impossible. A moment later, the man who'd saved her life grabbed her arm and yanked her toward the street.

"Quickly," he said in Korean. "We cannot stay here."

"But . . ." Sung Kim said. "I can't . . ." She tried to pull the man's hand away. "My parents," she said. "I can't leave my mom and—"

"Now!" He jerked harder on her arm. "The Americans are monsters. They murdered your parents. They won't quit until they kill you, too."

Sung Kim pried at his fingers but he was too strong.

"No!" she hollered, as he dragged her toward a waiting taxi. "You can't make me . . ."

Her voice died as he pulled the taxi door open and shoved her inside. The Mercedes accelerated hard. Sung Kim swung around in the seat, desperate to see her parents. The crowd had finally realized what happened. A tall woman was the first to reach her mom, to extend her hand and close Sung Kim's mother's eyes. Sung Kim stared at the tall woman until the Mercedes turned the next corner. Her shoulders slumped as she began to cry.

Back at the Salon de Thé, the tall woman stepped into the street to make sure the Mercedes was out of sight before she turned back to Sung Kim's parents.

"Okay," she said in English. "They're gone."

Sung Kim's mother rose from the chair first, followed by her husband. They came around and stood facing the crowd, which had grown even larger as word of the shooting raced up and down the street. The tall woman smiled at the astonished faces around them.

"Sorry if we startled you," she said in French. "But your reaction will make the movie all the better."

She turned toward Sung Kim's parents and began to applaud. A teenager in the crowd started to clap, as well, and suddenly everyone was doing so. Sung Kim's parents bowed, but her mother couldn't help looking up the street, at the corner where the Mercedes had disappeared.

SEPTEMBER 1997

BUENOS AIRES, ARGENTINA

Tonight Sung Kim was a whore.

And eager to get on with her mission.

At twenty-one she was well aware of her position in the spotlight. As the first of the *ipyanghan* considered ready by Division 39 of the Central Workers Party to be relocated in America, the success of the Division's "sleeper" program would be judged by her performance here. For five years she'd been studying fine art, psychology, and a number of languages from the finest English-speaking tutors Pyongyang had managed to recruit. Away from the classroom her training had been every bit as good. She'd learned her tradecraft from world-class murderers and saboteurs, from cat burglars and prostitutes, all of them disaffected Americans from every level of criminality in the United States, and now it was time to see how it worked in the real world.

By ten o'clock that night, Buenos Aires was ready to party. The street called Macacha Guemes was bursting into life. A stream of diminutive Fiat Uno taxicabs arrived and departed from the wide sidewalk in front of the Hilton Hotel toward which Sung Kim strolled. Groups of expensively clothed young Argentinians strolled toward the hotel as well. With their slicked-back hair, silk turtleneck shirts, and linen jackets, the men looked like movie stars, but it was the women who made Sung Kim shake her head. It was hard to disguise yourself as a prostitute these days. Despite her micro-mini leather skirt, the four-inch spikes on her come-fuck-me pumps, her "big hair" curly brown wig, and the huge shoulder bag swinging against her hip, she didn't look all that different from the women around her.

But different enough, she discovered a few moments later, as she approached the tall glass entrance to the hotel.

"*¡Dios mío!*" a slouching man in a cheap suit said as he blocked her way on the sidewalk. "*¿Tienes algo para mí?*"

Sung Kim laughed. Did she have something for him? "*Lo siento, chico.*" she told him. Sorry, pal. "*Puede ser la próxima.*" Maybe next time.

He stepped aside as she pushed past him and continued into the entrance to the hotel. The doorman in his blue blazer and gray slacks looked her up and down, but only for a moment. This was Buenos Aires, after all, and the Hilton was a popular hotel for businessmen from all over the world. Sung Kim wasn't the only hooker expected here tonight. He held the door open. She tossed her head as she passed, and caught him grinning.

She crossed the enormous lobby, glancing up at the underside of the hotel's glass roof, seven stories above. The place was really quite elegant. Had to be costing Kwon Jong a fortune to stay here. Money he'd stolen from his own government, her government. Money that could have bought food for the starving children who lay dying all over Pyongyang. The thought darkened her mood and made her even more eager to get to him.

Kwon was in suite 491, she'd been told, along with his bodyguards, and they were staying in tonight. Her contact in Buenos Aires had checked only ten minutes ago. At the bank of elevators on the left side of the lobby, she pushed the button and a door to her right slid open almost immediately. There were two men in the elevator as she stepped in and pushed the button for the fourth floor. On the way up she could feel them staring at her legs, until one of them broke the silence.

"Christ," he said in semislurred English to his companion. "I wouldn't mind having those legs wrapped around my neck."

In your dreams, Sung Kim thought, although she knew better than to say it out loud. Later, when the cops talked to these two fools, she didn't want them remembering the Argentinian whore who spoke idiomatic English.

The elevator arrived at the fourth floor and she got out. She could hear the two men talking about her ass as the doors slid shut. In the hallway, her eyes turned hard. Suddenly she could hear the words of her trainer as clearly as if he were standing next to her.

In fast, Sung Kim. Out fast. No mercy.

She read the sign opposite the elevator. Suite 491 was to her left and would be near the end of the corridor. She kicked her ridiculous high heels off and headed in that direction. As she passed the rooms on both sides she could hear the muted sounds of television but nothing else, until the soft scrape of a door opening behind her brought her to a dead stop. Sung Kim whirled, one hand reaching for the weapon in her shoulder bag, but stopped when she saw a little girl with huge brown eyes staring at her. A moment later an adult arm reached out and snatched the child back into the room. Sung Kim's heartbeat took a moment to steady again as she turned and continued toward the end of the hallway.

Suite 491 was coming up, Sung Kim saw as she passed 481. The fifth door on her left. She stopped for a moment to reach into her shoulder bag and withdraw the Beretta 92FS nine-millimeter pistol with three-inch silencer she'd chosen for tonight. She held the brutish black weapon close to her body, out of sight of anyone who might step out into the hall, then advanced toward the door.

At the door she tapped softly. *"La camarera,"* she said. The maid. *"Está listo su traje."* Your suit is pressed and ready.

There was no answer. Sung Kim knocked again, but as she did so she heard a door opening behind her, then a rush of footsteps. She pivoted toward the sound but wasn't able to completely face the bear of a man hurtling toward her before he kicked her in the back, a blow that sent her flying into the wall to the left of the door. The Beretta spun from her hand and arched through the air before tumbling to the floor a dozen feet away. Her shoulder bag slid off as she crashed to the carpet, but she jumped instantly to her feet to face the man shuffling toward her.

She stepped back against the wall to give herself room and an instant to assess the danger. The man was half a head taller and at least a hundred pounds heavier. He wasn't Korean. Her contact had been wrong about something else as well. There wasn't supposed to be another hotel room involved. The two bodyguards were never supposed to leave Kwon Jong alone. Which meant the other one had to be close by.

The big man bent his knees for an instant, then sprang at her with amazing speed, his hands up, an eager smile on his face. His right fist shot toward her head, all his body weight behind the punch, but Sung Kim deflected the blow. As his fist passed her head, she used both hands to grab his shirt, to pull him toward her in a classic *akido* response. Off balance now, he had no strength to resist as she pivoted and moved her shoulder under his body, used the momentum of his superior weight to throw him over her and onto the floor. He fell hard, but was up in a flash and facing her again. His smile got bigger now, as he appeared to relish the idea of her worthiness as an opponent.

She took a fighting stance, feet shoulder-width apart, her body turned until her right shoulder was facing him, "blading" herself to present a smaller target. He did the same, then advanced toward her more slowly this time. She waited for him to attack, to give her an idea of how he'd been trained, to reveal a vulnerability she might use. He approached to within kicking distance and raised his knee, preparing for a snap kick. Sung Kim waited for the twitch of movement that would send his foot flicking toward her head. He kicked but she danced out of range. He shuffled forward and tried again—like a boxer using his jab to measure the distance—but again she moved away. His smile seemed a little more forced now.

He was using a mixture of *hapkido* and *akido*, Sung Kim decided. A combination of fists and feet. But he had a problem with his arms. Both times he'd kicked at her, his arms had gone wide in an attempt to maintain balance. Not as wide as an amateur, but a dangerous flaw anyway.

Now he was as bladed as she was. She slid toward him, inviting another kick, her eyes locked on his midsection, waiting for him to telegraph which leg he'd use. He rocked back, "unweighting" his front leg, but the instant his foot swung toward her, his arms went wide. Now his fists were useless. She slipped into his body, inside the effective arc of his kick, then used both hands to parry his thigh and throw his leg past her. The movement served to cock her right arm for her own strike. She crouched slightly and felt the energy gathering in her legs. *All power comes from the ground.* She fired her elbow up and out, directly into the base of the giant's nose. In the quiet of the hallway, she could hear the cartilage tearing away as it slid upward into the sinus cavity above his eyes. He staggered back, his hands on his face, trying to stop the blood that was pouring through his fingers, and Sung Kim slid her foot behind his ankle. He tripped over her foot, twisted as he fell, and crashed on his stomach. Before he could turn over and continue fighting, she leaped on him, all her weight on her knees as she drove them into his back. He grunted as the air rushed from his lungs. She reached for his head, one hand grabbing his greasy brown hair, the other gripping his chin. She pulled his head back, then wrenched his chin around and back toward her. The sound of the bones in his neck breaking echoed in the corridor. His body seemed to deflate as she let go of his head and watched it bounce against the floor.

She was up in an instant, her eyes searching for the Beretta, but she heard the knob turning on Kwon Jong's door before she had a chance to start for the pistol. She grabbed for her shoulder bag on the floor instead, managed to pull out her knife just as the door swung open and the second bodyguard stepped into the doorway. Sung Kim brought the stiletto up hard. The point of the blade struck just below his sternum and traveled from there directly into his heart. He frowned for an instant before falling. Sung Kim stepped up close, left the knife in him as she caught his body and pushed it back into the room.

She had to hurry now. She hadn't made enough noise to bring anyone out into the hall, but that didn't mean one of the guests hadn't called hotel security. Or that Kwon himself hadn't loaded up a shotgun and was now lying in wait for her inside the suite.

She darted back into the hallway and scooped up the Beretta before returning to the doorway. Holding the weapon with two hands, she stepped through. The living room of the suite was deserted. She glanced at the couch and chairs, at the computer work station near the glass doors out to the balcony, then to her right. Through the open door she saw a bedroom. She crept through the door and swept the room with the Beretta. It was empty. She retreated through the door and stepped across the living room to the closed door on the left side of the suite. She paused outside the door for an instant, then turned the knob and burst through.

Kwon Jong sat upright on the king-size bed. He was wearing a white hotel bathrobe and holding a small revolver. His hands trembled as he tried to train the weapon on her. Sung Kim swung the Beretta into place and fired. The silenced pistol coughed quietly. Kwon's round face was expressionless, as a crimson-black hole appeared in the center of his forehead.

ONE

In her rented Lincoln Navigator, the massive black SUV that allowed her to see over traffic, it wasn't difficult for Sung Kim to follow Lyman Davidson from his three-story house in Kalorama Heights to the O'Bannon Gallery on Thomas Jefferson Street in Georgetown.

She watched him leave his silver Mercedes coupe with the gallery's parking valet, before she tailed the valet half a block down the street to the pay lot the O'Bannon was using for the opening of the Bourney exhibit. Satisfied the Mercedes would be there when she returned, Sung Kim drove up to M Street, turned right, and parked in the first lot she came to. She switched off the engine and sat for a moment, uneasy with the nagging sensation that something wasn't right.

The steady beat of her pulse was too slow, for one thing, and her breathing was far too regular. Had she been doing this too long? After eight years, had her work become too routine? She forced herself to picture what Pyongyang would do if she botched this job. The images made her shudder, but they did the trick. Now her palms were moist, her breathing quicker and shallower, as she slipped out of the SUV, grabbed her canvas book bag, and started back toward the Mercedes.

The overcast sky had brought some serious humidity, and she was sweating by the time she got to the rear of the valet lot. She stood for a moment on the narrow sidewalk, under the canopy of a dogwood still heavy with summer foliage, waiting for her chance. In her sleeveless gray Georgetown University sweatshirt, blue jeans, and Reeboks—with her shoulder-length blond wig tied back in a ponytail—she looked exactly like the all-American girl she'd been trained to become. Like Gidget, Sung Kim couldn't help thinking. Like the girl in the old movies she and her parents used to watch in Pyongyang. The thought of her dead parents still brought an ache to the back of her throat and made her even more anxious to get to the work that would continue to avenge them.

As she watched the parking lot, the same dark-haired valet who'd delivered Davidson's car pulled in with a white Mazda sedan. When he sprinted back toward the gallery, she hurried to the Mercedes. She dropped to the ground behind the right front tire and pulled her book bag with her as she slid underneath and went to work. Three minutes later she was finished. She listened as one of the valets brought another car, and waited until the running footsteps receded before zipping out from under the Mercedes and hustling back toward M Street.

At her Navigator, Sung Kim opened the heavy rear door, climbed in, and closed it behind her. The black tint on the windows made it impossible for anyone to see in. She sat on the carpeted floor and wriggled out of her jeans before pulling the sweatshirt over her head. In her black panties and bra, she reached for her makeup kit, a leather-covered carryall that opened like a fisherman's tackle box. Now she had to risk turning on a light. She toggled a switch in the lid to illuminate the built-in mirror. Tugging at her blond wig, Sung Kim pulled it away from the custom-made skullcap covering her real hair. She blinked at her image in the mirror. No matter how often she did this, the sight of herself completely bald never failed to startle her.

Next she grabbed a new applicator pad and a round container of L'Oréal True Match No. 6, the darkest shade she could risk without calling attention to herself. She used the makeup on her face and neck, then lightly on her arms. For her eyes she applied black mascara on the lashes, black eyebrow pencil to darken her brows, and a thin streak of liner to make her eyes look bigger. She used a crimson shade of volumizing lipstick with an added collagen complex that thickened her lips and changed the entire look of her face.

From the bottom of the makeup kit, she brought out a single strand of pearls and fastened it around her neck. Back into the kit, she retrieved her panty hose and a pair of open-toed Isaac Mizrahi pumps with three-inch heels, half price at Nordie's the same day she'd bought the dress.

Sung Kim had to work a little harder as she slithered into the panty hose, before slipping her shoes on and rising into a kneeling position. She reached for the garment bag hanging on the hook over the window to her right, withdrew the dress she'd bought for the mission: a killer black sheath that accentuated the length and shape of her legs. She pulled the dress over her skullcapped head, tugged it down until the hem settled into place a few inches above her knees.

Careful not to damage her panty hose, she knee-walked to the front passenger seat and picked up the jet-black wig she'd chosen for tonight. She slid into the seat, where she used the mirror in the back of the sun visor to put on the wig, making sure the double-sided tape on her skullcap kept it in place. From a midsize white leather purse lying on the console between the seats she pulled a brush, then used it to smooth the short straight black hair that extended to her jaw line, as well as the razor-edged bangs that extended down her forehead.

Back into the purse, she grabbed her contact lens case. Using the mirror, she put the lenses on her eyes, then stared in the mirror to check on how she'd done. She saw that Gidget had disappeared. In her place was Sarah Freed, a dark-eyed woman as beautiful as an Egyptian princess. As beautiful as a princess on her way to meet the pharoah.

A few minutes later—her Navigator safely in the hands of a parking valet—Sung Kim stepped through the double doors of the O'Bannon Gallery and looked around the narrow room until she saw Lyman Davidson. According to Thomas Franklin, the lean and immaculately suited multimillionaire with shaggy dark hair and suggestive brown eyes was a leg man. In her high heels and above-the-knee sheath, she would give him exactly what he wanted to see.

She ignored him to stroll among the thirty or so people in the room, pausing to pluck a glass of Chardonnay from the tray of a passing waiter before moving to the wall farthest from where she saw Davidson inspecting one of the larger of the Bourneys. She pretended to study the painting in front of her, shifting her weight from hip to hip, sensing his eyes on her. She turned suddenly and saw that she'd been right. He started to smile, but she swung back to the painting. Davidson was a sophisticated man. To be blatant with him would be a mistake.

Half a minute later she crossed the room. Those movie-star eyes were still watching her, Sung Kim noticed, so she tossed her hair just enough to make it swirl, and caught him staring again. This time she was the one who smiled as she made her way toward the painting he was examining. A moment later she was standing next to him, giving him a chance to smell the woodsy fragrance of her Paloma Picasso perfume before she leaned in to take a closer look at the small white card next to the picture.

Museum, the painting was titled. Under the title was the name Hanson Bourney, and the year 2001. The picture—about two feet by three feet— showed a young woman sitting on a bench in the center of a room, the walls of which were covered with paintings. Beyond the woman were shadowy figures of people staring into the room in which she sat. Sung Kim shifted her weight until one bare shoulder was touching Davidson's arm. He turned to her.

"So what do you think?" he said. "Does Bourney have a future?"

"Not with this one. It's too derivative." She looked at him. "He should have spent less time studying Hopper and more learning how to do his own work."

"Ouch." Davidson paused. "But couldn't you say the same thing about Hopper himself? He was hardly original either . . . Few painters are. Last time I checked, he didn't have a patent on urban realism."

"I'm not talking about the realism. I'm talking about what Hopper called the 'decay,' the destruction of perception by painting a picture of it."

Suddenly Davidson was looking at her differently. His heavy-lidded eyes stopped glancing at her boobs and stayed fixed on her face.

"Hopper's way of dealing with the decay," she continued, "was to add story elements to make up for it." She turned to the picture. "At first glance the woman seems to be enjoying the museum. Then we notice the figures behind her, staring in at her, and we see that to them she's just another part of the exhibit. Hopper did the same thing in 1927 with *Automat*. A woman at a table drinking a cup of coffee, a window in the background. It becomes clear that she's just as packaged at her table in front of the window as the food behind the little windows of the automat. But the decay of first-hand perception is neutralized by our interest in Hopper's story . . . the woman's story." Sung Kim glanced at Davidson. "It's a good technique to emulate, but it's still a rip-off."

Davidson looked at the painting again, then at Sung Kim. "I know the Hopper you're talking about. I think you may be right." He smiled. "You talk like a teacher, or a collector."

"Close. I was married to a collector."

He smiled again, his brown eyes on her brown contacts. "I'm a collector myself."

"That's a shame." She added just a trace of teasing in her voice. "One art collector per lifetime is my motto."

"But we can still be friends, I hope."

"I don't know about that." She shook her head playfully. "I already have quite a few."

He grinned. "You're not making this easy for me."

"You don't look like the kind of man who needs much help."

"I didn't think so either, but I have the feeling I could use some now." He looked toward the door, then back at her. "Tell you what. Let me buy you a drink. We can walk down the street and still make it back here to catch the rest of the exhibit."

"Ordinarily, I'd love to do that . . . but not tonight."

He frowned. "I caught you looking in my direction. A couple of times. Did I read that the wrong way?"

"Not at all. It's just that I came here straight from the office, and I'm exhausted. The only thing I want to do is look around and go home."

He nodded. "I can certainly relate to that . . . but if you change your mind, I'll be around for another hour."

Sung Kim smiled. "You'll be the first to know," she said, then turned and walked away.

· · ·

But Davidson didn't wait an hour.

Thirty-two minutes after she'd walked away from him, Sung Kim saw him heading out the door.

She followed him as far as the gallery's front window, where she watched him give the valet his ticket. The young man sprinted off toward the parking lot as she moved closer to the double front doors. Five minutes passed. The second of the two valets went for a car and was back with it in two minutes. Now Davidson was looking at his watch and beginning to pace. Another three minutes went by before Davidson's valet came running back. Sung Kim stepped through the doors as the young man pulled up, out of breath.

"Sorry, sir," he told Davidson, "but I can't start your car."

"Impossible," Davidson said. "Damned thing's brand-new."

"Gotta be the battery, but I've never seen one so dead. I couldn't even get a sound. No clicking, no grinding, nothing."

Davidson looked around, saw Sung Kim and shook his head. "Hundred and ten grand for a car and it won't even start."

Sung Kim handed her ticket to the valet, who ran off into the darkness.

"Where do you live?" she asked Davidson.

"Not far. Kalorama Heights. I'll grab a cab and take care of my car tomorrow."

"Kalorama? I'm going that way myself. I'd be happy to drop you off."

His eyes brightened. "Thank God for dead batteries."

She smiled. "Be careful what you pray for."

There was a moment of silence, the two of them looking at each other, before Sung Kim's Navigator pulled up. She walked around the car and gave the valet a five-dollar bill. He held the door open while she slid behind the wheel. By the time she got there, Lyman Davidson was already in the passenger seat.

Half an hour later they pulled up in front of Davidson's house, a three-story Federal-style brick mansion just off Massachusetts Avenue in Kalorama Heights, with a balcony over the front door and creamy white wood-work around the windows.

"Won't you come in for a drink, Sarah?" he asked. "It's the least I can do to reward you for your kindness."

She shook her head. "It's kind of you to offer, but I've had a long day. Perhaps another time."

"What if I confess I have an ulterior motive? You know a lot about art. I buy a lot of it. I'd really like to know what you think of my latest purchase."

Sung Kim smiled. "You want to show me your etchings?"

He used his index finger to make an X across his chest. "No etchings, I promise. And no ham-fisted passes either, if that's what you're worried about."

She reached out and touched his hand. "I'm not trying to be rude, but I really am exhausted."

He glanced toward his house, then looked at her again. "Well, if I can't thank you with a drink, or lure you inside with my new paintings, I guess I'll just say good night."

Sung Kim held out her hand. "It was a pleasure to meet you, Lyman," she said. "Perhaps we'll run into one another again."

His smile was forced. "I suppose it could happen."

He opened the door and got out, closed it, and started up the brick walkway toward the house. Sung Kim let him get a full twenty feet away before she zipped down the passenger window.

"Lyman," she called. "Hold on a second."

T W O

After their second Courvoisier, Sung Kim decided he was ready.

"Okay," she told him, as they sat together in upholstered chairs across from his unlit fireplace in the living room. "Let's go see what you bought."

Davidson nodded, then held up his nearly empty glass. "Let's refresh these first. We can take them along."

Sung Kim smiled. "I never say no to Courvoisier."

He reached for the bottle on the small round table between the chairs and refilled their glasses. She uncrossed her legs so that her dress rode up her thighs, then rose from the chair, glass in one hand and white purse in the other. Davidson took his eyes off her legs and looked at the purse.

"You can leave that here," he said. "The house is locked up tight . . . and my housekeeper has been with me for twenty years."

Sung Kim shook her head. "A lady doesn't go anywhere without her purse, Lyman, surely you know that." She paused. "I would have thought your housekeeper would greet you when you come home." As good a way as any to verify what Sung Kim had been told, that it was the house-keeper's night off.

"We have a deal. She doesn't bug me for a big-screen TV, and I let her watch her favorite nighttime shows in peace."

Sung Kim nodded, but he hadn't really answered her question. She reached out and took his arm. Davidson turned and led the way out of the living room, then to his left down a wide corridor. They passed two open doorways on the right. Sitting rooms, with expensive furnishings and mostly-red Persian carpets. Davidson stopped at the next open doorway, this one on their left. He went through and she followed him into a library with a fifteen-foot ceiling and book-filled shelves lining two of the walls. The other two walls were filled with paintings. Sung Kim's eyes ranged across the collection—many landscapes—and nodded her approval. The man knew how to collect.

Davidson led her past leather couches and chairs to the library's back wall. On the gleaming maple floor, leaning against the wall, stood three oil paintings.

Sung Kim stepped up to them. "Interesting," she said, gesturing toward the first of the paintings, a William Aiken Walker oil on canvas entitled *Noon Day Pause in the Cotton Field*. A little over a foot high, two feet across, the picture showed a horse-drawn wagon filled with cotton and surrounded by the slaves who'd picked it. Sung Kim glanced at the wall to their left, toward the paintings hanging there. "I don't see a lot of figures in the rest of your collection. What made you decide to buy the Walker?"

"Walker's going to be big again. I paid seventy-five thousand, but I'll hold it five years and get ten times that much."

She nodded. He was right. One day she'd be stealing Walker herself.

"Nice Meeker, too," she said, looking at the second of his purchases, a painting she knew to be entitled *Sunlight on the Bayou*. "*Sunlight's* one of his best, don't you think?"

"Another good investment, that's for sure."

"They're all nice," she said, gesturing toward the three paintings on the floor. "But not quite what I was expecting, Lyman. A man with the good sense to jump on a Walker has to have something else in the house. Something to knock my socks off." She sipped brandy from her glass and smiled. "Or all the rest of my . . ." She shook her head. "Jesus, listen to me. A couple of drinks and I forget all about growing up in Boston."

He leaned toward her. "The stuff down here is what I speculate with.

My real keepers are upstairs, locked away for safekeeping. A few close friends get to see them. Nobody else."

"How close a friend do you have to be?"

"I think you just might qualify."

She allowed him to lead her out of the library and back toward the front of the house, to the wide staircase leading to the top two floors. The steps themselves were built of the same polished maple that filled the rest of the house, and a crimson carpet formed a runner up the center, held in place by bronze rods.

On the second floor they moved to the end of a long corridor, the walls lined with exquisite paintings of every period and style. The door at the end looked ordinary enough, but the alarm panel set into the right-side jamb bothered Sung Kim. It was part of the same Ademco Vista-40 system she'd seen when they came through the front door of the house. A good system, too good. She couldn't beat the Ademco, not without spending the whole night working on it, and that was clearly out of the question. She would just have to do the best she could with the equipment she'd been born with.

Davidson moved up close to the door, his body between her and the keypad. Sung Kim glanced back down the corridor. The housekeeper was supposed to be visiting her kids in Baltimore tonight but she might pop out of any one of these doors. Sung Kim checked her watch. It was after eleven. Maybe the housekeeper was asleep. *Maybe.* As a professional, Sung Kim detested the word.

She turned back to Davidson, stepped up to his right side, close enough that her right breast pushed into his arm. He made no attempt to get away so she pushed harder. This time he edged closer to her, encouraging the contact.

"Sorry," she said. "I know I'm crowding you, but I can't wait to see what you've got." She laughed, low and in the back of her throat. "In your secret room, I mean."

He reached for the keypad and she looked around his arm, saw him touch the numbers 1-6-3-9. A green light on the control panel began to blink. Davidson pulled the door open and stepped into the room. Sung Kim started to follow, but he put out his hand to stop her.

"Give me a second," he said, "to punch in the security code. If I don't shut off the motion detectors, we'll trip every alarm in the house. The cops'll be here before I can call them off."

She nodded, but her eyes stayed on him as he turned back into the room and reached to his right, to what had to be a second keypad, although Sung Kim couldn't see it from where she was standing. Which wouldn't work. Knowing the code to get through the door didn't help if she couldn't disable the alarm once she was inside. She heard three distinct beeps as he touched the keypad before reaching for her hand and pulling her into the room.

He flipped a switch and the interior lights came on: museum-quality baby spots from track lighting that crisscrossed the ceiling. The walls were painted flat black in the three-hundred or so square foot space, and the effect was elegant. Almost as though the paintings were suspended without any support at all. Sung Kim couldn't remember seeing an exhibit lit better.

She saw the *Madonna* immediately. There was no use pretending she didn't. It was much more important to pretend she was surprised to see it here.

"My God," she said, as she stepped toward the famous da Vinci, a fourteen-by-twenty-inch depiction of Mary with the baby Jesus, the infant reaching for a yarn winder, a Renaissance-era machine shaped like the cross he would eventually die on. "You've got one of the copies Leonardo himself may have painted."

Davidson joined her in front of the painting, entitled *Madonna with the Yarn Winder*, a copy of the da Vinci masterpiece believed lost in antiquity. One of three copies art historians continued to argue about.

"I haven't had it long," he said. "Bought it in New York last April."

"I didn't see anything in the papers."

"Got it from a private collection. People like that don't want publicity. Art theft is so brazen nowadays, the collectors don't want anyone to know what they own. Half the time they don't even report what's stolen."

Sung Kim nodded. Rich people went to great pains to keep from alerting the wrong people to the presence of their collections. Thomas Franklin was a good example of one, and Franklin—her own billionaire—would have no problem at all with keeping this *Madonna* to himself.

Davidson smiled. "I have a bar in the master suite. Let's freshen our drinks in there and come back here later." He turned toward the door. "If you'll step out into the hall I'll reset the alarm. That way we can take our time with our drinks."

Sung Kim moved toward him and he turned back to her. She couldn't allow him to lock the door again. She stumbled as she got to him and he reached out to steady her, his hands on her shoulders a lot longer than they needed to be.

"You know," she told him, her words slurred perfectly. "I'd really like to see the resht . . . the rest of your collection first." She reached out and stroked his arm. "Then we won't have to worry about coming back in here at all."

He grinned. "Sounds great to me. Let's get started." He glanced over his shoulder. "I've got a Matisse over here you might enjoy." He started toward the back wall. Behind him, Sung Kim reached into her purse and withdrew the weapon she'd chosen for tonight. She lifted it and pulled the trigger.

Davidson stopped dead. "Jesus!" he said. "What the hell was that?" He started to turn toward her, then stiffened suddenly, his arms and legs jerking wildly, before he slumped to his knees and toppled to the floor.

Sung Kim turned and hurried back to the door. She checked the corridor for any sign of the housekeeper, saw nothing, then started to close the door before realizing she couldn't do that. Without punching in the correct code on the Ademco panel to her left, the silent alarm would go off. The police would be here in minutes, maybe—in a ritzy neighborhood like Kalorama Heights—even faster.

She swung the door almost closed, then turned and went to work.

Eight minutes later, she'd finished cleaning up the traces of her presence.

She left her brandy glass—wiped clean of prints—on the dark carpet and searched the rest of the carpet until she'd gathered up anything else that might tie her to this room.

Satisfied she'd done everything she could, Sung Kim removed the *Madonna* from the wall and held it by the edge of the frame in one hand as she returned to the door and opened it again to check the corridor. She stuck her head into the hallway and listened intently. Now she could hear it. A television set. Damn it. She hadn't heard it before. The housekeeper was here. And she'd just opened her door.

Sung Kim stepped out into the hallway, turned back and once again closed the vault door almost all the way, then hustled toward the stairs. As she approached the landing, the housekeeper came around the corner and stopped dead. Seventy, at least, Sung Kim guessed, dressed in a dark blue bathrobe and brown slippers. Her gray hair was going in every direction at once, as were her brown eyes.

"Who . . . ?" she said. "I heard a noise . . ." She saw the painting in Sung Kim's hand. "What's going on here? Who are you? Where's Mr. Davidson?"

Sung Kim started toward her. The housekeeper turned back toward the stairs, surprisingly quick for her age, and Sung Kim stopped when she heard the sirens.

Shit.

Somehow she'd tripped the silent alarm. Or the housekeeper had called the police. Now there was no time to get to the SUV.

Sung Kim turned and sprinted toward Davidson's bedroom. When she got there, she veered toward the big bed against the far wall, grabbed an oversized pillow, and managed to stuff the *Madonna* inside the case. She darted toward the French doors leading out to a small balcony above the back yard, through the doors, and out to the black iron railing. It was ten feet to the thick lawn below, maybe a little more. She held the *Madonna* in the pillow over the railing and let it go, careful to keep the soft side down. She reached for her high heels and snatched them off, tossed them over as well.

The sirens were closer now.

She considered jumping, but only for an instant. Even with the cushion of the grass it was too far. A twisted ankle would get her caught, and she couldn't get caught. Prison would be the least of her worries. She'd never be allowed to make it as far as a trial.

She turned to her right. There was a drain pipe she might be able to reach if she jumped at it. She looked down and shook her head. If she missed . . . She wouldn't miss. Scrambling over the low railing, she stood on the very edge of the balcony and gathered her strength. The sirens were a block away now, maybe less. She jumped. Her right hand grabbed for the iron drain pipe, caught the pipe, but her downward momentum tore her grip loose. She was falling now . . . her hands desperately trying to find something to save her . . . when she hit a patch of climbing ivy. She clutched it with both hands . . . and felt it tear away from the brick wall.

She hit the lawn hard, but knew how to land. She bent her knees at impact, then rolled immediately into a ball. She was up in an instant, pulling the *Madonna* from the pillowcase. Grabbing her shoes. Racing into the darkness.

THREE

"You can't be serious," Trevor Blaine said, when Monk told him Lyman Davidson's *Madonna* had just been stolen.

It was very quiet in the living room of Blaine's penthouse apartment in the Watergate complex overlooking the Potomac. Monk looked past the thin-faced art dealer, out the window at the lights across the river. On the blue leather couch across from the matching club chairs occupied by Monk and his partner, Roger Forbes, their suspect sat perfectly still.

"When, Agent Monk?" Trevor Blaine asked. "When did it happen?"

Monk allowed the question to hang in the air while he watched for a tell, for something in the man's body language to indicate that Trevor Blaine already knew the answer. He saw nothing. Despite the late hour—half an hour past midnight—Blaine showed not the slightest sign of discomfort. Even his clothes looked relaxed. His light gray silk suit hung on his spare frame as unwrinkled as if it had just come from the cleaners. Monk wasn't surprised. If what he and Roger Forbes had heard about the art dealer from Monk's informant in jail was true, it would take more than just their showing up to rattle him.

"The *Madonna* was stolen from Lyman Davidson's house in Kalorama

Heights about two hours ago," Monk told him. "A woman Davidson was entertaining in his home attacked him and walked out with it."

"Attacked him?"

Monk nodded, but again he said nothing. Davidson was alive, but Monk wasn't about to be more specific about the details of the robbery, not with a suspect, not this early in the investigation.

Trevor Blaine frowned. "What does the FBI have to do with the theft of a painting? I would have thought the Metropolitan Police Department handled something like this."

Monk glanced at Roger Forbes, signaling his partner to answer the question, to give himself a better opportunity to observe Trevor Blaine's reaction. He paid particular attention to the man's eyes, looking for Blaine to glance to his left, a shift of his gaze in that direction, something to indicate his mind's eye might be looking backward as he "watched" the robbery go down. Or a shift of gaze to his right, to "see" the painting Blaine might even now be waiting to fence.

"The money," Roger said. "That's what gets us involved. Davidson claims the *Madonna*'s been appraised at fifteen million dollars. That kind of money, there's a presumption it'll go interstate, or out of the country. If we recover the painting here in the District, the case goes back to the locals."

"Then my next question is, Why are you here? At my flat, I mean. How can I possibly help you with this?"

Monk had to hand it to the Englishman. There wasn't the tiniest variation in the pitch or timbre of his voice, not the slightest lean of his shoulders away from them. Even his hands stayed in the right position, palms open and up. He appeared to be sincerely puzzled by their visit. Monk glanced at Roger and saw his partner's eyebrows lift. Perhaps coming here was a mistake, Roger's expression suggested. Maybe they'd leaned too hard on Monk's informant when they'd sweated him in the interrogation room at the Federal Detention Center downtown. Made it too easy for the criminal informant to trade Trevor Blaine's name for a kind word to the judge before the informant's sentencing next week. It wasn't impossible. Sure as hell wouldn't be the first time a snitch had lied to save his own ass.

But then Trevor Blaine made his first mistake.

"I know I'm an art dealer," he said, "but really." He smiled. "Surely that isn't the only reason you've come to me."

Now Monk wanted to smile himself. One of the hardest things for a liar to do was keep his mouth shut. Unable to let it alone, Blaine had tried to make the same point a second time, and Monk was so surprised he almost changed expression himself. Unfortunately, he couldn't give the man an answer. To give up his CI—get his informant killed in prison—was not an option. Made it too damned hard to recruit the next one. But maybe there was a better way.

"Why you, Mr. Blaine? Is that what you want to know?"

Trevor Blaine nodded. Monk glanced at Roger, then reached into the inside breast pocket of his summer-weight silk jacket and pulled out a folded sheaf of papers. He unfolded the pages and examined them for a moment before staring at Blaine.

"According to Interpol, we have very good reason to come to you about the *Madonna*. According to our friends at Scotland Yard, we should have come to you the moment we heard the *Madonna* was—"

Monk's voice stopped as the cell phone in his pocket rang.

Damn it. Concentrating hard on Trevor Blaine's reaction to his words, Monk tried to ignore the phone, but he saw that it was already too late. The Englishman had been leaning toward him, toward the papers in his hand, but now he was sitting back, grinning as he recognized his reprieve. Monk felt a sudden warmth up the back of his neck. Shit. A good interrogation was as intricately choreographed as a tango contest. He'd been on the verge of pulling Trevor Blaine onto the dance floor when the orchestra dropped dead.

He grabbed his phone. "What!"

"Listen carefully, Special Agent Monk." The voice was dead flat. "This is the counterintelligence unit at the Hoover Building. These orders come from the director himself."

Monk glanced at Roger Forbes as the voice continued.

"You and SA Forbes will return immediately to the Special Operations Group headquarters. To the wire room. Be alert for countersurveillance. Park no closer than a quarter mile from the SOG. Do not walk to the building until you are certain you are not being observed."

"Who is this?" Monk demanded. "We're right in the middle of some-thing here. I can't just—"

"Ten minutes, Agent Monk," the voice said. "You will not want to be late."

F O U R

Downstairs in Monk's SOG car—a black Saab 9-3 Turbo—he realized that Roger Forbes was staring at the side of his head, clearly upset by Monk's refusal to tell him what had just happened upstairs.

"Christ, Puller," he said at last. "I can understand why you didn't want to talk inside the building, but it's just the two of us now. What the hell's going on?"

Monk lifted his finger to his lips, then used the same finger to point at the radio mike hanging at the end of the black cable that spiraled out of the center console. It was the universal signal between agents to check to make sure the microphone switch wasn't stuck in the on position, a calamity that had led to some of the worst horror stories in the FBI.

Roger bent down and keyed the mike. The short raspy squawk told them the radio was safe. Roger turned his attention back to Monk.

"We're going back to the SOG," Monk told him. "One of the surveillance teams must have come up with a new lead on the *Madonna*. But for some reason they want us to dry-clean first." Bureauspeak for evasive maneuvers to detect the presence of surveillance.

Roger unfastened his seat belt, preparing to turn around and watch through the rear window. "Whenever you're ready."

"I'll get on the Whitehurst. If you notice anything before then, we'll stay on the surface streets."

Monk got on H Street out of the Watergate parking lot and took a left on Twenty-fifth as the quickest way to K Street and the Whitehurst Freeway. But as he drove, he couldn't keep his brain quiet. What he'd told Roger about the possibility of a new lead didn't seem a very likely reason for the cryptic phone call. For one thing, the director of the FBI wouldn't be personally involved in a robbery, regardless of the amount of money involved. For another, the bureau's counterintelligence division wouldn't be either. So what did it mean? Monk wondered. Why had they been interrupted and ordered back to—

"Jesus Christ, Monk, look out!"

Roger's shout snapped Monk back to life.

He slammed on the brakes, but it was too late.

He'd blown the red light at K Street and was halfway into the intersection. Directly into the path of a white Cadillac Escalade, its tires screaming as the driver fought to stop before running right over the top of the Saab. Monk stomped even harder on his own brakes, but could only stare wide-eyed as the man driving the SUV clutched the steering wheel with both hands. Monk braced for the impact.

But the Cadillac skidded to a stop just inches from his door.

The driver glared at him, then slumped over the wheel for a moment before looking up and shaking his head. Monk lifted his hand in an "I'm sorry" gesture, then continued through the intersection, his heart pounding and his hands shaking. He turned to Roger Forbes, who was staring hard at him.

"Christ," he said. "I didn't see the light. I was thinking about that damned phone call."

Roger shook his head, but said nothing.

Until they got all the way up to M Street without turning left.

"Now what are you doing, Puller? I thought you wanted to take the freeway."

Monk stared through the windshield, perplexed. Where the hell was he going? Not only had he almost killed them at K Street—where he'd planned to turn left to the Whitehurst—he'd gone right past L Street as well, past the Columbia Hospital for Women, and was now halfway through the intersection at M.

"What's the matter with you?" Roger said. "If I hadn't been with you for the last hour, I'd swear you were drunk."

"Drunk?" Monk scowled at his partner. "I didn't even have wine with dinner tonight."

Roger shook his head. "Your driving has been getting worse and worse, Puller. To the point where I don't want to ride with you anymore. It's like you're in a fog or something." He paused. "Are you feeling okay? Are you getting enough sleep?"

Monk nodded. He was getting way too much fucking sleep. And it seemed like the more he slept, the fuzzier his head became. He felt a stab of fear in the pit of his stomach. Roger wasn't the first to mention his fog, it was becoming a daily issue at home with Lisa as well. Had his behavior become that obvious? Monk hoped not. He needed this job, needed to keep his head together enough to hold on to it. He couldn't help thinking about the MRI test his doctor had scheduled for Thursday. There was no doubt he needed the brain scan, but he wasn't nearly as sure he wanted to find out the results. Without the possibility of a cure, what good would it do for him to know?

"It's just that goddamned phone call," he repeated, as he took the next left to loop back to the freeway. "And that business about dry cleaning."

Three minutes later they were on the Whitehurst and heading toward the Special Operations Group building near the foot of the Key Bridge. He glanced at the light traffic around them. "The last exit," he told Roger. "Be ready to watch when we hit the bridge exit."

Ninety seconds later they approached the exit for the Key Bridge, the last one before the Whitehurst ended in Canal Road. Monk stayed in the far left lane, accelerating past the few cars to his right until he was almost on top of the bridge exit, when he jerked the wheel and swerved to his right, cutting off a slow-moving truck to take the exit and swing around the big loop that would take them up on the bridge. He turned to Roger, who had climbed around in his seat to watch the traffic they'd left behind.

"Nothing," Roger said. "Trucker gave us the finger, but that was about it."

Monk didn't bother telling his partner to watch for the same thing on the other end of the bridge. It was standard operating procedure. When he got to the Rosslyn, Virginia, side, he took the first exit and circled around to get back up on the bridge.

"Still nothing," Roger said.

Monk nodded. Satisfied they were alone, he got off the bridge onto M Street and took a left on Thirty-fourth, continued for half a block before pulling to the curb and parking. Roger got out of the car first and looked around before tapping on the roof as a signal to Monk to follow. Together they hurried through the clammy night, and five minutes later approached the nondescript entrance to the converted trolley-car barn just off Canal Road that served as headquarters of the Special Operations Group. Monk used his card key on the battered metal door before he and Roger stepped through into the vast, dimly lit garage that served as the heart of the group. Despite the fact that Monk had been working at SOG for almost a year, the sight of the garage still made him blink.

The FBI had field offices in more than fifty cities—public offices anyone could walk into—but what most people didn't know was that in many of those cities there was a second office as well, one with no public face, with no visible connection to the bureau at all. Designed to serve as command and control centers for covert operations, these secret offices were home to the FBI's special operations groups. And nowhere in any of these SOG facilities was the mission more apparent than in the garages that housed their vehicles.

Fifty yards long and at least that wide, this garage had been built in the 1800s as a trolley-car barn to house the streetcars that traveled back and forth across the Francis Scott Key Bridge. A century and a half later it was still a car barn, although the rolling stock was vastly different. Filling every available square foot, nondescript Dodge sedans cozied up to slouching Ferraris, Winnebagos to massively chromed Harley Hogs. Only the breathtaking Rolls-Royce Corniche convertible in the farthest corner escaped such democratization. The cream and brown Roller sat by itself and gave off the distinct impression that it knew the reason why.

Monk led the way as he and Roger navigated through the vehicles toward the far end of the garage. Half a minute later they stood in front of a dull gray steel door that had been deliberately beaten and dirtied to make it match the rest of the place. Monk used his card key again. They went through the door and into a long corridor, then moved up the hallway to the second of two doors on the left. The same gray steel as the outer door, but this one was spotless. It featured a combination lock the size of a grapefruit set just under eye level. The door was ajar, probably left that way for their arrival. Monk glanced at Roger, who shrugged before following him into a room no civilian would ever see.

At eight hundred square feet, the wiretap-monitoring room was still too small. Fluorescent light fixtures lined the twelve-foot ceiling and kept the room bright as day no matter the hour. Gray carpetlike soundproofing covered the floor, walls, and ceiling. A dozen or so FBI agents sat in black-fabric chairs in front of metal tables pushed against three of the four walls. On the tables sat the machines that the room had been specially built to house. Electronic wiretap receivers predominated—squat black boxes that looked like overgrown DVD players—but there were reel-to-reel audio and videotape machines as well, and portable cassette recorders, too. In the little bit of space left over, desktop computers sat side by side with flat-screen monitors.

On the wall opposite the door hung a sign on white posterboard:

QUIET!!!

IF YOU DON'T HAVE TO—DON'T TALK!

Headphones clamped to their ears, the agents were straining to hear conversations in a cacophony of languages. Mostly Spanish and Arabic these days, but still lots of Russian, more and more Korean, and several other tongues. The last thing the agent-monitors needed was more chitchat, and the only sounds to break the silence were the annoying buzz-hum of the lights, the whir of computer cooling fans, and the clicking of fingers against keyboards. The rule against bringing food in here was just as strict as the no-talking prohibition, but a lot more easily ignored. Monk saw no physical evidence, but the place carried the unmistakable odor of furtive burritos and surreptitious pizza.

Midway down the room stood three men. The tall one—almost seven feet tall—in the green windbreaker was Kendall Jefferson, the Special Operations Group supervisor. The deadly one in the dark blue suit was Burt Malone, the bureau's assistant director in charge of the FBI's counterintelligence division.

The sight of the third man brought Monk to a stop.

What the hell? he thought. What was William Smith doing here?

Monk stared at the NSA spook from Fort Meade. Monk had trained himself to show no reaction to surprise—pretty much a necessity for a man who spent his days off sitting over a poker table—but he damned near allowed his eyes to flicker. William Smith had gained some weight in the five years since Monk had last seen him, but he was getting close to forty and that was to be expected. His black mop of hair showed no gray and was still just as slicked back as ever, and he was dressed even better than in the old days. A tan linen suit tonight, with a crimson tie, and brown Italian loafers that hadn't come off any sale table. And he'd kept his mustache too. Just as black as his hair, and a perfect match for his deep-set eyes.

Kendall Jefferson motioned for them to approach.

Monk saw that Jefferson was sweating—his milk-chocolate skin glowing despite the chill in the room—but that was as it should be. With an AD in the room, a middle manager was expected to sweat. The AD was not only dry as a bone, but scowling as Monk got closer. Monk smiled. Smiling confused assistant directors.

"This is Puller Monk," Jefferson told Malone, "and his partner, Roger Forbes." He didn't bother announcing the AD's name, before turning toward the third man. "And this," he said to Monk and Roger, "is William Smith from NSA."

Monk extended his hand. "William," he said. "Been a long time."

William Smith stared at his hand for a long moment before shaking it. "Monk," he said. And nothing more.

In the suddenly less than comfortable silence, Assistant Director Malone turned to William. "You know each other? Did you mention that earlier?"

"No," William said. "No, I didn't."

There was another short silence as the AD appeared to be waiting for the customary pleasantries that should be attending such a reunion, but

Monk knew better. It would snow in August before William Smith would say anything the least bit pleasant to Puller Monk.

Again it was Burt Malone who broke the silence.

"We'll go to Jefferson's office to talk, gentlemen," the AD said, "but we have to stay here to watch the elsur intercept first. I don't want any of the electronic surveillance video to leave this room."

Malone nodded at Kendall Jefferson, and everybody turned to the table against the wall to their right. Jefferson leaned over and picked up two sets of headphones, handed one to Monk, the other to Roger, before touching a key on the gray keyboard in front of a twenty-inch flat-panel monitor. Monk adjusted the phones over his ears.

The blue screen turned fuzzy for an instant before the picture appeared, a crystal-clear picture of an apartment living room, with numerals in the lower right corner, showing the date and time of day. The date was today, August 8, and the time 0047—12:47—just over half an hour ago.

Monk watched as the video began to run. His eyes widened as he saw the three men in the living room, as he realized he didn't need the date-time readout at all. Not when he'd been there in person.

F I V E

"What the hell's going on here?" Roger Forbes whispered to Monk, as the two of them hung back on the way upstairs to Kendall Jefferson's office. "What have you done this time?"

Monk shook his head but said nothing before they hurried to catch up.

To get to Jefferson's office, they had to pass through the deserted squad room, another of the SOG's bizarre departures from cookie-cutter FBI conformity. The place was a mess. Stacks of brown cardboard boxes littered the room, many open to display electronic gear of one kind or another. Audio and video recorders predominated, but there were all kinds of cameras, along with a wide selection of magnetic tapes and a variety of other devices for looking and listening.

Against the wall to the right, a long table held a couple dozen battery chargers, half of them filled with the portable handie-talkie radios the SOG people used out on the street. Ten gray metal desks sat amid the clutter, shared by the forty or so agents assigned to the group, crummy and outdated desks that had been thrown away by the field office downtown but were considered plenty good enough for the trolley barn.

If the point was to make the place look like anything but a government office, the bureau had done a hell of a job, and the cover story they'd created was the best Monk had ever heard. Any civilian stumbling in wanting to know what kind of business they were running was told the same thing. That this was a car-storage facility, that the people working here were repo men—and women, of course—doing contract work for banks across the city. Paid to grab vehicles from deadbeats, to store them until the banks could dispose of them. What made the cover so effective was that it explained everything at the same time. Not only the bizarre collection of cars and trucks, but the rag-tag clothing of the agents as well.

Inside Kendall Jefferson's glass-walled cubicle in the far corner there wasn't enough room for all five of them to sit, so nobody did. Assistant Director Malone went around Jefferson's desk and stood facing the rest of them. Monk and Roger lingered near the open doorway.

"Close the door," the AD told Monk.

Monk did so, but he wasn't happy about it. In the bureau, closing the door meant a number of things, none of them good. Malone turned to look through the glass wall into the squad room. Monk followed his gaze. The agents had been glancing in their direction, but suddenly became intent on the far wall as they realized the AD was staring at them.

"Damn it, Monk," Malone said, turning back. "What were the two of you doing in that apartment?"

Monk took a moment before answering. He couldn't help noticing that Malone was no longer calling them "gentlemen," as he'd done in the wiretap room downstairs. He also knew that from here on his partner was just along for the ride. At forty-five, Monk was ten years Roger's senior, and in the bureau that meant he had to take the hit. Glancing at Kendall Jefferson, he wondered if he'd misunderstood Malone's question. It seemed pretty clear from what they'd just seen in the wire room what they'd been doing in Trevor Blaine's apartment, but that wasn't the sort of answer one gave to an assistant director.

"We're working the *Madonna* case," he said. "The da Vinci that was stolen from a private home a couple of hours ago." It was easier to call it a da Vinci than get involved in the argument about who might actually have wielded the brush. "The *Madonna with the Yarn Winder*, they call it."

"That's not what I asked you. What we want to know is how you ended up with Trevor Blaine."

"One of my criminal informants, Mr. Malone. He's sitting in jail for sentencing . . . burglary, possession of stolen property. He was the first one we went to, and we offered him a deal. He gives up the names of fences who might handle something as valuable as the *Madonna*, we put in a good word to the judge. The informant gave us half a dozen names. We knew all but two of them already, no way they were big enough for a job like this. Trevor Blaine we never heard of, so we started with him." Monk glanced at Roger. "I guess I should say we were starting with him when my phone rang."

Malone glanced at William Smith, and William took over the questioning. The sour look on his face was augmented by the tone in his voice.

"I don't give a damn how you got there, Monk. What I'm more interested in is that report you pulled out of your pocket. The Interpol stuff . . . at least that's what you told Trevor Blaine. And something about Scotland Yard."

Monk reached into his jacket and pulled out the sheaf of paper in question. "This?" he said, as he fanned the pages to show William they were blank on both sides. "I was just running a game on him. Just wanted to see what he'd say. Never hurts to try."

William Smith stared at the paper, then laughed out loud, a sharp bark of cynicism that seemed to echo off the glass walls. "Christ," he said. "Why am I not surprised?" He looked at Monk. "Why would I ever have imagined you'd be telling the truth?"

Monk ignored William, turned to Malone instead. "What's this all about? What's going on here?"

"You know better than to ask something like that," the AD told him.

Monk felt his shoulder muscles tightening. He glanced at Roger Forbes. Roger's brown eyes were telling him to shut the fuck up, but Monk shook off the signal.

"It's our case, Mr. Malone. It's part of a year-long investigation, an international series of similar robberies. I'd think that qualifies us to know what NSA is doing here. And why the bureau's counterintelligence division is running a wiretap I know nothing about."

"It isn't your case anymore, Monk, that's the simple answer. National security matters are handled at headquarters level . . . and you no longer have a need to know."

Need to know. It was the classic basis for dissemination management when it came to keeping secret things secret, but still Monk frowned. "National security? A woman in a tight dress seduces some poor bastard and it's national security?"

He turned to look at William before going back to the AD.

"I grant you the *Madonna*'s worth a pile of money, but what possible interest could NSA have in the theft of a . . ."

Monk's voice died as he finally put it together.

"It's not the painting," he said. "Not directly anyway. It's the—"

"That's enough!" the AD snapped. "Don't say another word! You and Forbes may already have alerted the target. It's too late to fix that now, but your part in this operation is over."

Monk took a short step toward the desk, closing the distance, before he felt Roger Forbes's hand reach out to restrain him. He pushed Roger's hand away.

The AD's voice rose. "You're out of line, Monk. If you want to keep your job you'll—"

William Smith raised his hand and Malone closed his mouth. Monk stared. He couldn't remember ever seeing such a thing. A pretty good indication of who was really running this show.

"I know Monk very well," William told Malone. "Too damned well." He turned to Monk. "I've seen your act before, but this time it's different. This time the White House is serious about controlling access. Not only can't you and your partner be cut in, I'm ordering both of you to go home and forget all about it."

Monk opened his mouth to argue before realizing he didn't want to do that. William Smith might be running this show but Monk knew better than to rub the AD's nose in it.

"Are those your orders, Mr. Malone?" he asked, then winced. Somehow it sounded even more insulting this way.

The AD glared directly into his eyes. "Get out," he said. "Both of you. Get out of here while you still can."

· · ·

Two minutes later they were back out on M Street, standing on the broad sidewalk outside the pedestrian door. Monk had barely closed the door when Roger turned directly into his face.

"Jesus, Puller, have you gone completely mental? I thought you were going to take a swing at somebody in there."

Monk's voice rose, loud enough for the microphones installed outside the door to hear. "I lost it, Roger . . . I completely lost it." His voice got even louder. "I don't know what happened to me in there, but I ought to go back and apologize."

Roger shook his head. "What you ought to do is exactly what the NSA guy said. Forget all about this and go home."

"I got no problem with going home, it's the forgetting part that's tough. The way I acted upstairs is going to come back and bite me in the ass . . . you know it will."

Roger stared at him. "Not this time," he said quietly. "Trust me, Malone's got bigger asses to bite than yours."

Monk laughed. "You're probably right." He looked up the street, in the direction of the Saab. "You want to get a drink before I take you back to your car? Or a cup of coffee?"

"If we can't work, I'd just as soon go to bed."

"Yeah, I guess you're right. Right now, bed sounds pretty good to me, too."

Monk started toward the car, but Roger's voice stopped him. "If it makes you feel any better, I was just as angry as you were." He paused. "What the hell just happened up there?"

"What difference does it make?" He was almost shouting now. "We got our orders, we follow them. End of story."

"End of story? When did you start talking like—"

Roger's voice died as Monk raised his finger to his lips, then grabbed his partner's arm and pulled him up the sidewalk until they were at the corner of the building, safely out of reach of the mikes and TV cameras guarding the entrance. The listeners inside had heard all they needed to. They would report Monk's words to Burt Malone. The AD would be satisfied with Monk's groveling. It wouldn't be five minutes before Malone forgot all about him.

On the way up M Street toward Thirty-fourth, where Monk had left the Saab, he thought for a moment about asking Roger to stick around and help, but only for a moment. Roger had a lot of career ahead of him, a brand-new wife, and plans for starting a family. Plans Monk had no right to jeopardize. A friendship he had no right to abuse.

S I X

Monk had to take Roger back to his own car in the parking lot at the Watergate, but he managed to get back to within half a block of the SOG just in time to see William Smith emerge on foot from the trolley barn, turn left and walk up M Street. Behind William, Monk slowed to a crawl and watched as the NSA man turned left at Thirty-fifth Street. Monk accelerated quietly, aware that the sound of his engine might alert William to his presence. As he passed the intersection at Thirty-fifth, he looked to his left and saw William pulling away from the curb in a Chevy sedan. Dark blue or green, it was hard to tell. Monk hit the gas, hurried to Thirty-fourth and turned left. Moments later he came to Prospect Street, where he sat at the stop sign until he saw William go by.

He gave the spook a block or so head start—easy to do at this time of night—then followed. He didn't have to bumper-lock the guy. William was only going one of two places, both of them in Maryland. To his house in Cheverly, or up the highway to NSA Headquarters at Fort Meade. Monk could afford to hang back, and that's exactly what he did.

. . .

But William surprised him.

He didn't go home. He didn't go to his office at Fort Meade, either.

Where he went was across town, up New York Avenue to the campus of Gallaudet University, where he made a right turn on Florida and continued a few blocks down to a nondescript two-story brick office building. Monk hung back as William parked the Chevy and walked toward the front door, then hit the gas and closed up fast, jumping out of the Saab and catching William just as he entered the building. Monk pushed through the door before William could shut it behind him. William's eyes widened, then glittered with hostility as they stood together in the tiny lobby.

"What the fuck are you doing here?" he demanded.

"What do you imagine I'm doing here?"

"A couple of things come to mind. How far back do you want to go?"

"Just as far as you like, but right now I'm only interested in one thing."

"It's classified, Monk. Even if you had a need to know, I wouldn't tell you."

"You're running a FISA wire out of my office." He was referring to the secret wiretap provisions of the Foreign Intelligence Services Act. "Which I'm guessing means you already know where the *Madonna* is, and who stole it. Which also means you don't give a shit about the painting at all. It's the woman you want. The thief who's not a thief at all, but a—"

"Goddamit, Monk, shut up!" William's eyes darted out toward the street. "For Christ's sake, anybody could be listening!"

"So let's go somewhere where nobody's listening."

William shook his head, then turned away and started back toward the door. Monk grabbed his arm and spun him back around before stepping up into his face. William tried to shove him back, but Monk held his ground.

"You are seriously out of bounds, Monk." William's voice was gravelly with fatigue. "I could have you arrested for following me here."

Monk reached into his pocket for his cell phone, held it out. "Make the call. Let's get somebody down here right now."

William batted the phone away. "What the hell's this to you, anyway? Why can't you follow the rules for once in your life?"

"The bureau's been working these art thefts for five years. Obviously you people know who's doing them. You can't possibly think I'm going to go away until I find out as well."

"What about your partner, what about Forbes? He feel the same way?"

"It's just me now. Roger's got too much to lose."

"And you don't?"

Monk stared at him. "We used to be friends. I understand why we're not anymore, but this is business. I want in. I have plenty of reason to be included. Malone won't make it happen, but you can."

But William's eyes only got harder, as he took a took a half step toward Monk. "Go to hell, Puller," he said. "I don't ever want to see your face again."

S E V E N

Sung Kim hated Paris.

For some reason her controller continued to insist on using Paris for their infrequent face-to-face meetings, but she'd never been able to get over the horror of the day the Americans slaughtered her parents. From the moment she landed at De Gaulle to the moment she left again, she had to shut down that part of her mind and pretend the murders had never happened. Today—in the tan cotton walking shorts and bright red silk blouse that made her fake ponytail look even more blond than usual—she couldn't wait to get back to Washington.

It was close to three o'clock in the afternoon when she joined the crowd of tourists on the Pont Neuf, careful not to give the slightest impression of looking around for a tail as she crossed the bridge. She knew the Paris protocol inside and out, and was far too well trained to slip up this close to a contact point. She was being watched, of course. Her controller would be tracking her every step. He wouldn't approach for the meet until he was sure she was alone, that the Sûreté, the Paris Police Judiciare, the CIA, or anyone else, wasn't following her into the Ile de la Cité. Her job was to keep walking, to keep meandering like a tourist until the coast was clear for a meeting he insisted was too critical to trust to their normal methods of communication. Which meant "wet" work. Despite knowing better than to speculate, she couldn't help wondering who the target would be this time.

When she reached the steps leading down to the Ile de la Cité, Sung Kim descended to the Quai de l'Horloge. She stopped for a few moments to gaze at the Seine on her left, to watch a red and white bateau mouche glide under the bridge, tourists crawling all over the boat as they scrambled to take pictures. Satisfied her controller had her well in sight—that he hadn't lost her in the crowd coming off the bridge—she continued with the throng moving down the quai.

When she got to the Rue de Harley she turned right and strolled along the Conciergerie with its sharply pointed turrets until she came to the Quai des Orfèvres. This time she turned left, continued along the quai on the south side of the massive Palais de Justice. She glanced up at the ancient sundial, set high above the street in the side of the building. *Hora fugit*, Sung Kim read, the first two words of the Latin inscription beneath the sundial. Time flies. It certainly does, she told herself, especially when you've crossed the Atlantic for a ten-minute meeting before jetting directly back to Washington.

Moments later she came around the corner into the Boulevard du Palais and passed the front of the Palais itself. She checked the ornate clock above her head. She had just under a half hour before the three-thirty rendezvous. There was a flower market just ahead in the Rue de Lutèce. She would stop there, Sung Kim decided, kill another few minutes, and give her controller a further chance to scour the vicinity for watchers.

As usual, the Marché aux Fleurs was packed with shoppers as Sung Kim strolled through. Her senses sharpened by the danger of her presence so close to the meet-point, the flowers were almost overpowering: the sweet scent of crimson roses and fire-engine red carnations, the white and yellow clumps of chrysanthemums, and the stately drooping poses of sunflowers as tall as her head.

Ten minutes later she left the market and idled her way toward the Rue de la Cité, and from there—walking even more slowly now—toward Notre Dame. If it was safe for them to meet, her controller would show up exactly five minutes after she entered the cathedral. If he didn't, she would go directly to the Gare de Lyon, take the train back to De Gaulle, and return immediately to Washington. Sung Kim hurried now, striding toward the west facade of the cathedral, to the north door—the Virgin Portal— eager to get it over with and return to the anonymity of her life in America.

It was five minutes to the second when her controller showed up.

Sung Kim knew better than to look directly at the man, who was tall for a North Korean, a few inches taller than she was, with shiny black hair, wire-rimmed glasses, and a jagged scar that ran from the corner of his right eye, through the edge of his lips, to the middle of his chin. She'd heard all about the wound from the other teachers in training school. About the CIA agent who'd cut him, the American thug her controller had killed with his bare hands even as blood and muscle spilled from his butchered face. Cho Hyun was a Division 39 legend. His facial damage kept him out of deep-cover field work, but there'd never been a better "wet" man. Just his proximity made Sung Kim sweat.

But his presence meant something else as well. That they hadn't been followed. Still they stuck to protocol. To anyone watching, they were tourists, strangers to one another, just a man and a woman visiting the world's most famous Gothic church. Cho closed the distance between them as they milled along with the others making their way under the vaulted arches of the nave arcade to the left of the rows of wooden pews. Sung Kim strolled from there to the side altar in the choir room. She was standing with a dozen other men and women near the base of the steps up to the altar itself, her eyes on the six huge candleholders that dominated the altar, when she heard his voice. As usual he spoke English, slightly slurred from the dead nerves at the corner of his mouth. It would not do to have anyone become interested in a blue-eyed blonde who spoke Korean.

"Follow me," he said, before turning to his left and heading for one of the two massive stained-glass windows behind the altar.

Sung Kim strolled toward the same window and moments later they stood together in front of it. For the moment, they were alone.

"You have disappointed me," he said softly. "Two million from the *Madonna* was not what you promised."

Sung Kim's scalp began to tingle. It was never a good idea to disappoint this man. "Franklin knew I couldn't sell it anywhere else," she said just as quietly. "Not without the risk of holding it for months." She paused. "He's getting tougher about these paintings."

"You asked for more, of course."

"Five million. I was lucky to get two."

He stepped closer to the window, examining the lower right portion for a moment before moving back to her.

"I have a new assignment for you," he said.

She waited for him to continue.

"We must use Franklin for something else," he said. "For something more important than money."

Sung Kim almost looked at him, but caught herself in time. "I'm not sure he's ready yet."

"We can't wait longer."

"Who's the target?"

He told her, using the target's code number. Sung Kim didn't react. She'd been reading the papers, of course. Pyongyang no longer had any choice.

"We expect an opportunity soon," Cho said. "An opportunity that necessitates our using Franklin."

Sung Kim leaned toward him, uncertain she'd heard right. Use Thomas Franklin? Now, with all his potential still intact? This time she had to work harder to control her response, and even harder to change his mind.

"Franklin won't . . ." That was too strong, she realized. "He might not agree to do it," she told him instead. "Stolen paintings are one thing, but . . ." She glanced around to make sure they were still alone. "He could very well refuse to do it."

"Of course he could. That's why you're not to tell him."

"Not tell him? But how? How can I . . ." She didn't bother to finish.

"He won't know until it's too late. He won't know what he's done until it's all over."

Sung Kim opened her mouth to repeat her question but she knew better, so she tried to go at him from a different direction. It was dangerous to argue, but as a professional she had to.

"We use him now, we'll have lost him forever. And the millions he pays for the paintings, the billions his company funnels into Pyongyang. Along with his access in Washington." She paused. "I might never develop anyone to replace him." Again she hesitated, clearly overstepping her boundaries now. "Might there be another way? Might the job be done before the target visits America?"

His voice hardened. "The Division has decided. You will eliminate the target. You will use Franklin to do it."

Sung Kim swallowed a response. Her chance to change his mind had passed. And she understood something else as well. Once Thomas Franklin was blown—when he was no longer of value to Pyongyang—she would become damaged goods herself. If she could do the job and walk away, good for her, but to her controllers it would be infinitely better to die trying than to fail.

"When will I know more?" she asked.

"Soon. The materials you'll need are already on their way."

E I G H T

"Pull!" Thomas Franklin shouted.

He snapped the Cogswell and Harrison twelve-gauge to his shoulder, leaned into the shot, pulled the front sight past the spinning clay pigeon and squeezed the trigger. The clay disintegrated as number-nine birdshot tore through it, the roar of the antique shotgun reverberating across Battle Valley Farm before dying in the Gettysburg forest.

Franklin spun to his left. "Mark!"

This time the target came out of the low house at the level of Franklin's waist, climbing rapidly, but the result was the same. Another quick track of the barrel, another shattered pigeon. He brought the shotgun to his chest, broke the action to allow both barrels to swing away, removed the empty shell casings, then turned to the president of the United States.

"Clean through sixteen," he told his best friend. "But don't let the pressure get to you."

The president stepped up to the firing line. He was sweating from the noontime heat, his broad chin dripping, but he wasn't smiling. Franklin realized he hadn't smiled since stepping out of his helicopter an hour ago. Normally the first to trade insults, the most powerful man in the world wasn't having a whole lot of fun today. Maybe it was the heat, or the fact that it was Monday, and that he'd just returned from an exhausting trip to Japan and South Korea.

The president adjusted his yellow-lensed shooting glasses, snugged his ear protectors tightly over his ears. He stood with the Remington shotgun in his hands for a long moment, then shook his head. Stepping back to the gun rack, he put the gun away, pulled off his "ears" and dropped them to the ground.

"You win, Tom," he said. "I've had enough for today."

Franklin nodded. "It is hot out here, isn't it? Why don't we go inside and have a beer. I think Grace sent out some sandwiches."

The president turned away without a word, strode directly toward the skeet house to their right. Franklin hurried after him, following the president through the door and into the gun room, the deliberately informal clubhouse where Franklin kept the weapons he furnished to a constant stream of guests who loved the sport as much as he did. About the size of a racketball court, the gun room was a far cry from the baroque splendor of the mansion, more like a hunting cabin in the woods of Maine than an air-conditioned retreat from the swelter of a Pennsylvania summer.

Franklin paused in the sudden chill as the president stepped past the table to the wood-framed windows, tall windows that let in more than enough light to make using the electric fixtures unnecessary. The president looked out toward Franklin's golf course in the distance before turning to the wall to his left, to the photographs on that wall, pictures of many of the guests who'd enjoyed Franklin's hospitality over the years.

He was looking, Franklin saw, at the latest addition, the large photograph of Vladimir Putin that Grace had hung in here only yesterday. The Russian president had been a dead shot with both skeet and trap, not surprising given the former KGB chief's background with weapons. The president glanced at Franklin before turning back to the table and grabbing the nearest chair. He grunted as he settled into it.

"Your back okay?" Franklin asked, as he took a chair across the table from his friend. "You seem a little tense today."

"Back's fine. Good as it's ever going to be, at any rate."

Franklin waited for more, but the president just stared at him. Franklin leaned toward his friend "What's going on? You look like you want to punch somebody in the mouth."

"I'm just hungry," the president said. "Did you say Grace sent something over?"

Franklin rose from his chair and stepped around the table to a small door set into the wall on their left. In keeping with the "good old boy" spirit of the place there were no servants in the skeet house, but that didn't mean there was no service. Of all the innovations he'd brought to Battle Valley Farm, Franklin was most proud of the minisubway system he'd designed to transport food and drink throughout the property. The dumbwaiter was part of a circuit that ran in a loop through the farm, assuring that Franklin and his guests would never be far from refreshment. Starting in the immense kitchen back at the mansion, the tunnel came here first, then hit the fishing house on the bank of the stream running a half mile west of the golf course, before heading for the golf house at the far edge of the estate, and finally back to the kitchen.

Franklin opened the dumbwaiter door and reached in to retrieve the silver serving tray. He carried the tray back to the table, set it down, and lifted the cover. On the tray were two barbecued chicken sandwiches and two bottles of Samuel Adams, their favorite beer, along with a pair of tall crystal glasses. The president stared at the food for a moment, then looked up, directly into Franklin's eyes.

"You're right," he said, as Franklin sat down again. "I am tense today. More than a little bit, as a matter of fact." He paused. "But it doesn't have anything to do with my back." Suddenly the president's eyes were granite hard. "I know what you're up to, Tom. I know what you've been doing."

Franklin's mind went numb. He stared at the president and tried to respond, but his tongue was suddenly thick in his mouth.

"I . . ." he began. "I don't know what you're—"

"Stop it!" the president snapped. "How could you imagine I wouldn't find out? How could you think the people you've been talking to behind my back wouldn't come straight to me?"

What? Franklin thought, as his shoulders sagged with relief. *That's what this is all about?* His legs began to quiver as the adrenaline drained away.

"You're making a mistake, Mr. President," he said. "I can't seem to make you see that, so I went to Jimmy Allen and Fred Baxter. To ask the senators to talk you out of this thing with Japan. To save you from a decision you won't survive." He leaned forward. "I owe you that much. You know I do."

"What you owe me is loyalty, Tom. What you owe me is not to go to my two biggest enemies on the Hill." He continued to stare directly into Franklin's eyes. "Disloyalty is an everyday part of my job . . . but you?"

"A yes-man, is that what you want from me? Someone to validate you even when you're wrong?"

"That doesn't even deserve an answer."

"Then listen to me, that's all I'm asking. Give me another opportunity to show you how wrong you are."

The president grunted, then lifted his hand and gestured for Franklin to continue. Franklin paused to gather his thoughts, his stomach beginning to churn. The stakes were huge. He wouldn't get another chance to change the president's mind, and he couldn't allow himself to think of the consequences should he fail. What would happen to Global Panoptic should he fail.

"You think giving Japan a bomb will force North Korea into line," he began, "but you're wrong."

The president frowned. "You'd rather we do it ourselves? Use American men and women to protect the region instead?"

"Nobody has to do it, is what I'm saying. Not when Korea's on the brink of reunification. The new government in Seoul is pushing even harder for it. Give them a chance first. Give them time to make it happen."

The president shook his head. "The only way Kim Jong Il's going to reunite is if he's in charge, and that's never going to happen."

"His people are starving. He has no choice."

"He cares about his people? You're talking about a man who has hungry children cutting his lawn with scissors."

Franklin stared at the untouched sandwiches on the table, at the untouched beer. He looked at his friend. How could he make the president understand the necessity of a unified Korea? He fought to keep his tone moderate, and his argument alive.

"Kim's already convinced you're trying to destroy him. You arm Japan, you'll give him even more proof of that. He'll react by isolating himself even further from the south. Reunification will go down the drain. He'll build even more nuclear weapons to protect himself from us."

Franklin heard his voice rising. He had to stop himself from standing up and shouting.

"You've got to negotiate with Kim Jong Il, Mr. President. Make him see that one Korea is the only way to save his people." He paused to take a breath. "Offer him money, for Christ's sake. Write him a big enough check, he'll do whatever you want."

The president looked away, over Franklin's shoulder toward the wall with all the photographs. When he turned back, his eyes seemed even harder. "He won't stop building the nukes. Surely you're not naive enough to think he would."

"That's why we have spy satellites."

"Satellites can't see underground, or inside mountains. If we can't find the facilities, we can't do a damned thing about them."

"So what you're saying is that we have no idea whether he has nukes or not."

"He admits having two warheads capable of reaching Tokyo. CIA tells me he has three. We can't stand by and hope for the best. Either I give Prime Minister Nakamura what he wants, or I send more troops to add to the ones we already have in Japan. And more, and more. Forever."

Franklin reached for his beer, but withdrew his hand and leaned toward the president. "You'll be adding them to the nuclear club. Adding another country with weapons we'll have to worry about."

"I'll take my chances with Japan. If that's what it takes to keep peace over there."

Franklin took a deep breath and let it out slowly. Maybe there was a better way to go here. Another way to survive this thing.

"Let's say you're right," he said, "but I'm still convinced that now is not the time. At least wait until after the election. Until you get your second term. If you do this before November, you're going to lose."

"I don't have any choice about the timing. Ishii Nakamura's term ends soon, and he's the only leader in Japan with the guts to ask for a bomb. Hatred of nuclear weapons is born into his people . . . they'll despise him for what he's doing. It could be generations before we get another prime minister like him over there."

The president glanced again at the wall of photos. At several ex-presidents, along with all the others.

"George Bush," he said, turning back to Franklin. "George W. had a similar problem. Don't go after Iraq, his people told him . . . you're going to get blown out of office if you take on Saddam now. But he knew he had no choice. 'I'll probably lose the presidency over this,' Bush told them, 'but this is the right thing to do and I'm not going to shy away.' "

Franklin nodded, but he still wasn't finished. "At least make Nakamura go to the United Nations first," he insisted. "At least do that much to pro-tect yourself."

"The U.N.? By the time they do anything it'll be too late. Nakamura will be out of office."

The president pushed his uneaten sandwich out of the way, then put his elbows on the table.

"I've always appreciated your candor, Tom, but the time for arguing is over. Nakamura will be here a week from today. He'll spend the afternoon with you on the golf course. I'll join you for a few minutes in the evening. We'll minimize the press coverage, and get this thing done."

Franklin stared at the president. He managed to choke back the first response that came to mind, then forced himself to nod instead. "Of course, Mr. President. You can count on me."

"I know I can." The president's eyes caught and held Franklin's. "And I know you won't disappoint me again."

N I N E

It was all Monk could do to keep from screaming.

He'd heard the stories about these MRI machines, but he'd had no idea.

And what made it even worse was that he had only himself to blame.

"What about claustrophobia?" the radiologist had asked him. "We can give you a sedative if it's a problem. Or send you to a facility that uses the newer more open machines." Monk had shaken his head, but what else could he do? He was an FBI agent, for God's sake. How could he possibly admit to cowardice in the face of a routine medical exam?

Now, wedged inside a steel tube that enveloped him like a coffin, his head locked in a cage to keep it rigid, the only things Monk could move without violating the technician's orders were his eyelids. The problem was that opening them only made it worse. The sight of the shiny metal just inches from his nose brought on a cold sweat that bathed Monk from head to toe.

He forced himself to breathe deeply, pulling the stale air in through his nose, blowing it out slowly past tighter and tighter lips. *Let it go . . . let it happen.* Forty-five minutes, the radiologist had told him, but he must not have heard right. Surely he'd been in here an hour already. Surely they'd made some kind of . . .

A metallic voice interrupted, distant in the headphones they'd attached over his ears to drown out the hammering of the magnets.

"Halfway there, Mr. Monk," the technician told him. "You still okay?"

Monk scowled.

Halfway? Are you fucking kidding me?

He mumbled a response that must have satisfied the voice, because a moment later the banging started up again, like someone standing outside the tube with a wooden mallet, pounding like a madman trying to get through to him. Monk tried to ignore it. The trick was to think about something else, of course, but that wasn't easy when you were locked into a machine that was scanning your brain, peeling away the layers as it searched for the reason behind your increasingly disturbing symptoms.

Drawing a deep breath through his nose, he went to work distracting himself. He thought about sex and tennis, about blow jobs and topspin backhands down the line. He tried to conjugate the dozen or so Spanish verbs he remembered from his childhood in San Diego, but gave up when he couldn't get past *tenemos* to the third person plural. Three English words came a whole lot easier: fear, rage, and loneliness. Pillars of the human condition, a woman had once told him. Right now Monk knew she'd been right. He tried to drive her words from his mind. Tried not to admit to the fear, give in to the anger that it had come to this, or the lonely emptiness of his cold dark tube.

But it only got worse.

No matter what he tried to think about, his skin continued to crawl, the sweat running down his forehead into his eyes, soaking out of his armpits through the cotton fabric of his dark green golf shirt. He had no choice, Monk decided. He had to use Lisa early. He'd been trying to save fantasizing about his FBI agent girlfriend for later, in case it came down to shouting into his microphone for help, but he couldn't wait. First he pictured Lisa's face, imagined the herbal scent of the shampoo she used on her long brown hair. He visualized her naked body, the two of them in bed together. Saw her . . .

Suddenly Monk realized it *wasn't* her . . . that it wasn't Lisa Sands anymore.

That Lisa had somehow turned into Bethany Randall.

Christ, he thought. What was William Smith's ex-fiancée doing in the middle of his fantasy?

He opened his eyes to kick Bethany out of his head, but she refused to leave. Suddenly he could see her with magical clarity, the two of them alone in a place they should never have been. Good God, Monk told himself, startled at the images, so vivid he was sure the radiology technician was watching right along with him. He opened his eyes again, but couldn't keep them open. The steel surface just beyond the cage seemed to shrink even closer. It was either Bethany Randall or the tomb around him, and Monk didn't have to think for even a millisecond to know which one he preferred. So he shut his eyes even tighter, let Bethany take him wherever she wanted to.

And where she took him was directly back to that night in the hot tub.

The three of them had gone skydiving earlier in the day. Bethany had grown up in a family of fliers and had been a pilot since her college days. Fixed wing, at first, but later on she'd flown helicopters and did a short stint in the right seat of a corporate jet. Early in their relationship she'd convinced William to take up skydiving, and William hadn't had to work very hard to get Monk involved as well.

They'd spent the afternoon in Frederick, Maryland, jumping out of a small private airport in the woods outside the city: the same airport where Bethany kept her plane, a distinctive dark-blue and white Beechcraft Baron twin-engine with a bright red eagle painted on the rudder. Exhausted, they'd dragged themselves back to William's house in Arlington for dinner. Before they could even think about eating they decided to have some drinks and unwind. They changed into swimsuits and climbed into the hot tub built into the back deck. William brought the booze with him to the hot tub, a big blue bottle of Bombay gin, along with a couple bottles of tonic and a bucket of ice. Enough of the good stuff to relax the entire neighborhood.

After an hour, however, and way too many drinks, the water got too hot for William. He left the tub to go to the kitchen and start the process of fixing something to eat, leaving Bethany and Monk behind.

· · ·

Monk realized that Bethany had caught him staring at her, and that she was sliding around the circular edge of the hot tub to get closer, close enough now that she could reach out and touch him. He shrank from the sudden proximity, but not for long. Despite knowing better—despite being far too cocktailed to take on such danger—he felt himself moving even closer to the woman whose yellow thong bikini he couldn't seem to ignore. Bethany Randall was a puzzle, he'd found himself thinking. How could a woman so demure in regular clothing be so deadly in a bikini?

For one thing, her body was absolutely flawless. Her legs seemed impossibly long in the high-cut swimsuit, and the flat ripple of her stomach only accentuated the bulk of her breasts in the wisp of a halter top.

Monk had been staring at her from the first moment they climbed into the hot tub, guardedly at first, but more and more brazen as the gin had worn away his resolve. That Bethany had noticed was certainly no surprise. Twenty-seven years old, she must have been dealing with men like him for at least a decade already. As though reading Monk's mind, she leaned toward him. The ends of her wondrous red hair brushed her shoulders, damp with sweat. She lifted her glass and pointed with it toward where William had gone into the house to escape the heat of the water. Clearly as unbalanced by the gin as he was, her green eyes sparkled playfully as she slid an inch closer to Monk.

"William couldn't take the heat," she said, "and you look a little warm yourself."

"I can take it if you can," he told her. "A few more minutes anyway."

She sipped her gin and tonic, held the icy glass against her cheek, then reached across and held the glass against his cheek as well. "How's that?" she asked. "Better?"

"Much." Monk held up his own glass, showed her that the ice had pretty much melted away. "But you better stay close."

She chuckled, deep in her throat, then raised out of the water far enough to expose the top of her bikini. This time she applied her glass just above her right breast, and held it there for a moment. "Get up," she ordered. "This is way better."

Monk hoisted himself out of the water. Bethany transferred her glass to his chest and held it there until he slid back down. Jesus Christ, he thought, as he realized what was happening. What in the hell was he doing here? He slid a full three feet to his right. This wasn't a date, for God's sake! This was William's fiancée. Sure, they'd been having a few problems, but that didn't make her fair game. It was time to get out of this tub. To get out of this house and back to the safety of his own life.

But in the next second he realized he couldn't.

That he was trapped by his own body.

He had sprung an erection, Monk realized. A hard-on he could use to pole-vault with, and much too protuberant to bring to Bethany's attention. He slid away from her as he waited for it to shrink.

"Where are you going?" she wanted to know. "I can't reach you over there."

Before he could answer, she stood up. Now he could see the rest of her, the thong bikini bottom, the unmistakable area she'd shaved in order to wear it. His tongue seemed to thicken in his mouth. The bulge in his trunks grew even harder.

This time Bethany held her icy glass against the tiny gold ring in her pierced navel. "God, that's good!" she said, her voice husky. "That's really good!" She turned to him and held out the glass. "Get over here," she ordered. "You've got to feel this."

All Monk could do was shake his head. How in the hell had he gotten himself into this? How was he going to . . . Before he could complete the question, Bethany was gliding right up next to him. In the next instant he felt her body against his.

"Stand up!" she cried. "I won't take no for an answer."

She grabbed at the waist of his trunks to pull him to his feet, but she missed. Instead of his waist, she struck lower, then drew back, her eyes wide.

"My goodness, Puller," she said. "I had no idea you were armed." She paused. "And that you're packing a magnum!"

She laughed softly, then stopped to stare directly into his eyes before hoisting herself directly onto his lap.

Monk shrank back, but only for an instant before his arms rose and circled her neck. Oh shit, he had time to think, before his mouth was on hers. And hers on his.

He felt her glass tumble from her hand down the side of his torso, into the water. He let his own glass go an instant later. Bethany's tongue was in his mouth now, and his hand was groping for her thong. He tried to tell himself to stop, but not very forcefully, as she . . .

"Mr. Monk?"

Lost in his memory of that night—of William's reaction when he'd stepped out of the kitchen and caught the two of them in the hot tub—Monk was slow to acknowledge the voice in his headphones. He felt someone tugging at his right foot, and heard the voice again, sharper this time.

"Mr. Monk! We're finished!"

The table on which he lay began to slide out of the tube. Monk shook the fog from his head, blinking as he came out of the darkness into the bright fluorescent lights. A moment later the technician removed the restraints. Monk lifted his head and shoulders, rested for a moment on his elbows, then swung his legs over and stood. He took a step toward the door, but the stocky young man reached out and held his arm.

"Hold on a second," he said. "You were in there a long time. Give your head a little time to get back to normal."

"I'm fine," Monk said. "Just point me toward the doctor's office. Or wherever it is he'll give me the results."

The technician shook his head. "Not today. The films won't be ready until tomorrow afternoon. Your doctor should have told you that."

"Tomorrow?" Dr. Gordon hadn't said a damned thing about that . . . had he? "Isn't there some way to—"

The technician took Monk's arm again and started him toward the door.

"Not if we want to be absolutely sure of the results," he said. "I'm sure you've heard the old line: You can have it fast, or you can have it right." He opened the door at the rear of the room. "Dr. Gordon will call you. You probably won't even have to come back to his office."

Monk nodded, then went through the door. He walked down a short corridor, through an archway, and out into the reception room. The receptionist, a thin, middle-aged woman, smiled as he passed, but said nothing. Trained, Monk guessed, to be careful with the people who came from the machines, people with problems that didn't lend themselves easily to chitchat.

Out in the Saab, Monk sat behind the wheel for a few minutes, staring through the windshield. Tomorrow afternoon. Thirty-six hours before he'd know. Despite a temperature in the high eighties—much hotter inside the parked car—he felt a distinct chill. He tried to recognize the cognitive errors, to apply rationality to the problem, but the other part of his brain— the much more primitive limbic part—would not be stopped.

His final years with Pastor Monk, the long years before his father finally died, had been a struggle, and not just for Monk himself. Even though they'd never talked about it, he knew the retired preacher had been terrified, and Monk realized he was now beginning to understand why. Even a bastard could be scared shitless, and not just about dying. Dementia and the decline into full-on Alzheimer's wasn't simply a matter of dying. Just the thought made Monk queasy. There were no atheists in fox-holes, and he didn't imagine there were many in brain-scanning machines either. Dear God, he felt like saying. Please don't turn me into my father. *Please don't let me turn into that.*

He reached out and slid the key into the ignition, but didn't have a chance to start the Saab before he was interrupted by the sound of knuck-les banging against the passenger window. He turned to see William Smith's face glaring in at him.

TEN

Monk stared back. William here? After what had just happened back in the hot tub? Monk felt a jab of uncertainty, suddenly unsure that what he was seeing was real, and it was almost a relief to hear the sound of William's voice as he knocked again.

"Damn it, Monk, open the door!"

Monk hit the power switch to unlock the door and William Smith opened it and slid into the seat.

"What are you doing here?" Monk asked. "How did you know I was—" He didn't bother finishing the question. If they wanted to, there wasn't much the NSA couldn't find out. About anybody.

"The director wants to see you," William said. "My director, I mean."

"Fort Meade wants to see me?"

"Trust me, it's not my idea."

Monk stared at him. "They sent *you* to get me?"

"I told them I was the wrong guy."

"Who else is coming from the bureau?"

William ignored the question. He pointed out the window toward his dark blue Chevy Caprice, parked a few cars away. The same car he'd been using the other morning. "You can follow me."

"To Fort Meade? We're going out to Maryland?"

William opened the door and got out of the Saab, then looked back at Monk. "Not Fort Meade," he said. "You already know the way to the office I've been using. I'm going to follow you there." He paused. "I've been ordered to make damned sure you make it."

William stayed close behind as Monk headed east on Reservoir Street, past the Ellington School of the Arts to Wisconsin Avenue, then across town to William's sad little building on Florida Avenue. They parked out front, went through the front door together and took the tiny elevator up to the third floor, then down a corridor to a door marked POTOMAC ENGINEERING. William used a key on the door and they went through.

The small reception room featured a faux-wood secretary's desk, a yellow vinyl couch, and two light brown vinyl armchairs. On the walls hung photographs of civil engineering projects—a couple of dams and a section of freeway—along with some framed blueprints. A plastic ficus benjamina stood beyond the desk, and a plastic philodendron leaned pitifully from a fake clay pot next to the couch.

The woman sitting at the desk smiled as they approached. A brass placard identified her as Esther Valenzuela. About forty, Monk judged, with remarkably white teeth and round brown eyes he suspected had been trained to miss nothing. What he knew for sure was that Esther was just as faux a secretary as was the imitation wood in her desk. Her only job was to get rid of anyone who might wander by in search of an actual engineer.

"He's inside, William," she said to her boss. "Got here about ten minutes ago." She stopped smiling. "Be careful. He seems extra tense today."

William stepped directly toward the door to the left of Esther's desk, tapped on it before opening the door and moving through. Monk followed. He knew the name Philip Carter, but he didn't recognize the NSA director standing near the small window behind the desk, and he wasn't surprised. You'd have to ask half a million Americans to find one who knew the guy's name, much less what he looked like. The man who ran America's biggest corporation of spies was virtually invisible himself.

William closed the door behind them. "This is Puller Monk, Mr. Director," he told Carter, before turning to Monk. "Director Carter," he said.

Carter extended his hand and Monk shook it. The director was close to seventy, Monk decided, and had to be a fitness fanatic. His prominent cheekbones accentuated the leanness of his tanned face, and his head was almost completely bald. He wore a dark blue suit with a blinding white shirt and crimson tie. Monk could see his cuff links as he held on to the man's hand for an extra beat. White enamel with tiny red birds in flight. Carter's blue eyes radiated power, as they flicked up and down Monk's standard SOG attire, his tan cotton Dockers and wrinkled tennis shirt. It was hard not to feel inferior to the impeccably tailored director, and Monk knew that was exactly the point.

Carter stepped around behind William's plain wooden desk and sat. William looked at Monk, then took the closest of the two lime-green vinyl armchairs in front of the desk. Monk sat in the other one. He glanced at the desktop. Except for a black telephone it was completely bare. No blotter, no calendar, not a photograph . . . nothing. On a narrow table to the left of the desk sat three framed photos, one of them featuring an attractive woman, the other two showing a couple of high-school age young men. Monk didn't know who they were and he would have bet a month's pay that neither of the other two men did either. The NSA director leaned forward in his chair. His thin lips moved very little as he began to speak.

"Forgive me if I'm blunt, Mr. Monk," he said, "but I don't have time to be polite."

"Blunt works for me, too. I'm just as busy as you are."

Carter's eyes indicated he wasn't used to such a response. He glanced at William, and William was quick to speak up.

"I told you this was a mistake," he told his boss. "There are fifteen thousand FBI agents. Why should we bother to use someone like—"

Carter glared at him and William closed his mouth and sat back in his chair. The director turned back to Monk.

"Please forgive Mr. Smith. I share some of his misgivings, but the time for arguing about you is over." He paused. "You're here because you have a . . . let's just call it a dark side. An extraordinary aversion to letting go long after it's time to quit, and an alternative approach—to use the kindest description—to getting the job done." Again he paused. "Ordinarily, fatal flaws for an FBI agent, but your results somehow manage to overcome your methods. Either you're the luckiest man alive, or you . . ."

Director Carter's voice died as Monk rose from his chair and started for the door.

"Where are you going?" the director snapped. "You will not leave until I finish."

Monk turned back, but stayed on his feet. "Look. You people told me to back off the *Madonna* case, and that's exactly what I did. You don't have to haul me in here and—"

"You did not back off, Mr. Monk. You followed Mr. Smith to this office. You were ordered to leave this case alone, but you did exactly the opposite."

"I wasn't about to quit, not without a better explanation. The case I've been working isn't simply about the *Madonna*. There's a major art-theft ring operating in this country and around the world. My job is to recover the loot and prosecute the thieves." Monk took a step toward the director. "The *Madonna* may be connected to the same ring, and I needed to make that clear to William. To make damned sure he understood that I had to be cut in at the finish of whatever you've got going."

"That's bullshit," William said. "He talked about a lot more than—"

Again Carter's chilly blue eyes swung to William. Again William's mouth closed.

"You mentioned the FISA wire to Mr. Smith," the director told Monk. "You indicated you weren't about to leave this case alone. Your history of persistence presents a problem."

"I have no damned idea what you're talking about." He took another step closer to the desk. "Let me say it again. You don't have to threaten me. You don't have to worry about me intruding. I'm not about to throw away my career like that."

Carter leaned back in his chair. "I'm afraid there's been a misunderstanding, Mr. Monk. I'm not here to threaten you. I'm here to ask for your help."

Monk stared at him. "My help?"

Carter pointed at the vacant chair. Monk sat.

"What do you know about North Korea's Division 39 program?" the director asked.

Monk sat up straighter. North Korea. Division 39. He felt a tickle in the back of his mind. "Jog my memory."

"They operate out of a building near the Russian embassy in Pyongyang. The division has two arms, one of them allegedly legal, but both have the same purpose."

Monk nodded. Now he remembered the piece in the *Wall Street Journal*. Division 39 was a slush fund, a holding company of businesses set up to funnel money directly to Kim Jong Il. Enough money to fund his intelligence activities around the world.

"I've read something," he said. "But I didn't get the sense that Division 39 is a secret."

"The commercial side isn't. It's the other end of the house we're concerned with here." Carter turned to William, who took over.

"The secret arm of Thirty-nine—the illegal activities directorate—is modeled on the Russian *mafiya*," he said. "Illegal arms smuggling, robbery and extortion, currency counterfeiting. But the biggest moneymaker is drug smuggling. Kim Jong Il orders every farming collective in North Korea to plant twenty-five acres in poppies. The annual yield in opium, morphine, and heroin is fifty tons, with a return of close to fifteen billion dollars a year, roughly equal to the country's reportable GDP." William paused. "Every cent is used to keep their spies in place around the world, including right here in Washington."

Monk glanced at Carter before returning to William. "You're saying Division 39 stole the *Madonna*, but how can that be? The thief—she used the name Sarah Freed—was an American. From Boston, according to what she told the victim."

"Not even close. She was born an American, but she hasn't been one for a long time."

"An American working for Pyongyang?"

"For the illegal activities directorate of Division 39. She's one of what the division calls the *ipyanghan*. A Korean word for adopted children."

Monk frowned, but William continued before he could say anything.

"But they weren't adopted, of course. They were kidnapped. As an off-shoot of Pyongyang's program to kidnap Japanese nationals in the 1970s."

Monk nodded. He'd read the stories.

"In the same decade," William continued, "Division 39 began to steal American infants as well."

William looked at his boss, and Carter nodded for him to continue.

"We have a source in Pyongyang who's identified ten kidnapped American girls who were sent to North Korea for training. Schooled together. Taught perfect English. Kept abreast of everything current in the United States. Raised to think and act as Americans, then conditioned to hate us. Trained to come back here, one or more at a time, to live with us. To carry out missions ranging from robbery to extortion to assassination."

Monk found himself sitting up straighter. "Sleepers. You found a sleeper." He paused. "And you've got a mole."

"Took me ten years. Money wouldn't do it—we offered millions—but two months ago I found a man working inside Thirty-nine who's convinced Kim Jong Il is destroying the country, so convinced that he's willing to risk his life to help us. So now we have a mole . . . I should say we think we have a mole. Until we can corroborate what he tells us, evaluate his reliability, we can't be sure who he's really working for. Can't be sure he's not a double agent."

"And your mole knows who stole the *Madonna*."

"He knows it was one of the *ipyanghan*. He knows her Korean name—Sung Kim—but that's all he knows. He works in the illegal activities directorate, but he has no access to the *ipyanghan* files. He can't get into them without risking discovery and I don't want him to do that. Not yet, for sure. Not until we've determined his usefulness. Dead, he's no good at all. If he's legit, we can use him forever."

"So you haven't really identified her, this Sung Kim."

"We know she's in the States, but that's about it. We don't know her cover name or names, her legend, or where she lives."

"Or where she is at the moment."

"She was in Paris immediately after the robbery, we do know that. . . . We think we know that. And we've been told she's back now."

"You didn't follow her in Paris? Follow her from the airport when she got back?"

William shook his head. "Our information comes from the mole. We didn't see the meeting . . . didn't have anyone on the ground." Again William glanced at his boss, again Carter nodded. "Our man says Sung Kim is here, somewhere in this country, preparing for her next assignment." He hesitated. "A job we have to . . ."

William stopped. Monk waited for him to continue, but he didn't. Seconds passed in silence. Monk turned to Director Carter.

"That's it?" he said. "That's all you've got?"

"We did get a name from our man," Carter said. "The name of an American supposedly involved with Sung Kim. But there's a problem. A bunch of problems." He paused. "That's why you're here."

Monk grunted. "I assume you're prepared to be a bit more specific."

"Not a whole lot, I'm afraid. Not until you agree to come on board."

"What's that supposed to mean, on board?"

"We need you to work with us to catch the sleeper. To catch Sung Kim before she can complete her next mission."

Monk stared at him. "That's what this is all about? I'm already on board . . . I'm already working the art thefts. Surely Burt Malone made it clear that whatever you need from the bureau is a done deal."

"I'm not talking about Burt Malone, or the bureau. I'm talking about you, Mr. Monk. Just you."

"Just me?" He shook his head. "I have no damned idea what you're . . ."

"Basically this, Mr. Monk. Our asset doesn't trust the FBI, not after that bureau supervisor got caught spying for the Russians a couple of years ago. He's terrified about being exposed and killed before we can get him out of North Korea. Frankly, I have the same concerns about the Hoover Building, but we need an FBI agent who's familiar with the string of art thefts." Carter paused. "Bottom line, we need you but we don't want your bureau."

"To work for NSA." Monk knew his tone was sarcastic, but he continued anyway. "Without telling my bosses."

"Worse than that, I'm afraid. We want you to work for us without telling anybody. Not the bureau, not your girlfriend, not your buddies at the SOG. Nobody. Even NSA will be off-limits. Outside of Mr. Smith and me, nobody from Fort Meade will know about this." Again he paused. "If you get caught, the two of us will abandon you as well."

Monk looked out the small window to the right of the desk. The sky was clouding up, but the tops of the trees were dead still. From the outer office he could hear the secretary typing at her computer. He turned back to Philip Carter.

"You said I have a dark side, that I take too many risks, and that I won't quit when they tell me to stop." He glanced at William. "Mr. Smith doesn't want me . . . neither one of us wants to work together. So why me?"

"Because you have the skills, for one. Because you function best outside the box. Because we can be certain you're not a spy. No double agent in his right mind would work the way you do." Carter's smile wasn't all that friendly. "But most of all because you're a winner. Because somehow you always manage to come out on top."

Monk stared at the director. A winner? Wouldn't it be great to believe that? But even if the director were right, there were table limits with every game. What Carter was asking was off-the-charts stupid. A real gambler knows when to throw in his cards and walk away. Monk started to get up, then heard himself asking one last question.

"Who's the target?"

"I can't tell you that until you agree to help."

"Has to be a big player, though," Monk said. "Somebody too powerful to risk alienating."

Carter did not respond.

"And you're not sure of your mole," Monk said. "Not sure enough to risk a disaster by going all out on the word of an untested asset."

"Let's just say we can't take the chance. Not with the kind of man he's telling us about."

Monk chewed the inside of his cheek. He could still hear the clicking of the keyboard from the other room, but now he could hear the faint groan of the air-conditioning system as well. He checked William's face, but the NSA spook turned away. Monk slid forward in his chair and faced Carter.

"I have a good job, Mr. Director. A job I like, and one I need to keep.

You're asking me to work as a double agent inside my own bureau, but I won't do that. I won't even consider doing that."

"I understand exactly what you're saying. You need time to make your decision."

"That's not what I said at all. I've made my decision. I don't need another minute to think about it."

Philip Carter smiled again, and this time it appeared genuine. "Of course you don't, Mr. Monk. But just in case, I'll keep the offer open till noon tomorrow."

ELEVEN

Monk was slicing a banana over his bowl of Kellogg's Mini-Wheats when the phone rang the next morning. He dropped the remaining banana into the cereal and grabbed the phone. His eyes widened when he heard who was calling. Dr. John Gordon, his primary-care physician at Georgetown University Medical Center.

"Yes, Doctor."

"I just spoke with the radiologist about your MRI films. Do you have time to come by for a few minutes this morning?"

Monk felt a tingle climb up the back of his neck. "What's the problem?"

"I have an opening at eight-forty-five."

"What did you find?"

"I'll see you at a quarter to nine."

Dr. Gordon's office was a small one, lit by a single large window behind the doctor's plain wooden desk. The right wall was covered with books, the left with framed diplomas and certificates. Dr. Gordon went around the desk and sat. Monk took the upholstered armchair in front of the desk. The doctor was young—couldn't have been much over forty—and that was one of the things Monk liked about him, that and the fact that he looked like a nerd. In his white lab coat, with his receding hairline and thick glasses, Gordon didn't seem like the type to have messed around in medical school, and that was just fine with Monk.

This morning, however, he couldn't help noticing that the doctor looked even more serious than usual as he gestured toward a large yellow envelope on his desk. Monk glanced at it, saw his name in black lettering, below his name the letters MRI in red. Monk looked at the doctor's face, but Gordon wouldn't meet his gaze. Monk felt a tightening at the top of his shoulders.

"What did you come up with?" he asked.

"Not enough, I'm afraid."

Monk stared at him. His shoulders grew even tighter.

"The radiologist concentrated on the parietal and temporal lobes," Doctor Gordon said. "Where we would expect early evidence of dementia . . . for pathology that might explain the symptoms you've reported. The good news is the films show no evidence of stroke or tumors."

"And the bad news?"

"The radiologist did notice something that concerns him."

Monk looked past the doctor, out the window at the tops of hemlock trees moving with the unusual morning breeze that was holding off the heat of the day. Is this how it happens? he wondered. Is this the way you get such news as this? Somehow—sitting in this drab little office with this drab little doctor—it didn't seem nearly dramatic enough.

"New York University did a study," the doctor said, "of markers for early detection of Alzheimer's. They claim they can predict to a ninety percent accuracy rate which patients are at risk."

"And I'm one of them."

"Not necessarily. I only mention the study as a lead-in to what the radiologist wants to explore further."

"What did he see?"

"The brains of patients with mental decline show a shrinkage of the medial-temporal lobe. About seven-tenths of one percent of its volume each year."

"But this was my first brain scan. You don't have a baseline to use for comparison."

"That's why we need to take the next step." The doctor paused. "The films show that your medial-temporal lobe is undersized. Microscopically so, but given the symptoms you claim are getting worse—increasing forgetfulness, problems with concentration and everyday functions like remembering passwords and common vocabulary for your written reports—we think a PET scan is the way to go." He paused again. "If for no other reason, to ease your mind."

Monk sat forward in his chair. "Amyloid plaque. That's what you'd be looking for, right?" He'd spent more than an hour on Google last night.

Dr. Gordon nodded. "The standard MRI you took can't show it. To find the amyloid plaque, the radiologist has to use PBI, a dye he'll inject, then watch as it circulates through your brain."

"It sticks to the plaque. Highlights the plaque."

"Exactly."

Monk glanced at the diplomas on the doctor's wall, then out the window again for a moment, before turning back to the doctor. "I'm only forty-five years old."

"Your father died of complications from Alzheimer's. How old was he at the onset of dementia?"

"Late fifties, I think, but I can't be certain. We didn't have much of a relationship."

"You told me last time you were here, but refresh my memory. How long has it been since he died?"

"A couple of months, maybe three."

The doctor glanced at Monk's chart on his desk, at his notes from the last visit. "Almost seven months, actually." He paused. "I have no training in psychiatry, but have you considered that your symptoms might be part of a reaction to his death?"

"Maybe for a few weeks. Not this long."

"Perhaps not. And you're considerably younger than he was when his symptoms started. You can look at the PET scan as a way to put your concern behind you."

"What if I don't take it at all?" Monk hesitated. "There's no cure. What good would it do me to know?"

"Your medial-temporal anomaly could be congenital, could be indicative of nothing . . . You wouldn't have to give it another thought. And even if we do measure further shrinkage, researchers are coming up with new discoveries every day. A cure could be found tomorrow. And you would have dodged a bullet."

Monk studied his hands on the arm of his chair for a moment, before looking at the doctor again. "Would you do it? If you were me, would you do it?"

"As a doctor I'd like to think I'd trust the science."

"I'm not a doctor."

"I'd still do it. It might be a gamble, but I'd still do it."

Monk chewed the inside of his cheek. A gamble. Ordinarily that would be all he needed to hear, but now? With this? No matter the payoff, some wagers were just too scary. This one sounded way too spooky. He opened his mouth to tell the doctor as much, but something else came out instead.

"When?" he asked. "How soon can I get an appointment?"

Even before he reached the Saab in the medical center parking lot, Monk knew the PET scan wouldn't be enough. To prove to himself he wasn't losing his mind to the disease that killed his father, he had to have something more than an examination of his brain. No matter how the test came out, he still had to make a living, and he couldn't do it in a state of fear. The only way to beat the fear was to run headlong at it, to tackle it directly between the numbers, to dare it to kill him or leave him alone. And to do that required a massive test of his abilities, every one of his abilities. A wager bigger than anything a casino would ever allow him to make. He thought about such a wager. About what losing would do to him . . . and winning. Winning would literally make him well, would do more for him than any poker pot he'd ever raked across the table to his stack. As he thought about it, Monk's stomach began to churn. The vibration seemed to expand in every direction at the same time, until he was giddy with it. But over the euphoria, an insistent voice in the back of his mind fought to be heard.

You're actually considering working for NSA without telling your bosses? the voice was saying. *Then why bother with the PET scan? Going after Sung Kim on your own is all the proof you need that you're completely crazy!*

Monk allowed the small voice to rattle on, but at the Saab he snatched the door open and reached for his phone. Philip Carter's offer was good until noon, but there was no reason to wait any longer to get started.

TWELVE

"Damn it, Charles," Thomas Franklin told Charles Emrick, his most senior vice president, as they stood together in the doorway of Franklin's office in the Global Panoptic Building. "I know I pay you to worry, but don't be ridiculous."

They were on their way to the boardroom just down the hall, to an emergency board of directors' meeting, and Emrick wouldn't be dissuaded.

"They've been reading the *New York Times* again," Emrick said. "And they're scared to death about what's happening in South Korea."

"They're *always* scared about something. That's their job. That's how they're supposed to be."

"This time it's different. We've got a lot of money in Seoul. The board's worried about what the *Times* is reporting. They're afraid to open the papers anymore, and they want to hear from you that they have nothing to be concerned about."

"Well, I guess that's *my* job, isn't it?" Franklin smiled. "To tell them what they want to hear."

Before Emrick could respond, Franklin started for the boardroom. Emrick hurried to catch up, and a moment later Franklin pulled open the ten-foot mahogany door and moved directly to the head of the magnificent table that dominated the room. Emrick stepped past him and took the chair to the right of Franklin's. Franklin slid into his own chair, laid his hands on the table with a feeling of pride. Eighteen feet long, burnished walnut with crimson mahogany inlays, the conference table gleamed like polished leather under the glow from twin crystal chandeliers suspended above it. Franklin glanced at the faces around the table.

To his right—beyond Emrick—Stanley Ballinger's nearly lipless mouth was as lifeless as usual. The man was a zombie. There was no way in hell to read his mood, and a waste of time even to try. To Ballinger's right, Jeffrey Cox sat smiling, his gray mustache quivering at the tips, but Franklin knew the smile meant nothing. Cox smiled even when somebody died. Past Cox, Sarah Hundley was busy with the paperwork in front of her, and hadn't even bothered to look up when he came into the room.

Franklin swung to his left, nodded and smiled at the directors down that side of the table. Gordon Fairclough nodded back. Jim Adams raised his eyebrows, and the Devore brothers lifted their right hands in a miniature wave. Franklin smiled at the twins. They'd been the first members of his first board of directors, more than twenty years ago. He could announce a plan to nuke Washington and theirs would be the first hands raised to support him. No matter what happened here today, Eric and Pat would back him all the way.

"Please forgive my being late," Franklin said. "What can I do for you today?"

Stanley Ballinger's lackluster gray eyes swung toward him. His thin voice sounded more mechanical than human.

"I won't mince words, Thomas. We're troubled about the situation in Korea . . . about the series the *New York Times* is running." He paused. "Especially yesterday's story. The one about the automobile executive who jumped out the window when the *Times* disclosed his financial ties with North Korea."

Ballinger glanced up and down the table before continuing.

"We all know why he'd been giving his company's money to Pyongyang. Everybody wants to get in on the windfall of contracts for the development of the north when the two countries reunite. It's going to be a multitrillion-dollar market, but it's still illegal in South Korea to provide financial support for Kim Jong Il. And it's every bit as illegal here."

Ballinger paused to stare pointedly at Franklin.

"A big share of the money the automobile executive gave Pyongyang came directly from American corporations eager for reunification. The Justice Department's going to nail the American companies the *Times* has outed, but that won't stop the attorney general. He's not going to quit until he gets everybody who's been doing the same thing."

Ballinger glanced at the other board members before turning back to Franklin.

"What we want to know, Thomas, what we want you to tell us, is that Global Panoptic has nothing to hide. That this company has nothing to hide."

Franklin nodded. The stories out of Seoul were indeed troubling, and not just the one Ballinger was talking about. The *Times* had obviously developed a hell of a source inside the South Korean government. Every day the reporters uncovered more and more of the growing scandal . . . the illegal transfers of American corporate money to North Korea through business executives and politicians in Seoul.

"I've been following the stories just as closely as you appear to be, Stanley. There hasn't been a word about Global Panoptic, but I hope that doesn't surprise you." He smiled. "Do you really think that if the attorney general suspected us of funneling Global money to Pyongyang, we'd have to wait to hear about it from a newspaper?"

Ballinger did not return his smile. "We've got a billion dollars working in Seoul alone, not to mention the rest of South Korea. There's no way to take proper care of that kind of money, not in that part of the world anyway." He looked up and down the table, into the faces of the other directors, talking to them now as much as to Franklin. "How can you know for sure that some of it isn't going to Kim Jong Il instead?"

Franklin stared at Ballinger. The North Korean dictator goddamned well *better* be getting some of that money. A whole lot of that money. For a fleeting instant Franklin was tempted to tell these people the truth about Global Panoptic's investments in the Koreas. About how he was pumping money through Seoul to Pyongyang as fast as he could, just to keep the North Korean people from starving to death before the inevitable reunification. To keep them and their nearly one hundred percent literacy rate alive long enough to go to work for Global Panoptic. To give Global an inexhaustible supply of educated and hardworking technicians, a workforce second to none for the emergence of North Korea into the twenty-first century.

Franklin felt a surge of excitement. Global would be the first corporation into the new Korea. Every inch of the north's brand-new telecommunications infrastructure would be designed and built by Franklin's company. Every mile of fiber optic cable, every one of the thousands of cell phone repeating towers, all of the millions of cell phones themselves, along with the cutting-edge wireless computer technology that was sweeping the world, would be provided by the company he'd built from the ground up. To bring the north up to the standard of the south—admittedly a long-term operation—would eventually result in billions of dollars of profit for Global Panoptic. Franklin glanced at the faces around the table. It wouldn't happen overnight, but one day the members of this board would understand the risks he was taking and appreciate his foresight.

"We've got the biggest accounting firm in South Korea watching our money," he told them. "I wouldn't swear to you about anything when it comes to Asian politics, but I can guarantee one thing. Global Panoptic hasn't authorized one penny to do business with Pyongyang."

Which was the truth, technically anyway. Franklin's corporation hadn't authorized anything of the sort, hadn't left so much as a smudged corporate fingerprint to identify Global as dealing with the north. And it would take a hell of a lot more than the *New York Times* to prove otherwise, to follow a trail of money that God himself would have trouble tracing back to Thomas Franklin.

"It's not the pennies we're concerned about, Thomas," Ballinger said. "It's the billions. And you want to put even more money over there. Your insistence on increasing the size of our existing infrastructure all over South Korea borders on irresponsible."

"Especially," Jeffrey Cox interrupted, his higher-pitched voice coming in a rush. "Especially with Pyongyang's nuclear arsenal growing stronger and stronger every day. Good God, Thomas. Kim Jong Il has made no secret about his dream of invading the south. If his weapons program gets any bigger, he might just do it. We could lose everything we've invested over there. We could be ruined."

Franklin nodded. *We might be, if a doormat like you were running this company*.

"I appreciate your input, Jeffrey, but an invasion's not going to happen. The *Wall Street Journal* is reporting that Seoul is considering paying off Pyongyang if Kim agrees to freeze his nuclear program. I'm on top of that situation. With my access to the president and his national security advisor, I'm not about to let us get caught by surprise."

"My point exactly," Pat Devore said, his eyes sweeping the table. "You would know as soon as anyone if the north makes a move to invade." Next to him, his twin brother nodded in support.

Franklin forced a smile, but Pat Devore's words brought no comfort. Pat hadn't been at Battle Valley Farm the other day. He had no way of knowing about Franklin's meeting with the president. No way of knowing that when Ishii Nakamura got his bombs, Global would be ruined. That the hundreds of millions of dollars Franklin had spent would be wasted. Franklin felt a weakness sweep his body as he admitted there could be an even worse outcome.

If the Justice Department discovered what he was doing, the attorney general would act quickly. Franklin pictured the FBI arresting him, handcuffing him, and leading him to a bureau car, TV cameras crowding against him, reporters shouting, as he completed the infamous "perp walk." In the end he'd lose everything, most of all the company he'd founded, that he'd given his life to creating and developing.

Jesus, he thought. *There has to be a way to . . .*

Sarah Hundley's calm voice interrupted the noise in his head.

"Let's get back to the money thing," she said. "I'm not as worried about an invasion as an audit. If somehow—accidentally or any other way—our money is getting to Kim Jong Il, we could go to jail." She glanced at the people around the table. "We could all go to jail."

Franklin forced himself to concentrate on her words. "You're right, Sarah, of course you're right. What would you recommend we do?"

"A special internal audit. I want to see an accounting for the funds we have in Korea. Every penny."

Franklin looked around the table. "And the rest of you?"

Voices rose in agreement, but Stanley Ballinger's stood out.

"At least," he said. "An audit at the very least . . . although I'm not sure what good it would do." He shook his head. "There are too many ways to get around an audit, but it would be a start. Show good faith on our part, if nothing else."

"Done," Franklin said. He turned to Emrick. "Make it happen, Charles."

Emrick made a note on the pad in front of him.

"Anything else?" Franklin asked. He stared at Jim Adams and Gordon Fairclough. "You two haven't said anything."

Fairclough shook his head. Next to him, Jim Adams appeared to have something to say. He sat forward for a moment, then relaxed back into his chair.

"I've got nothing to add," he said, then looked around the table at his fellow directors, before turning his eyes back to Franklin. "As long as you keep making the kind of money we're seeing, I'm just fine."

Now there was a murmur of agreement and nodding of heads. Franklin could feel the tension drain out of the room. He looked at his board of directors. They worked hard at their job, made every attempt to pretend they ran the company, but in the end they were happy to let him do it.

Sarah Hundley had mentioned going to jail, and everyone in the room knew the best way to avoid such a disaster was to make sure the CEO made all the decisions: to make doubly sure that Thomas Franklin would take all the blame if things went sour. All in all, it was a good system, a workable system that made it unnecessary for these people ever to know the truth.

THIRTEEN

Monk stared through the window of the massive Bell 412EP helicopter as it swept across Thomas Franklin's estate on the way to the mansion that dominated the gentle hills of Battle Valley Farm. Despite the size of the chopper, he still had to fight off a twinge of claustrophobia, but was less successful against the shiver of doubt that swept through him as they passed over the billionaire's private golf course, the stables, the skeet range, and on to Franklin's twenty-thousand-square-foot house. Seeing all of this grandeur through the haze of an August twilight, Monk had to wonder if he'd made a big mistake by accepting Philip Carter's assignment. Gambling was one thing, but this just might be ridiculous.

He glanced at Lisa Sands. She grinned at him and he felt a twinge of guilt. His FBI-agent girlfriend carried the same credentials and badge he did. She could be a big help to him tonight, but he couldn't allow her to participate. If this mission for Carter and William Smith failed—if he got busted in the attempt to validate the information from their asset in Pyongyang—Lisa would at least have "plausible deniability" when the shit hit the bureau fan.

He surveyed the other guests in the helicopter, recognizing three senators and a lady congressman, and that was only in this chopper. Franklin had leased a fleet of them for the evening: ten of the beefy 412s to ferry the more than one hundred gowned and dinner-jacketed guests from the Global Building in Crystal City, Virginia, out here to Gettysburg. Tonight's party to honor America's newly appointed ambassador to the United Nations was the hottest ticket in town. Even the president was expected to drop in to say hello. Monk still wasn't sure how NSA got Lisa and him included on the guest list.

On the ground nobody moved until the rotors stopped spinning. A lot of money had been spent on hair and makeup, and no one was about to make an entrance to Franklin's party looking like a tornado victim. Again Monk glanced at Lisa, but this time he felt nothing but pride. These were beautiful people, but Lisa was the most gorgeous of all. Her backless red gown highlighted the tan she'd been working on all summer, and with her dark hair hanging straight to her bare shoulders she made him want to reach out and touch her. In his own white dinner jacket, Monk was indistinguishable from the other males, which was precisely the point.

A few minutes later, he and Lisa stood with the others inside Franklin's front door, in a marble foyer big enough for a parking lot. Gilt-framed mirrors lined the entry hall. Cast-bronze figurines and multicolored ceramic treasures filled the niches and crannies between the mirrors. Lisa took a long look around before turning to Monk.

"What a dump," she murmured.

Monk glanced past her toward the great room just beyond the foyer then gestured toward the reception line inside. "There's Franklin, talking with Harrison Ford."

Lisa's head snapped around, and she took a couple of steps toward the movie star, then turned back to grab Monk's arm. "C'mon," she said. "Before he gets away."

Lisa led the way toward the receiving line, striding as hard as she could in her formfitting gown, but they didn't make it in time. Before they were halfway there, Harrison Ford was shaking Franklin's hand and walking away. Lisa stopped dead.

"Damn it," she said. "I'm going after him."

But she'd only taken one step before Monk touched her shoulder.

"Why don't we start with Thomas Franklin first. Trust me, Harrison's not going anywhere you won't be able to find him." Monk glanced around the room. "And he won't be the only celebrity here tonight. The place is crawling with them."

A moment later they were standing in the reception line, one couple short of Franklin himself. He was a tall man, Monk realized, taller than he looked in the photographs William had provided. At least as tall as his own six-two. In his late fifties, Franklin's gray-streaked dark hair was still full, and combed straight back above his high forehead.

As Monk had been told to expect, he was asked by Franklin's assistant—a slender man in a white dinner jacket—to identify himself and Lisa, so the assistant could make the introduction. Monk did so, and a moment later they were in front of Franklin.

"May I present," the assistant said, "FBI agents Lisa Sands and Puller Monk. They're with the Washington Field Office."

Franklin stepped toward Lisa and extended his hand, exposing several inches of gleaming French cuff and a gold cuff link the size of a half dollar. Lisa took his hand.

"How very kind of you to join us, Special Agent Sands," he said, then chuckled. "I trust that you and your partner aren't working here tonight."

Lisa smiled. "Not tonight. Tonight we're just here to enjoy ourselves."

Again Franklin laughed, but Monk ignored it as not worth trying to read. He waited for a smile instead. You could tell a lot more from a smile.

"And Special Agent Monk," Franklin said as they shook hands. "You are most welcome as well."

Monk was afraid for a moment that he wasn't going to smile at all, but an instant later he did, his perfect teeth made even whiter by his world-class tan. It was a big smile, but not in the right places. The corners of Franklin's mouth were turned up, but the creases in the skin to the outside of his eyes, his crow's-feet, didn't move at all, and the orbital muscles were totally uninvolved. "Nonzygomatic" was the technical term, but Monk needed more. In this setting a less-than-heartfelt smile was actually more normal than the other kind. Most likely it had nothing to do with the fact that they were FBI agents. Monk decided to up the ante.

"Your home is magnificent," he said. "Especially your art collection. I hope you won't think us rude if we have a look around."

"Not at all," Franklin said, but Monk noticed his body turning as he said it, very slightly, but enough so that he was no longer facing Monk head on. An unconscious shift from an aggressive posture to a defensive one. "I'm very proud of Battle Valley Farm," Franklin added. "You have my permission to look at every inch of it."

Unlike his body, Franklin's voice was anything but defensive, although Monk couldn't miss the irony of his words. Without a warrant there was only one legal way to search this house—with the permission of the own-er—and Franklin had just given his permission. The idea made Monk smile, but Franklin didn't notice as he turned to the next couple in the re-ceiving line. Monk and Lisa moved a few feet away and stood for a mo-ment as Lisa glanced around the room.

"Come on," she said, her voice eager. "Let's go see who we can find."

Monk followed her for a few steps, but stopped when a white-jacketed waiter appeared at their side. "Drinks?" he said. "What may I bring you tonight?"

Monk turned to Lisa. "Champagne for me," she told the man.

Monk decided to test Franklin's cellar. "Cabernet," he said. "Do you have any Fallbrook in the house?" A boutique winery that was helping es-tablish Southern California's growing reputation as wine country.

"Of course," the waiter said. "As a matter of fact, we just opened a cou-ple bottles of the 2001 Cabernet."

They hadn't taken a dozen steps into the thick of the party when the waiter returned with their drinks. They stood sipping, then began to wan-der through the room. As they passed among groups of people in ani-mated conversations—toward the string quartet playing at the far end of the room—Monk didn't bother looking at the paintings hanging on the walls along the way. The last place the *Madonna* would be was down here. He turned toward the magnificent staircase behind them and to their left, covered with guests on their way up to the second floor or coming back down. If Franklin had a secret cache of stolen paintings, it would be some-where closer to where he actually lived, somewhere up in the residential area on the third floor.

As he thought about where he'd have to go to find those paintings, what he'd have to do when he got there, Monk almost stopped walking.

Now that he was actually inside Franklin's house—surrounded by the people who ran this country—he couldn't help questioning his decision. Had he finally gone too far? Had his addiction to risk finally caught up with . . .

"Puller?"

Monk felt a tug on his arm. He turned to Lisa. Her dark eyes were concerned as she moved closer to him.

"¿Qué te pasa?" she asked in the flawless Spanish her father had brought from Spain and taught her as a child in Texas. "What's the matter with you?" she repeated. "You haven't heard a word I've said . . . and you look terrible." She touched his face. "Feels like you're running a temperature."

Monk shook his head. "Sorry, Lisa, I was daydreaming. But it is awfully stuffy in here." He pointed in the direction of the huge open doors at the far end of the room. "Why don't we check out the veranda."

But it was even warmer outside, the August night soggy with humidity.

"My God, Puller," Lisa whispered in his ear. "You were right about the celebrities. That's Paul Newman over there. Can you believe it?"

Monk followed her discreet effort to point with her head, and damned if she wasn't right. Paul Newman—older than you'd expect, but still every bit the larger-than-life figure Monk had grown up watching—was talking with a man Monk didn't recognize. Next to Newman, Teddy Kennedy was laughing with Jimmy and Roslyn Carter, and behind them Senator Hillary Clinton—no hubby in sight—was surrounded by a gaggle of admirers, the familiar insistent pitch of her voice clearly audible as Monk and Lisa passed by. He wasn't about to gawk, but he came close. Lisa didn't even try to be cool. She might be an FBI agent and a former district attorney, but right now her eyes were wide as a fifth-grader's.

Monk used her distraction to do some business. He turned around and looked up, examining what he could see of the back of the three-story mansion from his position on the terrace. There were a few lights in the windows of the second floor, but the top floor appeared to be completely dark.

Lisa nudged his arm. "When's the president supposed to show?"

Monk spotted a couple of strapping young men with bulges under their white dinner jackets and earpieces in their ears. "Can't be long," he said. "The detail's here already." He thought about the Carters and Hillary. There'd be Secret Service with them as well.

He checked his watch. A quarter after ten. The Secret Service body-guards down here meant there would be a few more upstairs, but they wouldn't be at peak vigilance until POTUS was actually on the premises. Monk had to get moving before that happened.

"I need to find a bathroom," he told Lisa. "Do you mind if I leave you alone for a few minutes?"

She didn't answer, her eyes still riveted on the celebrities. Monk touched her arm and she spoke without looking at him. "Go . . . Take your time. I'll be right here when you get back."

He hurried through the double doors and headed for the main stair-case, halfway back toward the front of the mansion. On the way he spot-ted an alcove leading to what had to be a bathroom, and suddenly he needed to use one. Inside the baroque powder room, he stared into the mirror over the sink and once again saw the face of his father. He blinked it away—getting used to Pastor Monk's ghost by now—but still it was un-settling. It had been seven months now, Dr. Gordon had reminded him, and the old bastard shouldn't continue to show up like this.

Monk turned on the cold tap and bent over the sink, used his cupped hands to throw water on his face. Picking up a towel from a stack next to the basin, he dried his face, then flipped the towel into an ornate basket against the wall to his right. He didn't risk another look in the mirror be-fore opening the door and heading back to the party. Another helicopter had arrived, Monk guessed from the increased noise level in the room, but the president was still nowhere to be seen.

He threaded his way through the crowd to the base of a curving stair-case wide enough to climb in a Hummer. As he stood there, two couples approached, glasses in hand, laughing as they started up the steps. Monk began to laugh himself as he fell in with them, as he stuck close all the way to the second floor.

FOURTEEN

When he reached the landing, Monk saw that the second floor was every
bit as impressive as downstairs. A wide corridor stretched in both directions. Crystal chandeliers hung in a sequence that carried all the way to
both ends, creating a gentle light that made the crimson Persian carpets
seem to shimmer underfoot.

He followed the two couples he'd come up the staircase with as they
started down the corridor to the right, but no longer bothered to laugh at
their wisecracks. He stayed with them just far enough to verify that
William's mole had been right about the second level, that the sitting
rooms and galleries were primarily display areas for the billionaire to show
off his art collection.

He hurried back to the staircase leading to the third floor. There was a
small white sign hanging from a blue velvet rope across the bottom of the
steps. PRIVATE, the sign read. PLEASE DO NOT DISTURB. Monk glanced
around. He saw no one looking his way, but he found himself hesitating
anyway. From here on he was trespassing, which was an extremely polite
word for what he was really doing. He straightened to his full height and
felt the "juice" rise through his body.

Life's a gamble, he reminded himself. Sometimes you just have to let it ride.

He stepped over the low velvet rope, and started up the staircase. The temptation was to skulk, but the trick was to do just the opposite. The only way to go up these stairs was to march up with his head up and shoulders back. When you act like you belong, people take if for granted that you do. But halfway up he couldn't help pausing anyway, as he listened for the voice of anyone trying to stop him. Better now than later. Better here on these steps than deeper inside the privacy of the mansion.

He heard nothing as he mounted the remaining stairs, his eyes scanning the brilliant white crown molding. He didn't see any cameras, but that didn't mean much. These days the cameras weren't much bigger than the head of a match. There could be dozens of them built into the woodwork. Whatever the case, there was no point worrying about it. He'd know soon enough if he were being watched.

On the landing he turned right again, but this time he hurried straight toward the tall double doors at the end of the corridor. The doors to the master bedroom, he was willing to bet. When he got there he reached for the gold-plated knob on the right-hand door, twisted the knob and pushed, but it was locked. A run-of-the-mill Schlage keyed-tumbler, Monk saw, not even a deadbolt, and not meant to do much more than keep the doors closed. He reached into the pocket of his dinner jacket for his picks, then took a deep breath and let it out slowly before dropping to one knee.

Long and skinny, the two black-steel extrusions looked like dental instruments. Monk inserted the first one—the torsion bar—into the keyway of the lock, followed it with the second pick. He used the second one to move the tumblers out of the way and the torsion bar to hold them there, exerting gentle pressure until twenty seconds later the lock turned. Monk straightened up, then stepped to his left, to an immense ceramic pot containing a leafy green tree he couldn't identify. He bent to the pot, picked up a handful of sphagnum moss, laid the picks under it and replaced the moss. Now no matter what happened, the burglar tools wouldn't be found in his pocket.

Back at the doors, he pushed them open and stepped through before stopping to stare. Franklin's master bedroom gave new meaning to the word "master." You could play a pretty good game of tennis in here. The ceiling wasn't quite high enough for a desperation lob, but there'd be plenty of room behind the baselines. Through an enormous skylight came more than enough moonlight to see everything. A platform dominated the room, on which stood a bed big enough for half a dozen Samoans. Oil paintings littered the walls. Narrow alcoves featured life-size statues and other sculpture. Antique French nightstands flanked the bed, each of them bearing a museum-quality bronze lamp.

Monk was on his way toward the far end of the room when he saw it.

On the far side of the bedroom, past the bed and in the corner, was the doorway into a second room. One of those "panic rooms," Monk realized, although he'd never actually been inside one. The newest fad of the superrich, it was a last-resort hiding place in case of criminal invasion. Monk started toward it. The door was open, of course, it was the way these rooms were designed. When the bad guys were chasing you, the last thing you needed was to stop and open the door.

Moments later he was standing in front of the opening.

From up close the enclosure looked like a bank vault. The door jamb was solid steel, at least four inches thick, and contained the recessed door that was ready to slide out and slam shut to seal off the entrance. Monk didn't need to go into the room to see the layout, to realize he couldn't see all of it from where he was standing. Shaped like an L, the rear section was hidden from view around a corner. The wall to his right was filled with TV screens, computer equipment, and a telephone console with dozens of buttons. A suite of comfortable furniture—leather couch and matching chairs—sat across from the electronic gear. The wall behind the couch bore a number of paintings, oils and watercolors, but no *Madonna*, not in the front part of the L at any rate. He stood there for a moment, thinking.

He had to see the rest of the panic room, had to go inside to do that, but what was the mechanism that would close the door behind him? Was there a switch inside—just on the other side of the door—or was it automatic, a sensor beam that slammed it shut whenever the beam was broken? Probably a switch, Monk decided. Sensor beams were notoriously unreliable. A number of things could trigger them. Worse, a beam might close the door too quickly, injure somebody before they could get all the way into the room. Then Monk realized he was wasting time. No matter what the setup was, he couldn't leave here without seeing every inch of the place.

He stepped over the threshold and into the room. From his left he heard a loud click, followed by a *swoosh* as the door shot out of its enclosure, then a solid *chunk* as it slammed tight against the other side. He turned to his right, looking for the switch, but saw nothing. Damn it . . . nothing was ever easy. He hustled to the corner of the L. The other section of the room was smaller than the first, and the *Madonna* wasn't there, either. The walls were completely bare.

He dashed back to the electronic gear on the right-hand wall near the door, searching for the door-release switch, but he didn't see anything obvious. He felt his heartbeat quicken. He could have explained his presence upstairs, in the bedroom even, but in here? He looked above the door for a camera, didn't see one, and realized there wouldn't be one in here. The reason was obvious. There'd be a security room downstairs, more monitors just like the ones in here. In a home-invasion situation you wouldn't want the bad guys to be watching what you were doing in this room. He turned back to the electronic array. There were too many switches, none of them marked, no way to tell what they controlled. So he tried them all. Pushed, pulled, toggled, pounded, and swore at every last one of them.

Nothing.

Then Monk saw the computer keyboard on the shelf beneath the video monitors. Grabbing at it, he began to punch the keys. Enter and Shift and Delete and Backspace, then the F keys, one after another, until he got to F8, when he heard a sound from around the corner of the L. He hurried back to the corner. The sound he'd heard was a door opening at the rear of the back section. The panic room had two exits, he realized. He was halfway to the opening when he saw that he was wrong . . . that this was no exit. He continued into what was yet another room. Lights had come on when the door opened, and Monk felt his eyes widen.

The room was huge, and stuffed with works of art. Like a museum, the space was crammed with paintings and sculpture. Directly in front of him stood a life-size female nude, beyond her at least a dozen Greek and Ro-

man statues. Oil paintings covered the walls and stood on easels throughout the space.

Monk's eyes swept the room for the *Madonna*, for the muted colors of
the picture of Mary with the Christ Child. He didn't see it, but the da
Vinci had to be in here. He started toward the rear of the room, but hadn't
gone three steps before he heard a shout behind him.

FIFTEEN

"*Stop!*" the deep voice yelled. "Stop right there and raise your arms. Put your hands on your head and turn around . . . slowly."

Monk did as he was told, until he was facing two large men in the doorway of the second room. Shorter than he was, both of them, but with much thicker necks and closer haircuts. The chrome-plated automatic pistols in their hands made them look even bigger. Not Secret Service, Monk decided. Too ape-like for the presidential detail.

"There's an explanation," he said, before either of the men could speak again. "I know this looks awful, but it was an accident. I came up from downstairs. From the party downstairs."

The taller of the two shook his head. "Then you should have realized the rest of the house is private. You must have seen the sign on the staircase." He paused. "How the hell did you get into this room?"

Monk stared at the floor for a moment, careful to keep his hands on his head, just as careful to keep his tone as meek as possible. As far removed from his official bureau voice as possible.

"I came with my girlfriend," he told them. "I couldn't find a bathroom downstairs, so I came up to the second floor to use one. Then I . . . I just got carried away looking at the house. I don't know what to say. I . . . I can't . . ." He looked at the floor again. "This is so humiliating, I can't begin to tell you."

"Maybe so," the second man said. "But the door was locked. The door into the master bedroom was locked up tight."

"Locked? No . . . no, it wasn't locked. It was wide open . . . that's the only reason I would ever have come in." He shook his head. "Mr. Franklin told me himself. Feel free to look around, he said."

The taller man scowled. "That door was supposed to be locked, but that still doesn't explain the rest of it. How you got all the way into this room."

"An accident, I told you. The door to this vault was open. I poked my head in and the darned thing closed. I hit all the buttons, and the other door opened." Monk took a short step toward the two men and allowed his voice to rise. "I was just trying to get out. All I wanted to do was go back down—"

"ID," the shorter man said. "Let's see some identification." He slid back his jacket and replaced his pistol in the holster on his belt. The taller man kept his weapon trained on Monk.

"Can I lower my arms?" Monk asked. "And reach into my pocket?"

The shorter man nodded. Monk's hand moved to the inside breast pocket of his dinner jacket. He pulled out the wallet he'd chosen for this evening, opened it, and extracted a Maryland driver's license, which he handed over. The shorter man examined the picture on the license, stared at Monk's face, then back down at the license.

"Okay, Mr. Towne," he said, "but I have to keep this until we can run a check to verify it."

"Of course," Monk said. "But why don't we just go back down and talk to Mr. Franklin. He'll tell you who I am. He'll vouch for me."

The taller man glanced at his partner, who gave a quick shake of his head. "The president's downstairs, pal," the shorter man said. "The last thing Mr. Franklin wants to hear about is you."

Monk nodded, unsurprised that his bluff had worked. The locked door he'd picked to get in here was their responsibility. As long as they thought they were the ones who'd left it open, these guys weren't about to tell their boss about him. As long as they knew they should have spotted him before he'd gotten halfway to the third floor, Thomas Franklin wouldn't hear a word about this. The only problem now was the lock picks themselves, and in a place this size it might take forever for anyone to find them.

Now the taller man put his gun away as well. "Let's go, Mr. Towne. Let's get you back downstairs where you belong."

Hearing their sudden return to politeness, Monk realized the dynamic had changed. Maybe he could push them a little harder now. Maybe he could still pull this mission off.

"What is this place, anyway?" he asked. He took a couple of steps toward the interior of the secret museum, his eyes searching in every direction, but it didn't work.

"Hey!" the shorter man snapped. "That's far enough! We may not be going to see Mr. Franklin, but you're definitely leaving this room."

Monk turned around. "This is unbelievable!" he said, as his eyes continued to scan as much as he could in the next few seconds. "Just look at all this stuff!"

"Now!" the man barked.

"Okay, okay."

Monk followed them toward the door, then through it into the panic room, around the corner of the L, until they stood next to the security monitor screens. His mind raced in search of a solution. Once he was out of here there was no way he'd ever get back in.

"Wait here," the taller man said before turning to his partner. "Go back in there and reset the alarm."

The shorter man walked back into the secret room and Monk turned toward the bank of TV monitors to his left, the dozen or so displays connected to cameras throughout the mansion. One image showed the front lawn. Monk recognized the helicopter sitting there as Marine One, the forest green chopper used by the president. He scanned the other screens and saw that the party downstairs was in full swing. His eyes skimmed over the crowd, looking for Lisa's distinctive red gown, but he didn't see her. The screen farthest to his right showed no people at all. Monk's eyes focused hard as he realized what he was looking at.

The camera was inside the secret museum, he saw, mounted on a swivel as it panned slowly from left to right across the paintings and sculpture. He took a half step toward the monitor to get a better look. The clarity of the images was far from perfect—the surveillance camera was designed to scan for intruders, not showcase the art—but at least it gave him another chance to look. He watched the camera reach the end of its travel and start back the other way.

Marble statuary dominated the foreground, but in the background—at the far edge of the camera's depth of focus—Monk could make out a couple of paintings standing on easels. The first was an abstract jumble of colors, a Jackson Pollock, maybe, although it passed out of view too quickly for Monk to be sure. The second painting brought his eyes to within inches of the screen. Christ, there it was . . . or was it? The damned camera had gone by too fast. But it *was* Renaissance . . . he was sure of that . . . pretty sure anyway. And that *had* been Mary, the Madonna . . . hadn't it?

Damn it, this wasn't good enough. He had to get another look.

He started for the other room, but the second guard came around the corner and blocked the way.

"Alarm's set," he told his partner. "Let's get this guy back downstairs where he belongs."

"Just a second," Monk said. "Let me tie my shoelace."

He knelt on one knee, his eyes on the monitor screen. The camera was continuing across the secret room, not yet back to the painting Monk needed to see. He fiddled with his shoelace while he waited, fumbling with the . . .

"Hey!" the taller guard barked. "Do that on your own time. You can take all night with it downstairs."

Lisa wasn't happy.

In the rear of the black Lincoln that was taking them back to the District—one of a fleet of chauffeur-driven cars Franklin had provided for those who had to leave early—she made little effort to hide it.

"Damn it, Puller," she told him as they pulled away from the mansion. "I paid two hundred bucks for my hair . . . just for my hair!" She stared out the side window for a moment, than glared at Monk again. "You don't even want to know how much this dress cost me . . . and these shoes."

Monk tried to touch her hand, but she brushed his fingers away.

"First you go to the bathroom and I don't see you again for damned near an hour. And when you do show up, we have to leave!" She paused. "What the hell's going on here?"

Monk opened his mouth, but closed it again. He looked at Lisa's dark eyes and wished he could tell her.

"So that's it?" she said. "You're not even going to try to explain?"

"Something came up. I've got to go to work."

"You're on standby? Tonight . . . when you knew we'd be at this party?" She scowled. "Why didn't you switch with somebody?"

Monk stared at her. It would be easy to lie, but he wouldn't do it. Not with Lisa. There was so much bullshit in his life already, he wasn't about to turn their relationship into the same thing.

"I have to work," he repeated, ignoring the part about being on standby, sticking hard to the truth. "You know the rules. You know I can't say anything more than that. Not unless you have a need to know." It was the first principle of information sharing in the FBI.

"Damn it, Puller . . ."

Lisa shook her head and gave up. She slid to her right, up against the door, her face turned to the window. Monk wanted to reach out and touch her, but he knew better. She was right, of course. He did owe her an explanation, but this time she'd just have to settle for his marker.

The next forty-five minutes passed in silence, until the limo pulled up in front of their building, a loft-conversion off P Street, near Logan Circle in the Northwest area of Washington. The driver came around and opened the door. Lisa got out first and headed for the front door of the building. Monk hurried to catch up.

"I'm exhausted," she said, as he approached. "All I want to do is go to sleep and forget this ever happened."

Monk stepped to the door and used his key, then moved aside to let her pass. Lisa went through, then realized he wasn't following. She turned back to him.

"You're going to work like that? In those clothes?"

Still holding the glass door open, Monk looked down at his white dinner jacket, considered running upstairs and changing, but decided not to. It didn't make any difference what he was wearing. William Smith sure as hell wouldn't care.

"I should be home in a couple hours," he said.

Lisa just stared at him and shook her head before turning to the elevator and punching the button. Monk let the door swing shut, then headed around the side of the building, to the ramp down to the basement garage.

In the foyer, Lisa told herself to relax, but her finger jabbed at the elevator button anyway, and her mind was just as surly.

She'd become used to Puller's increasingly strange behavior, but this was really too much. He was right, she couldn't come right out and ask him what he was up to tonight, but he sure as hell could have volunteered more than he did. It was just another example of what had been going on ever since his father died.

Lisa hated to admit it, but Puller was turning into a different man. He was no less loving—once she got his attention—but he'd become increasingly distant. Bit by bit he seemed to be moving away from her. "Preoccupied," was the first word to come to mind, but "unavailable" was more apt. More and more he seemed to be unavailable to her, and the realization brought a painful twinge. Unavailable was often the final step before "completely gone."

She reached out and rammed the elevator button again, over and over, then looked upward as though her impatience might bring it down faster. She shouldn't be so surprised, Lisa admitted. Puller had showed definite signs of the same thing almost from the start. From the day she'd met him as a brand-new agent assigned to his SPIN squad—Special Inquiries for the White House—she'd sensed that Puller was wearing a disguise. That he was keeping something to himself, hidden away and unavailable. It was ironic, though it gave her no comfort to admit it. His determination to hide was what had seduced her in the first place, and she had to admit that he wasn't the one who'd changed. He was still just as determined to hide, but now it was driving her nuts.

From her left, Lisa heard a car pull up to the curb out front. Despite the industrial thickness of the glass in the doors, she heard the deep boom of rock music from the car's radio. She turned toward the sound, saw the passenger door open and a beautiful young woman emerge. It was Jillian, from the penthouse loft at the top of the building. Jillian's husband, Rick, was dropping her off before parking the car downstairs. Jillian was laughing as she leaned in toward her husband, saying something Lisa couldn't hear, although she could see Rick laughing in response. They were having a great night, and suddenly Lisa didn't like either one of them very much.

She stepped up closer to the elevator and whacked the button with the heel of her hand, and all at once—almost as though it had been reading her mind—the damned thing arrived. Lisa darted inside and pushed the CLOSE button before Jillian could see her, then leaned against the wall of the elevator and looked forward to going to bed.

SIXTEEN

"Go back?" William said, half an hour later, across the desk in his under-cover office.

His tired eyes had grown more and more narrow as Monk told him what had happened back at the mansion, and now his voice was down-right hostile.

"You want to go back to Thomas Franklin?" William shook his head. "You've got to be crazy."

Hearing the words—the same words he'd been saying to himself in the limo all the way back to the District—Monk had to admit that William could be right. But that didn't mean he was about to agree.

"Do I *want* to go back? Hell no, I don't." Those were the words William would want to hear. "I have to, is what I'm saying."

"But you saw the *Madonna* . . . you just told me you saw it."

Monk looked away for a moment. "I just can't be sure. Franklin's guards were all over me. The security camera was panning too fast. Five seconds . . . I had maybe five seconds." Monk shrugged. "I can't sit here and tell you I'm certain."

"But it's possible, right? The secret room was definitely a stash."

"It was private, that's for damned sure . . . And it was certainly secret, the way the guards rushed me out of there. Hell, I suppose you could call it a stash." Monk hesitated. "But what difference does it make? I'm almost certain I saw a *Madonna*, but I can't tell you for sure it was Lyman David-son's da Vinci. Not sure enough to go after a man as connected as Thomas Franklin."

William looked away, toward the window to his left. Monk followed his gaze. At two-thirty in the morning the sky was lit by a moon partially obscured by a thin patchwork of clouds, their edges silvery against the darkness. The sort of night sky you see in the opening credits of a horror movie, Monk couldn't help thinking. Add a clap or two of thunder, you'd have the whole thing. He turned back to see William watching him. Monk leaned forward in his chair.

"It won't be long until Franklin knows about what happened with me in his vault, if he doesn't already know. His security people might wait overnight to make their report, but we can't count on that. They'll identify me as Derek Towne, but Franklin will put it together. He'll remember Lisa and me from the reception line."

"So let him stew. We wanted him to know you were at the party, and you made damned sure of that." William paused. "Actually, your getting caught upstairs might work to our advantage. Franklin's got to be wonder-ing what's coming next."

"What's coming next has got to be me. Straight up, straight into his face." Monk heard his voice quicken. "You want him to stew, give him even more reason to. Give him a chance to make a mistake. If your mole is telling the truth, if Franklin's really buying stolen art from Sung Kim, he has to be scared shitless about what happened with me. He has to be contacting her. By going back, I'll make it even more necessary for him to talk to her."

"The *Madonna* won't be there, Monk." William sounded like a tired schoolteacher with a particularly dull child. "If the mole is right about him, Franklin's already moved the *Madonna* somewhere we'll never find it."

"But we can't know that for sure unless I go back, that's what I'm trying to tell you. We can't get a FISA wire with what I *think* I saw, and we've got to have the wire. It's the only way we'll ever get to Sung Kim."

"Carter will never go for it."

"Then I'm afraid we've got a problem."

"With you there's always a problem."

"The *Madonna* robbery is still my case. Regardless of your Sung Kim, I'm still the case agent on Lyman Davidson's da Vinci. I may have been ordered to stay away as long as you were working Trevor Blaine, but that ended when you took your FISA wire down. Now it's back to business as usual, and that means I keep looking for the *Madonna*. Thomas Franklin is my best lead. With you or without you, I'm going back to him."

William sat back in his chair. "You're bluffing. I've played enough poker with you to know."

Monk raised his eyebrows but said nothing, happy to stand pat with the cards in his hand. The silence grew longer, and Monk wasn't about to break it.

"You made a deal," William said at last. "You agreed to the deal."

"When do we talk to Carter?"

"Goddammit, Monk, I told him this would happen if we cut you in." William leaned forward. "But this time you're going to lose. You pull this shit with the director of NSA, you're going to—"

Monk raised his hand like a traffic cop. "Forty-eight hours. With Philip Carter's permission or without it, I go back to Franklin in two days."

They hadn't talked about Bethany Randall.

But Monk knew they would.

On his way back to Lisa at the loft—and despite his tired brain—he had no trouble bringing up the images of that night in the hot tub, the worst part of the night, at any rate. The quick jolt of humiliation at getting caught . . . Bethany's leap off his mostly naked body as William stood over the two of them with a gin and tonic in his hand. The shouting, all three of them yelling, mostly a slurred and drunken mixture of threats, apologies, and promises. Then William throwing him and Bethany out into the night . . . and Bethany's desire to keep the party going at her house. Finally, Monk's better angels coming to the rescue and taking him home.

Christ.

He and William hadn't talked about it yet, but it would happen.

Sooner or later it had to happen.

SEVENTEEN

Thomas Franklin loved this room.

Which made the thought of losing it all the harder to take.

His study was the only part of the mansion he'd designed himself. From the two-story floor-to-ceiling windows—arched and mullioned windows, framed in flawless maple, that stretched all the way across the far wall—to the built-in bookshelves that occupied two of the other three walls, Franklin's imprint was all over the room. He'd brought the antique cherry desk in the center of the room from France, the red, blue, and green carpets from a Persia that no longer existed, and the custom-made club chairs from North Carolina. The red oak floor was local, straight from the Pennsylvania forest surrounding Battle Valley Farm, and this morning the wide planking took on a fiery glow as it reflected the sunlight streaming through the windows.

Franklin settled into the high-backed swivel chair behind the desk and sat quietly, tipping back in the chair and closing his eyes for a moment before starting to work again on the Nakamura problem. He couldn't go back to the Hill, that much was certain. The president would never forgive his meddling a second time, and he needed the president more than ever, especially in the next four years. If he got another four years. And Franklin couldn't argue directly with the man again, the president had made that pretty damned clear. Which left . . . which left what?

Franklin opened his eyes and swung toward the desk. There had to be something. Some way he could still save this thing. He reached for the phone. If he couldn't use Congress, he could try something more powerful. He could go straight to the money behind the lawmakers. Global wasn't the only company at risk should the president give Ishii Nakamura what he was asking for. Maybe the way to do this was to go directly to the people who really ran the country.

He reached for his private phone directory, the beige leather notebook with numbers few people in the country would ever dial, but before he could open his desk drawer he was interrupted by a knock on the door.

"Yes," he called. "Come in."

The door swung open and Manny Johnson walked in. Franklin motioned for Battle Valley Farm's chief of security to approach the desk.

"What is it?" Franklin said. "I'm busy."

Johnson shifted his weight from foot to foot, lifted his hand to his face to stifle a short cough. "It's the panic room," he said. "I didn't want to bother you with this at the time, but it happened again. At the party."

Franklin stared at him. "Damn it, Manny, what's this make? Four . . . five times?"

"Six, I'm afraid. I've already talked to the factory rep. We can recalibrate the door, but that's about all they can do."

Franklin shook his head. The panic room had been Johnson's idea, but it was turning into a giant pain in the ass. Installed to keep bad guys out, it was turning out to be a lot better at keeping good people in.

"What about the lock on the bedroom door?"

"The guy said it wasn't locked. That the doors were wide open." Manny Johnson paused. "He said you told him to feel free to look around."

Franklin grunted. "I tell everybody that."

"Our log shows that the door was locked at nine o'clock. Did you go into the bedroom after that?"

"Of course not. I was downstairs the whole—" Franklin stopped. "Wait a minute. I did run upstairs for a second, but I locked the door again when

I left." At least he thought he had. "You said you didn't want to bother me with this when it happened. So why're you bothering me with it now?"

Johnson looked at the floor for a moment before his eyes came back up. "Uh . . . ," he began, then stopped. "Uh . . . This time . . . Well, it wasn't just the panic room this time."

Franklin glanced at the phone, impatient to get back to his own problem. "Yeah, I know. The bedroom lock. You just told . . ." His voice died as he realized what Johnson was saying. "The collection? Goddammit, Manny, the *collection?*"

"I don't know how he did it. No way he could have known."

"And you didn't come for me?"

"He wasn't in there ten seconds. We caught him on the monitor downstairs . . . he just barely got through the door when we nailed him."

"What was he doing up there? When you got there, I mean."

"Just standing in the doorway. Didn't say anything about what he saw. Probably figured every house like this has a secret room filled with art."

"Who was he?"

"Derek Towne, according to the driver's license he gave us. We ran him through Maryland Motor Vehicles. License checked out."

"Towne," Franklin said. "Derek Towne. Never heard of him." He paused. "You checked the guest list, of course."

"He was on it. His girlfriend, too."

"His girlfriend?" Franklin looked past Manny Johnson, in the direction of the great room down the hall. Girlfriends were unusual at such a formally diplomatic function. Lots of wives, but not many lovers. He would have thought he'd remember a girlfriend. He closed his eyes again, but opened them immediately when he felt a tightening in the back of his neck. He sat forward, his eyes on Manny again.

"What did this Towne look like?"

"Tall. Six-two, maybe. Brown hair, blue eyes. Forty-five years old, according to his driver's license."

"And his girlfriend?"

"Dark hair. Red gown. Legs a mile long. Gorgeous, but not too happy."

Franklin closed his eyes, trying to see the woman in his mind's eye. "But you say this guy was alone upstairs."

"Up in the vault he was, but we put him and the girlfriend into a limo afterwards."

"You threw them out?"

Manny shook his head. "He couldn't wait to leave. I've never seen anybody so embarrassed." He chuckled. "His date was giving him a pretty good ass-chewing when I closed the car door."

Franklin leaned back, his mind racing, before he told himself to relax. It couldn't have been those two . . . That just wasn't the way it worked. He swung forward again. "You've got video, of course. From the panic room."

"I made a cassette in case you wanted to see it."

"I do want to see it." Franklin rose from his chair. "I most certainly do."

EIGHTEEN

Legal training went the whole two hours.

Despite the claustrophobic afternoon heat that the antiquated SOG air-conditioning system had no chance against, the agent who'd been sent over from WFO to lecture on the latest federal criminal court decisions took every last second of his allotted time. Monk and the rest of the special operations group people sagged with relief when the clock finally hit five. Fifteen minutes later he was climbing into his Saab, anxious to get to the loft, where it would be at least ten degrees cooler. But before he could turn the ignition key, his cell phone rang. It was Lisa.

"Don't wait for me," she told him. "I'll be lucky to get home by nine, so go ahead and eat."

"What's going on?"

"Gotta run over to Dulles. One of the Customs dogs smelled out an explosive in an air-freight shipment. ATF says it's C4."

Monk frowned. "Why call you guys? Surely they don't have anybody under arrest."

"They don't, no, but we have all these new protocols. If the shipment involves certain countries, the Customs people at the airport have to call us immediately. Iraq, Afghanistan, Syria . . . the usual suspects."

"Which one we talking about this time?"

"North Korea."

Monk felt himself frowning. "A shipment from North Korea? We don't do business with them."

"The flight originated in China, but it stopped in Pyongyang on the way."

North Korea? Suddenly Monk didn't feel the heat.

"I've got an idea," he said. "Instead of going home, why don't I tag along. We can go to dinner in Alexandria when you finish."

"Are you sure? Could get late before I break free."

"If it does, I can go out and get us some food, bring it to you at the airport."

Lisa laughed. "Doesn't sound like much of a date to me, but sure. Do you good to get away from the SOG. See how the real bureau works for a change."

It took Monk almost an hour in the going-home traffic to get to freight terminal building 5, at the far edge of the immense runway system at Washington Dulles International Airport. Lisa was already inside, the Customs agent at the door told him when Monk presented his credentials. She and two other members of her counterterrorism squad from WFO were still with the suspect shipment, although the ATF people had taken the C4 back to their lab already.

Monk stared into the cavernous warehouse, lined on both sides with immense steel racks filled with containers, and saw Lisa standing with a man and woman in business clothing about halfway down the building. He dodged his way among a number of beeping forklift trucks and stacks of freight until he got to them.

"Puller," Lisa said when he walked up. She gestured toward the agents with her. "Do you know Laura Ridley and Henry Benitez?"

"I don't think so," Monk said. The beefed-up counterterrorism program had brought scores of agents into Washington from all over the country. It was impossible to keep up with the new faces. He stepped over and shook hands.

"Puller Monk," he said. "From the SOG."

Lisa pointed toward the wooden container to their right, a shipping crate the size of an SUV. It had been opened, and the contents laid out on the concrete floor.

"Shipment started out in Taipei," Lisa said. "Consumer electronic gear . . . DVD players. The plane made a stop in Pyongyang to off-load freight before coming straight to Dulles." She paused. "Customs did their routine, ran the sniffer dogs around the container to check for drugs or explosives. The drug dog didn't react at all. The other one didn't signal, but was acting funny about the container, so Customs opened it up and transferred the individual boxes to the floor here. The drug dog still found nothing, but the bomb sniffer signaled when he got to the box with the plastique."

Lisa led the way to a table that had been set up next to the container. Monk could see the suspect DVD box, lying open on the table.

"ATF X-rayed the box," she said. "There was no DVD inside, no electronic or mechanical devices of any kind. What they saw was a brick-size container with a lump of something inside it."

Lisa glanced back toward the front door of the warehouse.

"They cleared the area outside, then used their robot to open both the DVD box and the one inside it, the one with the plastique. It was an aluminum container, sealed with a dozen layers of duct tape. It had been cleaned with some kind of solvent before being placed in the DVD box. That's why the dog didn't catch the C4 while it was inside the air-freight container . . . not until he could put his nose right up next to the DVD box itself."

"And it was C4," Monk said. "We're sure it was a plastic explosive."

"I didn't see it—ATF took it to their lab before we got here—but Customs told us it looked the same. Like a block of gray putty. And the way the dog reacted made them even more certain."

"What about fuses? Blasting caps."

"None, thank God."

Monk stared at the stack of boxes next to the table. "Where are they going, these DVDs? Who's the customer?"

"Outfit called Digital World, Inc. Stores all over Maryland and Virginia. Dozens of them."

He walked over to the boxes, ran his eyes up and down the stack, then glanced back at the box out of which the C4 had come, before looking at Lisa. "The black mark on your suspect box. Did Customs do that?"

"Good catch, Puller. I forgot to mention the mark." She pointed at the suspect box. "That's the only one marked. For obvious reasons, I would think."

Monk nodded. How else was the intended recipient supposed to pick up the C4? He walked back to Lisa.

"Gonna be a ton of leads on this," he told her. "Gonna take more than just the three of you."

"I expect so. Let's hope my supervisor agrees with you."

"But even if he does," Lisa said, "it's still a question of manpower."

It was thirty-five minutes later, and Monk and Lisa were sitting in a booth at the Taste of Bombay Restaurant in Alexandria.

"Barry Sonenburg is a great supervisor," she continued, "but we've only got twenty-two agents on the squad, and every one of us is loaded to the gills with work."

"The assistant director in charge will have to give you more people. Loaners from the other counterterrorism squads."

Lisa shook her head. "The ADIC will do what he can, but everybody's in the same boat."

"It's C4, Lisa. It came from . . ."

Monk stopped talking and glanced around. At nine-thirty on a summer evening the restaurant was still full enough that he recognized the danger. It was tempting to break the rule in a place as familiar as their favorite low-price restaurant, but Monk knew better than to talk business over a public dinner table. Especially in Washington. Half the breaking news stories in this town came directly from waiters and waitresses, and a surprising amount of their gossip found its way into one file or another around the District.

Lisa had seen his glance, and as usual had read his mind. One of these days, Monk was going to ask her how she did it. She held up her menu.

"I'm going to start with the chat papri," she said. The small appetizer salad included yogurt and chickpeas, and was Lisa's usual starter.

"Bhaji for me." He was addicted to the potato-onion fritters.

As a matter of fact, Monk admitted, he was pretty much addicted to everything on the menu. The Taste of Bombay featured northern Indian food and prices low enough to suggest money laundering, although only to a government investigator. He and Lisa could stuff themselves with food and drink and not come anywhere near eighty bucks. That the place was small—thick Indian rugs and dark red wall hangings made it look even more intimate—and pretty much unknown to tourists only made it more perfect.

A lithe young lady in a powder blue sari glided up to the table and took their drink order. Manhattan on the rocks in a bucket, extra cherry juice, for Lisa, and a Grey Goose martini for Monk, with two onions. The server glided away and returned momentarily to set down their drinks and take their dinner order. Lisa stuck with her usual, a vegetarian selection of eggplant, potato, chickpeas, and homemade cheese. Monk went the other way. Lamb vindaloo, chicken curry with lentils, and a small bowl of fenugreek-laced fish curry.

"And a plate of the onion-baji bread with our drinks, please," he added.

Again the server seemed to shimmer away. Monk lifted his martini in a salute to Lisa. "Confusion to our enemies," he said.

"And may their children be acrobats," she replied, a toast she'd been told at Quantico was popular in China, for a reason Monk couldn't begin to fathom.

In due time the food came. They ate in companionable silence, punctuated by tidbits of small talk that nobody in their right mind would eavesdrop to hear. Lisa's hairdresser had left her shoulder-length dark hair too long again, despite Lisa's explicit instructions to cut the damned ends off. Monk's real estate agent wanted to spend more money on ads for his late father's persistently unsellable dome house in Fredericksburg.

"Darcy Edwards thinks I should advertise in San Diego, Los Angeles, and Seattle. That we should expand the market to the West Coast. Not a bad idea, but she wants five thousand bucks to do it." Monk shook his head. "Might as well be a million. The way it is now, I can barely keep making the payments. That goddamned house is killing me, Lisa. And Darcy just keeps asking for . . ."

Monk stopped when he caught Lisa staring.

"What?" he said. He reached to brush at the corners of his mouth, expecting to find the piece of chicken curry she had to be looking at, but there was nothing on his face.

"You did it again," she said.

Monk grinned. "I guess I did. I shouldn't let it get to me, but that house . . ." He paused. "Just thinking about it pisses me off, but I shouldn't bitch about it over dinner."

Lisa shook her head. "I'm not talking about that, Puller." She hesitated. "You told me the same thing yesterday, in exactly the same words. You told me what Darcy wants to do with the West Coast ads. You called me as soon as you got off the phone with her."

Monk frowned. "Yesterday? What are you talking about?" A chill ran through his body. "I already told you this?" He couldn't have. She must be mistaken.

Lisa laughed. "You ought to see the look on your face. I wish I had a camera."

"Jesus, Lisa, I don't really see the humor."

She reached out and touched his hand. "Take a breath and relax. This isn't the first time. You must have a lot on your mind. You did the same thing last week."

"Last week?"

"You told me Kendall Jefferson's getting a divorce. That you guys are going to take a day off and help him move."

He nodded. "On the thirty-first, yeah. Get him into an apartment by the first of September."

"You told me twice . . . the same story twice. Back-to-back days, just like the Darcy stuff."

Monk stared at her. "You didn't say anything . . . or did you?"

"I was busy, I was paying bills." She laughed again. "I shouldn't admit it, but I was hardly listening to you." She paused. "Like I said, you must have a lot on your mind."

He frowned again, and she continued before he could respond.

"Saturday night. The party . . . rushing away early, going back to work the same night." She shook her head. "You work that hard, you're bound to get confused."

"Yeah, sure, but that's no reason to . . ."

Monk stopped, then told himself to keep quiet. This was not a conversation he wanted to get into tonight, or anytime soon. He forced himself to grin.

"Maybe I should put in for disability right now," he said, reverting to the blackest of humor. "Get the paperwork out of the way while I can still remember my name."

Lisa patted his hand. "That's what I'm here for, darling. I'll make sure you get a nice room at the home. Look at the upside. They say the best thing about losing your memory is all the new friends you keep meeting."

Monk stared at her, then laughed, and he was damned if it didn't make him feel better. Talking about what he feared the most did make it seem a little ridiculous. He looked at what was left of the food on his plate. Suddenly it looked better, as well. He picked up his fork and stabbed a piece of lamb.

He was lifting it to his mouth when he saw Bethany Randall.

NINETEEN

Monk lowered his fork with the lamb still attached.

Where had Bethany come from?

As he did every time he was in a public place, Monk had scanned every face in the room as he and Lisa had come in, but he hadn't seen Bethany sitting alone in that booth in the far corner. Until just now. He leaned in her direction, suddenly unsure he wasn't imagining her, that seeing William again hadn't set him up for conjuring Bethany. It wasn't dark in here, but just dark enough to make him wonder.

Then she turned face on to him, and he realized he was wrong. He'd never seen Bethany without her long red hair sweeping to her shoulders. This woman's hair was pinned back behind her ears. Bethany wore glasses—for some reason she couldn't wear contacts or have laser surgery—and this woman wasn't wearing glasses. Monk smiled at her anyway, but she turned away as though she hadn't even seen him.

"Puller?"

Monk felt Lisa's hand touch his.

"Puller?" she repeated.

He turned back to her.

"See someone you know?" she asked.

"I thought I did, but I was wrong."

"The redhead in the corner?"

"She looks like someone who used to date a friend of mine."

"She's pretty."

"I prefer blondes."

Lisa grinned. "You'd best learn to live with disappointment."

He squeezed her hand, ready with a wisecrack that died on his lips as the redhead slid out of her booth. Christ, he thought, those have got to be Bethany's legs. She was walking toward them now, and Monk couldn't take his eyes off her. She glanced his way, her green eyes on his for a moment, but she didn't react at all, just kept walking toward the front door. Monk felt a warm flush climb his face. He didn't want to make a fool out of himself, but he couldn't just let her walk by without knowing for sure.

"Bethany?" he called. "Bethany Randall?"

She turned to him, her eyes puzzled, before she stepped closer to their booth.

"Puller?" she said, in that voice Monk could still hear in his head when he wasn't careful. "Is that you, Puller?"

Monk rose from his chair as Bethany approached. He stuck out his hand, but she put both arms around him and hugged him. Monk couldn't see Lisa, but he felt her eyes on them before Bethany stepped back. Dressed in a black tailored suit, with a dark green silk scarf at her throat, she looked nothing at all like she had the last time he'd seen her. That night. That night in William's . . .

"Bethany," he said. "I thought it was you, but your hair is different, and you're not wearing glasses."

"And I can't see five feet in front of me. That's why I didn't see you earlier." She smiled. "What's it been? Gotta be five years."

Five and a half, Monk could have told her. "Has to be," he said.

"Do you come here often?" she asked. "We—the three of us—used to eat here, remember?"

Monk nodded. He did remember now, although a Freudian might have tried to convince him it was the only reason he kept coming here.

Behind him, Lisa coughed quietly. Monk turned to her.

"Lisa," he said. "This is Bethany Randall. She used to date a friend of mine." He swung back to Bethany. "This is Lisa Sands. We . . . we work together." Somehow that didn't sound quite right, but before he could revise it Bethany extended her hand. Lisa took it, held on a moment too long, Monk thought. "It's a pleasure to meet you," she said.

Bethany said pretty much the same thing, then turned to Monk.

"How is William?" she asked. "Are the two of you still working together?"

"No . . . no, we're not," Monk told her. A small lie, the kind so often necessary in his line of work.

Silence fell awkwardly, the three of them standing next to the table, until Lisa broke it.

"We like this place, too," she said. "I didn't get much Indian food in Texas." She laughed. "If you can't grill it or deep-fry it, a Texan doesn't have a whole lot of interest."

Bethany smiled. "Ohio wasn't much better."

Monk was trying to think of something to add when Lisa's cell phone rang. She bent to grab it from her purse, talked into the phone for a few moments, then dropped the phone back into the purse.

"Damn it," she said. "I've gotta go."

"What's going on?"

Lisa glanced at Bethany before answering. "Believe it or not, the same thing we just did. But it's Baltimore-Washington International this time."

Monk frowned. "Why isn't the Baltimore field office handling it?"

"Because of what happened at Dulles. They want me there." Again she glanced at Bethany, clearly uncomfortable about talking in front of her, even in terms as inexplicit as these. "But you don't need to come this time, Puller. Stay and finish your dinner." Lisa hesitated. "Catch up on old times with your friend."

Monk nodded. "If you're sure you won't need me."

Lisa's smile included Bethany this time. "Listen to him," she told William's ex. "All he'd do is slow me down."

She grabbed her purse, then stepped up to Monk and kissed him on the lips, something Monk had never known her to do in public. "See you at home, sweetheart," she said. "I shouldn't be all that late."

. . .

"I hope this isn't a problem," Bethany said, after Lisa was gone. "Lisa doesn't look too pleased." She paused. "And I gather the two of you do more than just work together."

Monk ignored the last part. "Lisa's fine," he said. He hoped she was. Because there was no way to explain Bethany to her. No way even to start. "Would you like a drink?" he asked.

"I'd love one . . . but can we walk across the street? I feel like a brandy, but they don't have anything decent here."

Monk looked at her. It wasn't brandy that had started their problem that night, but something damned close. He opened his mouth to beg off, and was shocked to hear what came out.

"Great," he said. "Brandy sounds great." He hesitated. "I think I could really use one."

Half a block from the restaurant, Lisa slid behind the wheel of her bureau-issue Grand Prix, shoved the key into the ignition and started to crank the engine, before dropping her hand into her lap and sitting back for a moment. Two shipments of C4 intercepted in the same day, she thought, both on their way to Washington, both in containers addressed to Digital World.

Puller had mentioned getting some help from the assistant director in charge of WFO, and he was right. The ADIC might very well turn out the whole field office for something like this . . . not that such a move would guarantee success. The frustrating part of her job was its near impossibility. Even with a hundred agents it would take weeks to run any sort of investigation on every employee of Digital World, and the overwhelming probability was that it wouldn't turn out to be an employee at all. Whoever was shipping the plastique wouldn't address the stuff to anyone the bureau could trace so easily. Which left any one of the scores of other people who'd have access to the boxes of DVDs before they ever got to the stores. But that didn't mean she could shortcut the process. She and her people had to eliminate Digital World before they could go on to the next step.

Lisa stared through the windshield and admitted something even more frustrating. These wouldn't be the only two shipments, Dulles and BWI wouldn't turn out to be the only two entry points. If Customs agents had caught these two, how many others would get through? How many had already gotten through?

She started the car and looked over her shoulder, let a black convertible go by, then pulled out into the heavy traffic. Reaching for the air-conditioner switch, she turned it up to high. It was a quarter to nine, she saw on the dashboard clock. She'd be at the airport well before ten, but she wouldn't get back to the loft until after midnight, and wouldn't be able to go to sleep until at least one. Tomorrow morning would come way too soon, and with the Digital World leads ahead of her she wasn't sure when she'd ever get back to bed. Christ, Lisa thought. Sometimes she wondered what she'd been thinking when she quit her job in the DA's office to come to Washington. Sometimes a life in Texas didn't seem all that . . .

She hit the brakes when she saw them.

Puller and Bethany, walking across the street ahead of her.

Puller offering his arm and Bethany taking it. Bethany turning to him and brushing something off the sleeve of his shirt. The two of them heading for the front door of a bar as she slowed down to avoid having to wave to them.

Lisa felt a surge of . . . she wasn't sure what . . . anger most likely . . . trepidation maybe, or . . . or premonition. Something. From behind, she heard the bleat of an angry horn. She stared into the rearview mirror and resisted the urge to raise her middle finger, then hit the gas hard. The car surged forward. The last thing Lisa saw was Monk holding the door for Bethany, a smile creasing his big fat face.

TWENTY

Monk followed Bethany through the door and into a green leather booth at Johnny's, one of Alexandria's oldest saloons, a mixture of 1700s ambience and twenty-first-century booze that attracted a full house every night of the week. Fortunately for them, it was about an hour early for the usual crowd, so they didn't have to shout at each other to be heard. The seating arrangement helped keep the noise down even more. The booths circled the room, separated by an immense saltwater fish tank that distorted the customers' view of each other, and blocked their conversations as well. In the center of their table a candle set in an amber bowl flickered with exactly the right amount of illumination for after-dinner conversation.

After they'd ordered brandy in snifters and the drinks had been delivered, Bethany dug into her purse for a pair of brown, very thin horn-rim glasses. She put them on before looking at him and smiling.

"Hope you don't mind," she said. "I've been dying to put these back on. I didn't wear them at dinner, but there's no need to be vain around you."

"You should wear them all the time. They make you look . . ." He searched for the right word. "I always thought they made you look dignified." He laughed. "Wait a minute, that's not what I meant. Dignified makes you sound like a . . . like a . . ." He stopped trying. "Oh hell, you know what I'm trying to say."

"Like a teacher? Like a schoolmarm?"

"Not like any schoolmarm I've ever seen . . . but a little like a teacher, yes."

"A good thing then, because that's what I am."

Monk stared at her. "When did that happen?"

"I had all my course work for my doctorate—bioinorganic chemistry, you might remember—so after William I took a year off work to do my dissertation at Georgetown. Got my PhD a couple of years ago."

"Where are you teaching?"

"A community college in Maryland, in Prince George's County. Just a couple of lectures a week, but I've got my application in all over the country for a full-time university job."

"How do you like teaching?"

"I'm really a researcher at heart. I'm not real comfortable in front of large groups of students. My plan is to work my way into a graduate program, then hide away in the lab and do my work."

"Bioinorganic, did you say? Should I know what that means?"

Bethany laughed. "If you want to be about one in a million, you should. My interest is in metals. Magnesium, molybdenum, tungsten, and the chemistry involved. It's not very sexy, I'm afraid . . . not like recombinant DNA or cancer research, but I find it fascinating."

"You weren't doing any of this when we used to hang out together."

"I was trying to keep William interested, not drive him away. You know what they say about girls who wear glasses." She leaned forward. "What about you, Puller? Obviously you're still with the FBI, from what I heard at the restaurant."

"I've got too much in the pension fund to quit now."

"And your friend, Lisa." Bethany hesitated. "How long's that been going on?"

"We've been living together for about a year."

"I hope she wasn't upset that you didn't go along with her just now. I know she said she didn't need you, but she looked at me kind of funny when she left."

"Lisa's fine. She isn't like that at all."

"We're all like that, Puller. Some of us are better than others at hiding it, but trust me, we're all like that."

"She's been working night and day lately. She loves the job. She doesn't have time for jealousy."

Bethany smiled. "If you say so. What do I know except chemistry?"

They fell silent as they sipped brandy. Monk checked out the fish tank. It ran floor to ceiling and was filled with a variety of miniature sharks, swimming around in circles, eyes wide with what looked like honest disbelief at what they were seeing. And it was true, Monk remembered from a TV show he'd seen on the Discovery Channel. A shark's memory was so short-term that each turn around the tank was a brand-new experience, each sight as mind-boggling as walking around a corner and bumping into Mount Everest. As he watched, a brown and white speckled beauty wheeled toward him, then stopped dead to stare—no self-doubt, no guilt—before swooshing away to the next incredible sight. Monk turned back to Bethany.

"Are you married?" he asked her. "I don't see a ring, but these days you never know."

She shook her head. "Almost happened about a year ago, but . . ." Her eyes dropped to her hands on the table. "He got a job in South America. I would have had to give up my career, or put it on hold." She looked up. "I'm thirty-two, Puller. If I don't keep at it, I won't get tenured until the week I retire."

Monk smiled, but he was aware of an uncomfortable feeling of . . . of what? He wasn't sure. All he knew was that he wasn't upset about her impending marriage having fallen through.

"Forgive me for bringing up William again," she said, "but I still feel guilty about the two of you." She paused. "And what happened."

Before he could stop himself, Monk reached out and touched the back of her hand. "It wasn't my best night either."

"It was a mistake. We were drunk . . . we were all drunk."

"Not drunk enough. Not too drunk to keep me from remembering."

"We were already over, William and I, but that's no excuse for the way I acted."

They fell silent, drinking brandy, until Monk looked at her again. "You still flying?" he asked. "Skydiving?"

"Every chance I get. It's a lifesaver for relieving stress."

"Still keep your Baron in Maryland?"

"Same airfield, exact same hanger, as a matter of fact." She paused. "What about you? Still diving?"

"Not since that last time."

The silence was a bit longer this time, until Bethany shook her head. "William shouldn't have blamed you, Puller. I deserved to get thrown out of his life, but he was a fool to do the same thing with you."

"I would have . . . I would have punched me in the nose. I don't know a man who wouldn't."

"You wouldn't have. You're one of the few I know who wouldn't have."

"You're a pretty smart lady, but you're dead wrong about that."

"You're saying you'd have banished William?"

"I'm saying I'd have tried harder than William to keep you in my life."

The words had come out before Monk could stop them. He sipped brandy to keep himself from continuing. He looked at her green eyes again and noticed for the first time the tiny golden flecks surrounding the iris, highlighted by the candlelight from the center of the table. Then he stared at the fish tank, and through the tank to the front door. There was danger here, he told himself. *Make sure you know how to get to the emergency exit.*

"But you didn't try," she said, and now her voice carried reproach. "We were friends, but after that night I never saw you again."

Monk held up his glass, swirled the brandy, buying time to form a response to something he wasn't prepared to deal with right now. Or maybe ever.

Suddenly Bethany reached across and touched the back of his hand. "I've got something to say," she told him. "I haven't had nearly enough to drink, and if I don't say it quickly I won't say it at all."

Monk tried to pull his hand away from her fingers, but it refused to obey his command.

"The reason William and I never made it was you, Puller. The way I acted that night was exactly the way I felt about you. I never would have done it without the gin, but there was nothing dishonest about it back then." She looked away for a moment, then back at him. "And there wouldn't be now."

Monk shifted his weight. Suddenly it was awfully warm in here. It was also time to leave. He saw that Bethany's glass was empty, so he drank the rest of his.

"I better get going," he said. "Lisa might need my help after all."

Bethany's eyes dropped to her hands again, and when she looked up, her eyes were somehow even softer in the gentle light. "I've done it again, haven't I? Embarrassed both of us." Her voice dropped, a deflated sound that had lost its spirit. "I've got an early lecture tomorrow, myself."

Monk risked a glance at her face, careful to stay away from those green eyes as he reached into his pocket for his money clip, peeled off a twenty, and threw it on the table. He slid out of the booth. As Bethany came out on her side, he saw enough of her legs to make him turn away. Before they started toward the door, she moved up close to him.

"I . . . I'm sorry, Puller. I think I just made a fool out of myself."

Monk shook his head. "Don't be ridiculous. We're old friends. You can say anything you like to me."

Before he could turn away, she stood on her tiptoes and kissed him on the cheek, a quick kiss before she started for the door. Monk followed her. On the way past the shark tank, he took one last look. They seemed astonished to see him. His eyes swung back to Bethany. To her hips. To those legs.

The trick was to forget her, Monk knew, but the question was how.

Without jumping into that big tank and turning into a shark himself, how was he ever going to make her go away?

TWENTY-ONE

Monk spent much of the next day with Russian farmers. SOG Team 3—the team Monk led—had been assigned to follow a group of award-winning Russian farmers who were enjoying their prize of a visit to Washington, New York, and Boston. According to the CIA, two of them weren't farmers at all, but agents of the FSB, the new name for the Soviet KGB. The name was new, but the two agents' mission was the same: gather information, maintain contact with their old networks inside the United States, and construct new ones. The FBI's role hadn't changed, either. To watch and listen, to find something that might come in handy down the line.

Today was shopping day.

Monk and his team spent six hours watching Russians move from Nordstrom on Fifteenth Street to Robinsons-May on East Capitol, from Banana Republic on M to Discount Mart on Alabama Street. Trying on clothing, touching and feeling everything else, the farmers were indefatigable. Neither Monk nor any of his people had seen anything they could identify as a "brush pass" or a "dead drop," but that didn't mean much. Russian intelligence officers—IOs—were good. The best you could do was forward to New York the hundreds of photos you'd taken and hope

the agents up there could match some of them with current counterespionage files.

He was halfway back to the trolley barn when William finally called.
He didn't sound so much angry as resigned. Philip Carter, William told
him, thought Monk's idea of going back to Thomas Franklin was a perfect
way to put more pressure on the man, force him, perhaps, into some kind
of a mistake. Carter wanted Monk to do so as soon as possible.

"Good to hear it," Monk told William. "I was sure Carter would—"

He stopped talking when William hung up on him.

He forgot about the trolley barn and headed for Crystal City instead.
It was three-ten that afternoon when he walked through the big bronze
doors of Franklin's Global Panoptic Building.

He strode across the marble floor of the lobby and prepared himself
for a long delay. As a rule, FBI agents didn't spend much time waiting to be
seen—few businessmen were capable of ignoring a G-man's presence for
more than a minute or two—but Thomas Franklin would be an exception.
A man whose closest friend was president of the United States had little to
fear from an FBI agent, and to prove it Franklin was easily capable of making him sit around for at least an hour.

So he was surprised when the blond young woman behind the reception desk had no more than glanced at his credentials when she picked up
a telephone and spoke a few quiet words into it, then hung up, turned to
Monk, and smiled.

"The chairman asks if you'd care to use his private elevator." She
pointed across the lobby. "It's the last one on the right. Mrs. Waverly will
be down in a moment to get you."

Monk thanked the receptionist and turned just in time to see the elevator door open and a middle-aged gray-haired lady step out and smile in
his direction.

"Welcome, Special Agent Monk," she said when he got to her. "The
chairman is happy to make time for you. He's always been a great fan of
the bureau."

The elevator was lined in dark walnut with polished brass inserts.
Against the back wall the letters GP were fashioned from the same brass,
and a faint smell of very expensive pipe tobacco hung in the air. But de-

spite the trappings, Monk hated it as much as he hated all elevators. At least there were only two of them. His claustrophobia was much worse when the tiny cars got crowded.

They rode together in silence to the top floor. The doors slid open and Monk saw that they were inside Thomas Franklin's office. Franklin was standing by his desk, and came forward immediately with a huge smile on his face.

Somehow—in his office at the top of the building he owned—Franklin appeared even taller than Monk remembered. And even better dressed. In his light gray silk suit and pale yellow necktie, Franklin looked like an ad in the *New Yorker*. Monk couldn't help glancing down at his cotton Dockers and blue golf shirt, but the moment passed as Franklin offered his hand.

"I'm pleased to see you again, Agent Monk. May I offer you coffee . . . or a soft drink, perhaps."

"Nothing, thank you. I won't take up any more of your time than I have to."

"I've got all the time you need. Why don't we just get started."

They turned to the furniture grouping on their right, a round table surrounded by five brocade upholstered chairs. On the table sat a silver carafe and four crystal water glasses. They sat across the table from one another. Franklin waited for Monk to begin.

"I'm here about the party Saturday night," Monk said. "About something that happened at the party."

Franklin shook his head. "I'm really embarrassed about that, Agent Monk." He grinned. "Or should I say Mr. Towne? That panic room hasn't done much but *cause* panic. I wanted to apologize to you but I only just heard about it."

Monk stared at the man. He'd expected a number of reactions to his visit, but not this one. He'd been the one in the wrong place. He'd been the one using the phony name.

"About that name," he said.

Franklin held up his hand and grinned. "Forget it. Actually I'm glad you didn't tell them who you really were. My security guys would have overreacted, and Saturday night was not the time to make a scene." He paused. "There's absolutely no reason for you to apologize."

Monk smiled. It was almost a shame to ruin the mood. "Unfortunately, that's not why I'm here. Not directly anyway. I'm relieved you're so understanding, but there's more to it than that."

Franklin leaned forward. "Sounds serious."

"It is serious, I'm afraid." Again Monk hesitated, but his eyes never left Franklin's body. It was important to catch his initial reaction.

"I saw a painting up there, in your private collection room. A *Madonna* I know to be stolen. A da Vinci. Perhaps you saw the story in the paper."

Monk watched Franklin's face, but he showed nothing you wouldn't expect. Slight lift of the eyebrows was all. Pretty damned normal considering what Monk had just told him.

"I need to see the painting again, Mr. Franklin." He paused a beat longer this time. "And I'm afraid I have to ask how you came to have it."

Franklin smiled. "You sure don't waste a lot of time getting to the point . . . but you're mistaken. Trust me, if I had a da Vinci, I'd know about it. I'd know everything about it."

"I'm sure you would, but I still need to see for myself."

Franklin's tone was suddenly less pleasant. "Of course. Have you any particular time in mind?"

"Would today be convenient?"

Franklin glanced at his watch. "A bit late in the day for you to drive out to Gettysburg, isn't it? With the commuter traffic it would take you three hours. And a couple more to get back."

"It's important."

"I can see that it is."

Franklin stared to his right, out the window. Monk followed his gaze. In the distance he could see the Washington Monument against the blue sky. The single black cloud he'd noticed during his shopping spree with the farmers had vanished. Franklin turned back to him.

"How about this," he said. "Why don't I give you a ride out to the farm in my helicopter. You can look at every painting I've got. My pilot will bring you back to your car afterward. We can get the whole thing done in two hours."

"I couldn't impose on you like—"

"Nonsense. You have a problem, I have a big stake in helping you solve it. Making things happen is what I do for a living. Let's get this resolved as quickly as possible." He picked up the phone on the table. "Call John, Mrs. Waverly. Have him warm up the chopper. We'll leave for the farm in ten minutes."

On the rooftop, Monk was happy to get out of the elevator, but as he stepped out and saw the size of the red and white Sikorsky sitting on the pad, its main and tail rotors spinning and ready to go, he cursed under his breath. It was much smaller than the one the other night, way too small as far as Monk was concerned. He didn't mind flying in the slightest, but the passenger compartment would be narrow, the roof low, and leg room non-existent. He could already feel the tension rising through his body as he considered getting back in the elevator and trying this again another time, but he kept going. Now he could see the pilot in the cockpit, reaching over his head and adjusting switches. Even though the rotors were not yet moving at flying speed the noise was deafening, and the turbulence was enough to blow Monk's hair sideways.

Outside the chopper, the copilot, a slender young woman in a dark blue skirt and matching jacket stood at the passenger door waiting. Franklin led the way. The woman touched her hand to her cap as they moved past and climbed the single step up into the compartment. Once they were inside, she slid the door shut.

Six gray leather seats filled the confinement of the passenger compartment, arranged in two rows of three, opposing each other. Franklin sat on the right-hand side. Monk lowered himself into a seat opposite. Franklin reached to the carpeted floor beside his chair and came up with a headset complete with microphone attached. He gestured for Monk to do the same. Monk bent to get his own headset and slipped it on just in time to hear Franklin's voice.

"Have to use these," he said, his voice extraordinarily clear. "Or make hand signals all the way to the farm."

Monk nodded, then tried to keep his voice casual. "A twenty-minute flight? At least that's how long it took the other night."

"A little longer today. The birds I lease for parties are bigger and faster." Franklin looked at his watch. "We'll be at the house by four."

Monk checked his own watch. Damn it. Almost a half hour until they landed again.

The pilot's voice came through his headset.

"Whenever you're ready, Mr. Franklin."

"Take us a little east today, John. I want to show off for my guest." He smiled at Monk. "My little part of the forest is gorgeous right now, Agent Monk. The golf course, too. Please forgive me if I take a couple of extra minutes to show you."

Monk forced a smile as the helicopter lifted suddenly, accelerating with a swoosh that he felt in the pit of his stomach. The District of Columbia swept past beneath them, but before long they crossed the Beltway into the dense forest of southeastern Pennsylvania. Monk had time, however, to notice the traffic, the gridlock below them on every street and highway. He glanced at Franklin and realized that despite his discomfort he was grateful for the ride.

"Something to see, isn't it?" Franklin said, his voice jolting Monk back to reality. "I've been commuting like this for years, and I still can't get used to how quickly the city turns into country."

Monk nodded, but said nothing. The next twenty-seven minutes felt like two hours before the Sikorsky was descending toward the farm.

"These are my woods," Franklin said, pointing out the window. "I hated to cut even one tree down when I built the golf course. As it is, I probably should have cut more." He grinned. "At least that's what my golfing buddies tell me."

Monk watched as they hurtled past the golf course, the skeet range, the airstrip with the big Gulfstream jet in the same place it had been the other night, then the mansion itself, before making a sweeping turn. He looked for the front lawn, expecting to land there, but the chopper flew directly to the roof of the mansion instead. There was a helipad atop the only flat portion of the many different rooflines. A moment later they were hovering above the pad, then settling onto it. The pilot cut the engines. The rotors slowed to a stop. The copilot came around and opened the door.

"Be ready in an hour," Franklin told the young woman as they left the chopper. "You'll be taking Agent Monk back to town when he's finished here." He turned to Monk. "An hour . . . will that be long enough for you?"

Monk nodded, then followed Franklin into yet another elevator, and a few moments later they were downstairs on the main floor of the house. A tall woman—middle-aged, with short, stylish hair, and wearing a severe blue suit—stood waiting.

"Mrs. Woods," Franklin said to her. "I'd like you to meet Special Agent Monk of the FBI." He turned to Monk. "My housekeeper," he said. "Grace Woods."

She smiled and held out her hand. Monk took it. Her handshake was firm and dry. Monk could smell her perfume, a hint of jasmine. Her blue eyes appraised him without any suggestion she was impressed, and Monk wasn't surprised. Considering the status of most of the people who passed through her house, it was a wonder she bothered offering her hand to an FBI agent at all.

"Mrs. Woods runs the house," Franklin said. "I'd be lost without her."

"It's a pleasure," Monk said. "I won't disrupt your routine any longer than necessary."

"Anything you need," she said, "just ask."

"What he needs," Franklin told her, "is to see my bedroom."

Her eyebrows lifted, but just barely. "Of course. If you give me a moment, I'll be glad to take you upstairs."

Monk turned to Franklin. "I would prefer to have you show me."

What I would really prefer is that you not get out of my sight before I see that secret room.

Franklin's eyes flickered for an instant before he smiled again, but Monk had seen his displeasure, and realized he was happy to see it. Franklin and his people were very good at smiling. Monk wondered what they were like when they weren't.

"I'd be happy to take you upstairs," Franklin said. "Please follow me." He turned to Monk and this time his eyes were dead flat. "Although I'm sure you remember the way."

Franklin led as the three of them climbed the sweeping main staircase to the second floor, and on to the top floor. They walked down the wide corridor—across the collection of Persian carpets, past the alcoves with the marble statuary Monk had admired the other night—to the open double doors of the master bedroom. Not locked today, Monk saw. He glanced at the potted tree next to the doors. It would be nice to get a moment alone to retrieve his lock picks.

Franklin took them straight into the panic room. The door slid closed behind them. Franklin touched a key on the keyboard under the closed-circuit TV monitors, and Monk heard the secret-room door slide open around the corner of the L. They moved around the corner and into the private gallery. Franklin turned to Monk.

"Now," he said, "you say the da Vinci was in here, in this room."

"It was in here . . . but I didn't actually see it while I was in here."

Franklin frowned. "I'm afraid I don't understand."

"I didn't see it until I was back out in the panic room. On one of the monitors." Monk looked up at the ceiling. "Show me where the cameras are and I'll get my bearings."

"There are only two." Franklin pointed to their left, at a small camera mounted on the wall just beneath the ceiling. "That one covers the front of the room, up here where we're standing. The second one is halfway back." He pointed again. "There." He started toward the back of the room. "Come along, I'll show you."

Monk followed him. He looked for the paintings he'd seen on the monitor the other night. He recognized the Jackson Pollock immediately, and turned to his right. There it was, the *Madonna* he'd seen. He took two steps toward the painting on the easel in front of him.

"Here," he said. "Here it is right . . ."

Monk's voice died.

He stared at the painting in front of him. He stepped right up and touched the frame. It wasn't the da Vinci, not the *Madonna with the Yarn Winder*, not any kind of Madonna at all. He scowled. Damn it. The painting was similar. The same size, the same muted Renaissance colors. A religious theme, a saint of some kind, but decidedly not the mother of God. Franklin coughed quietly, and Monk forced himself to turn to the man.

"This isn't it," he said. He looked around the room. "I'm . . . I'm confused. This is the only room, the only private gallery?"

"The only one, I'm afraid."

Monk glanced to his left. "Do you mind if I look around? Make sure I haven't lost my bearings?"

"Take all the time you need."

Monk started with the Pollock, then moved to his left, all the way to the far end of the room, his eyes examining the paintings. He touched the frames of a couple of them, absentmindedly brushed away an inch-long streak of dust from the largest of the frames. He toured the entire gallery, then stood staring at the floor. This time Franklin didn't bother to cough, but Monk knew he had to be staring. That he and his housekeeper both had to be staring. Again Monk forced himself to turn around and face them.

TWENTY-TWO

"Mary Anne!" Steve Batcholder said, when Sung Kim pulled her white Dodge Grand Caravan up to the guard shack at the entrance to Battle Valley Farm. "What are you doing back here so soon?"

The size of the gate guard's smile showed that he wasn't a bit disappointed to see her again, as he glanced over Sung Kim's shoulder at the plants and flowers in the back of the van.

"What was it?" he said, "Two days ago? Three?" He laughed. "Look at me, asking you . . . when I'm the one who's getting paid to keep track."

Sung Kim tossed her long brown hair. "The day before yesterday, and I'm flattered you care."

Steve blushed, then turned away for a moment before looking at her again. He was clearly flustered by her flirting, and why wouldn't he be? She'd spent almost as much time learning to use her sexuality as she had learning how to kill.

"I . . ." he began, then started over. "I don't really get too many through here I do care about." Steve straightened his tie and ran a hand through his thick black hair. "Not many who look as good as you, I mean."

Sung Kim stretched through the van's open window to touch his hand. "I could say the same thing, you know."

His face got even redder before he shook his head and changed the subject.

"Good thing you're here today," he told her. "Better hope you won't have to come back soon."

She arranged her features in a look of surprise. "Why? What's going on?" Steve glanced over his shoulder in the direction of the mansion in the distance, then turned back to her and lowered his voice. "I don't know who's coming, but the Secret Service has been all over this place for days."

"I was wondering why Mr. Franklin wanted so many plants and flowers." She looked at him. "I don't know when I'll be back . . . it's not really up to me. You know the man. He's liable to call me at midnight tonight and order more." And he was likely to call, Sung Kim knew, although Franklin's needs had nothing to do with flowers.

"Well, if you do have to come, just be ready for a real hassle." He pointed at the ID badge pinned to her white smock, the badge she made it a habit to wear to the farm because she never knew when the Secret Service would be around. "I know you always have your badge, but be sure not to forget it. Even I won't be able to get you in without it." Then he gestured toward the plants behind her. "And make sure what you bring isn't too delicate. The Secret Service people will manhandle your flowers until there won't be anything left of them."

She nodded. "Thanks for the heads-up. I hope I don't have to come back that soon, but if I do, you can be sure I'll be ready."

And Steve could count on that, Sung Kim thought, as she smiled one last time, then waved at him before stepping on the gas and heading through the gate toward the mansion. A few minutes later, she was at the rear of the big house, at the delivery door, and ringing the bell. To her surprise, the door was answered by Grace Woods herself. Thomas Franklin's impressive housekeeper was frowning.

"He specifically asked to talk with you today, Mary Anne," she said, "but I don't want you taking a lot of his time. We're very busy, and he's a little . . ." Grace appeared to be looking for the right word to use with the hired help. "Mr. Franklin's a little testy today. He's in his office with the door closed, but I've already heard his voice a couple of times. Didn't sound happy."

Sung Kim nodded. "I'll only be a few minutes."

Grace gestured toward the front of the house. "He's waiting for you, but stop and check with me on your way out. We'll need some special floral arrangements in the next few days. I want to make sure we choose exactly the right things."

Sung Kim smiled. "Of course. Anything I can do to help."

Franklin was sitting behind his desk when she entered his office, but rose quickly to come around the desk and meet her before she got there. She took one look at his face and guessed what had happened, and that it was going to take all her skill to work him through this thing.

"Damn it, Mary Anne, what took you so long?"

Sung Kim reached out and touched his arm. "I was in the middle of a delivery, Thomas." She smiled and moved up close to him, only a few inches from his face. "You want me on a shorter leash, you've got to hire me full time."

He scowled. "Yeah, that's all I need. People are already wondering why I need so goddamned many flowers."

"You could make an honest woman of me." Still teasing, but he didn't even smile. As a matter of fact, he looked awful. His eyes were lifeless, as if someone had drained all the fluid out of them, and he was shifting from foot to foot in a way she couldn't ever remember seeing. "What's the matter, Thomas?" She took his arm and tried to lead him toward the chairs near the fireplace, but he shook her hand away.

"The FBI was here again," he said. "Puller Monk. The same agent as Saturday night." He stared at the floor before looking up at her. "We've got a problem, Mary Anne . . . a big problem."

Sung Kim looked away, toward the windows beyond the desk, and the golf course across the driveway. It was important to play this just right. She turned back to Franklin.

"Tell me what happened. Exactly what happened."

Franklin turned toward the chairs, then walked slowly to the closest one and sat. Sung Kim followed and sat in the other one. She listened as Franklin told her about Puller Monk showing up at his office downtown and his insistence on looking for the da Vinci. The helicopter ride out here, and the rest of it.

"I moved it out of the vault right after I talked to you," he said. "I moved all of them out of there."

"So he saw nothing."

"But he didn't buy it . . . I could tell from the way he went all through the vault." He hesitated. "Monk will be back, Mary Anne. The bureau will be back. And when they do, they're going to . . ." He stopped and shook his head. "We've got to . . ." Again he stopped, and suddenly his voice was a lot tougher. "I'm not going to let him destroy me."

Good, Sung Kim thought. She needed him tough. For a few more days he had to stay tough.

"He's not going to destroy anybody. Your nosy agent was on a fishing expedition. If Monk had any evidence, he'd have come with a search warrant. You and I would already be in jail."

"That's what I keep telling myself, but . . ."

"But nothing. It's over."

"You sound so damned sure."

"I'm a thief, Thomas, a professional, and I know exactly what happened. Trust me, Monk wasn't sent to your party to conduct an illegal search. There wouldn't be any point. As a matter of fact, what he did would destroy their case."

Franklin stared at her. "A coincidence? He just happened to show up after the robbery? Just happened to walk into the vault where I put the da Vinci?" Franklin shook his head. "Give me a fucking break."

She knew better than to argue. Especially when he was dead right. "So what do you want to do about it?"

"Get the da Vinci out of here, for one thing. Get the other five out of here." He rose from his chair. "You're right about one thing, Mary Anne. If Monk had any evidence, he wouldn't have asked for my consent to search. If I get rid of the paintings, there's no way any of this can come back to me. Or you, either."

Sung Kim nodded. "I'll have them out of the house in an hour." She grinned. "But before I do, I've got to put a smile back on your face."

Franklin frowned. "Now? Christ, Mary Anne, how can you think about . . ."

His voice died as she stood and came to him, pushed him gently back down into his chair, and got on her knees in front of him. She reached for the zipper on his pants, but he deflected her hand.

"No way," he said. "Not after what's happened. Even you aren't that good."

She looked up at him, her brown eyes playful. "You know how I love a challenge."

"The door's unlocked, Mary Anne."

"Someone could walk in," she told him, staying with the game they always played. There wasn't a chance in hell anyone would walk into Thomas Franklin's office without his permission.

But this time he shook his head. "You're wasting your—"

He stopped abruptly as her hand found his flaccid penis and pulled it out of his pants. He was sure as hell right about his lack of motivation, Sung Kim saw, as she lowered her head and began to work with her lips and tongue. She couldn't help thinking about the first time she'd done this to him, three and a half years ago in this very chair. She could still hear his tortured breathing, still see his eagerness to get it out of his pants, and feel his gasping release only moments after she'd started. No challenge in it at all, back then. This time it would take all her skill, but she had more than enough in reserve. More than enough to keep him firmly in line.

Afterward, Sung Kim went back to her Dodge van for a wheeled cart filled with plants and floral arrangements, along with a folded canvas tarpaulin, then headed upstairs, where Franklin accompanied her from room to room as they placed the floral displays. The cart empty, their last stop was a locked room on the third floor, at the opposite end of the wide corridor from the master bedroom. Franklin had already boxed the six paintings, none of them large enough to attract any attention. He set the paintings on her cart and she covered them with the tarpaulin from the van. Then he accompanied her back downstairs and out to the van.

"Thanks, Mary Anne," he said loudly, for the benefit of anyone who

might be in a position to hear. "I get a lot of compliments about the flowers, and I owe it all to you."

"I still have to see Grace for a few minutes," she told him, "before I
leave."

"Good," he said, then dropped his voice to barely above a whisper.
"Then get these fucking paintings as far away from here as you can take
them."

Steve Batcholder grinned and waved at Sung Kim as she drove through the
main gate and turned right toward Washington. As soon as she got out of
his sight she pulled over to the side of the road and reached into the console for a cell phone she tried never to use. She dialed a number that
started an electronic signal that bounced off three satellites over a dozen
countries before ending up in Paris. A voice answered in Korean. This
time she and her controller had no need to speak English, although she
still had to be circumspect.

"There's a problem at the farm," she told him. "I suspect some kind of
burrowing animal."

"I'll need to know more, madam. Can you be a bit more specific?"

It was the signal that the phone connection was secure, that she could
be a bit less cryptic, although nowhere near the level of what they called
plaintext.

"We've had a visitor who seems to know all about this animal," she
said, "but he didn't mention a specific name. Which makes it hard to treat
the problem."

"Of course," her controller replied. "We will make inquiries at this end
and let you know. I'm certain we can take care of the situation before it
gets out of control."

Inquiries. Just the word made Sung Kim shudder.

"And our visitor?" she said. "Are you telling me there's no longer any
point keeping him around?"

She listened to her controller's blunt response, then nodded as he
added a specific instruction. "Yes," she said. "Yes, of course. I will make sure
of that."

TWENTY-THREE

Monk's mood was seriously rotten. His failure at Franklin's mansion continued to eat at him, and he couldn't wait to get to the loft and start the process of putting it behind him. When he drove through Dupont Circle and continued on P Street to the front of his building, he was surprised to see Lisa sitting in a strange car with a man he'd never seen. The car was a two-door red Infiniti G35, with Texas plates. A year old, maybe two, but not a bureau car, not one that would be assigned to the field office at any rate. The bureau bought only American cars for routine use.

Monk looked at the man behind the wheel. Young, younger than he was, black hair combed straight back. White shirt and tie, tan jacket. His face was pretty much inexpressive, but Lisa's sure as hell wasn't. She was shouting, Monk saw, although he couldn't make out anything she was saying over the noise from the air-conditioner in the Saab. He reached to turn the fan off, but his hand stopped as he focused on Lisa's face. Her features were twisted with rage, and Monk had the feeling she was about to strike the man.

He pulled to the edge of the row of parked cars, about to jump out of the Saab and make sure she was okay, when Lisa saw him. Her eyes widened for an instant before she threw the door open, jumped out of the car, and turned back to the driver. Now she was smiling at him, her face just as friendly as a moment before it had been furious. Monk heard her thanking the man for the ride home before she closed the door and lifted her hand in a brief wave as he pulled away from the curb.

Lisa glanced at Monk before she turned and headed for the front door. Monk took the parking place the man had vacated, jumped out of the car, and tried to catch up with her before she took the elevator upstairs. He didn't make it, but when he got upstairs and went through the front door of their loft she was waiting for him. They stood awkwardly, just inside the door, facing each other

"What was that all about?" he asked her. "Who *was* that?"

"Just a ride home, Puller." She stepped closer to him, and he could see the vacant look in her eyes. "Christ, I'm so tired I can't even see straight."

He stared at her. "You haven't been home yet? You're still going from last night?" She'd been gone when he got up this morning, but he'd just assumed she'd gone to work.

She nodded. "You know how the Hoover Building can be. They want the C4 traced right now, right this minute. We've been on it ever since I left you at the restaurant. Things got pretty hectic, and somewhere along the line my bureau car got left behind. The guy offered to give me a ride home."

"I saw you shouting at him. I thought you were going to slug him."

"He made a move on me is all." She tried to smile. "I am a single woman, you know. But he took it a little too far."

Monk nodded, but he didn't believe her. Her tell was nothing as obvious as touching her nose or tugging an ear, but it was there nonetheless. When Lisa was playing with the edges of the truth, her voice dropped a barely perceptible tone in pitch, and right now that's exactly what she was doing.

"Who was he? Do I have to go beat him up?"

She shook her head. "I think he got the message."

But she hadn't answered his question, Monk realized, not both parts of it at any rate, so he tried again. "Is he on your squad? Is he working terrorism?"

Lisa frowned. "This is starting to sound like an interrogation. I told you it was nothing. The guy hit on me, I overreacted. End of story."

"The car had Texas plates." Monk stared at her. "Seems to me he came a hell of a long ways to make a pass."

She took a step toward him, and her voice developed a hard edge. "Drop it, Puller. I don't need this. Especially when I'm exhausted . . . and most especially after Saturday night." She paused. "Seems to me you're the one keeping the secrets around here."

"Damn it," he said, then closed his mouth as he realized he didn't want to fight about this. He couldn't fight about this without showing his cards, and he wasn't ready to do that, especially when he didn't even know himself what those cards were.

"God, Lisa," he said. "Listen to us. Listen to *me*, I should say." He shook his head. "How often do we get the chance to get home for dinner together? . . . And we spend the time fighting?" He grinned. "How about we say you win and go to bed early."

Lisa stepped back. She scowled and made a sound in the back of her throat. "*Now?* You want to make love *now?*" She shook her head. "You walk in here and treat me like a bank robbery suspect, then expect me to fall into *bed* with you?"

Monk said nothing, just held out his arms and kept grinning, but Lisa's scowl turned into a steady glare.

"Damn it," she said. "I'm serious about this." She turned away from him, started toward the kitchen, then turned back to face him again. "You haven't shared anything with me for six months, and I'm not letting it go this time." She took another short step toward him. "I'm not . . ."

Her voice died as he reached for his crotch. "You want me to share," he said. "Well, I've got something right here we can both use."

Lisa shook her head, then put up her hands.

"You just stay where you are," she said. "You're not going to . . . I won't let you . . ." But in the next moment—as Monk pulled his golf shirt out of his suddenly bulging pants—a smile began to tug at the edges of her mouth. "Oh shit, Puller," she said with a shrug. "Why the hell not."

She stepped into his arms. Monk enjoyed the warmth of her body as he breathed in the herbal scent of her hair and felt his demons drifting away. After a long moment he pulled out of her arms, holding her hands as they stood looking at each other. The gaze from her deep brown eyes seemed to go all the way through him. For the first time in months he felt a surge of power, and an irresistible impulse to use it. Lisa's eyes widened as he put one arm around her shoulders, and bent to put the other one around the back of her knees.

"Puller," she said. "What are you . . ."

But she couldn't finish her question before he straightened up with her in his arms and held her for a moment before turning toward the big bed at the rear of the loft. Halfway there, she looked up into his eyes again, but this time she smiled. "I hope you don't think this is the end of the argument. I hope you don't think . . ."

Her words died as he pulled her up and kissed her mouth, then lowered her again, grinning now as they approached the bed.

"Quit thinking, Lisa," he told her. "We spend way too much time thinking."

When they reached the bed, he lowered her onto it before stepping back. Christ, she was beautiful, Monk thought, as he looked at her black hair fanned out across the pillow, at her now half-lidded eyes as she reached for her shoes and flipped them off over the end of the bed before starting on the top button of her blouse.

Monk pulled his shirt over his head, tossed it on the floor, then kicked off his shoes. He lifted his leg and removed his ankle holster with the big Glock. He walked over to the wardrobe and put the pistol on the top shelf, then unbuckled his belt, dropped his pants, and booted them away. Next came his Jockey briefs, which took a little maneuvering to get down to his knees and all the way off, and finally his socks.

He returned to Lisa naked.

She had stopped unbuttoning her blouse to watch him undress. He sat on the bed next to her and went to work on her clothes. Her blouse first, finishing the last four buttons, sliding it off and throwing it on the floor with his clothes. Before he could get to her black bra, Lisa was releasing the clasp in the front. The bra fell away and she slipped out of it.

Monk stared at her breasts. She claimed they were too small, but he knew better. He bent over and took one of her nipples in his mouth. She gasped as he swirled his tongue across its hardening surface. Lisa arched her back, thrusting herself toward him, before he pulled away. She was working on her skirt now, tugging at the clasp to unfasten it before using her arms to hoist herself so Monk could pull the skirt off, along with her pantyhose and her black bikini panties. He tossed them on the floor before stepping back once more to look at her.

His eyes ran up and down the length of her naked body, at the tan that covered most of it, at the lighter spots around her breasts and her dark pubic hair. He felt a sudden welling of joy that rose through his body as he lowered himself onto her and kissed her again. She kissed him back, tugging at him to get him into position over her. He lowered his head to kiss her breast, to flick his tongue over her nipple. He heard a gasp, but she pulled his head up.

"I love what you're doing," she said, "but we're wasting time."

She reached between his legs, tugged him toward herself. Monk was more than ready as she opened her legs and smiled. He lowered himself toward her, his own breath much faster now. He bent to kiss her mouth again, but he didn't get that far before the phone rang. He turned to look at it, then at Lisa as it rang again. She shook her head.

"That's what answering machines are for," she said, then reached to pull him inside her. Their bodies were moving in unison when the machine picked up and Bethany Randall's voice rang through the room. Monk's eyes shot to the machine.

"Puller?" Bethany was asking. "Pick up the phone, Puller . . . You've got to be there."

Monk turned back to Lisa. Her face was tight with anger. She rolled out from beneath him, turned her back and pulled the bedspread over her naked body.

Monk reached for the phone. "Bethany?"

"Can you talk?" Bethany asked. "Is it all right that I called?"

"Of course. What's going on?" Behind him he heard Lisa turn back toward him. He could feel her eyes boring holes into him.

"I've got a problem," Bethany said. "There's a car sitting outside my house."

"A car?" He frowned. "I don't understand what you're telling me."

"A white Lexus with New York plates."

Monk glanced at Lisa, and she turned away again.

"I went to the movies this afternoon," Bethany said. "I noticed a guy looking at me in the line for popcorn . . . I saw him again in the lobby after the movie, on the way out. He didn't do anything but stare at me again, but I didn't like the way he . . ." She paused. "I saw him get into his Lexus and drive away." Again she hesitated. "When I went out half an hour ago to turn off my front sprinklers, the Lexus was parked down the street. I've been sitting here ever since, trying not to overreact, when I thought about you. And I realized you'd given me your phone number."

"Maybe he lives in the neighborhood. Maybe that's why he was looking at you at the movies."

"I've never seen him around here before." She paused. "But I have seen him . . . That's what's got me worried, Puller. I saw him at school last week, too. In the parking lot when I was about to go home."

Monk chewed the inside of his cheek. "Is he still there?"

"I'll go check."

She came back after ten seconds or so.

"I can't see him anymore . . . but I'm afraid."

Monk glanced at Lisa.

"Puller?" Lisa said when their eyes met. Just the one word, but her jaw was set in that way she got when all hell was about to break loose. He lifted the phone back to his mouth.

"Call the police, Bethany. They'll be there before I even get my car out of the garage."

There was a long silence on the other end.

"Bethany?" Monk asked. "Are you still there?"

"I feel foolish calling the police. Now that he's not there anymore, I feel kind of . . ." She paused. "I really wish you could come. I need to talk about this with someone I can trust."

Monk glanced toward Lisa. Her dark eyes were getting darker by the second.

"Thirty minutes," he told Bethany. "I'll see you in half an hour."

He hung up and turned back to Lisa.

"There's a guy stalking her and she's terrified. Bethany's alone. She doesn't have anyone else. I can't just pretend she didn't call."

"That's what the cops are for, Puller. She ought to be calling them."

"The cops? They can't do a damned thing until the guy rapes her . . . or worse. Their hands are tied, and you know the kind of animals out on the . . ."

His words died as she jerked the bedspread around her shoulders and spun away. He reached out and touched her, but her whole body went rigid.

"Lisa," he said. "You're just tired. And I wouldn't do this if I didn't have to."

She grunted and he turned away. He headed for the wardrobe for his clothes, and his words seemed to hang in the air behind him. Regardless of what he might or might not have meant by them, the words themselves had been the absolute truth.

TWENTY-FOUR

There was no white Lexus.

There was no white sedan with New York plates anywhere on Bethany's street in McLean, Virginia, no car of any kind with a man lurking behind the wheel anywhere in her neighborhood.

Monk drove up and down the streets for ten minutes to double-check, before parking the Saab in front of her house, the same house she'd lived in when William Smith had been in her life. The small one-story brick colonial was just as well kept as he remembered, the white framing around the front windows looked freshly painted, and the front yard was postcard pretty. Twin maples towered over brightly flowering shrubbery, all of which bordered a small patch of grass as green as a country club's.

A brick walkway led up to the house, and by the time Monk slid out from behind the wheel and strode up to the front steps, Bethany had opened the door and stood waiting for him. He took one look at her—standing there in a thick white bathrobe—and took a step backward.

She'd come directly from the shower, he saw. The hand holding the top of her bathrobe together was still beaded with water. The ends of her long red hair were damp, and from this distance he could smell the flowers in the shampoo she'd used. An intimate aroma, intimate enough to move him another full step back.

"Tell you what," he told her. "I'll take you out for dinner. Get dressed. I'll wait in the car."

She frowned. "Don't be ridiculous, Puller. What do you think I'm going to do, attack you?"

"I just think it's better if we go somewhere."

She stared at him, her green eyes not as lustrous as last night. "I suppose I should be flattered, but I'm not thinking very well right now." She glanced down at her bathrobe. "The way I look I can't imagine a man being interested."

Now it was Monk's turn to stare. Was she kidding? He'd walked into every man's fantasy: to ring a doorbell and be greeted by a woman all wet and fresh and . . .

"Come inside," she ordered. "I'm the schoolmarm, as you put it. Standing here in my bathrobe with a strange man. My neighbors are going to be scandalized."

He followed her through the door and directly into the living room. Bethany closed the door and stood in front of him. Monk shoved his hands in his pockets to keep from reaching for her. Christ, he thought, it was the same every time he saw her, the same as every time he'd ever seen her. He couldn't explain how or why, but somehow Bethany seemed to generate her own field of gravity. In her presence he felt like a small planet in the tug of a star.

He told her about checking the neighborhood. "I couldn't find your Lexus anywhere."

She shook her head. "It's out there though, I can feel it. Maybe not right now, but that guy's not finished with me."

"I'll stick around for a while and check again. I won't leave until we're sure. Or as sure as we can be, at any rate."

"Have you eaten yet?" she asked, then shook her head. "Listen to me. Of course you haven't, or you wouldn't have asked me to go with you." She reached out and grabbed his arm to lead him toward a hallway to their left. "I ate enough popcorn at the movie to fill me up till tomorrow afternoon, but I'll fix you something. We can talk while I cook."

He followed her to a modest kitchen. The countertop was black granite, laid in squares, and the cabinets were white, with glass doors. There wasn't a lot of room between the cabinets and the refrigerator and range on the other side of the kitchen. Bethany turned back to Monk.

"You mind standing here and watching me work?"

He didn't, he told her. Didn't mind watching her at all.

"I've been a little lazy about shopping," she said, "so the cupboard's a mite bare."

"Whatever you've got would be great."

Her smile was a little embarrassed. "A Denver omelette? Does that sound too ridiculous for dinner?"

"My favorite, but I could really use a drink while I watch."

She glanced at him. "Still drinking gin?"

He looked for a smile. Gin was what had happened to them the last time they drank it together, but her face showed nothing more than a civil question.

"A martini, if you've got any vermouth."

"I think there's a bottle somewhere in the cupboard."

She went to a cupboard next to the refrigerator, pulled a couple of bottles down and mixed martinis for both of them. She looked over at him.

"Two onions, right?"

"You've got a good memory."

"I do have." She looked at him. "I remember everything."

To avoid responding, Monk looked for some lint on his tennis shirt. Bethany added the onions and brought his drink over. She held hers up and smiled.

"To old friends," she said. "And absent friends."

Monk held his glass out and touched hers. "Friends," he said, thinking about William as he said it. Talk about absent. Talk about no longer absent.

They stood together, chatting comfortably, until their glasses were empty. "Another?" Bethany asked. "I'm going to cook first."

"I'll wait for you." The last thing he needed was to have another drink with this woman.

They set their glasses on the counter, and Bethany grabbed a stainless-steel omelette pan from a cabinet over the gas range. She lit the

burner and allowed the pan to heat while she went into the small GE refrigerator for the makings. Back at the range, she cracked three eggs into
the pan, then added a little milk. She sliced some ham, chopped the slices
into little cubes, threw them into the mix, grated a small mountain of
cheese and threw that in, along with chunks of onion and tomato. She
pulled a plate from another cabinet and handed it to Monk, then gestured
toward a table just beyond an archway leading to what looked like the
dining room.

"You can set the table while I watch the omelette," Bethany told him.
She reached into a drawer next to the sink and pulled out a knife, fork, and
spoon, handed them to Monk. He took them, along with the plate,
through the door to the table, laid a place for himself. A few moments
later she joined him with the omelette pan. She lowered the pan to his
plate and slid the omelette onto it.

"Salt and pepper?" she asked. "Or some toast?"

"No toast, but hot sauce would be great. Or salsa, if you've got it."

"That's right, you are a California boy, aren't you?"

She zipped back to the refrigerator, returned with a plastic tub of fresh
salsa. Monk spooned it over his omelette, then put the salsa aside and used
his fork to eat a bite. Bethany was watching. He looked at her.

"What can I say? It's a masterpiece."

She smiled as she sat down across the table from him. Monk put his
fork down and looked at her. Suddenly Bethany's eyes were not as cheerful.

"It's going to be okay," he said. "Your white Lexus guy has probably
gone on to somebody else by now." He looked at her. "I'm not going to let
anybody hurt you."

She lifted her shoulders and dropped them. "I don't know what's the
matter with me. You're right, I know, but . . ." Her voice died. Her eyes
seemed to focus on something very far away, before they swung back to
him. "Listen to me. I invite you to stay for dinner, and I won't even let
you eat."

He started to protest, but she reached over and touched his arm.

"Eat," she said. "Enjoy your omelette. Then we can talk."

• • •

He left Bethany's house at a few minutes after nine o'clock, but before Monk started the Saab he reached into the glove compartment and pulled out his spare house key to replace the one he'd just given her. He slipped the key onto the same ring with his car keys, then fired up the engine and headed back toward Lisa at the loft. As he looked for Dolly Madison Boulevard to get him back to the George Washington Parkway, he shook his head.

What the hell had he been thinking back there with Bethany?

Their conversation after dinner had been a lot more intimate than he'd liked. The gin she'd kept drinking after they moved to her living room had hit her much harder than his one martini had hit him. Her insistence on apologizing again for her behavior in the hot tub had been far too detailed—way too anatomical—than was necessary. Detailed enough that Monk began to see a reprise on Bethany's big couch, specific enough to get him out of her house before anything could happen.

The two different Bethany's continued to surprise him, Monk admitted, although he'd seen it often enough to know better. There was sober Bethany—a subdued chemistry professor dedicated to research—and there was drunk Bethany—dedicated to getting into somebody's pants. No wonder he was drawn to her. He had a history with such a woman, with a bunch of women like Bethany.

Annie Fisher had been exactly the same way, a respectable veterinarian by day, a staggering harlot by night—in the best possible meaning of the word. Until she started the twelve-step program and turned into a respectable veterinarian twenty-four hours a day . . . and not nearly as much fun.

Annie and Bethany, Monk thought. And him. Flawed, all three of them. Baggage enough for an entire airport. He'd loved Annie to spite his father, she'd told him in the bloom of her self-improvement, and she was probably right. The old pastor would have shit. And now Bethany was rearing her very attractive head. The two of them were a match made in . . . Monk almost said heaven, before he laughed out loud. Definitely not heaven. The electricity they seemed to generate was a whole lot more earthly than heavenly. And something he had no interest in pursuing. Not when he had someone like Lisa, and Monk recognized the contradiction.

Lisa Sands wasn't a drunk, she didn't gamble, but she excited him more than the other two put together. So what was that all about? Monk admitted he had no damned idea. What he did know was that he wasn't about to make a mistake that would send Lisa away.

So why had he done what he'd just done? Why give her a key?

Bethany was frightened, but giving her his address would have been enough. Inviting her to come directly to the loft if she had any more trouble with the guy in the Lexus would have been enough, but giving her a key was way dumb. Monk pictured Bethany coming through the door and surprising Lisa as she came out of the shower. Jesus. He banished the picture from his mind, then made the left turn onto Dolly Madison Boulevard.

Lisa would be waiting in the living room, he told himself again. She would want to know how it went with Bethany.

Jesus.

TWENTY-FIVE

At Division 39 Headquarters in Pyongyang there were seven possibilities.

Besides the lieutenant general and his top colonel—the two men who ran the covert operations directorate and were therefore above suspicion—there were only seven men familiar with Sung Kim's art-theft operations in the United States.

None of them knew about her mission to assassinate the prime minister of Japan, but that didn't matter. Now that Sung Kim had reported the FBI's interest in Thomas Franklin, the wet job was just as imperiled as the rest of it. And she had to be right about her suspicion that the Americans had somehow developed a mole in Division 39. There was simply no other explanation for the FBI agents' presence at Franklin's mansion the night of the party.

Which meant that one of the seven was a traitor.

General Pak Yong-sik had begun the process of discovery by administering polygraph tests to each of them. At the end of the day, there were only three men left, three whose lie-detector test results were inconclusive. Further interrogation of the three began around midnight, in the basement chamber beneath Pyongyang's Central Prison.

Lee Song-jun was first.

The civilian intelligence analyst's eyes darted toward the general as he was dragged through the chamber door by two uniformed guards, but he knew better than to speak. That it would only be worse if he begged.

General Pak waited patiently while a stumpy man in a white butcher's apron and thick eyeglasses strapped Lee into the plain wooden chair that sat in the center of the room, directly beneath a wide fluorescent light fixture bright enough to cast shadows on the subject's sallow terrified features. As the leather belts were tightened around his arms and legs, holding his arms tightly pinned to his sides, Lee began to writhe in the chair. His head swung to the right, his eyes on the table next to him, on the apparatus itself, then at the small man. Again he looked at the general, but this time he couldn't make himself keep quiet.

"Why?" he asked, his voice barely discernible. "I told you I know nothing . . . I told you this morning I don't—"

Lee shut his mouth when he saw General Pak nod at the small man. The small man reached to the table and picked up a pair of bolt cutters.

"No," Lee whimpered. "Please, no." His eyes were wild now. "Ask me anything . . . but I don't know what you . . ."

His voice drained away as the small man stepped up and grabbed Lee's right hand. Lee tried to jerk it away, but the strap was too tight.

"I don't know anything," he pleaded. "Why would you do this to—"

Lee's face blanched as the small man tightened the jaws of the bolt cutter around his manacled wrist. Lee's eyes widened and he began to shout.

"No! Not my hand! *For the love of mercy, not my hand!*"

General Pak nodded at the stumpy man, who applied pressure on the jaws. Lee began to scream as blood formed around the dull steel blades.

But the little man released the pressure, then pulled the bolt cutters back.

Lee quit screaming and began to sob.

"Thank you," he said. "Oh, God, thank—"

His voice stopped as the dwarfish torturer slipped the jaws back on, this time around Lee's pinky finger, and with a quick movement snapped them closed.

Lee's finger fell to the floor.

It was rolling toward the recessed drain under the chair before Lee began to wail, a siren of a scream that had to have been heard by the waiting ones.

"That was to capture your complete attention," the general told him. "You told me you don't know what I want, so let me reiterate. I am not interested in what you don't know."

Again he nodded at the short man, but this time the man returned the cutting tool to the table, next to the electrical generator that took up most of the tabletop. The short man picked up a pair of jumper cables, returned to Lee and clamped the copper jaws at the end of one cable to Lee's right arm before bending to attach the other cable to a steel bar extending from the concrete floor. Then he picked up a control switch—it looked like a TV clicker—and handed it to the general.

"It is my wish," General Pak said, "that you survive this interrogation, but in the end it will be up to you."

Lee's head went up and down, tears running down his cheeks, a wet stain forming on the front of his trousers. "Anything, General . . . please . . . I'll tell you anything."

"Just one question, then. Have you sold your comrades to the Americans?"

This time Lee shook his head side to side, and his voice was barely a croak. "I told you already . . . earlier today. How could you even suspect—"

General Pak touched a button on the clicker.

Lee's body stiffened and he began to howl.

The general touched a second button and Lee slumped back, his eyes closed. A few moments later they opened again, but now they were filled with hopelessness. General Pak asked the same question. Lee gave a variation of the same answer, bucking and straining at his leather bonds, howling even louder now as the general lifted the clicker.

Twenty minutes later, the general decided that Lee Song-jun was not the mole. He motioned to the small man to unfasten Lee from the chair. Then he turned to the guards standing at the door to the room.

"The next one," he told them. "Bring us the second man."

TWENTY-SIX

Sung Kim made three complete circles around the camera store in Towson, Maryland with her radio scanner tuned to the FBI's Washington Field Office channels before she was certain she wasn't under surveillance. Knowing they'd be using secure radio channels, she wasn't expecting to hear the agents talking with one another. Her scanner wasn't able to decrypt the digital codes that carried their voices, but if the agents were out there, she would know it anyway. Whenever she stopped at a red light, whenever she made a turn to a different street, the brief raspy cough of a carrier wave when they used their radios would tell her all she needed to know.

The timing was critical for this part of the Nakamura job.

Yesterday at this time, Sung Kim had watched from her Volvo wagon in the parking lot across the street from Yardley's Camera Exchange, as the big brown Konitax Camera distribution truck pulled away from the store and disappeared into traffic on its way back to the warehouse in Rockville. The shipment was there, right on schedule. The first part of the operation was complete.

Now, Saturday morning, she was in the same parking lot as ten o'clock arrived and the store opened for business. She waited until she saw Yardley's small parking lot begin to fill with cars, then hurried across the street and into the store.

Good, she said to herself, as she saw that the salespeople were busy with the dozen or so customers already inside. She didn't need a salesclerk for what she needed. She passed beneath a large yellow banner that read ANNUAL CLEARANCE SALE on her way to the Konitax display at the rear of the store. The freshly unloaded boxes of digital cameras were stacked head high back there, and she moved directly to the stack.

Sung Kim's eyes ran up and down the boxes, until she saw the one she wanted, the one packed especially for her by someone she would never meet. She had to be careful not to topple the stack as she withdrew the box, before she turned and walked to the cash register up front. On the way, she couldn't help thinking how well the box had been prepared. It was tricky to get the weight just right, and this time it was perfect.

The middle-aged register clerk with reading glasses hanging from a braided leather strap around her neck smiled as Sung Kim walked up and set the box on the counter. "Did you find everything you needed?" she asked.

Sung Kim smiled back. "I found exactly what I needed."

The register clerk turned the Konitax box over, found the bar code and ran her handheld scanner across it. Then she frowned and picked up the box, examining it now. Sung Kim saw that one of the corners was very slightly crinkled, hardly noticeable but damaged nonetheless. It was the corner opposite the short black-ink mark Sung Kim had been looking for on the carton.

"Look's like this one might have landed on its edge, honey," the clerk said. "I'm sure there's no damage, but we could open the box and make sure." She glanced back toward the rear of the store. "Why don't I just run get you another one?"

"Please don't bother. These cameras are packed so well you'd have to throw one off a building to hurt it."

The clerk laughed. "You're right about that. I've never seen a Konitax damaged in shipping, but if we're wrong you just be sure to bring it back."

TWENTY-SEVEN

Monday was cleanup day at the SOG.

Unlike the field office downtown, which had a nightly gang of security-cleared cleaning people, the men and women assigned to the Special Operations Group had to do the work themselves. The covert nature of the place made it too risky to employ a janitorial service, which meant that every Monday, unless a fast-breaking case intervened, one of the eight teams had the duty of cleaning what little office space there was, along with the bathrooms and shower, the locker room, the wiretap room, and the garage itself.

This week it was Monk's team's turn.

So he and the rest of Team 3 spent most of the morning with brooms, with bottles of Formula 409 and Windex, spraying and wiping, cleaning and dusting, tidying up enough to make the place bearable for another week. Not very glamorous, the Monday duty, a far cry from what you see on television, but a lot more real. They finished about noon, and Monk filled out an annual leave slip for the rest of the day.

Back in the Saab and on his way down I-95 toward Fredericksburg, Monk reached to turn up the radio, tuned as usual to WJZW, the jazz station he preferred. He recognized the distinctive guitar of Ottmar Liebert.

He sat back and tried to enjoy the music, hoping to drown out the increasing wave of negativity that threatened to fill up the car. On his way for another hopeless try at getting rid of the dome house his father had saddled him with, Monk couldn't hold back his resentment at what appeared to be the rest of the old man's legacy.

The *Madonna* wasn't the only thing.

It was all the rest of it. His memory. His driving. All of it. Pastor Monk had been the same way, before his mind slipped all the way over the edge, before the day the Fredericksburg police had called Monk at the office. Had told him his father was picked up wandering downtown, unable to give his name, address, or phone number. Without the wallet in his pocket, they still would have been trying to figure out what to do with him. A week later the doctor had given Monk the final diagnosis. Remembering her words, Monk's hands tightened on the steering wheel. He still avoided using the actual name of the disease.

He came up on a slower moving car and switched lanes.

What was he going to do, he wondered, if his own PET scan went the same way? How would he make a living? He couldn't be an FBI agent anymore, that much was certain. Without a memory, he would be useless to the bureau. Pretty much useless to everybody. His shoulders sagged as he formed an image of his father's eighty-pound body on his deathbed. He forced the image away and reminded himself that the disease was not necessarily inherited. Having a father die from it doubled the odds against him, but there were lots of other factors just as important. Just because Pastor Monk had died not knowing who he was didn't mean Puller Monk would end up the same way. It was just as unlikely as his becoming the rest of what his father had been. The pastor had destroyed his own family, driven Monk's mother to suicide, refused even to speak to Monk in the years since, not until the day the son of a bitch had needed a place to die. No matter what the PET scan ended up discovering, Monk knew he would never turn into something like that.

At least that's what he kept telling himself on the way to Fredericksburg. Until he was pulling into the driveway of his father's ridiculous dome. He saw that his Realtor, Darcy Edwards, was already there. She had the buyers with her in the Cadillac. Monk couldn't make them out very well, but he tried to tell himself they were smiling. By the time he got out of the car, the three of them were waiting near the front door. As he approached, Darcy gave him a big grin and a furtive thumbs-up. Monk felt his own smile forming. After so many disappointments—after dropping the price three times already—he was ready for her optimism.

Darcy made the introductions.

"Sam here is an engineer," she said. "Microsoft just transferred him to their new facility over in Spotsylvania, and Janet does interior design."

Sam Fitzpatrick was thin, but only halfway down. He was narrow in the shoulders, but potbellied and wide-hipped below, and wore tan khaki pants and a worn-out blue dress shirt. His wife was much better dressed, in a no-nonsense dark green suit with a purple scarf, and appeared to be a whole lot more attentive as well. The interior designer was already looking past Monk at the dome, but her brown eyes were narrow now, and his smile began to fade as he found himself wishing she were a schoolteacher instead.

He opened the front door and stood aside as the Fitzpatricks went through. Darcy stayed behind for a moment.

"This is it, Puller, these are the people. Sam went to grad school in London, actually met Buckminster Fuller just after Fuller started the geodesic movement. Sam's always wanted to live in a dome. Couldn't believe he'd found one when I took him through last week."

Monk looked at her. "Damn it, Darcy. His wife's never seen it?"

"Don't worry. Janet's a nice lady. It's Sam's dream. She's not going to ruin it for him."

But she did, of course.

Before Monk and Darcy could even get inside to join them, Mrs. Interior Design came back out, Sam in tow.

"Thank you so much for the chance to see your home," she said to Monk on her way past. "We'll talk about it and get back to Darcy."

She strode back to Darcy's Cadillac, Sam hustling to keep up. He opened the door for her, but she couldn't wait till they got inside before she went to work on him.

"Jesus, Sam!" she snapped. "What's the matter with you? It's got no *corners!* How do you expect me to furnish a house with no goddamned corners?"

"But honey," Sam told her, "it's state of the art. Think about the—"

"Think about nothing! Just get in the car and take me someplace I can decorate."

Darcy started for the car, turned back to Monk and shook her head. "He was so *certain.* I just don't know what to say."

She glanced toward the car. Monk could see the missus right up in Sam's face, her mouth working him over like a middleweight with a lightning jab.

"I'll talk to her," Darcy said. "Give me an hour to change her mind, but don't give up hope. Even if I can't persuade her, I'll find *somebody* else. I'll find somebody with *round* furniture."

But Monk felt his shoulders sag as they drove away. He was no expert on real estate, but he knew a lot about relationships. Enough to realize that Sam Fitzpatrick getting his dream house was about as likely as prime rib at a vegan picnic. Darcy could talk herself silly, but Pastor Monk's dome still belonged to his only begotten son. The dome the old man had been convinced would start a revolution in home design—a demand so great he'd be able to sell it and use the profit to build another church—was still safely in the family.

He walked out to the curb. Even the FOR SALE sign appeared to have given up. The post tipped like an Italian monument, the hanging signboard with Darcy's smiling face swinging crookedly from its chains. Monk pulled it upright, but it sagged again the instant he let go. He looked in the flower garden next to the sign for a rock or two, found a couple of beauties, round and smooth, took them back to the sign. He straightened the post again, then wedged the rocks around the base to keep it that way. He stepped back and stared at it, daring it to tip again, but it didn't. I'll be damned, Monk thought. At least the drive out here hadn't been a total waste. Then he turned and scowled at the dome as he headed back inside. He had plenty of rocks, he told himself. He could keep that sign upright forever, but he couldn't help wondering how many it would take to bury the whole damned place completely.

Inside the dome, he realized he was starving. He walked through the circular entry into the circular living room, from there to the circular dining room and on into the circular kitchen. He swung the refrigerator door open. He kept a few things in there for the days he checked on the place and did the necessary upkeep chores. It was lean pickings, he saw. Two nearly empty jars of Gray Poupon, half a gallon of orange juice, and an uncapped mayonnaise jar. He closed the door and tried the closest cupboard, where he spied a can of Campbell's tomato soup, which he opened and poured into a bowl. He popped the soup into the microwave and pushed enough buttons to heat it. Grabbing a big spoon from the drawer to the right of the sink, he plucked the soup from the microwave and took it to the small round dining table next to the kitchen. It didn't take him five minutes to finish it off, and he'd just gotten the bowl washed and put away when the phone rang.

"I thought I'd catch you there," Lisa said when he answered. She paused for a long moment. "Well?" she said. "I'm waiting . . . or were you going to surprise me when you get home?"

"They didn't want it. The wife seemed a little upset."

"Darcy have anybody else in mind?"

"Says she does, but I wouldn't count on it."

There was silence on the line. "So what are you going to do?" Lisa said at last. "I hope you're not thinking we can move out there."

"I can't keep making this payment forever. Not with the rent we're paying downtown."

This time the silence was shorter. "We talked about this, Puller. I hate to be a problem, but I can't move out there with you. I'd have to get up at four in the morning to get to the office by seven."

Puller found himself nodding. "I'll think of something."

And he would try, of course, but the bottom line was against him. He could make the double payments for another couple of months, at the most. After that he didn't know what he was going to do. He closed his eyes and ran a hand through his hair. His stomach began to churn with a familiar anxiety, the same feeling that always came over him when he tried to clean up the mess his father had left behind. And he knew just what he had to do about it.

"I need to go back to work for a while," he told Lisa, and it wasn't really a lie. "I'm not sure when I'll get home."

"Call me if you're going to be real late, okay?"

"Count on it."

On the way out to the Saab, Monk had to pass the FOR SALE sign once more. It was leaning again, but he realized he no longer cared. Now he had a plan. If it worked out, he'd be able to stay in the loft with Lisa, at least for another month or two. He reached to the sign anyway and pulled it straight, but the moment he took his hand away it fell back to where it seemed determined to stay. He glared at the damned thing for a moment before turning away and going to the car. Behind the wheel, he'd barely made it to the road that passed through the Civil War battlefield when his cell phone rang.

"It's the PET-scan center at Georgetown University," a woman's voice told him when he answered. "Reminding you of your appointment tomorrow morning at eleven."

Monk stared through the windshield at the battlefield where so many brave men had been slaughtered. A PET scan wasn't anywhere near the same thing as the Union Army's suicidal assault on Marye's Hill, but he could use some of that kind of courage himself.

"Mr. Monk?" the woman said. "Are you still there? Did you remember your appointment?"

Monk exhaled. What was wrong with the woman? Did she imagine there was any chance he'd forget?

TWENTY-EIGHT

Monk had to go to Atlantic City, and there were two reasons why.

He needed the money, true enough, but he needed something else just as much.

Another failure with selling the dome meant he had to come up with the means to keep making double payments until the damned thing finally sold, and the continuing disintegration of his mind meant he had to prove to himself he could still use it at the tables.

It was five o'clock in the afternoon when he got to Bally's.

As he walked through the massive glass doors into the tumult of chimes, buzzers, and mind-numbing electronic musical ditties, he found his strides growing longer the closer he got to the poker room at the rear of the casino. The room wasn't as noisy as the rest of the house, Monk saw when he got there. It wasn't crowded—not like it would be in a few hours—and with luck, he'd make his score early and be back at the loft by midnight.

He wandered around the poker room, watching the action for a few minutes, looking for the best game to join. It was pretty much all Hold 'em these days—the movies and ESPN had made Texas Hold 'em the game du jour—and that was fine with Monk. It was the perfect game for a man with his skills.

He saw a table in the back. Three men and a woman. Had to be careful about women. They could play, for one thing, and they were by far the hardest to "pick." He didn't have the time for the five or six hours it would take to learn to read her. So he moved toward the table nearest the entrance. That one would do, he decided, after watching the six men around it. It was a pot limit table, for one—which meant semiserious players—and their faces were impassive, which was another good sign. Contrary to the stereotype, the very best poker players weren't stone-faced. The top players confounded their opponents with movement, gave off so many tells that you couldn't pick the one that counted. But these guys weren't top players, and he'd have no problem reading them. Didn't mean he'd win every hand, of course, but all a serious gambler needed was an edge.

He moved up to the table and took an empty chair. The dealer nodded as he sat down. "Good afternoon, gentlemen," Monk said. "Good day to win a little money."

The man to his left blew a lungful of cigar smoke across the green felt. "Shoulda been here earlier, pal," he growled. "Coulda had a bunch of mine."

"Chips, sir?" the dress-shirted dealer asked. Good, Monk thought. The dealer hadn't made him as a player or he would have used the insider word "checks."

Monk pulled a roll of hundred-dollar bills from his pocket, peeled away twenty of them, handed them across the table. "Two thousand. Mix 'em up."

"Counting two thousand dollars," the dealer said, as he counted the money, then pushed several stacks of red, yellow, and green chips—five, twenty, and twenty-five dollar chips—to Monk, before stuffing the cash into a slot in the table.

The man to his right glanced at his chips, a small stack for a pot limit game. "Hope you're not planning to stay long."

"Just long enough."

God, he loved the lingo of gambling. From his buy-in for chips to the good-natured taunting of the players, it was all so damned good. He glanced around, listening for a moment to the raucous laughter, the brief but colorful language. Robert Frost had said it best. "Home is the place where, when you have to go there, they have to take you in." Frost had to have been a player himself. At least Monk liked to think so.

But for Monk, the "juice" had started way before he actually got here.

It started back at the dome, when he took the credit cards out of his pocket and stuffed them away in the drawer of his desk. When he opened the secret compartment in his briefcase and removed the cash he was willing to wager, and when he slid his lucky gold-nugget ring on his pinky finger. The electric tingle got better and better on the plane and heightened even further when he walked through the casino doors. In the same way a new lover sets your whole body aflutter, the noise, the smoke, the stink of too many people in one room, all of it made Monk feel more alive.

It was the one place where he could be as irresponsible as an infant, the one place where the horrors of the world didn't exist. In here, nobody was dying of cancer, nobody'd been dumped by a lover. In here nobody was losing his mind to dementia. Nobody was lying, except to himself or herself. They didn't even have clocks in the casino. Noon was the same as three in the morning. Time was suspended, and your money was as good as anyone's.

In a casino there were only two absolute truths.

The first was that winning or losing was less important than playing. It was more fun to win, of course it was, but in the end it was the thrill of putting it on the line, of letting it ride, that really mattered.

The second truth was that anything could happen in a casino, and a casino was one of the few places on earth where that was true. When a player drew three cards that turned his hand into a royal flush, it was as though the planet stopped spinning, and gravity disappeared. The player would stare at his hand for a moment, but his first thought wouldn't be about the money. What mattered first was telling somebody, and the knowledge that he'd be telling people for the rest of his life. And that others would carry his tale. Gamblers everywhere would hear about the day the earth stood still. It was an achievable way to immortality. One day the player would die, but as long as people rode into town on gambler-busses, his name would live on forever.

And the beautiful part was that he might be anybody in this casino . . . sitting at any one of these tables.

He might even be Puller Monk.

Just the thought of it made Monk eager to start.

He tossed a red chip into the center of the green-felt table. The man to his left added two red chips. The dealer burned the top card off the deck and dealt two facedown cards to each of the players. Monk looked at his. Jack of hearts, nine of hearts.

The betting started to his left and went clockwise. There were several raises and Monk had to slide out two greens to keep himself in the game. He looked at his cards again. Several possibilities came to mind, although it was far too early to get excited. Hold 'em was a much quicker game than stud. Worst thing you could do was get caught up in the pace.

Again the dealer burned his top card, then dealt the flop, the three cards that now lay faceup on the table. A "rainbow," Monk saw. Ace of spades, queen of hearts, nine of clubs. He thought about his possibilities. Flush. Straight. Straight flush. He grinned. He scratched his head, bounced a little in his chair. The guy to his right looked at him and shook his head.

Everyone was aggressive, and when the bet came around, Monk had to toss in two greens and two reds to stay. The dealer burned the top card again, then dealt the turn, the fourth up card, or fourth street. Six of diamonds. There goes the flush and the straight. Forty dollars to Monk, when the betting came around. He threw in two greens. "And ten," he said.

"Big-timer," the guy at the far right end said, as he threw his cards facedown on the table. Two others folded but didn't bother to comment. Three left, three to beat. The dealer burned his top card before dealing the river, the last card. A four of diamonds.

Monk looked at the board and began to identify the "nuts," the best possible hand that could be made with the faceup cards on the table.

Anybody holding two aces was the automatic winner. Nobody could beat three aces. Anybody who had a pair of any other card in the flop would beat his pair. The man to his immediate right called the twenty dollars to him and bumped another ten. Thirty dollars for Monk to stay. He didn't like the feel of it. He tossed his cards on the table, facedown. The hand played out and went to the man on the right with three nines.

Three hours passed in a blink. Winning and losing, down maybe eight hundred, nothing to get worried about. Fidgeting, groaning, scratching. Bluffing, losing, grimacing, bluffing even more. The others really getting tired of it.

And finally getting the hand he'd been waiting for.

His first two cards were both fives, a spade and a diamond. The flop gave him the two more he needed. "Yes!" he yelped.

The guy to his right snorted. "You ever get a hand you don't like?"

Monk laughed far too loudly as he threw in twenty dollars. By now they were all convinced he was nothing more than a "fish" ready to be gutted. Three bumps later, the dealer dealt the turn. Jack of diamonds to add to the diamond on the board now, with the nine. Monk still liked his quad fives, and bet them hard. This time there were four raises before it got back to him. He bumped it another twenty. Everybody stayed.

The river turned up the eight of diamonds. Monk stared at it, and did the nuts. His fives beat anything but a royal flush and a straight flush. He grinned even more broadly. The two guys to his far right glared at him.

"Goddammit," the first one said. "I just don't know about you."

"Only costs a few bucks to learn."

"Phooey!" The guy threw in. His seatmate did the same.

Now there were five.

The betting went around the table until there were only two players. Monk and the guy sitting next to him on the right. Monk looked at his chips. Not many left, but the pile in the center was a beautiful thing to see.

And it got bigger as they faced off, each of them raising, trying to run the other out of the game.

The last bet was to Monk. To call, he had to throw in all but one of his green chips. He looked at his opponent. He'd been watching the guy for hours, but hadn't seen any sort of tell, not one he could rely on anyway. Not for this kind of money.

"To you, sir," the dealer said to Monk.

He nodded, but never took his eyes off his opponent. And that's when he saw it. The guy had bags under his eyes, and one of them had twitched. There it was again. Almost unnoticeable, but definitely there. He was bluffing. He didn't have the straight flush.

"I'll have to see 'em," he told Baggy Eyes.

"You know the price."

Monk tossed three green chips onto the pile.

Baggy Eyes laughed as he laid down his cards. Diamonds, both of them. Seven and ten. Monk felt the blood run out of his face.

"Jack high," the guy said. "All red, all in a row."

"Fuck," Monk said quietly. He rose from his chair, slid his last chip to the dealer, and walked away.

TWENTY-NINE

"You feeling okay, Mr. Monk?" the heavyset radiology technician asked him, after Monk had been strapped to the table that would slide him into the PET scan machine at Georgetown University Medical Center. "You look a little pale."

"I'm fine," Monk said. "Just a little tired is all."

"We'll go ahead and start then. Straighten your arm," the technician said, "I need to find a good vein for the dye."

Monk did so. This part was easy. Needles weren't his problem, but as he thought about the rest of it—the feeling of being buried alive he was about to undergo—he had to force himself to breathe deeply and evenly, to stop his legs from twitching, to stop himself from leaping from the table and bolting out of the room. The technician used his index finger to snap gently against the prominent vein in the inside of Monk's elbow, then bent over to inject the dye. Monk felt the prick of the needle and a sudden chill sensation as the dye entered his vein and began the lightning journey up his arm, through his heart, and all the way to his brain. He'd spent an hour doing a Google search, and knew exactly what was about to happen.

The positron-emission tomography would use powerful subatomic particles to take pictures of his brain, incredibly detailed three-dimensional images. The medium the technician had injected was designed to circulate inside his brain and adhere to any amyloid plaque that might have formed in there. It would highlight the gummy substance that was one of the indicators for the onset of dementia, that could forecast the probability of Alzheimer's as well. Just keep going, Monk wanted to tell the dye. Don't stick to anything in there. *Just keep on going all the way out the other side.*

The technician applied a Band-Aid to the puncture site, then reached to a table to his right and came back with the head cage. Monk felt his body turning rigid as the man fastened the cage into place to keep his brain perfectly still inside the tube. Jesus, he thought. His brain wouldn't be moving, but that sure as hell didn't mean it was going to be quiet.

"Music?" the guy asked. "What would you like to listen to today?"

Monk tried to shake his head, but couldn't. He'd taken the music last time but it hadn't worked. "No," he said. "I've got plenty to think about."

"You sure? I've got you for fifty minutes today. It can be a long time without something to distract you."

The son of a bitch had no idea.

"Okay, then," the technician said. "Let's do it."

He pushed a switch. The gurney slid silently into the tube. Monk stared at the shiny steel just inches from his nose. His chest tightened, he could feel the cold sweat already bathing his head, could hear his heart hammering in his chest. He closed his eyes, then began to breathe in and out, in and out. He tried to think about Lisa, but couldn't. He waited for Bethany to show up, but she didn't. What came up instead was his latest disaster at the poker table. Christ, he thought. Two thousand dollars . . . and it could have been worse. If he hadn't been careful to leave his credit cards at home, it damn well would have been worse.

And the money wasn't the worst of it.

He'd lost more than money in Atlantic City. He'd lost the one thing he was counting on, the one thing that had sent him to the casino to validate. He'd been certain Baggy Eyes was bluffing. How could he have misread the guy so completely? He might as well have walked into Bally's and thrown the money into the air. Or flushed it down the toilet at the SOG, and saved himself the airfare.

Maybe it was time to admit that Annie Fisher had been right about him from the very start of their relationship. That he needed the twelve-step program even more than his gambling-addicted ex-girlfriend did. Then he thought about the PET scan tracing the dye through his brain. Jesus. Gambling could very well be the least of his problems.

He decided to think about something else.

But before he could decide just what that might be, Monk found his mind returning to Thomas Franklin's secret vault, the billionaire watching as Monk moved from painting to painting, looking for something—anything—he might have mistaken for having been there the night of the party.

Suffocated by the steel machinery pressing against him, Monk's mind delivered images of startling clarity, so vivid he could almost smell the carpeting in Franklin's vault, almost hear the gentle whir of fans and pumps attached to the air-conditioning system that kept the climate inside the vault a perfect combination of temperature and humidity, as free of airborne contamination as the chip-assembly building at Intel. He saw himself stepping up to each of the paintings, actually reaching out to touch several of the frames, using the tip of his index finger on one of the frames to wipe away a tiny streak of . . .

Monk's eyes opened, but this time he didn't react to the sight of steel just inches from his nose.

Dust.

He'd wiped away a streak of dust from one of the frames.

And dust was impossible.

Inside Franklin's private collection vault, dust was completely impossible.

Franklin himself had said no paintings had been moved in or out of the vault, but that was bullshit. At least one new one had been brought in.

Damn it, why hadn't he thought to check all the others for dust?

But one was all he needed, Monk knew, because this changed things . . . This changed a whole bunch of things, the least of which were the stolen paintings. The paintings could wait until Sung Kim was safely in handcuffs, and finally there was a way to make that happen. There was no longer any doubt that the road to Pyongyang led directly through Battle Valley Farm.

Monk's legs began to twitch. He wanted to call out to the radiology tech, to tell the guy they could skip the rest of the PET scan.

Suddenly he had better things to do.

THIRTY

An hour after he made it out of the PET tube, Monk walked into the tiny office of assistant United States attorney James Campbell near Judiciary Square. It was a hell of a long shot to expect help from Campbell, Monk knew that much going in, but maybe he was finally walking around lucky.

Campbell sat surrounded by cardboard boxes crammed with files. They covered much of his desk, as well as the two plain wooden chairs in front of it, and testified to the fact that Monk's longtime colleague was just as swamped as every other AUSA in the District. Monk shoved his way into the nearest of the chairs, sat down, and stared for a moment over Jim's mostly bald head at the prosecutor's "glory wall." The Yale Law School diploma was the centerpiece, but there were another dozen or more certificates attesting to his excellence, and Monk continued to be surprised that he was still around. That Jim hadn't gone on to greener and more lucrative pastures a long time ago.

Monk cleared his throat and Campbell looked up from the file he was scribbling in. He stared over the top of his half glasses. His forehead seemed to extend all the way over the top of his head, and it looked even more wrinkled today than usual. Monk had never noticed it before, but

Jim's thin eyebrows were a completely different shade of brown than his close-cropped beard. Monk waited for a smile from the man with whom he'd worked dozens of cases over the years, but there was none.

"Christ, Puller," he said, "you should have called first." He nodded toward the biggest stack of files on his desk. "I'm dying here."

"Five minutes. All you have to do is listen. You can call it a break."

"Three minutes."

"Four. And I bring you a Coke afterward."

Now Campbell did smile. He pulled his glasses off and sat back. A good sign, Monk knew, but four minutes wasn't going to do it, and there was only one way to get more. Despite the fundamental weakness of his argument, he might just pull it off if he could set the hook quickly and deeply enough.

It didn't work.

Even before Monk finished with his story, and what he wanted to do about it, Campbell's round face was scowling.

"Damn it, Puller, I told you I'm busy. Whattya come in here with something like this for?"

"You don't even have to leave your desk. All I need is your okay, I'll do all the work."

"My okay? That's all you need?" Jim shook his head. "You walk in unannounced to ask for a search warrant for Thomas Franklin and I'm supposed to start writing?"

"Look, I know who Franklin is. I know who his friends—"

"You don't know shit. None of you bureau guys do. All you see are cops and robbers. I'm the one who has to live with the mess you make."

Monk stared out the single window to Campbell's right, but wasn't aware of seeing anything outside before he turned back to the AUSA.

"The guy's dirty, Jim."

"Prove it."

"Give me a search warrant."

"How about a primer on federal law instead."

"I saw that painting. I can describe exactly where it is . . . and you're telling me I don't have probable cause?"

"Hell no, you don't." Jim Campbell put his elbows on the desk. "You were trespassing, for starters. You had no right to be in Franklin's bedroom in the first place, much less inside that panic vault. And the other room? You had to push some kind of a secret switch even to *see* that one. Just by being there, you were conducting an illegal search."

Campbell stopped for a moment, then shook his head.

"Fruit of the poisoned tree, Puller . . . the phrase ring any bells? Anything you might have seen once you broke into Franklin's private collection is clearly and irrevocably inadmissible. Can't be used as evidence, sure as hell can't be used as the basis for a search warrant."

He glared at Monk.

"How can you be so sure you saw the damned thing in the first place? A couple of seconds, you say, that's all the time you had. How do you know it was even the same painting?"

Monk leaned forward. "Are you saying I imagined the whole thing?" Monk wasn't about to go into his epiphany about the dust on the frame.

"What I'm saying is that we have two problems: your warrantless search and the phony ID you gave Franklin's guards. Even if we wanted to argue that you stumbled on the painting accidentally, how do we explain that you were doing it as an undercover FBI agent?"

Monk tried to interrupt, but Campbell held up his hand.

"No way . . . no way in hell. It's hard for me to believe you'd even come in here and ask." The AUSA leaned back in his chair and laced his hands together behind his head. Monk recognized the posture for what it meant. Authority. Jim was no longer arguing. Now he was ordering. "You just don't have what I need," Campbell said. "You've got to bring me something I can use, but you'll have to do it the old-fashioned way. I know it's grunt work, but . . ." He shrugged. "I don't have to tell you what it's going to take."

Monk had to nod. The man was right, of course, about the warrant, about the work involved. All Jim was doing was his job. Most people think the FBI runs roughshod over the law. Too bad they can't see the process the way it really is . . . can't watch FBI agents begging and pleading in offices like this one all across the country.

"Okay," Monk said. "I'll see what I can do."

. . .

William's eyebrows lifted as Monk told him about the dust on the picture frame in Franklin's vault. They were sitting together in William's Chevy Caprice on Twenty-second Street, just south of the State Department.

"Your mole," Monk said when he'd finished. "How quickly can you contact him about this?"

"We can't find . . ." William started over. "We seem to have lost contact with him." He stared at Monk. "Have you been talking to the Hoover Building?"

Monk knew better than to be offended. Even with their history, William's question was nothing more than routine.

"Not a word," he said. "But that's going to be a problem." Monk paused. "I can't go on much longer this way. I've got to cut the bureau in on what you and Carter told me. The C4 is directly related to Sung Kim and whatever she's planning to do. And they're both connected with Thomas Franklin. I can't sit on that kind of information."

"A few more days . . . That's all we need. I've been up forty hours straight. I think I've talked to half the countries in the world in the past two days, and it's only a matter of time till I get something we can use."

"Even if you do we still need the bureau, and NSA. We're too far behind the curve without them."

"Carter's still afraid of leaks."

Monk nodded, but Carter was wrong. Their mole could only be protected so far. "Something's close, William. The C4 at Dulles and BWI, the Franklin connection, the sudden quiet from your man in-country. Doesn't spell it out in big letters, but . . ."

Monk shrugged. He didn't have to elaborate for William. Much of what the two of them did for a living was based on hunches and leaps of faith, far too often on downright luck. A notable exception was a good informant. Of all the things William had mentioned, the sudden disappearance of his mole was the most disturbing.

"What about the C4?" William asked. "The bureau getting anything decent on those shipments?"

"Leads. Hundreds of leads . . . but they'll take forever to run down."

Monk paused again. "That's all the more reason I've got to tell the bureau. I can't be the only agent knowing about Franklin's ties with a North Korean assassin. If something were to happen to me . . ."

"If something happens to you, we'll make sure your people get cut in."

"If you're still around yourselves."

"Where else would we be?" He paused to stare at Monk. "All three of us?" William shook his head. "You're the gambler. What are the odds of that happening?"

Monk looked through the windshield again. Now the sidewalk was deserted. He turned to William, but the man's question didn't deserve an answer.

"I'm going after Franklin," Monk told him. "It'll take me a couple of days to do the research, but the only way I can get to Sung Kim is through him."

"I'll be doing the same thing. I've already got calls out. Anything comes up with Franklin's name connected, I should hear about it." He looked at Monk, and his voice hardened. "I don't need a cowboy on this thing, Puller. Do you understand what I'm saying? Are we on the same page about that?"

Monk took a breath and let it out slowly. Once again the question didn't deserve an answer.

Parked in her Volvo wagon half a block behind William Smith's Caprice sedan, a blond Sung Kim with wide-lensed sunglasses watched Monk get out of the Chevrolet and walk south toward his Saab. Her face was pensive as she waited for Smith to pull away from the curb. She gave him a two-car lead, then followed.

According to the traitor in Pyongyang—who'd been very reluctant to provide the information before he died—it was William Smith to whom he was reporting about her operations in America. Now Pyongyang had given new orders, but first she had to find out where Smith was working these days. Where NSA had sent him to conduct his mission to destroy her.

THIRTY-ONE

What with his unplanned meetings with Jim Campbell and William Smith, Monk was late for his noon-to-eight shift and had to join Team 3 in progress.

Today it was drugs . . . the absolute frustration of drugs: the wholesalers who sold them and the traders who bought and resold them to the pathetic bastards in the community who used them. Team 3's job was to tail the local gangbangers to the buy site, photograph the deal, and support the task force arrest team when they swooped in at the end.

The Colombians were supposed to show up at four o'clock, but Monk had known better than to count on it. Three hours late was about right for drug lords . . . if they showed up at all.

Four o'clock came and went, as did the next hour, and the next. The Colombians finally left their rented house in the Southeast part of the District, Team 4 on them with the help of an airplane, following them to the warehouse district near Union Station, where Monk and his team were waiting. Waiting in vain, as it turned out, as it so often turned out in cases like these.

The Colombians were two blocks from the meet when something must have spooked them. There were four of them in a black Mercedes sedan, and the car turned right at the very last moment, away from Union Station before heading straight back to Southeast and their rented house.

"Three-o-one from four-o-one," Monk heard on the bureau radio in the Saab, before responding to his signal number as team leader of Team 3.

"Go, four-o-one," he told Debbie Glengarry, his counterpart on Team 4.

"Package put away for the night," she told him. "See you at the barn."

Monk acknowledged her message and laid the radio mike back in the console. He hated drugs, but not as much for the reasons he should have as for the days he'd spent like this one. You sit around watching for hours, days, weeks sometimes, waiting for the scum of the earth to transact a five-minute deal, and half the time the irresponsible motherfuckers can't get it together long enough to go through with it. He loved SOG work—it was the closest thing to gambling for getting the juice he required—but drug cases sucked. He hadn't seen tomorrow's schedule yet, but he suspected it would be a reprise of the same thing. Monk shook his head. Maybe the bastards would try to cook up some meth tonight and blow themselves all the way back to Bogotá.

He stretched his arms and shoulder muscles. It was amazing how stiff you could get just sitting in a car for a few hours. He started the Saab and began the short drive back to the loft. He checked his watch. Almost seven-thirty. Lisa would be home. They could have a drink or two together before deciding on what to do about dinner. He reached for the phone in his pocket to call her, but it rang before he could get to it. He smiled. Lisa had to be thinking the very same thing.

But it wasn't Lisa.

"Monk?" Kendall Jefferson asked before he could say a word. "I know you're finished for the day, but I need some help."

Monk stared at his tired reflection in the rearview mirror. "I'm on my way home."

"I only need an hour?"

Monk made the translation automatically. In special operations terms, an hour meant at least three, and more than a few times could turn into an all-nighter. He could feel the fatigue everywhere in his body, along with his desire to get home to Lisa.

"Sure," he said. "What have you got?"

"Chinese IO. All of a sudden he's headed for the Kennedy Center. On his way to the opera."

Monk wanted to groan. Another Chinese intelligence officer. The old SOG joke came to mind. What's the point of catching a Chinese spy? An hour later you just have to do it again.

"Who's on him?" Monk asked.

"Seven . . . but they didn't know about the opera until just a few minutes ago. They don't have anybody dressed for it."

Surveillance teams were ready for most contingencies, but it was impossible to be prepared for everything. In this case, Team 7 had been caught short, and there was no question about going to help them.

"I've got to run by the barn to get suited up. Tell Seven I'll be at the Kennedy in forty minutes." He paused. "And see if they can get a seat number . . . or some idea where the guy's going to sit."

Twenty minutes later he was in his locker at the SOG, pulling out the tuxedo he'd been issued, the formal clothing that everyone kept in their lockers just in case. He changed quickly, and eighteen minutes after that he was at the John F. Kennedy Center for the Performing Arts, next to the Watergate Complex on the east bank of the Potomac.

Brian Shanahan, the Team 7 leader, handed Monk a photograph of the spy, a ticket to the opera, and—thanks to the cooperation of a woman in the box office who'd been helping the bureau for years—the number of the guy's seat inside.

Monk took his seat just as the opera started, a dozen rows behind the Chinese IO, in a perfect position to make sure the man didn't slip out of the place unobserved. That he didn't go back to his car before 7 could drill a big enough hole in the tail light to make it a cinch for the airplane to follow him when the opera was over.

But the spy didn't go anywhere, and halfway into *Aida*, Monk found himself hoping to God he would. Dead tired, his mind filled with his failure at Bally's, Monk kept asking himself why Verdi hadn't gone to an editor somewhere along the way. When at last the curtain fell, the IO returned to his car and left the parking lot, Team 7 strung out behind him like water skiers behind a speeding boat.

Monk didn't bother returning to the SOG for his clothes. He drove straight toward Logan Circle instead, back to Lisa at the loft, and it was close to twelve when he parked the Saab in the basement garage. On the way upstairs he realized something was wrong, that his fatigue had somehow disappeared. Now he found himself wide awake and filled with nervous energy. He'd never get to sleep unless he burned some of it away, until he grabbed his bike and took a midnight ride. The problem would be doing it without disturbing Lisa.

The loft was dark when he opened the door. He pulled off his shoes and headed for the bedroom before veering toward the bathroom. He wasn't paying attention, however, and two steps from the bathroom door his foot came down on the loose board in the hardwood floor. He recoiled from the sharp screech as the edge of the board rubbed against the one next to it. Damn it! He turned toward the bed, hoping Lisa hadn't heard, but it was too late.

"Puller? Is that you?"

He walked toward the bed. "Sorry, sweetheart. I forgot about that damned board."

"It's okay. I just now closed my eyes." She looked at his tux. "Another night at the opera?" He nodded. "Come to bed," she told him. "You've got to be exhausted."

"I'm going for a ride first. I'm too wired to sleep."

"You're going riding now?" She turned to look at the red digital numbers on the alarm clock. "It's midnight."

"I just need to burn off some energy. Go back to sleep. I won't be more than an hour or so."

Lisa plopped back onto the bed and pulled the covers up. Monk stepped quietly to the wardrobe and changed into his black riding shorts and matching T-shirt, grabbed his thick-soled cycling shoes, and went back to the living room for his bike. A few minutes later he was out on the street again.

He would take Q Street to Rock Creek, Monk decided, then cross the creek on the Dumbarton Bridge—the buffalo bridge everybody called it—and continue on to one of the many bike trails in Rock Creek Park. He could sprint around the empty pathways for half an hour, then head back. If he put his mind to it, that would be plenty.

. . .

Monk had to be nuts.

Behind the wheel of the black Camry she'd just stolen, Sung Kim shook her head. Half a block in front of her on Q Street, the FBI agent was making it too easy. Riding a bicycle at this time of night, in clothing just as dark as the streets, was plenty dangerous enough on its own. Doing such a thing was either crazy or brainless, and she was certain he wasn't stupid.

She reached for the lever to the left of the steering wheel and turned her headlights off, then began to close the distance between them.

Monk felt the car behind him before he heard it.

He turned to look, but there was nothing there.

What the hell? He couldn't be mistaken. It must have turned down a side street. Or pulled over and . . .

No. There it was. No headlights. Right behind him, coming fast. Some drunken bastard on his way home.

Monk pulled as far right as he could as he moved past the first of the famous buffalo statues at the near end of the bridge. He kept his eyes on the low wall just off his right handlebar, careful not to catch the edge of the narrow sidewalk and rebound into the car's path. He pumped harder to keep his momentum going as he approached the center of the bridge. The car swung out to pass him. Monk waited for the driver to go around, but the car seemed to hesitate. He felt a jolt of fear . . . there was no more room to his right.

What the hell is the guy thinking?

He turned to shout, but had no chance to before the car hit him.

The impact against his back tire slammed the bicycle toward the low wall. An instant later his front tire struck the wall and the lightweight racing bike shot like a kite into the air. Monk wrenched his feet out of the toe clips, but in the next second he was upside down, still astride the bicycle, above the wall, then over it, and plummeting toward the creek below.

Time seemed to slow down.

He felt like he was floating as he fell toward the water, but he hit the shallow creek back first with a blow that knocked the wind out of him. He sank fast, under the water now, struggling to shed the bike and stand up. Stumbling, falling, getting back up. Gagging, gasping, he slipped to his knees, then toppled face forward. Chill water washed over his face and up his nose. He struggled until he was upright again, then dragged the bicycle to the nearby bank of the creek and stood shivering on the grass.

Jesus Christ!

Monk tried to focus his mind, to stop his body from shaking, but he couldn't seem to make his brain send the commands that would get him up the slope and back onto the street.

He wasn't sure how long it took but he made it to the slope at last, and stood for a moment to inspect his bike. The front wheel was bent double from where it had hit the wall, and the impact from the car had ruined the back wheel, but the frame was intact. Sinking to the grass, he lay there shivering, snot running from his nose, creek water from his hair. He released his chin strap and pulled the helmet from his head, then stared at the creek, at the slope he was on, and the bank on the other side of the creek.

He'd been lucky, Monk realized. Very lucky. Had the accident occurred a moment sooner, or a few moments later, he'd have missed the water, would have fallen to the ground instead. He'd have been killed. That imbecile behind the wheel would have killed . . .

The thought died as a new one took over.

Where the hell was the car?

Where's the son of a bitch who hit me?

It took Monk a few moments to understand what had happened. In all likelihood the driver hadn't even seen him. It wasn't impossible. People didn't notice cyclists, it was the first thing a rider learns. The driver couldn't have seen him, or he'd be here now, helping him, making sure he wasn't dead. As a matter of fact, the accident was nearly as much his fault as the driver's. He'd been preoccupied again, his mind filled with everything but what it should have been, and this time it had almost killed him.

· · ·

Unbelievable!

Sung Kim had stopped the Camry a block away, watching as Monk pulled himself out of Rock Creek. There was no way he could have survived a fall from that bridge, but he had.

She made a U-turn and turned the headlights back on. Monk was walking now, on the sidewalk, carrying his mangled bicycle as he started back to his loft.

Sung Kim accelerated, then slowed down behind him. Reaching for the silencer-mounted Beretta in her lap, she slid the passenger window down and held the pistol low until she was abreast of him. He was walking with his head down, oblivious to her presence. She lifted the Beretta into place, her finger curling around the trigger, before she lowered the weapon. Damn it, she thought, it would be so much easier this way.

But it was an accident her people wanted.

And it was an accident she was going to give them.

THIRTY-TWO

"Just fill in the file number, Mr. Monk," Alicia Donaldson told him the next morning, from behind her counter in the 1B vault on the second floor at WFO.

More commonly known as the bulky-exhibit room, the 1B vault was the field office storage locker for evidence too large to be kept in the manilla 1A envelopes attached to the case files themselves. It was also the most important room in the office. The bureau in Washington had hundreds of cases in court at any one time, virtually every one of which would be dismissed immediately should something happen to the evidence locked up in here.

Monk wrote the Lyman Davidson robbery file number on the form Alicia gave him, and handed it back to the gray-haired lady with the long yellow pencil stuck behind her ear.

"Give me a second," she said, and hustled away into the long rows of government-gray metal shelving behind her.

The bulky-exhibit room looked more like a humongous garage sale than anything connected with the somber business of the federal judiciary. Evidence too big to fit between the stiff cardboard file covers tended to run a gamut you'd have to see to believe. As a matter of fact, the black Lincoln Navigator the thief had used was currently a 1B exhibit, although it was being kept downstairs in the basement garage: Some things were too big even for this room. Looking around—without half trying—Monk could see dozens of computers and monitors, two old-fashioned floor safes that looked heavier than elephants, and a bicycle built for two. A bicycle built for two? He shook his head, then turned to Alicia as she came back with a cardboard box slightly larger than a case of wine.

"You taking this back to your desk?" she wanted to know. "Or looking at it here?" As long as he'd signed for the stuff, he could take it anywhere he wanted.

"Here's fine." He glanced to his left and felt a jolt of pain from his still-aching back. "I'll use the table for a few minutes."

Alicia carried the box around the end of her counter and took it to the library table in the corner near the door. Monk joined her, and she handed him the green sheet, the long green 1B form. He checked it over. The form served as a chain of custody log as well as the document to input the evidence into the filing system, and chain of custody was taken very seriously around these parts. When you got to court, you had better be able to prove not only where the evidence had been when you seized it, but where it had been every single moment since that time. In some cases it could be years before the start of a trial, but that didn't make any difference. Every moment the evidence was in FBI custody had to be accounted for, and there were no exceptions. Ever.

Monk saw from the form that the office crime-scene specialists had recovered the evidence from two places: from Lyman Davidson's house and from the rented Navigator that had been left behind at the curb outside the house.

The evidence people had signed the stuff in the box into the bulky vault at three-thirty-seven in the morning, about four hours after the robbery. He saw from the form that nobody but him had looked at it since. He took the pen Alicia offered and bent to sign his name. In the blank entitled OUT, he wrote the date and the time of day. He would repeat the process when he was finished, when he left the box for Alicia to put away until next time. When he finished his entry, she took the form and went back to her desk behind the counter.

At the table, Monk began to remove items from the box. The first and biggest was the portable makeup kit, a box about six inches high and fifteen inches long. It opened like a tool box or a fisherman's tackle box. He glanced at the contents. Makeup, costume jewelry—fake pearls, five or six pairs of earrings, a few fake diamond rings—and an assortment of brushes, sponges, and small square wiping cloths. He examined the makeup in the various containers: a little heavy duty for his taste, but perfect for disguise.

Obviously the woman Davidson had known as Sarah Freed was not what she'd appeared to be, but Monk already knew that. He was neither surprised by anything in here nor hopeful that it would help find her. He put the kit aside and pawed through the box for the hairs and fibers, found them in a large glassine envelope sealed with white tape on which the word EVIDENCE was printed in brilliant red lettering. He didn't need to look at the individual specimens, so he grabbed the attached paperwork, the sheets of paper detailing what was inside the envelope.

The searchers had found all kinds of hair, both in the front seats and in the rear compartment of the SUV, not surprising in a rental car that probably didn't get much more than a wipe-down and quick vacuuming between uses. Monk read the list, and shook his head. Christ, it couldn't be much worse. Black hairs—some from wigs, some from still-living heads—blond hairs, ditto. Same with brown, same with red. "No help," as a poker dealer might say when he threw you the wrong card.

There was one wig in there, too. Blond, with a ponytail. No label, no way to use it to find a trail leading back to her. The hairs in the glassine envelope did contain DNA, of course—the non-wig hairs—but that didn't mean shit either. There was no national DNA database—not yet anyway—and without a suspect in hand for comparison purposes, the DNA was useless. Sure as hell wouldn't lead him to Sung Kim. Monk looked at the green sheet again. The evidence techs had lifted a bunch of latent prints, but who knew which were hers and which had come from previous renters? And again there was the problem of using prints to catch her. One thing Monk knew as well as he knew the feel of a deck of cards in his hands was that Sung Kim's fingerprints wouldn't be on file at the bureau's identification division.

The fibers the techs had collected were pretty much useless as well. Plain cotton strands, polyester tufts, common stuff from clothing you could buy anywhere, recovered from a car that had been used by multiple renters.

But it didn't mean that what the specialists had gathered wouldn't one day be used. Despite the fact that all Monk cared about was catching Sung Kim before she struck again, he still had to observe every last detail of evidence gathering, analysis, and preservation. The case could end up in court—it damned well better end up in court—and when the time came, all the seemingly useless minutiae would come into play.

Monk turned and called to Alicia. She smiled and started toward him with the chain of custody log in hand. He glanced back at the box. He'd been hoping for something here, for inspiration if nothing else. Monk chewed the inside of his cheek. He wasn't sure what inspiration was supposed to feel like, but he was pretty sure this wasn't it.

THIRTY-THREE

"Hey, Mary Anne!" Steve Batcholder said, when Sung Kim pulled up at the guard shack. "Have I got a joke for you!"

She laughed. "You'll have to save it till I come back out. Grace Woods has been paging me for an hour."

He pushed the button that opened the gate. "You better get moving, then. I don't want you getting in trouble on my account."

She waved as she drove through and headed up the driveway toward the mansion. A few minutes later she was at the rear of the big house, at the delivery door, and ringing the bell. Grace Woods came to the door.

"Finally," she said. "Mr. Franklin is anxious to make the skeet house look right. He wants as many fresh plants as you can jam into the place." She turned in the direction of a noise behind her, shook her head, and turned back. "It's a madhouse around here today." She pulled a set of keys from the pocket of her gray tailored suit, handed them to Sung Kim. "You can give them to one of the staff when you finish."

Sung Kim nodded. "Shouldn't take me more than thirty minutes."

She turned and went back to her van, drove back up the driveway, then onto a second driveway that led to the skeet house, several hundred yards from the mansion. She backed up to the front door, then continued the charade of using the keys Grace had given her, although she'd long ago made her own set of keys to every door at Battle Valley Farm. With the double doors open, she turned back to the van and pulled out the first of two huge, brilliant red azaleas.

Inside the skeet house, a masculine space without a trace of the glamour that typified the rest of the farm, she took the azalea to the left-hand corner, set it down and went back outside for the second one. That one she stuck in the right-hand corner. Next she grabbed a large centerpiece from the Dodge, took it back to the plain wooden table, and set it in place. Roses this time, two dozen of them. Long-stemmed red roses, with delicate white baby's breath and slender green ferns to complete the arrangement. The largest and nicest display she'd been able to buy from a real florist. And it was perfect, she saw. The guest of honor would especially appreciate the colors.

Now for the important part.

Back in the van she grabbed a wreath this time: red and white carnations and chrysanthemums, more of the baby's breath and greenery, entwined in a circle of branches and festooned with a generic crimson banner that read "Welcome." The wreath under one arm, she picked up the metal stand that would hold it. The stand felt even heavier than it had when she built it. It was the C4. She'd decided on steel for the third support leg—steel that would make the plastique even more effective, and virtually impossible for the Secret Service dogs to smell—but it had increased the weight of the stand enough to trouble her. It wasn't likely anyone would notice, but it wasn't impossible.

Sung Kim took the stand and the wreath inside, dropped the wreath on the floor, and carried the stand to a second door in the room. Grace hadn't given her a key for this door, of course, but she had her own. She used it to open the door, then reached to her right and flipped on the lights before hurrying down the fifty-yard tunnel that led to the ammunition bunker, the steel-reinforced concrete tunnel that allowed such a thing to exist so close to Franklin and his guests. A few moments later she came to where the tunnel widened into a square room the size of a two-car garage, filled with cases of shotgun shells, with boxes of the dynamite used to clear land and demolish boulders all over the property.

She lifted the stand to the top of a stack of dynamite, slid it down end-wise behind the boxes, and stepped back. Perfect. She couldn't see the stand, but she could easily reach it when the time came. And nobody else would find it. Not even the Secret Service, if they even bothered to check. In a storage vault already filled with dynamite and gunpowder, their explosives-detecting equipment would be useless.

Sung Kim paused now, thinking about her next and last step, then reached into the breast pocket of her white shirt and pulled out a swatch of dark green cloth, a piece of cloth blended from an expensive strain of Egyptian cotton and an advanced extrusion of polyester manufactured in only one country in the world. Holding the swatch in her left hand, Sung Kim used her right hand to pull at the edges, to tug at the cloth until several minute strands of the blended fibers came undone and fell to the floor.

She looked down at them, had to bend over even to see them, then used her foot to nudge the fibers toward the bottom of the nearest stack of boxes filled with dynamite. Now the fibers were virtually invisible. The FBI's crime scene investigators would have their work cut out just to find them, but they would find them, of course. And when they did, the bureau would use its world famous laboratory to track the fibers to their origin. The rest would take care of itself.

THIRTY-FOUR

There had been no point going to the car rental counter at Reagan National and double-checking what the agents from WFO had already done, but Monk did it anyway. Sung Kim had used the name Gayle Kirk to rent the black Navigator, he was told, and provided a Maryland driver's license to match. The rental agency hadn't photocopied the driver's license as they sometimes did. Leaving the airport, Monk had run a 10–28 and 10–29 on both the name and DL, but neither Maryland motor vehicle records nor the bureau's National Crime Information Center could make an ID. The license was counterfeit, of course, but he'd known that going in.

So he went back to WFO and got started on the tough part.

On the fourth floor, he sat at a desk just off the rotor clerk's area in the Squad 13 bullpen. He'd chosen that particular squad room for a reason. He needed privacy, and using 13 would give him more chance to be alone than any other space at the field office. The squad worked "91s"—referring to the bureau's classification number for the crime of bank robbery—and, as usual, every last one of the agents was out of the office. BR people spent their days on the street, responding to the newest of the bank robberies that went down every day of the week, talking to victims and witnesses, working their informants, and attending lineups for the robbers they'd already caught. Or making up the clever names the media liked to print. Like the "Whistling Bandit," for the guy who whistled through his teeth while the victim-teller filled his canvas bag with money, and "Filthy Harry," for the older man who reeked of whisky and urine. Bottom line: There was no squad busier, and there was no better place to find an empty desk.

But sitting there, Monk realized he was still not comfortable. Despite the fact that the room was empty now, any number of agents might come wandering through and wonder what he was doing there; they might even ask him to explain his presence. The SOG would have been much better, but the off-site building wasn't an option. He was here to review files, and there weren't any files at the SOG. Bureau rules forbade the removal of files from the field office. You could charge out "serials"—the documents in the file—but not the file itself. He didn't have time to go through the hassle, so he'd have to risk exposure while he worked.

Monk sat back in his chair and considered how to proceed.

There were three main sources of possible information pertaining to Thomas Franklin.

The first was the computer on the desk he was using, and what he could gather from a search of Google, Yahoo, and MSN. It was astonishing what was available from the Internet without having to look for a word in official FBI files. These days one didn't have to be famous to be very well documented, and Thomas Franklin was more than famous enough to justify a warehouse filled with information. So Monk opened his briefcase, pulled out a long yellow pad and a government ballpoint pen, and got down to business.

He started with the Google search bar, typed in the name Thomas Franklin. A moment later the screen blinked, and Monk saw that he'd been right. The Google search engine had come up with more than five hundred hits on Franklin's name. Way too many for any kind of efficient research. He would have to refine the terms. He went back to the search bar and typed "Thomas Franklin + biography." Again the screen blinked, again there were far too many hits. His eyes ran down the list of publications, and he chose a magazine article from *Time*. He opened the article and pulled his yellow pad close, then stared at the screen and smiled. *Time* had made his job a little easier.

In the course of an extensive article on movers and shakers in the president's "kitchen cabinet," the magazine had included sidebars on several of them: separately boxed areas on the page that stood out sharply from the rest of the article. The sidebar he wanted covered nearly half a page, a capsule biography of Thomas Franklin that would provide much of what he needed.

He highlighted the bio, hit the print key, rose from the desk, and walked past Ginny Alexander, the Squad 13 rotor clerk—the lady who maintained the steel bin that held the hundreds of current bank robbery files. Ginny looked up as he passed, smiled, but said nothing. Monk walked over to the network printer on a table behind her desk. The big printer was whirring quietly as it discharged the page he'd sent over. He grabbed it and went back to his desk, where he sat and reread the bio.

Thomas Jefferson Franklin was born in 1946, just months after the Japanese surrender. He seems dedicated to building a corporate empire unlikely ever to fall. He was orphaned at the age of twelve when his parents, Edgar and Mary Ellen, died in the crash of their private plane into Chesapeake Bay. Franklin attended all the right schools, finishing with Princeton University, where he met and became friends with the man who would one day become president of the United States: the man with whom Franklin's life and fortune have been intertwined ever since. The charismatic chairman of the board of Global Panoptic was a multimillionaire well before his fortieth birthday, when he burst onto the international stage in a nearly two-billion-dollar deal with the struggling South Korean government. The deal provided most of the telecommunications infrastructure that would propel Seoul into the stratosphere of a rapidly industrializing Asia. The money did not come without a price, however. The wunderkind's best pal—by then a third-term congressman—was accused of playing favorites, and for the first time Franklin's link with the man now in the Oval Office looked like it was going to take both men down. Most Americans remember the bitterness of the hearings on Capitol Hill, but the controversy died in a maelstrom of political sound and fury that in the end signified nothing. One thing's certain: In the decades since those hearings, both men have made it all the way to the top, one way or another. *Forbes* lists Franklin as a solid top-tenner this year—enough billions to keep him from having to sweat the rent—but even so, his money hasn't made him immune from scandal. His seventeen-year marriage to Christina Atwood Franklin ended two years ago in the "divorce heard round the world." Despite their relentless efforts, the feverish paparazzi have failed to link him with anyone new.

There was more but Monk skimmed it quickly before tossing the page aside. Interesting stuff, but to find Sung Kim, he'd have to do a whole lot better.

He pulled the computer keyboard closer, brought up the Google search screen again and typed in the words, "Thomas Franklin + art." A moment later he scanned the results, then spent twenty minutes confirming what he already knew, that Franklin was a respected collector of fine art, of paintings and sculpture primarily, but ceramic pottery as well. There wasn't a word to suggest he was now or ever had been involved with anything stolen.

He went back to the search bar and typed in "Thomas Franklin + Madonna with the Yarn Winder." The screen blinked, no hits. He tried "Thomas Franklin + Leonardo da Vinci." Again no hits. Monk had to smile. If it were that easy, anyone could do it. He typed "Thomas Franklin + thefts of art." Nothing. What the hell, he thought, as he tried "Thomas Franklin + Sung Kim." Nothing . . . big shock there. "Thomas Franklin + North Korea." Nothing. He typed Franklin's name and added South Korea. The screen lit up with references, again far too many to be of value. Finally he tried "Thomas Franklin + FBI." This time there were seven hits. Monk pulled them up.

Every one of them dealt with the president's use of Battle Valley Farm for important meetings with foreign dignitaries, and the bureau's cooperation with Secret Service in the security necessary for those meetings. Nothing Monk could use. But looking at the articles triggered another thought.

He typed in "Thomas Franklin + foreign leaders," and this time there were twelve full pages of hits. It took Monk an hour to review the list, and what he discovered was that Franklin played an important role in the president's dealings with leaders around the world. Many of them had visited Franklin's farm at one time or another, but there was nothing Monk could see that might lead him to Sung Kim.

Next he tried Yahoo. He ran the same searches, but came up with little to add to what Google had provided. He did it one more time with the MSN search engine, and again found nothing particularly useful. Monk stretched his arms over his head and yawned. Almost two hours without much to show for it, but that was FBI work for you. Hours, days, months, and years. Sometimes you never found what you needed.

Now it was time to start on the field office files.

With a few keystrokes, he brought up the indices screen, the database containing all of the current and closed files in the Washington Field Office. More than a hundred thousand files, most of them closed, but thousands still current, still being worked by the hundreds of agents at WFO. He typed in the name Thomas Jefferson Franklin. The screen blinked, then showed the message *"486 files located containing the name Thomas Jefferson Franklin. Would you like to see main files only?"* Meaning the cases where Franklin was the principal subject of the investigation. Monk clicked Yes and the screen blinked again. *"Four files located. Would you like to see the abstracts?"* Single-paragraph synopses of the files. Again Monk clicked Yes, and a screen appeared with four abstracts.

Background investigations, all four of them. SPIN cases—White House Special Inquiries—that wouldn't tell Monk a damned thing. He'd supervised the same kinds of cases before being transferred to the SOG, and he'd seen enough of those files to know he wouldn't find anything surprising.

SPIN files were filled with accolades from people who had too much to gain by the nominee's success. In the case of those who made it through the process unscathed, there'd be nothing derogatory in the file. His mind went back to one of those SPIN cases, one he'd never be able to forget. The Brenda Thompson background investigation for her nomination to the Supreme Court. Justice Thompson's file was still maintained in the closed files section here at WFO. The final report contained not a single word of derogatory information, but it didn't come anywhere near telling the truth, either, and Franklin's SPIN file wouldn't be any different.

Then Monk considered the almost five hundred other files in the office containing Franklin's name, cases where Franklin was not the subject of the investigation but whose name had come up along the way. Five hundred files. Impossible. Might as well be zero. He'd need an army to go through that many files for tidbits of something he might be able to use. He had to do better than that. He had to see the files that dished the dirt, the ones that contained nothing but the dirt. He had to take a look at the confidential files.

Like every FBI office, WFO maintained thousands of informant files, filled with all kinds of criminality, but that was the problem with them. The informant files had no filters. The raw intelligence might not be true at all—too much of the time it was nothing more than wild speculation by informants with every sort of ax to grind—but that's just what Monk needed. He needed somewhere to start, something to link Thomas Franklin with stolen art. Or a woman. Or a North Korean sleeper. Monk grinned. He wouldn't find such a link, not spelled out as perfectly as that, but the truth might be in there all the same. When dirt was dished, you never knew what might rise up out of the mud.

But there was a problem, of course.

In the FBI, there was always a problem. In this case it was bureau security.

The confidential files were just that—confidential. They were stored in a special vaultlike room with a dreadnought clerk by the name of Betty Clement, who guarded them like a dragon at the mouth of her own rent-controlled castle. Monk glanced at the computer. He couldn't use it for what he needed, not even to check for references to Franklin in the confidential files. It was a separate computer system altogether—requiring a special password—designed to restrict access to the agents who operated the informants and to the support staff who maintained the files. Monk himself had informant files in that vault. Like most agents, he was expected to maintain a handful of confidential informants and he could see those files anytime he wanted to . . . as long as Betty Clement or one of her assistants was there to let him in. He could take the elevator to the third floor, go to Betty's lair, and request his files. She would check them out to him, check them back in, but he could do anything he wanted while they were in his custody.

Unfortunately, that wasn't going to do him any good.

His own informants were a bunch of lowlifes who couldn't have identified Thomas Franklin in a lineup, much less provide meaningful information on the man, and Monk knew he wouldn't be allowed to see any other
agent's informant files. There might be a ton of dirt about Franklin in
Betty's files, but he had no way of finding it. Not unless he took three or
four weeks to canvass every agent assigned to WFO, and there were two
problems with that. First, it would simply take too long; second, such a
survey would surely catch the attention of one or more supervisors who
would see Franklin's name and want to know what the hell Monk was
looking for.

He stared at his notepad, at the little bit of information he'd gathered.
There had to be a way to look at Betty Clement's files without her knowing, without anyone in the bureau knowing. Monk's mind began to play
with the problem, and thirty seconds later he had a solution. Maybe. He
stuffed his papers into his briefcase and hurried out of the squad room.

In the elevator on the way to the basement garage he checked his
watch. It was almost three. Betty got off at five. He could still make it to
the trolley barn and back here before she left for the day. Traffic would be
murder, but he could do it if he hurried.

THIRTY-FIVE

Now Sung Kim was puzzled.

Monk had been in the FBI field office for two hours, then come out and driven his Saab like an Indy racer toward the Key Bridge. It had taken every bit of her skill to stay with him, all the way to a grungy-looking warehouse near the foot of the bridge. He'd gone inside for less than an hour, then come back out and driven just as recklessly back to the field office.

What the hell was he up to?

She'd managed to jam her Volvo station wagon into an illegal parking space across the street from the down ramp into the WFO garage, but she didn't know how long she could hold on to it. She sat with one eye out for a cop, one eye on the ramp, and tried to relax. Monk was simply doing his job, she told herself. Just another day at the office. But despite her efforts to believe it, Sung Kim couldn't help the feeling that she might just as easily be wrong.

Monk made it back to WFO well before five, and was standing near the charge-out slips on the long chest-high wooden counter in Betty

Clement's office on the third floor. It was a large office, although most of it—the room containing the thousands of pending and closed informant files—was hidden from view behind the locked door beyond her desk. Betty was sitting at that desk, her back to him. Her computer screen was blank, Monk saw. She was working with a number of hard-copy files, two sizable stacks sitting on the desktop next to her computer.

Monk moved a few feet to his left along the counter, then set his red and white Igloo cooler on the counter as close to her keyboard as he could manage. He adjusted the cooler's position slightly, then moved away from it. He coughed discreetly and Betty Clement turned around.

"Yes, Mr. Monk." She glanced at the Igloo. "That thing yours?"

He nodded.

"Make sure you take it with you when you leave. I've got enough bugs around here as it is."

"Don't worry, I won't forget." She could bet every cent she had on that.

"What can I get you?" Betty asked.

"I'm trying to get my 137's ready for a file review next week. Can you check the computer to see when I last posted 137-1527?" Informant files had to be "posted"—information sent to them—at least once every thirty days.

Betty swung to her keyboard and her fingers began to fly.

Monk turned away, turned completely around until he was looking back into the corridor outside her office. He could hear the rattle of the keys as she typed, then a few moments later the sound of her voice.

"You posted to that file on August third," she told him. "You're okay for another couple of weeks."

Monk pretended not to hear, as he stood picking lint from his red golf shirt.

"Mr. Monk," Betty repeated, louder this time. "Did you hear me?"

He turned to her. "Sorry, I was daydreaming. Did you say I was current on that file?"

"I did. Is there anything else while I'm in the system?"

"That'll do, thanks." He turned to leave, but hadn't made it to the door before she stopped him.

"Hey!" she said. "Wait a minute."

He looked at her.

She pointed at the cooler. "You forgot your food." She shook her head. "FBI agents. I don't know how you find your way to work."

He was back at the SOG by six o'clock. Now there was no longer any hurry. He couldn't go back to Betty's office until later, much later, and he could take his time downloading the video from the camera in the Igloo.

Monk parked the Saab in an empty space in the big garage, between a black and chrome Harley-Davidson and a light blue Ford pickup truck, then made his way through the other vehicles until he arrived at the equipment room at the rear of the building. Pushing through the door, he moved to an empty table near the television gear stacked on metal shelving against the back wall. He set the Igloo on the table, opened it, and pulled the miniature digital camcorder out of the cooler, then removed the microcassette and turned to an array of playback machines on a separate table. He inserted the cassette into one of them and watched the seventeen-inch monitor to see what he'd come up with.

The fish-eye lens in the tiny video camera had done its job beautifully. There was a second or two of white noise—static—at the beginning of the tape, then a slightly walleyed look at Betty Clement, a view just enough off to her left side that her fingers were clearly evident as they flashed over the keyboard.

He waited until he could see the yellow letters on her monitor that asked for Betty's password, then reached for a switch on the playback machine to reduce the speed to super slow motion. Betty's fingers were barely moving now. Monk twisted another knob and the picture came into sharper focus. He took a pad of paper, ready to copy. He ignored the string of asterisks that appeared on the screen, watching instead her fingers as they touched the keys.

"S" was the first of the keys she struck, then, "K-I-N-S," before her fingers stopped moving.

SKINS.

Jesus, Monk thought. He'd known Betty Clement for at least ten years. Who'd have thought she was a football fan?

THIRTY-SIX

The beeping from the wristwatch alarm under his pillow woke Monk at two-fifteen the next morning.

He grabbed at the watch to turn it off before it could awaken Lisa. He swung around to check on her, saw that she hadn't reacted at all, and wasn't surprised. Lisa was a prodigious sleeper. The trick was to get out of here quietly enough to keep her that way until he got back.

He dressed quickly, in the Dockers and red Nike tennis shirt he'd been careful to leave on the floor next to the nightstand on his side of the bed, along with the socks and tennis shoes he'd left in the same place. Dressed, he headed for the bathroom, careful to avoid the loose board outside the door, and three minutes later he was out the front door and into the hallway. He glanced at the elevator, but didn't want to risk the noise it would make. Turning to his right, he hurried to the end of the hallway and the door to the stairwell.

This wasn't good, Sung Kim told herself, as she watched Monk's Saab disappear down the ramp into the FBI garage. This was definitely not good, but it did mean she'd been right to keep following him.

Monk's visit to WFO in the afternoon could well have been routine, and his quick dash to the building by the river hadn't necessarily had anything to do with her, either, but this was a different story. What he was doing now could no longer be considered routine. Now he'd gone back into an office that was virtually deserted, with no one around to challenge whatever he might be doing. There was no way to know what he was up to, but she couldn't just sit here and wait to find out. Sung Kim opened the door and slid out from behind the wheel. Time was running out. She could no longer afford to be a spectator.

It was quiet at WFO.

At three o'clock in the morning the only people around were half a dozen clerks and an equal number of agents to respond to emergencies. Monk didn't see anybody as he hurried to the third floor and Betty Clement's office. At her door, he reached into his pocket for the lock picks he'd grabbed at the SOG to replace the ones he'd left in Franklin's mansion.

He bent to the lock, the Kwickset he'd examined earlier. Crouching to get close, he slid his black steel torsion bar into the keyway, then the straight pick to manipulate the tumblers. Forty-five seconds later he was sitting at Betty's desk, the door shut and locked behind him.

Unwilling to risk the overhead lights, he switched on Betty's small desk lamp instead, and booted up her computer. The blue screen appeared, along with the FBI seal and the invitation to enter a password. S-K-I-N-S, he typed, and watched the menu screen come up. He mouse-clicked to the proper screen, then typed in "Thomas Franklin" and got a list of informant and asset file numbers identifiable with reports containing the billionaire's name. Next to the numbers were the names of the case agents, the handlers working those assets and informants. There were only six informants involved, surprisingly few, until Monk reminded himself that Franklin was an extraordinarily big player. He had scads of friends and associates, but not many of them would be willing to share what they knew about him with the FBI.

Monk thought about that for a moment—the kind of information

Franklin's associates might come up with—then reminded himself to take it easy, to keep in mind that in many cases the essence of informant files was garbage. A landfill of unsubstantiated rumor, innuendo, and just plain daydreaming.

An FBI agent handling a top-level source had no choice but to report what the informant provided, but there was little effort to evaluate or substantiate the information itself. The American people would shudder to know what went into Betty's files, but they should understand as well that virtually nothing was ever done with it. Ninety-nine percent of the time the only people who ever saw an informant report were the case agent and the source who provided it in the first place. It was a flawed system, of course, but that was the problem with intelligence work. You collect as much garbage as you possibly can, then paw through it for the bits and pieces that might do you some good later.

Monk jotted down the file numbers and rose from the computer, moved half a dozen steps to his right, to a second locked door, this one with a hell of a lot tougher lock to pick. He bent over it and shook his head as he reached for his picks. Mopping the sweat out of his eyes, he went to work.

Two floors below Monk, in the WFO mail room, Jack Bryant was up to his ass in work.

Jack was new, the newest of the night clerks, but his dream went far beyond the mail room. At nineteen he wanted more than anything to be an FBI agent, and he was taking full advantage of the bureau's help in assigning him to work nights so he could take classes at George Washington University during the day. Once he had his degree, he'd be able to apply for the agent position.

Right now Jack was sorting mail, standing in front of a gigantic wooden cabinet, shooting letters into the slots, keeping one eye on the security monitors to his right. Nothing ever happened on those monitors, especially at three in the morning, but he didn't dare stop watching. The last thing Jack Bryant needed was a screwup. If that happened he'd never be an agent, and just the thought of failure made him all the more determined.

He was just bending over the open mail bag, the third bright orange bag of the night, when he heard the alarm buzzer go off.

Jack stared at the electronic display built into the console below the TV monitors. The display resembled a blueprint of the entire building, and right now it was telling him that someone had just come through a door. The buzzing continued until he hit a switch to shut it off, replaced by a blinking red light at the site of the problem. He bent to examine the display and identified the location, designated on the schematic as GA/1. A pedestrian door into the garage downstairs. Someone had just come through the door. One of the hundreds of employees in the field office. No big deal, but Jack had to do a visual, had to eyeball the employee and enter the name and the time of day in the log.

He checked the TV monitor that covered the door in question, but saw no one. Still no big deal. Whoever it was had been in a hurry and had gotten out of sight before Jack got to the monitor. He tried the display covering the elevator in the garage. Nothing. Next he checked the roving camera, the one that scanned back and forth over the garage itself. He had to wait a few seconds for it to finish one complete trip, but still he saw no one.

Shit.

Now he had to go downstairs to check the door for himself.

He stared at his stack of mail. Leaving now would only put him further behind. He considered asking one of the other night clerks, but not for long. Everybody was busy, and the rule was simple. You identify a problem, you're the one who checks it out. Jack shook his head and started for the garage.

THIRTY-SEVEN

"Jesus Christ," Monk muttered, as he finally managed to turn Betty's second lock. Twelve minutes. Ridiculous. He'd done better in training school. It was hard not to wonder about the decline of his skills. He couldn't help thinking about Dr. Gordon's concerns, about the PET scan, before he told himself to shut up and keep moving.

He went through the door into the stacks, the shelves that held the files themselves. He flipped on the lights and the smell hit him, the musty odor of old paper. The files in here were both pending and closed, but at least the current ones got to see the light of day. The closed ones just stayed in this room and began to stink.

He didn't bother with the informants' so-called main files. Filled with administrative details—complete descriptions of the informant, credit and criminal checks, stuff like that—they wouldn't help with what he needed. Instead he went to the Sub-A files, which contained copies of the FD-302s, the "blind" 302s that didn't identify the informant but contained the results of the debriefings. The remaining copies of the 302s—documents increasingly more familiar to followers of Court TV—had already been sent to pertinent case files throughout the field office and around the country.

Thirty seconds later he had all six A-files in hand as he returned to Betty's desk. He stared at the closed door that led out into the corridor and felt a crawling sensation up the back of his neck. If he'd thought he was exposed before, he was even more seriously compromised now. Betty Clement wasn't likely to show up, but Betty wasn't the only danger. Her support-staff supervisor had a key to this room, too, and the agent supervisor in charge of monitoring the informant program also had one. But even if they didn't show up, he still wasn't safe. It wouldn't take a key at all to do him in. All anyone had to do was see a crack of light under Betty's locked door and he was finished. He felt his pulse quicken, his heart thumping behind his shirt. A shrink could probably tell him what he was doing here, why he *had* to be here, but it was too late for that now.

So he'd just have to work fast.

He picked up the first file and opened it. Franklin was not the subject of the file—not the informant himself—but there was no way he could be. The bureau didn't mind gathering raw data on public figures, but FBI HQ would never allow a man of Franklin's stature to actually be operated as an informant. The billionaire was much too powerful to fool around with, and the downside risk simply too great. If it ever came out that the bureau was operating the president's closest friend as an informant, the media would go crazy. Anybody and everybody with fingerprints on the case would perish. No FBI agent in his right mind would risk his career over such a thing. But that didn't mean Franklin's name wouldn't appear in these pages. That was a different matter altogether. No one could blame the bureau for making a record of what their legitimate informants reported.

And Franklin's name came up often, Monk saw, as he examined the first file. He used Betty's computer again, this time to identify the "serials"—the individual documents in an FBI file—that contained Franklin's name. A process that would save him from having to go page by page through the file itself. The computer listed twenty-three serials containing information about the man. Monk glanced one more time at the door, then turned to the first Franklin serial and began to read.

The informant report—bureau form FD-209—mentioned a party at Battle Valley Farm. Monk checked the date and let out a murmur of relief. It wasn't the party he and Lisa had gone to, thank God. The idea that an informant had been at that party, had reported what had happened upstairs, was unsettling enough to turn Monk's eyes back toward the door before he returned to the 209. This was a different party, and the informant was reporting the presence of a man at the party, a man whose name Monk didn't recognize. A name he decided was of no value in finding Sung Kim.

He flipped to the next serial.

Another party at Franklin's farm, again not last Saturday night's, but now he was concerned. Two parties in a row. An undesirable trend. He checked the next serial. Not a party this time, Monk was happy to see, but still nothing he could use. Franklin had hosted a group of engineers from South Korea, one of whom the informant suspected of involvement in an illegal transfer of American technology. Interesting. Monk pulled a small notebook from his pocket, jotted down the pertinent details of the report.

Then he went through the remaining serials in the first file. Two more parties at the farm, three business meetings at the Global Building, but nothing about da Vinci, the *Madonna*, or any sort of artwork at all.

The next file was even more innocuous. Two serials, old ones, both containing little more than gossip. Monk bent closer to the report. He needed the dirt, and this was more like what he was looking for. The first 209 reported that Franklin's wife was livid about rumors that Franklin was involved with a younger woman, rumors that had penetrated their social circle and were causing her embarrassment. The second 209 said pretty much the same thing, but added the fact that nobody could figure out who the woman was, or anything else about her for that matter. Monk felt his eyebrows lift. A younger woman. Now he had something to look for. Despite the fact that Betty's computer listed nothing else in this file identifiable with Franklin, Monk went through every page. Betty might have made a mistake. There might be something more in here about the mystery woman. There might be something to identify her as Sung Kim.

But there wasn't.

Monk tossed the file aside and went to the next one. The pertinent 209 was the last serial in the file, the latest addition. He looked at the date. Just a couple of weeks ago. He skimmed the report. According to the informant, the president had met with some of his closest advisors at Battle

Valley Farm. The stated agenda was economic development along the Pacific Rim, but the real purpose was a whole lot more serious. The informant had heard from someone at 1600 Pennsylvania, who'd heard from someone even closer to the West Wing, that the real purpose of the meeting was to talk about North Korea and the growing threat of North Korean nuclear proliferation. And what the rest of the world might soon have to do about it. Specifically, what Japanese prime minister Ishii Nakamura wanted to do about it. Despite the cultural contempt of his people for nuclear weapons, Nakamura was asking for nukes he could use to protect his country from North Korea and to keep peace along the Pacific Rim.

Reading the report, Monk was fascinated by the inside peek at what everyone seemed to be talking about these days, the ever-growing nuclear bluster from the lunatic in Pyongyang. Equally fascinating was the Japanese prime minister's extraordinary request. Not so long ago his country had been devastated by the same sort of weapon they now seemed ready to obtain.

And the fact that the meeting had taken place at Franklin's farm certainly underscored the man's influence with the Oval Office. Monk recalled the story in *Time*, the article that suggested Franklin was not only the president's closest friend but his most trusted advisor as well. He thought about that for a moment and felt his stomach tighten. The stakes were growing larger, weren't they? This was turning into a hell of a . . .

Monk froze as he heard footsteps outside the door.

He could do nothing more than stare at the doorknob, and watch it turn as the door began to shake.

Shit.

He looked around for a place to hide.

He reached for the light, but didn't dare turn it off. Whoever was out there would notice for sure.

The door stopped shaking.

The footsteps receded down the hallway.

Monk's body sagged. He glanced down at his shirt, half expecting to see the fabric jump with the hammering of his heart. He released the breath he'd been holding since hearing the footsteps. Christ Almighty. One of the night clerks, he realized. Rattling the door like a cop walking the beat, checking to make sure it was locked. Monk sat quietly for a moment, and when his breathing returned to normal he went back to the files.

He searched for more about the president's meeting at Battle Valley Farm but saw nothing. He wasn't surprised. It was amazing enough for the bureau to have one informant so close to the West Wing; more than one would be a miracle. He looked for anything to do with art, with paintings, with stolen paintings, with da Vinci or the *Madonna*, but found nothing. He glanced at his watch. He'd been here forty-three minutes already. Far too long. For all he knew, the night clerk had seen some light under the door and gone for help.

He grabbed the files and hurried back through the door into the file room, replaced them in the stacks, then shot back to Betty's desk and turned off her computer. Making sure her desk was exactly as he'd found it, he moved to the office door, cracked it open, peered out into the semi-darkness, and saw no one. He stepped through the door, shut and locked it behind him, then walked swiftly to the corridor and from there to the elevator that would take him to the garage.

Oh, for God's sake! Jack Bryant thought. Now what?

Someone had just gotten into the elevator on the third floor.

Still sorting mail, Jack checked the elevator monitor. A tall man stood inside, facing the door. Dark red tennis shirt, tan cotton pants. Jack didn't recognize him, but that didn't mean much. He hadn't been here long enough to know even a third of the people who worked in the field office. He looked instead for the ID card that should be hanging down the man's chest, but he couldn't see one.

Jack stepped over to the monitors and watched the screen that would show the man coming out of the elevator into the garage. A moment later he saw the elevator doors slide back and the man step through. Jack touched the button at the bottom of the monitor to zoom in with the camera. He still couldn't see an ID card. He reached for the microphone to his left to challenge the man. He lifted the mike as the man turned his back for an instant to look around at the closing elevator doors. Jack lowered the mike. There it was, the ID card, hanging down the guy's back.

Damn it, that had been close.

The last thing he needed was to piss off some agent who had to be dog-tired.

He stepped back from the monitors, turned toward the mail slots again, then realized he'd forgotten something. Jesus, what was the matter with him? He'd almost forgotten the security log, another good way to get your ass fired. Jack knew he was overly scrupulous—that the other night clerks laughed at his constant concern about crossing t's and dotting i's—but it was his life, his career, and he wasn't about to lose it through carelessness.

He went back to the clipboard hanging near the monitors. He jotted down the time, added the words, "unknown agent entered third floor elevator, exited into garage and drove out. ID badge verified."

There, Jack Bryant thought, as he initialed the log and returned to his mail. Any problem now, it wasn't going to be his. He picked up a letter, glanced at it, turned to fire it into a pigeonhole, then stopped with his hand in the air as he realized what he'd seen . . . or what he hadn't seen.

The agent had been on the third floor, working on the third floor, but Jack hadn't seen him. He'd just come back from walking through every squad room on that floor, and he hadn't seen a soul. Jack began to wonder if he hadn't made a mistake with the goddamned security log. Maybe he shouldn't have made any kind of note at all. Especially one that said he'd had an unidentified person on the third floor, a person he hadn't even bothered to identify. Shit. People had warned him the FBI was a dangerous place to work, but they had no idea.

He didn't need five seconds to decide what he had to do next.

His supervisor might chew his ass for failing to identify the agent, but the bureau would fire him if they found out he didn't report his mistake promptly. He was fucked if he did, but he was really fucked if he didn't. If he wanted to get his degree, to move up the ladder and become an FBI agent, there was only one way to go here. He took a deep breath and let it out slowly, then reached for the phone.

. . .

Back in the Volvo after her failed attempt to determine from the lights in the FBI building's windows which floor Monk had gone to, Sung Kim watched his Saab as it swung up the ramp and turned into the street. She waited for him to get far enough away that he wouldn't notice her, then pulled out of her parking place and followed. There was virtually no traffic, and she warned herself to be careful. She didn't have to risk exposure. She knew where he lived. She knew where he worked. She knew about the barnlike structure by the river. It was better to stay back tonight, better to lose him now than blow her assignment altogether.

Monk was too wired to sleep, so he drove around the deserted streets until the adrenaline level in his body had returned to something resembling normal. It was shortly after five o'clock when he finally made it back to the loft. Lisa was waiting for him. Sitting up in bed as he came through the door, her eyes on him as he approached.

"Where were you?" she asked. "I woke up about four, and you weren't here. When did you get up?" She frowned. "And where have you been all night?"

"My pager went off around two. You didn't hear it, and I didn't want to wake you."

"You had to work?"

"You sound like you don't believe me."

"The SOG? You and your team were out on the street?"

Damn it, she'd made a phone call to check. "I didn't say that at all." He paused. "What I said is that I had to go to work."

Lisa sat up straighter, her dark eyes narrow. "What were you doing? What were you working on?"

He stared at her for a long moment, but said nothing. Lisa knew better than to ask a question like that.

"I didn't know what to think when I got up to use the bathroom and you were gone." She paused. "You should have called me if you were going to be gone all night."

"I should have. I should have called, but I just got busy."

Lisa shook her head. She looked like she wanted to say something, but she didn't.

"What's wrong?" Monk asked her. "What do you imagine I was doing?"

"Why don't *you* tell *me*?" She shook her head. "Or is that something else I don't have the need to know?"

Monk stepped over to the freestanding wardrobe they used as a closet and began to unbuckle his belt, then stopped and turned to her again before approaching the foot of the bed.

"When did you go back to being a prosecutor again?"

Lisa looked directly into his eyes. "Were you with her?"

"Her?"

"Damn it, Puller, don't even start. Don't run one of your games on me."

"I'm not running a game. I don't know what you're talking about."

"Bethany Randall," she said. "That's what I'm talking about . . . That's who I'm talking about."

"Don't be ridiculous."

"I watched the two of you walking across the street together, going into the bar. You were gawking like an altar boy at her legs, she was touching your arm . . . brushing something off your sleeve." She paused, and when she continued her voice was different. Lower now, and sad. "She was brushing your sleeve like a lover." Lisa hesitated again. "I guess what I'm trying to say is that I worry, Puller. I see you with her and I worry."

Monk looked into her wounded eyes. He bent over the bed and spoke directly into those eyes.

"I was at WFO tonight. Checking on some stuff that I really can't talk about." He paused. "Bethany Randall was engaged to a friend of mine. We used to hang out together, the three of us, but that's it."

Lisa's voice softened. "Are you going to see her again?"

"I don't know why I would. I hadn't seen her for five years as it was."

He moved back to the wardrobe, pulled off his shirt and pants, and hung them up. Then he slid his shorts and socks off, opened the wicker hamper next to the wardrobe and tossed them in, before returning to the bed and sliding under the covers. He reached for Lisa, but her body stiffened as she edged closer to her own side. He followed her, nuzzling against the curve of her back.

"Lisa," he said into the back of her head. "I should have let you know I'd be working all night. I shouldn't have left without telling you. I'm a jerk and an asshole . . . but I love you." He put one arm around her and pulled her close. "Can we be friends again? Can I weasel my way back into your arms?"

She turned over, her face only inches away.

"You *are* an asshole," she said. "Sometimes you *are* a real jerk." She rolled away from him, got out of bed, and started for the bathroom. Halfway there, she turned back. "We're going to talk about this some more, Puller. I have to go to work now, but trust me, we will discuss this later."

THIRTY-EIGHT

"I hope," Roger Carmody said, "you can tell me you found Lyman David-son's *Madonna.*"

The short and gray-bearded Renaissance curator at the District of Co-lumbia Museum of Art smiled as Monk sat down across from his desk in Carmody's narrow office at the museum in northwest Washington.

"I'm afraid I can't. Not yet."

Carmody's thin lips curled with distaste. To a curator of fine art, the idea of thieves stealing the very finest art was abhorrent.

"But you're getting close," he said.

"We have heard something, Mr. Carmody. Nothing definite . . . more like a rumor." He paused. "It could be nothing . . . I've got to emphasize that. It's important not to make too big a thing of it."

"But it's a break. It's still a break."

"Break might be a stretch."

"Germany," Carmody said. "You're going to tell me the *Madonna's* in Frankfurt, or Berlin." He gestured toward the full in-box on his desk. "In-terpol sends me a new bulletin every other day."

Monk shook his head. "I'm more interested in Americans. Private collectors like Lyman Davidson." He hesitated. "I know some of the names, but you're the expert." He paused again, longer this time, as though wondering if he should continue with this. "Who are the serious collectors, Mr. Carmody? I need your help with identifying more of them."

Carmody stared at him. "Wouldn't it be quicker if you just told me the rumor?"

"I can't do that." Once again Monk hesitated. It was important to get this right. "Besides, it's purely generic information. A collector, that's all I've got. No name."

"You're suggesting a collector would buy a stolen da Vinci."

"I wish I knew enough to suggest anything."

"There's a black market for art, just like everything else, but a possible da Vinci *Madonna*? Who could fence it? Who'd dare display it?"

"What about a really *private* collection? There are people who need to own something more than they need to share it. If you know what I mean."

Carmody blew out a breath past pursed lips. "There are indeed such people. Certainly there are collectors who have a reputation for not bothering with provenance." He looked away for a moment, then back at Monk. "But you put me in an awkward position. I deal with rich people, extremely rich people. Privacy is an obsession with them. If they found out I gave their names to the FBI—that the FBI was targeting them because of me—I'd be finished as a curator."

"What if I give *you* a name?"

"That's different. I guess I'd feel obliged to comment."

Monk studied the desktop. Easy now, he told himself. You won't get a second chance at this.

"Clayton Stevenson," he said. "Lives in Los Angeles. A real recluse with enough money to buy almost anything he wants."

Carmody shook his head. "He must be a recluse, I've never even heard the name."

"How about Peter Bridges? Detroit auto money. Big into Renaissance stuff."

"Bridges? Peter Bridges?" Carmody frowned. "No . . . I don't know that name, either." He smiled. "I guess I'm glad I don't, if this Stevenson and Bridges are connected to your rumor."

"No assumptions, I said. These are just names, nothing more." And fictitious names, at that. "I only have one more."

Carmody nodded.

"Franklin," Monk said. "Damn it, I'm drawing a blank on his first name. Joseph, I think, or Edward, maybe." He grimaced. "You've got to know him. He's local. Lives in—"

"Gettysburg," Carmody said. "Of course I know him. He's on our board of directors, as a matter of fact. And it's Thomas, by the way, Thomas Franklin. He's a huge collector. Every museum in the world is after his stuff."

"Have you ever bought anything from him?"

"He won't deal with us while he's a director. But in a few years? Ask me again when he's not on our board."

Monk paused. This had to be put just right. Carmody had to understand perfectly what he was about to say. Franklin had to hear exactly the right words.

"I understand," he said, "that Franklin's got a private collection at his farm in Gettysburg. A collection nobody's ever seen."

"You've done your homework, but give me a break. Thomas Franklin stole the *Madonna?* You might as well go after the president himself."

"Does Franklin collect da Vinci?"

"Not that I know of. But I can ask him."

Of course you can, Monk thought. "If it's convenient," he said.

Carmody glanced at his watch. "I'm afraid I have to run. I'll call Mr. Franklin this evening, and get back to you tomorrow."

THIRTY-NINE

Christ, I hate running!

Some days, Sung Kim admitted, it felt like she was dragging tree stumps.

A little more than halfway through her daily five miles along the shore of Reston, Virginia's Lake Anne, she was tempted to stop and walk the rest of the way back to her car.

What she needed was a break, and not only from running. She'd been working too hard for too long. She needed to get away for a few weeks to recharge her batteries. She would insist on a vacation, just as soon as this Japanese thing was over. Somewhere she could lie around and do nothing. Bermuda, maybe, or the Costa del Sol. Distracted by visions of sun and sand, she was halfway around the last long curve on her way back to the car when she realized it was time to quit daydreaming and pay attention to business.

She ignored the lake on her left, intent instead on the familiar grouping of boulders coming up on her right. A dozen yards from the rocks, she slowed down to take a good look at the base of the boulder nearest the trail. Her eyes focused on the chalk mark, the six-inch line of white chalk her contact had drawn on the rock to signal that the dead drop was ready for her to clear. She glanced at her wristwatch. She had one hour to get to the drop. The fatigue vanished. Her long legs kicked into a higher gear, eating up the trail now as she sprinted for her car.

Twenty minutes later, still sweating from the run, Sung Kim drove her Volvo wagon west out of Reston to State Highway 28, then caught Highway 50 east for twenty-five miles to the turnoff for Highway 734 at the hamlet of Aldie, Virginia. She drove through Aldie on 734, and as she passed the city-limits sign reached to the dashboard and pushed the trip-meter button next to the odometer. Keeping a close eye on the trip-meter, she pulled over to the side of the road and stopped when she'd covered exactly seven-tenths of a mile.

Out of the car, Sung Kim walked around to the shoulder, then peered up and down the country road, saw nothing out of the ordinary, and turned to the grassy ditch that ran alongside the road. She didn't see the soft drink can she was looking for, so she started walking back along the road toward Aldie.

She hadn't gone a dozen yards before she did see it. She stepped into the ditch, reached down, and picked up the empty red Coca-Cola can. She carried the can back to the Volvo, opened the door, then turned to stare up and down the road again before sliding behind the wheel and dropping the can into the passenger seat. Satisfied she hadn't been seen, Sung Kim made a quick U-turn and headed home.

Inside her safe house, she used her one-time pad.

She sat at the desk in the bedroom she'd converted into a home office. The empty Coke can sat on the desk in front of her. She opened a drawer near her right hand and pulled out a short-bladed kitchen knife with a serrated edge, then used the blade to remove the top from the can. The inside of the can was bone dry, and when she turned it upside down a white card fell out onto the desktop. She picked up the blank card and turned it over. The other side bore a long sequence of hand-printed numbers. Sung

Kim reached to switch on the lamp over the desk, then bent to examine the numbers.

73918526186469128473

Twenty numbers. A simple substitution code, but without the use of a one-time pad, impossible to break.

She opened the center drawer of her desk and backed her chair far enough away to pull the drawer almost all the way out. She reached in, groping for the very rear wall of the drawer, and applied pressure at the far right end. The wall slid to the left, exposing a cavity the size of a deck of cards. From the cavity she pulled her one-time pad: a two-by-three-inch pad of gray paper that—together with the numbers on the white card—would contain her new orders. She set the pad on her desktop next to the card.

Her controller in Pyongyang had used an exact duplicate of her one-time pad at his end, bearing these same numbers. When he'd finished writing this message, he'd torn off the top page and burned it, then disposed of the ashes. When Sung Kim finished decoding her orders, she would tear off her top page and burn it. A simple, unbreakable method, and inexpensive as well, an important consideration for a country just now beginning to lift itself out of destitution. Sure it was slow—the almost primitive method of hand delivery they were forced to use—but the FBI had made utilizing the Internet simply too risky. The bureau's Magic Lantern program, an extension of the original Carnivore, now enabled the FBI to download every keystroke of an individual computer. It was a hazard Pyongyang was determined to avoid.

She began to decrypt the message, and ten minutes later sat staring at her orders, at the Korean characters that spelled out the specifics. Damn it, she thought. Did this give her enough time? She read the orders twice, just to make sure, then tore the paper into narrow strips, set them in an ashtray near her right hand, and used a cigarette lighter to burn them. She watched the small flames destroy the evidence, then gazed out the window at the clouds beginning to form in the sky to the west.

FORTY

"She's a pro," Monk told Lyman Davidson, as they sat together in the front room of Davidson's spacious home in Kalorama Heights. "You never had a chance." Monk smiled. "Not with the weapon she was using."

Davidson shook his head. "I'm still embarrassed." He reached to his knee to adjust the crease in his white linen slacks. "This kind of thing happens to other people, Agent Monk. The people who installed my security system warned me about the system's biggest weakness. Be careful about who you let in the house, they told me. We can't protect you once they're inside." He paused. "I just didn't see it coming . . . didn't see someone like her coming, that's for sure."

"I've seen what the computer came up with from the description we got from you and the people at the art gallery." Again Monk smiled. "Like I said, you never had a chance."

"It's good of you to say so, but you didn't come over just to tell me that."

"I want to try something with you."

"Will it help find my painting?"

Monk looked at him. "We will find your painting, Mr. Davidson. We'll get the *Madonna* back, but we want the woman at the same time."

Davidson sat forward in his chair. "Anything I can do, you've got it . . . but why today? What can you do now that you and your people didn't try the other night?"

"I couldn't do this the night it happened, not while you were still recovering from the drug she injected." Monk paused. "We'll need to go upstairs. Back into your vault."

Davidson rose. Monk followed him out of the room, then up the staircase to the second floor. Davidson pushed the buttons on the Ademco panel, then opened the door and stepped through to push the second set of buttons to deactivate the alarm. Monk waited until it was safe, then joined Davidson inside the vault.

As he had the night of the robbery, Monk took a moment to appreciate what he was seeing. The paintings were magnificent, the lighting dramatic, the entire room like something out of a movie.

"Okay," Davidson said. "What's next?"

"Humor me for a few minutes. This might seem strange, but it works."

Davidson's eyebrows lifted, but he had no objection.

"I need you to close your eyes," Monk said. Davidson did so. "I want you to go back to that night. Don't just think about it . . . I want you to actually see it."

Davidson smiled. "It wasn't one of my best nights, Mr. Monk."

"No talking. All you do is listen."

Davidson nodded.

"You poured her a drink downstairs. Courvoisier in a snifter. I want you to see the snifter, see the brandy in the glass, smell the brandy. Smell the scent of the woman sitting across from you. Smell your own scent as you react to the sight of her legs, as you grow warmer from the brandy and the proximity of a woman you're beginning to feel might like to see more than just your paintings."

Davidson was smiling now, his eyes shut, but still able to see.

"Now see the two of you moving upstairs," Monk said. "Closer to your bedroom. A few minutes with the paintings, you're thinking, then another drink up here, before . . . you're not sure of the rest, but you're starting to feel the excitement of possibilities.

"As you unlock the door to get in here, she stands so close you feel her breasts pushing against your back. Now her smell is much headier than the brandy, the scent of her perfume, her shampoo.

"She examines the *Madonna*, blown away by a painting she'd never ex-pected to see. She's looking at you differently, as well. Now it's clear that you're going to see the rest of that long lean body, and soon. All that's left is the charade of looking at the rest of your collection up here."

Now Davidson was nodding, as Monk continued.

"You suggest that the collection can wait, that a drink in the bedroom would make it all the better, but she disagrees. I'll look at them now, she tells you, then we don't have to worry about coming back. Suddenly you're aware of your own breathing, as you turn to lead her deeper into the vault. But before you get there, you feel a sudden pain in the back of your neck. A sharp pain, like a bee sting. You try to turn toward her, but before you can react you feel yourself falling toward the floor. But you're not un-conscious, are you? Not totally, anyway. On the floor you're somehow aware of what she's doing. You're like a camera now. You see, but you don't react, you can't react. You record, but you have no ability to identify what it is you're recording."

Davidson was stone-faced, but Monk could see his eyelids flickering, as his eyeballs shifted to the left, back toward the past. Looking now at what had happened then. Seeing what had happened then.

"But now you can," Monk told him. "Now you can see what she's do-ing. Exactly what she's doing. Now you can tell me exactly what she's do-ing."

Monk paused.

"Tell me, Lyman. Tell me what she's doing."

"She's pulling at my back," Davidson said, his eyes still closed but his voice entirely normal. "Then she's on the floor, on her hands and knees . . . like she's looking for something she dropped. The needle, probably, the needle she stuck me with. Twice, from the marks the paramedics found in my neck."

"Then what."

"Then she goes to the *Madonna*. She takes it back to the doorway . . . then she turns around and sees me . . . she sees me looking at her . . . she comes back to me . . . reaches down and . . ." Davidson shook his head.

"She . . ." He stopped. Seconds passed. "I don't see her anymore . . . I don't see anything anymore."

Monk reached out and touched his arm. "Good. Good work. That's a lot more than I was hoping for."

Davidson shook his head. "My God, Agent Monk, I *did* see her. I don't mean the rest of it, the drinks and my . . . my expectations . . . but the last part. She was on the floor, searching for something. I can't imagine why I didn't remember that the other night."

"Where was she searching? Can you point me in the right direction."

Davidson looked around. "The *Madonna* was right here." He pointed toward the rear wall. "I was heading back there. She was behind me. I felt the pain in my neck just before I fell to the floor." He took a couple steps to his right. "I think I was lying about here. So she would have been between me and the wall."

"And before you fell, you seemed to black out."

"Like I told you the other night, it was more like what I imagine a stroke would be like, or a seizure of some kind. Sort of a buzzing sensation in the back of my head, before I fell."

Monk settled to his knees on the black carpet, then looked up at Davidson. "Do the lights go higher? Can you make it brighter in here?"

Davidson stepped back to the door and used a sliding switch set into the wall. The lights blazed. So quickly Monk almost closed his eyes. He lowered his head to the carpet, his eyes searching along the floor. He saw nothing. He crept toward the wall, his face inches from the carpet. Still he saw nothing. At the wall, he pulled at the carpeting where it disappeared under the baseboard. He used both hands to press the carpet back toward him, and that's when he saw the three tiny white disks.

Monk rose to his knees and pulled his money clip from his pocket, peeled a twenty off the top, and put the rest back before bending over again. He plucked the three disks from the carpet and placed them in the twenty-dollar bill, then folded the bill carefully and put it in his pocket.

"Monk?" Wayne Nelson said, when Monk walked into the tech room at WFO. "Is that really you?"

Sitting on a stool behind the chest-high workbench he favored over a conventional desk, WFO's senior and most heavily bearded technical specialist peered at Monk over the top of his half-glasses. "I thought you finally got fired." He shook his head. "I haven't seen you down here for . . . what's it been? . . . gotta be *months*."

"Yeah, Wayne," Monk said. "A couple of weeks short of two *years*, but thanks for caring." He reached for the twenty in his pocket. "Got a second to look at something?"

Nelson scowled, then glanced at the mess on his workbench, a spread-out assortment of what looked like bits and pieces of a desktop computer, although they might have been the parts to a time-machine for all Monk knew.

"Damn it," Nelson said, "I don't have time for you. I've got to get this thing fixed by five o'clock." But he extended his hand anyway. "Whattya got?"

Monk stepped closer, then unfolded the bill and shook out the three white disks onto Wayne's workbench. Nelson frowned at the disks for a moment before reaching for a flexible-neck magnifying-lamp clamped to the edge of the workbench. He pulled it into position. The business end of the lamp consisted of a circular fluorescent tube surrounding a powerful magnifying glass. Nelson peered through the glass at the disks, then poked with his forefinger to position one of them under the strongest point of light. He lowered the lamp to just above the disk, taking his time now, as he continued to examine it.

Waiting, Monk looked beyond Nelson to the rest of the tech room Wayne was in charge of. Because the SOG had its own electronics inventory, Monk hadn't needed to come downtown to this one in a long time, and now he could see how much it had grown in his absence. Even more of the metal shelving these days, even more gear filling the shelves to overflowing. A whole section of video cameras and recorders now—much more compact units even than a couple of years ago—along with TV sets, FM walkie-talkies, cellular telephones, computer terminals, and flat-panel monitors, all of them smaller than ever before.

You'd think the room itself would get smaller, Monk thought, but there was no way the bureau was going to let that happen. The machines might vanish away to nothing, but the bureaucracy would only get bigger. No FBI director was going to go before Congress and ask for *less* money.

"Where'd you get these, Monk?" Nelson asked. "We had some training with them at Quantico last month, but these are the first I've seen in the field."

"I'm happy to hear that . . . I was pretty sure they were what I thought they were." Monk told him about the Davidson robbery. "It's part of a series I'm working. Art. Paintings mostly, all over the country." The rest of it—the Sung Kim part—he kept to himself. "I found these in the victim's house."

"Did you copy the serial numbers yet?"

"I thought I might as well let you do that, if you don't mind."

Nelson bent to examine the disk again. "You ready to copy?"

Monk grabbed a notepad from the workbench, and a government-issue ballpoint pen. "Go," he said.

"A–T–6–3–8–2–9," Nelson read. He straightened up. "I suppose you want me to look it up on the computer, too."

Monk grinned. "I was kinda hoping."

"As long as you don't tell anyone I did it." The famously grouchy tech specialist shook his head. "First thing you know, every son of a bitch agent out there'll want the same thing."

FORTY-ONE

It was nine o'clock the next morning when Monk walked into the office of Samuel Haggard, the general manager of Security Services, Inc., the company Wayne Nelson had identified as the seller of the Air Taser from which had come the disks Monk found in Davidson's house. The AFIDs. The Anti-Felon Identification Disks that were designed to identify a specific air-Taser gun whenever it was used.

The heavyset man wearing thick glasses stared at the disks Monk dumped out on his desk, then used a square magnifying glass to examine them more closely. He reached for a pad of paper, scribbled on the pad, then set aside the magnifying glass to pull his computer keyboard toward him. Haggard typed quickly. After a moment, he looked up.

"No problem," he said. "We sold the weapon you're looking for. It was part of a shipment of eighty-seven Tasers to Evans Medical two years ago. They run a chain of hospitals here in Washington. The tasers were shipped to George Mann, their director of security."

"Got an address?"

Haggard wrote on his pad again, ripped off the page, and handed it to Monk.

. . .

"Christ," George Mann said. "I wish I'd never heard of those goddamned stun guns."

The gaunt, hollow-eyed director of security for Evans Medical scowled.

"We own hospitals, Agent Monk. We have to be ready for anything. People go nuts around hospitals . . . you wouldn't believe it." He paused. "The tasers seemed like a perfect solution . . . a weapon to stop crazy people without killing them."

Monk nodded. "I would think so, too."

"What I didn't figure on was the people who were going to use them. Most security guards are good, but there are some real losers . . . mouth breathers about one notch smarter than a juniper bush. Give 'em non-lethal weapons they go ape shit. Spit out your chewing gum on the floor, some dipstick fills you with electricity." He shook his head. "It was a nightmare. Twenty lawsuits in the first three months. We got rid of them pronto."

"You don't have them anymore?"

"Couldn't even sell them. Corporate legal wouldn't let us. Liability, they said. Throw the damned things away, they said. Make sure they never hurt anybody again."

"But how? You can't just put something like that in a garbage can."

"Tell me about it. They laid around here for a couple of weeks before we took them to the Metropolitan P.D. I don't know what they did with them." He looked at Monk before shaking his head again. "I hate to tell you this, but some of them got stolen before we got them downtown to the cops."

"Any idea who took them?"

"Like I said, some of the guards are about half a step from doing time themselves. We try not to hire the bad ones, but it's a tough market. The pay . . . the hours . . ." He shrugged. "I wish I could help you, but what're you gonna do."

. . .

On his way to the woman whose singular skills he now needed, Monk called Dr. Gordon, but the doctor was out of the office until tomorrow. Was there anyone on call? Monk asked his receptionist. Anyone who could tell him about his PET scan? She would check, the woman promised, and get back to him. Monk shook his head as he hung up. Keep busy, he told himself. You'll know soon enough. He punched 4-1-1 this time, got the number he needed and dialed. Eleanor DeWitt was home, and she would love to see him again.

Monk tossed the phone aside, then realized he had to eat, that he was starving, and that he wanted nothing to do with Lisa's idea of healthy food. Eleanor DeWitt lived near Washington Circle, not far from George Washington University, and there had to be a Burger King along the way. He could swing past the drive-through and choke down a quick pair of cheeseburgers, maybe just the smallest order of their grease-soaked fries.

"You do know about me, Puller," Eleanor DeWitt said, after she'd let Monk into her apartment. "You do know the bureau considers me persona non grata."

Monk smiled. "Why do you think I'm here?"

"Well, you better come in and sit down then."

Eleanor toggled the joystick on the arm of her wheelchair, turned herself around, and glided back toward the brown tweed upholstered couch and contrasting armchairs that dominated her small living room. Monk followed. She motioned toward the couch. He walked past her and sat down. Eleanor zipped over until she was sitting in front of him. She reached up to smooth her gray bangs, then rearranged the burnt-orange and yellow afghan in her lap.

"Can I bring you some coffee," she asked. "Or a drink, maybe?"

Monk shook his head. "It's good to see you again, Eleanor, but I'm afraid I don't have much time to visit." He frowned as he realized how abrupt that sounded. "How are you?" he asked. "I mean how have you been?"

"Incredible," she said. "I liked it at the bureau . . . I loved my job there, but this is so much better."

Eleanor gestured toward a room beyond the living room, partly visible through an arched doorway. From where he was sitting, Monk could see a couple of computer monitors along one wall of the room.

"I'm doing the same thing here in the apartment," she continued. "The same sort of computer stuff I used to do for you downtown, but now I free-lance." She smiled. "And I make a lot more money."

He thought about the day she'd quit, the eyewitness accounts he'd heard of the way she'd stormed out of the office after a donnybrook shouting match with an idiot supervisor who hadn't realized what a treasure of a computer analyst she'd been.

"So it worked out okay then," he said. "In the end, I mean."

"Doesn't everything?"

Monk couldn't stop his glance at her withered legs, and she caught him at it.

"It's a philosophy, Puller," she said. "I don't believe it half the time, either, but I don't let a day go by without saying it."

Monk looked at her, at her long thin face, at the wire-rimmed glasses that dramatized her intelligent brown eyes. He tried to imagine what it would be like to live in a wheelchair, but couldn't begin to. The silence grew uncomfortable until she finally grinned and broke it.

"Okay, Monk, you're off the hook. No more visiting." She pushed her joystick and closed the gap between them by another six inches. "So tell me, what the hell are you doing here?"

"I need to find some connections. Something to connect Thomas Franklin, or Franklin's Global Panoptic Corporation, with stolen art. Worldwide." Monk reached into his pocket for the list he'd prepared back at the SOG. He handed the list of stolen paintings to Eleanor. "Specifically with the stuff on this list."

She studied the list, then looked at him.

"The da Vinci is the latest? The one from Georgetown just the other night?"

Monk smiled. "I knew I'd come to the right place."

"You said connections . . . plural. Something else to do with Franklin?"

"There's a rumor that he's involved with a younger woman, a much younger woman. Cost him his marriage, I've heard."

Eleanor nodded as Monk continued.

"He's a big socialite. Lots of parties, lots of press coverage. TV cameras, that sort of thing." He paused. "Can you do anything with that?"

She nodded. "I can access TV footage . . . and there are a few other tricks I've come up with over the years." She paused. "What's she look like?"

"I don't know. Like I said, it's just rumor."

"So we've got the stolen art and the secret squeeze. Anything else?"

"One more thing, yes. I need to find a link between Global Panoptic and a holding company called Evans Medical. They own hospitals all around the country, a couple of them here in the District."

Eleanor DeWitt stared at him for a moment. He could read the question in her intelligent eyes, but knew he was safe. She'd been far too well trained to ask.

"You've tried?" she asked instead. "You've already tried on this?"

"I'm not good enough to try." He glanced over his shoulder toward her computer room. "Not like you are, I mean."

"And you can't—for whatever reason—provide a file number to the bureau computer people. So they can do this for you."

"Not this time."

She looked past him, out the window behind where he was sitting on the couch. After a long moment she swung her head back to him.

"This man, this Franklin." She paused. "Is there any chance he's *not* the Thomas Franklin I'm thinking of? That Global Panoptic isn't *the* Global Panoptic Corporation?"

"None."

Again she paused, but this time she didn't look out the window. This time, her clear brown eyes were riveted on his.

"Am I going to regret this, Puller? Is this going to turn out badly?"

He raised his eyebrows. "Doesn't everything?"

FORTY-TWO

"Tell me," Sung Kim said to Franklin, as they sat in matching armchairs in his office at Battle Valley Farm. "Calm down and tell me exactly what Roger Carmody told you."

"It doesn't make any difference what he said, Mary Anne. That's the point. Just the fact that Monk went to Carmody says it all."

Of course it does, Sung Kim thought. Monk was trying to spook Franklin, and if she weren't careful, that's exactly what was going to happen.

"Monk doesn't know anything," she told him. "I told you before . . . and it's the same thing this time. If he had evidence he'd be at the U.S. attorney's office, getting ready to go to the grand jury for an indictment."

"How can we know he hasn't done that already?"

"Have you gotten a target letter? You're not just Joe Sixpack, Thomas. The government isn't about to go after you without letting you know." It was standard practice for federal prosecutors all over the country.

Franklin shook his head. "But Monk just started. How long will it be before I do get one? Before they do name me as a target?"

Sung Kim looked away, over his shoulder at the bookcase on the wall. There was no good way to ease into this, but she had to prepare him.

"What would you be willing to do to make him go away?" she said.

"Go away? Why would Monk . . ." Franklin stared at her. "Christ, you're talking about an FBI agent. You're talking about murdering an FBI agent."

He rose from his chair and moved to the unlit fireplace, where he turned to face her again. "How the hell did we ever let it come to this, Mary Anne?"

He paused.

"We had such a good thing going . . . such a good arrangement. You got my money to set up your flower business, I get your . . . I get the pleasure of your company whenever you're here at the farm. It couldn't have been better, but it was a mistake to get involved with you with the paintings. I knew better, but after you brought me the first one, I just let myself believe it would work out."

He came back and stood in front of her.

"Now you want to kill an FBI agent." He shook his head. "I can't believe I'm even talking about this."

Sung Kim hardened her tone. "Is it easier for you to believe that Monk will just go away?"

Franklin sat. "He doesn't work alone. Stopping him isn't going to stop the FBI."

Sung Kim nodded, but that wasn't her problem. Killing Monk wouldn't stop the bureau for long, but she only needed a few more days. A few more days to keep Franklin from discovering the real reason they'd been together for the past three and a half years. And to implicate him so deeply she could use him forever. Or as long it pleased her to do so.

"Trust me," she told him. "Monk came to you alone the other day, and that isn't the way the bureau works . . . not with someone as potentially dangerous to an agent's career as you. He should have had a partner with him, someone to counter anything you might later have complained about. The fact that he came alone means he's working alone." Sung Kim shook her head. "As long as the bureau believes his . . . his removal . . . is an accident, there's a good chance our problem will gradually fade away."

And pigs might one day fly, she could have added. She kept her eyes on him, willing him to believe, knowing he had the most powerful of motives for doing so. She let the silence grow, until he finally broke it.

"What are you going to . . . ?" He shook his head. "I don't want to know."

"I have friends who might be able to arrange something." She leaned forward in her chair. "But you're going to know, Thomas, there's no way I can leave you out of it." She smiled. "You know I can't let you skate on this, and you know exactly why."

It was one-thirty the next morning when Sung Kim drove the stolen Ford Explorer up the ramp of the parking lot beneath Union Station and stopped at the pay booth.

"Sorry," she told the attendant, a young black woman, "but I can't find my ticket anywhere."

The attendant pointed at the sign outside the booth. "Gonna have to charge you the all-day rate."

Sung Kim smiled as she reached into her pocket and pulled out her money clip. She peeled off two twenties and handed them through the window, but the attendant was shaking her head.

"What's the matter?" Sung Kim asked. "It can't be more than forty dollars."

"It's thirty-two, but that's not why I'm shaking my head. I can't believe you're not yelling at me."

She turned away for a moment before coming back with the change. Sung Kim waved the money away, and smiled.

"Keep it," she said. "Gotta be a long night for you in there."

"Thanks," the attendant said. "Thank you very much." She touched a button and the wooden arm lifted out of the way.

The smile disappeared from Sung Kim's face as she turned right and headed for Logan Circle. When she got to Monk's apartment building, her eyes swept the area for any sign of the opposition. She saw nothing, no unusual traffic, no parked vehicles that didn't appear to belong. She reached into the black canvas gym bag on the passenger seat and pulled out a portable police-radio scanner and turned the switch to fully automatic. The scanner began to search for radio traffic up and down the FM spectrum the police and FBI used in the District. She wouldn't be able to hear their voices—the scanner wasn't capable of decoding the FBI's encrypted radios—but she would hear a brief rasp of static, a short burst of carrier wave if someone used a radio of any kind while she was in the area.

Sung Kim found a parking place where she could watch and listen, then settled in to wait.

The last light in the windows of Monk's building didn't go out until a few minutes past three.

Even so, Sung Kim drove around the block twice, just to make sure the building security people weren't outside making their rounds. She saw no one, so she pulled the SUV to the head of the garage ramp, to the keycard reader outside her open window. Reaching into the pocket of her jumpsuit, she pulled out her card keys: the nine plastic master keys that allowed her to penetrate virtually any keycard system in Washington.

The first one didn't work, nor did the second, third, or fourth. Damn it, Sung Kim thought, nothing was ever easy. The seventh one did the trick. The steel gate lifted out of the way and she drove down into the garage. She parked in the first empty space, got out of the Explorer, and stood motionless next to the car until her eyes adjusted to the semidarkness.

The garage stretched away before her, the far wall fifty yards or so from where she stood. Concrete pillars thick as redwoods held up the roof, light fixtures on each of them providing a sort of greenish glow that passed for illumination. The smells were just as gloomy. Grease and oil, rubber tires, lots of wax and polish.

Sung Kim listened for the guards, listened without making a sound for five full minutes, but heard nothing. In her black jumpsuit, she'd be hard to spot in here, but she hadn't survived this long by taking unnecessary chances. She reached into her pocket and pulled out a black ski mask, fitted it over her head until her nose and mouth were comfortable, then used the giant support pillars for cover as she slipped across the garage to the dark blue Saab-Turbo parked nose first against the wall.

At the Saab, Sung Kim dropped to her knees just behind the left front tire and reminded herself to be careful. The car was alarmed, of course—FBI cars would all be alarmed—and the slightest motion would set it off and bring the guards running. She pulled a penlight from one of the many pockets of her jumpsuit, stuck it between her teeth, then went back into the same pocket for a black metal device the size of a deck of cards. She turned it over until the powerful magnet was facing the car.

Lying on her back, she used her heels to push herself underneath, then angled her head toward the rear of the car. She snaked her arm upward—careful not to touch any of the pipes and hoses—until she located the throttle linkage where it came through the firewall from the accelerator pedal. Very gently she brushed the surface of the firewall with her fingertips to make sure of a clean fit for the magnet, then snugged the magnet against the steel. She didn't have to worry about it falling off. A mechanic would need a crowbar to get rid of it.

Next she unfolded a three-inch arm attached to the same device, clamped it to the throttle linkage, reached into her pocket for a three-eighths end-wrench and tightened the clamp until the device was rigidly fixed to the linkage. Then she went to work on the electrical connection. Careful, Sung Kim told herself once again. Modifying the car's wiring—no matter how slightly—increased the danger from the alarm tenfold.

She located the alternator where it was attached to the left side of the engine, and the wire running from the alternator to the engine block. She took a breath and let it out slowly, then raised her slender chromium penknife and cut into the insulation around the wire. She felt the blade snick against the wire and held her breath. The alarm stayed silent. She stripped a half inch of insulation from the wire. Back into her pocket, she pulled out a two-foot length of insulated wire that matched the other wire perfectly. She attached one end of the new wire to her throttle device, the other end to the bare spot she'd scraped on the alternator wire. She used gaffer's tape to insulate the connection, then sat back to breathe. Now the throttle device had its own power source.

She inspected every inch of her work, then ran a test.

She tripped a recessed switch on the top side of the device, and a pinpoint of red light began to blink. The electrical connection was working perfectly. From her breast pocket, she withdrew a radio transmitter the size of a cigarette lighter, on its front side a toggle switch. She kept her eyes on the throttle linkage, then used a fingernail to move the switch to the ON position. With a metallic clank, the arm attached to the linkage shoved the throttle all the way forward toward the engine and locked it there. Sung Kim couldn't help smiling. The Saab-Turbo was quicker than most cars already. With its throttle jammed wide open like this, it would be like a runaway bullet. She switched the transmitter off, reached up and hit the reset button on the throttle device. The linkage fell back into normal position, and once again the tiny light began to blink.

Satisfied, Sung Kim made sure she had all her tools, then dug her heels into the floor to pull herself from under the car. She wasn't halfway out when she heard footsteps. She wriggled back underneath and lay motionless. The footsteps got louder, and a moment later she saw a pair of feet stop a few yards from where she lay. Cheap black shoes. One of the guards, she realized, and a moment later the man's voice as he used his radio confirmed it.

"Hey, Al," the voice said. "Where the hell are you? Can we get this thing done already?"

Sung Kim held herself perfectly still. In the silence of the garage, she had no trouble hearing the response over the guard's radio.

"Jesus, Burt, take a pill or something. These cars aren't going anywhere, for Christ's sake . . . We've got plenty of time."

Damn it, she thought. They were about to do a walk-through. A couple minutes more and she'd have been out of here. She considered her options.

She could stay where she was and hope their routine check of the parked vehicles was as careless as everything else rent cops did. Or she could slip away now, in the gloom, before Al showed up to help his partner. It only took her a second to reject the first option. No matter how slipshod, they might accidentally spot her. Lying under the car like this she was helpless. Under here she'd have no room to fight. She felt her muscles began to swell as she slid out from under the car.

She spotted Burt a dozen yards to her left. She moved in the other direction, darting from pillar to pillar—eyes and ears on full alert for the least sign of the other guard—as she made her way toward the pedestrian door at the other end of the garage. She could slip out the door and get away. There was nothing in the Explorer that would lead the cops to her. Moments later she was at the door, reaching for the knob, when the door swung open. Sung Kim leaped straight backward as she saw him. The guard was every bit as shocked as she was. He fumbled for the gun in the holster on his belt, finally managed to get it out and aim it directly at her chest. His eyes widened as he took in her black jumpsuit, and the ski mask covering her face.

"What the hell?" he said. "Who the h . . . ?" He advanced toward her. "Back up!" he ordered. "Put your hands on your head and get away from the door!"

She lifted her hands to her head and took three steps backward as he spoke into the radio clipped to his lapel. "Hey, Burt! Goddammit, Burt, get over here quick! I got a perp at the pedestrian door."

Sung Kim sighed. How much easier it would be if they just let her walk . . . how much less trouble for all three of them. She thought about trying to con them, telling them she was just a girlfriend, just trying to sneak away before the guy's wife showed up, but the ski mask was the problem. Rent cops weren't too swift, but they weren't completely stupid.

"Easy, Al," she told him, "I don't want any trouble."

He stared at her, reacting to his name, and she saw the briefest moment of uncertainty. "How do you know my name? Are you trying to tell me you're a—"

Suddenly Burt showed up, running out of the shadows with his own pistol in hand. Al turned to look at him and Sung Kim edged closer to them. Still too far away, but better.

"Hi, Burt," she said, and when he glanced at Al she slid another half step closer. "I wondered if you were working with Al tonight."

Al spoke without taking his eyes off her. "Jeez, Burt, she knows our names."

Burt snorted. "She's been listening to us talk to each other on the radio. Of course she knows our fucking names."

Burt turned to her, and now his tone was different. A lot harder, hard enough to match the dead stare in his eyes. She recognized the look. A cop. A real cop, making a couple of extra bucks on the side. She forgot about Al for the moment. It was Burt she had to watch.

"Don't even think about running," Burt told her. "We're going to hook you up and call M.P.D." He widened his stance and trained his black automatic pistol on her midsection. "Cuff her, Al," he said. "And take that fuckin' mask off her head."

"Don't do that, Al," she told him. "You really don't want to do that."

Burt grunted. "You been watchin' too many bad movies, sweetie. In the real world you don't get to take your secret identity to jail."

She shrugged, then dropped her arms behind her back so Al could cuff her. Her shoulders slumped, her head hanging, for all the world just another car-prowl loser ready to go back to jail. Al holstered his weapon and approached, then stepped around behind her and yanked the hood from her head. She stared Burt in the face, ignoring the gun in his hand. He wouldn't fire his weapon while Al was standing directly behind her, directly in the path of the bullet that would go right through her.

"Left arm back," Al ordered from behind her. "Palm out."

Sung Kim did so, but in the same movement she spun, hurled her leg in a round sweep that kicked Al's legs away and left the guard suspended for an instant in the air before he fell like a cut tree to the concrete. She dived sideways and came up with her own weapon in hand. She depressed the Taser's firing switch and twin wires leapt toward the frozen Burt. The steel points slammed into his chest with a clearly audible thud. She held the switch firm. Burt stiffened. His eyes rolled back, his body began to jerk, before he pitched forward onto his face.

She dropped the Taser—without a fresh cartridge it was useless—and whirled to face Al, who was back on his feet, snatching at the gun in his holster. She flipped her right leg and kicked him in the face. Blood exploded from his shattered nose as he fell straight backward and lay motionless.

She turned to Burt, still twisting and moaning on the floor. She stepped to him, jerked the darts out of his chest, grabbed the Taser off the floor and stuffed the weapon and the wiring back into her pocket. She stood for a moment, her breathing already back to normal as she considered her position. They'd seen her face. She'd warned them, but they wouldn't listen. Why did people do this to themselves?

She knelt at the side of Burt's head and pulled the chromium penknife from her jumpsuit pocket, the same one she'd used to expose the wire underneath the car. She unfolded the blade. It was only three inches long, but that was plenty. She set the point of the blade directly into the canal of the guard's right ear and used the flat edge of her hand to drive the blade directly into his brain. He sighed and went limp. She hurried to Al and repeated the procedure, then scooped up her ski mask and stared at the bodies. Now she had a problem. They couldn't be left here or there'd be cops all over the place when they were discovered.

Good thing she'd stolen an SUV, Sung Kim told herself. She jogged to the big black car, started the engine and drove over to within a few feet of the guards. Moments later she had them in the back of the Explorer. She looked at the area where they'd lain. Al had bled when she kicked him in the face, and that could be a problem. She checked the floor, found the blood spatters, used her ski mask to rub them away. She scuffed the area with her boots, but ignored the scatter of tiny white disks that stretched away into the gloom. By the time anyone figured out what they were, it would no longer make any difference.

FORTY-THREE

At her desk in the Squad 7 bullpen on the fourth floor at WFO, Lisa suddenly remembered that she'd forgotten to call Puller about tonight, to tell him she'd be late again—more of the hundreds of leads that had resulted from the discovery of C4 at Dulles and Baltimore the other night—and that he should grab something for dinner before he came home.

She dialed his cell phone and got a busy signal. She returned to the work on her desk, finished dictating another of the endless number of FD-302s stemming out of the C4 case. This one had been the manager of the trucking company that had delivered the DVDs from Dulles Airport to dozens of electronics stores around the District and into Maryland. Another 302 with nothing but failure, but no less important because of it. There was no great secret to investigating crime. You just kept talking to people until one of them had something useful to say.

The 302 finished, Lisa tried Puller again. This time he answered. She told him about having to work late tonight, but could feel her eyes narrowing as she listened to his response. Or lack of it.

"Tonight?" he said. "Is that what you said?"

She could hear him shuffling papers.

"Okay, Lisa," he said. "Say hello for me . . . and have a good time."

"Say hello for you?" Lisa realized her frown was deepening. "What are you talking about, have a good time?"

But he'd already hung up.

Lisa cradled the handset, then sat back and stared at the phone on her desk. What the hell was going on with Puller now? It sounded like he didn't even know it had been her he was talking to. Like he didn't care what time she got home. Like he had something a whole lot better to do than wait for . . .

You shouldn't be doing this, Lisa, she told herself as she reached for the phone again and redialed Puller. Now it was busy again. Quickly she slid her middle desk drawer open and pulled out a small sheet of paper bearing a single phone number. She dialed the McLean, Virginia, area code, then Bethany Randall's home phone number.

It was busy, too.

Lisa hung up and stared at the wall.

"Paris."

Just the one word, before the sudden click.

Behind the desk in his office, William Smith replaced the receiver, then rose from his chair and rolled the chair off the red and blue oriental carpet beneath it. He flopped the rug out of the way, then lifted a wood panel to expose the horizontal door of a steel floor safe. He bent to work the combination lock, opened the safe, and pulled out a silver-colored Toshiba laptop computer, then lifted the computer to the top of his desk and opened it up. Reaching to the edge of his desk, he pulled up a power cord, plugged the cord into the rear of the computer and hit the on button.

He waited for Windows XP to load, then used his thumb on the built-in mouse to get to the red and black screen that called for his password. He typed in the proper combination of numbers and letters, and seconds later he was downloading his message.

It was brief, and included two photographs. William started with the message, with the occult language of international counterespionage. The heading was characteristically terse.

Pyongyang/Paris: possrefJapanese PM/Battle Valley Farm.

The rest was much more cryptic, but only if you didn't speak the language.

SNKIO/P-AMAUNSUB. 100804.18. AVQP 'farm/Tokyo.' SSNOT. CEU.

William translated as quickly as he read.

NSA had received information from a source in Paris—Sûreté, most likely, or the intelligence division of the Paris Metropolitan Police—that a suspected North Korean intelligence officer had met in Paris with an unknown subject, an Asian male, on the tenth of August, for eighteen minutes. The source had covered the meeting with sound and video, but the quality was poor. Computer enhancement was underway. Presumably there would be better sound and images forthcoming.

The NSA supercomputers had processed the audio/video input and triggered on the words "farm" and "Tokyo." Because William had requested any and all hits concerning Thomas Franklin and Battle Valley Farm—because the word "farm" had come up in the conversation—the report, sketchy as it was, had been forwarded to him.

William thought about the rest of it, the "Tokyo" part. The possible reference to a connection between Japan and Franklin's farm. What was the connection? he wondered. Franklin had lots of foreign visitors, of course. The president himself did lots of business at his friend's farm, but there was nothing scheduled. And NSA would know if there were. Secret Service would already have been to Fort Meade as part of their regular advance work.

He turned from the message to look at the photos, grainy black-and-white pictures, not nearly good enough to make a positive ID. The first one showed two figures standing together at a railing with what looked like the Seine in the background. He couldn't even tell if they were men or women.

William reached into the center desk drawer and pulled out a thick round magnifying glass. He held the glass directly above the photos, then straightened up. Worthless, he thought. Why had Paris bothered to send something like this? How long would it be before the computers turned this into something he could use?

FORTY-FOUR

His mind preoccupied with Sung Kim, Monk faked his way through his shift with Team 3, and was relieved when it ended early.

They'd been scheduled to help Team 7 with the same opera-loving Chinese IO from the other night at the Kennedy Center, but the guy suddenly broke his State Department mandated itinerary—a major no-no— to head for Reagan National and take a flight to New York. Once he was gone, once Monk had alerted his counterpart in Manhattan, his team was finished for the night. He went back to the trolley barn and finished up the surveillance log for the case file, then grabbed a pile of the endless flood of administrative memos and other paperwork that filled an agent's mail slot.

But despite his best effort to keep at the stack until he finished with it, Lisa crept into his mind and he gave up. He couldn't concentrate while she was still angry with him, so he threw the paperwork back in his workbox and started for home. He made one stop along the way. To mend the damage with Lisa, he needed some tools.

"What can I get for you?" the young woman asked, from behind the counter at her flower stand near Georgetown University.

Monk stared at the overwhelming variety of flowers, colors, sizes, ribbons, and bows, then shook his head. "You're gonna have to do it for me. Roses, maybe."

"We talking wife here? Mother? Girlfriend?" She covered her mouth for an instant with her hand. "Oops, I'm supposed to say 'domestic partner.'"

"She's my . . . she's . . ." Hell, he didn't know *how* to describe her. Girlfriend sounded juvenile, lover sort of seedy, and "live-in" could just as easily be a Guatemalan housekeeper. "She's a friend," he said at last. "A real live grown-up gorgeous woman who doesn't fit into any category."

The flower lady laughed. "Well, listen to *you* . . . but I think I know exactly what you're trying to say."

She turned and went to work on the long bench behind her, and when she came back she was carrying a bundle of crimson roses almost big enough to fill the back seat of the Saab. She caught him staring at them, and laughed.

"Don't worry," she said. "By this time of day I need to get rid of everything I can . . . no extra charge. Trust me, she won't complain there's too many."

Twenty minutes later Monk carried Lisa's flowers into the elevator, and he was on his way up when the cell phone in his pocket rang. William Smith on the other end.

"We need to talk again," he said.

"What'd you come up with?"

"Not on the phone."

"I can be there in an hour."

"No good. Where will you be tomorrow night, late?"

"At work. We're scheduled for something downtown."

"I'll call you. Maybe I can meet you somewhere for a few minutes."

Monk frowned. "You sure we can't get together tonight?"

"Tomorrow," William said, before he hung up.

Monk put the phone back in his pocket just as the elevator arrived at the seventh floor. William's words continued to annoy him. Waiting was hard on anyone, but for an FBI agent it was especially maddening. Thank God for Lisa, he told himself, then glanced at the flowers in his hand and smiled. Together they'd think of a way to pass the time. He stepped out of the elevator and across the corridor to his front door, used the key and went inside.

"Lisa?" he called.

There was no response.

Monk turned around and shut the door behind him, then called out again, but still she didn't answer. "Damn it," he muttered. *How can I come home and apologize when you're not here?*

He set her bundle of roses on the small table next to the door and went straight to the booze cupboard in the kitchen area to pull down a bottle of Glenlivet. He poured an inch of Scotch into a water glass, then took the glass with him to the bedroom in the rear of the loft. Setting the glass on the nightstand next to the bed, he moved to the wardrobe. He bent down and removed his ankle holster, put his Glock high on the top shelf.

He might as well take a shower, Monk decided, while he waited for Lisa. If the flowers worked, he'd be ready for the makeup sex that almost made fighting worthwhile. Pulling off his clothes, he hung his khaki pants and his golf shirt in the wardrobe, tossed his socks and shorts into the wicker hamper, then stepped over to the nightstand, picked up his glass, and took the whisky with him to the bathroom.

In the bathroom, Monk stared into the mirror over the sink, ran a hand through his hair, and grunted. It was getting thinner up there every time he checked. A sudden image of his father's scrawny bald head flashed through his mind. To get rid of it he lifted the glass and drank half the Scotch in one long gulp, then set the glass on the vanity, turned away from the mirror, and reached past the heavy cotton shower curtain to turn on the water. He let the water run for thirty seconds before it got hot, adjusted the temperature before stepping under the spray. Slowly the whisky and hot water began to work. Slowly his knotted shoulders and neck began to relax.

He stood that way with his mind turned off for five minutes, then pushed past the shower curtain and reached for his glass, drank from it and set it back on the vanity. As he did so he heard a noise from the other side of the bathroom door. The unmistakable screech of a footstep on the loose board outside the door. He smiled. Lisa was home. His body got even warmer as he thought about spending the evening with her.

"Lisa!" he shouted. "I'm in the shower. I'll be right out."

He kept his head outside the shower to hear her answer, but she didn't respond. "Lisa!" he hollered, much louder this time, loud enough for the people downstairs to hear, but she still didn't answer. He shook his head. Shit. It was worse than he thought. Lisa was really pissed at him this time, but she must have seen the flowers, had to know why he'd brought them. He got back under the water and began to soap and rinse. Soap in his eyes, he reached blindly for the shampoo on the small ledge underneath the shower head. He fumbled for it, found the plastic squeeze bottle, and was raising it to his head when he came to a complete stop, when he realized there was a second possibility.

He turned the water off this time, stepped out of the shower, and faced the door. "Bethany? Is that you, Bethany?"

Christ, he hoped not. The way his cards had been running, Lisa would walk in the door and find Monk naked with a woman she already didn't much care for.

Then he thought about a far worse possibility.

He grabbed the towel from the rack next to the sink, cinched it around his waist, then searched the bathroom for a weapon. The choices were slim. Half a bar of soap . . . a bottle of shampoo . . . a can of Barbasol. Not much use against a stun gun. He saw the tumbler with what was left of his Scotch. He grabbed it, dumped the whisky into the sink, and held the glass in his hand like a baseball as he stared at the door, waiting for it to open.

It didn't.

Straining to listen for another footstep, Monk heard nothing.

He crept to the door, put his free hand on the knob, and raised the tumbler behind his head, ready to hurl it forward. He pulled the door open slowly, just a crack, just enough to see what was on the other side, but he saw no one. He opened the door a little wider, his arm still cocked. Now he could see farther into the loft, but still he saw no one. Opening the door wide enough to step through, Monk advanced slowly with the glass in throwing position. His eyes swept the entirety of the wide-open loft. There was no one there—no one he could see from here anyway—but there had to be. He'd heard the creaking board. He couldn't have been mistaken. He glanced down at the board. Surely he wasn't mistaken.

"Lisa?" he called again, feeling foolish now. Unless she were crouched down behind the bed across the way or hiding from him behind the storage cabinets at the rear of the loft, unless she were behind the furniture up front, near the windows that formed the front wall, she just wasn't here.

Gripping the glass even tighter now, he crept toward the bedroom, his eyes darting to the left and right, his ears straining. At the big bed, he bent quickly and checked underneath. Nothing. Stepping over to the wardrobe, he grabbed his Glock from the top shelf and left the whisky glass in its place. Holding the weapon in both hands, lifting it into firing position directly in front of his chest, he moved toward the rear of the loft, to the large wooden cabinets they used for storage. He paused for a moment, then stepped around the cabinets, all the way around to the back of them. No one. Nothing. He turned toward the front of the loft, moved quickly toward the furniture up there, the green-fabric upholstered couch, the high-backed chairs, his eyes sweeping back and forth. He circled the furniture, saw no one, saw nothing to indicate anyone had been there.

Next he went to the door.

He tried the knob, to satisfy himself that the door was still locked, but it wasn't. He stared at the door. Had he forgotten to lock it when he came in? It wasn't likely. In the District, you kept the dead bolt thrown all the time, even when you were home. But maybe he had forgotten. With his arms filled with flowers he might easily have done so.

He stepped back for a moment, breathing more quickly now as he pulled the door open just enough to see past it, to satisfy himself that no one was standing on the other side. He stepped through the doorway, looking left and right. Nothing. Across the hall, the elevator door was closed.

"Lisa?" he called. "Are you out here somewhere?"

Holding the Glock in both hands now, Monk turned to his right, then moved quietly toward the stairwell at the end of the wide corridor, to the back stairs that led to the rear of the building. Seconds later he stood next to the heavy door at the entrance to the stairwell. He listened for a moment . . . and heard footsteps, faint footsteps. The hair on the back of his neck began to tingle. He dropped his left hand off the Glock, and cracked the door.

"Lisa?" he called into the stairwell. "Bethany?"

No answer.

Monk took a breath and let it out, then jerked the door wide open and in the same motion swung himself into the doorway, his gun leading the way. His eyes widened as Lisa screamed. He dropped a full step back. On the other side of the doorway, Lisa did the same thing, her own eyes just as wide, as the echo of her scream in the hollow stairwell died away. She stared at the gun in his hand, then at the towel around his waist.

"What the hell?" she said. She looked past him into the hallway. "What in God's name are you doing?"

"Damn it, Lisa, I might have shot you! What are you doing hiding in the stairwell?"

"I'm not hiding." She hesitated. "I . . . I just came up the back way is all." She glanced at his towel and shook her head. "It seems to me I should be the one asking the questions."

"Did you see anybody? On your way up here? Or downstairs?"

She shook her head.

"I was in the shower," Monk said. "I heard the . . . I thought I heard that damned board squeal. I thought I heard someone outside the bathroom."

"And you were expecting Bethany Randall?"

"Bethany?"

"I just heard you call her name, Puller."

Shit. "Why would I think she'd be here?" This was definitely not the time to talk about giving Bethany a key. "You sure you didn't see anybody?" he asked again. "Or hear a car, maybe?"

He reached for her hand, but she pulled away, and in the next moment she was pushing past him on her way to the loft. Monk stared at her back for a moment, then followed. Inside, Monk moved to her, tried to put his arms around her, but she pushed him away.

"I can't do this anymore," she said. She turned and started for the kitchen, then turned back. "We have to talk."

Monk glanced at the roses on the table by the front door. He started toward them but Lisa's voice stopped him.

"I mean *now*, Puller. We have to talk right now."

"Just a second. Give me a second, then we can talk all night if you want."

He stepped to the table, brought back the roses, and handed them to her. She held them away from her body.

"What's this supposed to mean?" she asked.

"That I'm sorry. That I've been . . . I've been . . ." He started over. "I'm trying to apologize. To explain." Not an easy thing for an FBI agent to do, Monk wanted to add, but had the good sense not to.

"Why would you bother?" She took two steps toward the table by the door and tossed the roses on it, then turned back to him. "And when did you start explaining anything to me?"

"Right now. Tonight." He reached for her hand again but again she pulled it away. Monk felt a flush of anger. "Look, Lisa, I'm doing the best I can here. You have to give me a chance."

"I don't have to do anything," she said, before turning and heading toward the kitchen. A few steps from him, she looked back over her shoulder. "Right now I'm going to get myself a drink."

Monk started after her, then looked down at the gun in his hand and the towel around his waist and went to the bedroom instead. He put the gun away, back on the top shelf of the wardrobe, then slipped on a fresh pair of Dockers and a black tennis shirt. He grabbed the empty glass from where he'd left it on the shelf next to the gun and headed for the kitchen to fill it.

Before he could get there, Lisa was already on her way to the living room. In her hands she carried the bottle of Glenlivet and a single glass. Monk followed her, and when he got to the living room she was sitting in one of the chairs that faced the couch near the big windows, pouring Scotch from the bottle into her glass, then setting the bottle on the small round table between the chairs. Monk took the other chair, poured a couple inches of Scotch into his own glass. He took a long drink and realized Lisa was watching.

"Well?" she said.

Monk set his glass on the table and leaned forward in his chair.

"I know I've been a little . . . a little distracted lately." He paused as he considered how much he wanted her to know, how much of his preoccupation with the MRI and subsequent PET scan he wanted to burden her with. And what he might want to say about the bicycle accident he'd been so careful to hide from her. But before he could say anything at all, Lisa interrupted.

"I know you've been distracted, but that's not what's bothering me. That's not what I want to talk about." She paused. "There's only one thing I care about right now and that's Bethany Randall. And what kind of game you think you're playing with her."

He stared at her. "A game with Bethany?"

Lisa shook her head and rose from her chair.

"Where are you going?" he asked.

"I'm not going to sit here and listen to you pretend to be so stupid."

"Look, Lisa, Bethany needs my help. That's it. Nothing more."

She made a sound in the back of her throat. "Who do you think you're talking to? I'm a woman. I know what she's doing."

But Lisa did sit down again.

"I've only got one issue," she said. "One question." Her voice softened. "Listen closely, Puller, . . . and think hard about your answer." She paused for a moment, then stared directly into his eyes. "Are you going to continue seeing her? Are you going to keep running to her every time she calls?"

Monk reached for her. She pushed his hand aside. He sipped from his glass as he tried to think of a way to answer.

"It's not that simple," he began. "Bethany's scared. I can't abandon her."

"So that's your answer?"

Monk looked away for a moment, out the windows into the darkness. What was called for here was a lie. All he had to do was tell Lisa he understood her objection to Bethany and that he would agree to let her find help elsewhere. A simple lie would make the problem go away, but this was Lisa.

"You're the woman I love," he said, "but right now Bethany's the one I've got to help. I know what you want to hear, but there's no way to make this as simple as you'd like." He paused. "Surely you didn't expect anything else from me."

She shook her head slowly, then rose from her chair. Monk could only watch as she walked toward the door, as she turned back to face him. She reached up and brushed the sudden tears from her eyes.

"I'll come back for my clothes tomorrow, but right now I have to leave. Right now I can't spend another moment with you."

FORTY-FIVE

She had no intention of letting it get down to close work, but Sung Kim wasn't about to get beat because of a lack of preparation.

Sitting at a plain wooden table in the cellar of her modest safe house—an unfinished brick and drywall basement that ran the length of the house—she started with her favorite handgun. The flat-black nine-millimeter Beretta 92G Elite had the best features of the more famous Brigadier model, but Sung Kim preferred the serrated surface of the fast-cycling semiautomatic's front and rear slides. The sure grip of the serrations provided the lightning-quick racking of the action that could mean the difference between living and dying. But most of all she liked the removable sights. She wouldn't need the sights for hand-to-hand combat, and if the Nakamura job came down to looking into the prime minister's eyes when she killed him, there wouldn't be an instant to spare. When seconds mattered, there wasn't anything worse than snagging a weapon on your clothing.

Sung Kim had considered a bigger weapon, of course; you could never have too much firepower. But the only real option in her gun vault was the Heckler and Koch MP7A1, and the stubby machine pistol newly adopted by the German KSK was too big to be concealed. She could get it into the ammunition bunker beforehand, that wouldn't be a problem, but she'd have to carry it the rest of the way, and she couldn't walk around the farm with a sprayer like that. Besides, if she got into a shootout with Naka-mura's bodyguards, no amount of power would help. She was every bit as good as they were, but they'd have guns just as big, and against their num-bers she wouldn't have a chance.

She slid forward in her chair and reached for the unloaded Beretta, lifted it gently—a professional never allowed a fine weapon to slide across the wooden surface of a table—and set it on a rag in front of her, a red rag impregnated with the sharply alcoholic tang of Hoppe's Gun Cleaner. She reached into the gray metal toolbox to her left and pulled out a set of Allen wrenches, selected the right size, and used the wrench to remove the front sight first, then the Novak-type rear sight. Sung Kim hefted the weapon, enjoying its clean look without the sights. She raised it and dry-fired several times. The G configuration—so important in combat—en-abled the hammer lever to return to the ready-to-fire position the instant she pulled the trigger, another speed advantage whose value could not be minimized. Then, finally, Sung Kim smiled.

If worse came to worst, her weapon would be just as prepared as she was.

FORTY-SIX

Lisa put off going back to the loft for her clothes as long as she could.

An hour after she'd bolted out of the loft last night, she'd begun to regret it. She'd made her point, she was sure of that, but it was never her intention to leave Puller for good. All he'd done was refuse to abandon Bethany Randall, and if she were honest with herself, Lisa had to admit she'd known his answer before she ever asked the question.

She remembered Dr. Annie Fisher, the woman Puller had been in the process of breaking up with when Lisa entered his life. Had it been so different with Annie? Lisa would never forget how angry she used to get when Puller dropped everything to rush to Annie Fisher whenever the woman fell off the wagon, but she hadn't broken up with him then. This thing with Bethany was no different, so why was it bothering her so much this time?

The answer came just as quickly as the question, although Lisa hated to admit it.

The fact was she'd been in the thrall of first love back then. She'd yet to see even the tiniest flaw in Puller Monk, but that was no longer true. Boy, was it no longer true. Puller was tough to love, Lisa had become forced to admit, and that made it even tougher to understand her fear that

Bethany was stealing him away. She shook her head. She wasn't sure she wanted him anymore, but she was goddamned certain she didn't want Bethany Randall to have him.

Behind the wheel of her bureau Grand Prix, Lisa was just turning right on P Street when she saw the red Infiniti coupe parked in front of the loft building. Her eyes widened, her hands gripped harder on the steering wheel as she jerked it to the left and managed to continue up Ninth Street instead. She drove a full block beyond the building, then pulled over to the curb and turned the engine off.

Christ, she thought. He was here *again?*

The man who wouldn't take no for an answer was right in front of her *house* again?

Clearly he was making a point today.

Her shouting last time—the day Puller had caught the two of them in the Infiniti—had both startled and infuriated the man, but it hadn't dissuaded him. Clearly the son of a bitch wasn't giving up. As she sat there, Lisa's breathing slowly returned to normal. He'd accomplished one thing, she admitted, but it wasn't the effect he was hoping for. She wasn't beguiled by his persistence. She was angry. A hell of a lot angrier about him than she'd ever been before.

Lisa opened the door and slid out of the seat. Looking around to make sure he hadn't driven around the corner, she started walking toward the loft, toward the locked gate in the wall at the rear of the building. If she could get through that gate unobserved she'd be fine. She could use the same back entrance she used last night, the same stairwell she'd used when she walked out on Puller. Lisa stepped up her pace as she covered the block and a half to the gate. She slipped the key in and turned the knob, then darted through and closed the gate gently behind her. She didn't bother to look around. If the man in the Infiniti had seen her, he'd be calling her name.

Inside the loft she was careful to stay away from the windows, went instead to the bedroom, to the wardrobe across from the bed. She grabbed enough clothes for a couple of days. Surely she could patch up things with Puller by then.

She turned toward the bathroom to collect her things from there, but stopped dead when the phone rang. Damn it! He must have seen her, after all. She found herself holding her breath as the phone continued to ring. Three times . . . four times . . . until the machine picked up and she heard the caller leaving a message. A male voice she didn't recognize.

"This is Lieutenant Wade, McLean P.D. I'm trying to reach—"

Lisa picked up the phone. "Lieutenant Wade?"

"Ms. Randall?"

Lisa scowled. *Ms. Randall?* What the hell . . . ?

"Hello?" the lieutenant said. "Is this Bethany Randall?"

"No, it is *not*," Lisa said. Relax, she told herself. "She doesn't live here. Why would you call here to reach her?"

But Lisa had a pretty damned good idea why. Just thinking about it made the back of her neck burn. In a flash all her good intentions about Puller went out the window.

"What about Mr. Monk then?" the lieutenant continued. "FBI Agent Monk. He around?"

"He's not here, either, but at least he does live here." Silence now, the lieutenant obviously waiting for her to elaborate. Lisa forced herself to breathe evenly before continuing. "This is Lisa Sands, Lieutenant Wade. I'm an FBI agent, too. Sorry for the attitude, but I'm still wondering why you'd try to reach Bethany Randall here."

"Agent Monk called us yesterday. Asked us to keep an eye on her house, told us she's worried about a stalker. Told us if we couldn't reach her by phone, to try this number. That he would know where she was."

Lisa's forearm began to ache from the pressure of her grip on the phone. A stalker? *She* was the one with the stalker. She switched hands, held the receiver up to her other ear. The lieutenant was still talking. ". . . any idea where I might reach her?" he was asking.

Lisa took a deep breath and let it out slowly, but it didn't help. This was fucking ridiculous. First the restaurant, and the two of them sashaying across the street to that bar, then Puller stays out all night before dragging home at dawn. *Then she calls, and he literally pulls out of me to run to her.* What the hell was he . . .

"Agent Sands?" The lieutenant's voice jolted her back to the present. "Are you—"

"Yes, I'm here!" Lisa shouted. "For Christ's sake, I'm still here! What is it you think I can do for you?"

"Hold on, lady," he told her. "I don't know what's going on with you, and I don't give a damn. Just tell me how to find Bethany Randall or Puller Monk." He paused. "For the last time, do you know where they are?"

"No, I don't, Lieutenant." Lisa gripped the phone even harder. "But you can bet I'm going to find out."

It didn't take her ten minutes on the phone with the computer wizards at WFO to come up with Bethany's address in McLean.

From the loft, Lisa called the congressional staffer she was supposed to interview this afternoon and postponed their appointment until tomorrow, then hung up and crept to the front windows. The red car was no longer there. She hurried to the back door, went through, and slipped down the stairs and out to the gate. After a quick peek, she hurried to her Pontiac and drove away. She caught Twenty-third Street, took a left and drove down to Constitution Avenue, then across the Theodore Roosevelt Bridge to the George Washington Parkway, and north to McLean. Traffic was fierce, and it took longer than it should have to get to Bethany's house.

When she got there, Lisa pulled up in front of the modest house with the tree-filled yard and sat for a moment. She looked for Puller's Saab but wasn't surprised when she didn't see it. There was probably a garage behind the house. She slid out of her car and went to look. In the alley she saw that she'd been right about the garage, but that it wasn't going to do her any good. The garage had no windows. The doors were shut, so she had no idea what was inside. She stood under a tree next to the garage and thought about what she was doing. The drive to McLean had dulled her rage. It had been an hour since she hung up on Lieutenant Wade, and it was becoming tougher and tougher to hold on to her fury. Now she looked around and wondered if she wasn't just another foolish woman, trying to hold on to a man in the thrall of someone new. You can't beat "new," Lisa reminded herself. It was impossible to compete with "new." Maybe it was best just to let this go. To let Puller go if that's the kind of jerk he wanted to be.

Lisa thought about the man in the Infiniti, her ex-fiancé from Texas, the biggest mistake she'd ever made in her life. The man who wouldn't leave her alone, whose obsession with her had now turned into stalking. Wasn't what she was doing right now the same thing? Wasn't chasing after Puller exactly the same thing?

Just the thought of becoming a stalker made her turn around and start back to her car, but she hadn't gone a dozen steps before she stopped. No, Lisa told herself. I won't just walk away like this.

Not until I see for myself.

She turned toward the house, then strode to the head-high brick wall attached to the garage. She found a foothold and pulled herself to the top of the wall, rolled over, and slid down the other side, then hustled across the lawn and a few moments later stood quietly at the rear of the house. Elbowing her way through the bushes, she headed for the closest window. She crouched near the window, then raised up slowly, until she was look- ing straight into what she realized was the kitchen. There was nobody in it. Lisa looked to her left, at the corner of the house, and decided to try a window over on that side.

She started in that direction, but had barely cleared the corner when she heard a car, the sound of a car engine near the garage. Then she heard the garage door opening. She glanced at the wall she'd just come over, but she couldn't use it to escape. Bethany would see her for sure. So she turned instead, and ran toward a dense group of bushes halfway down the side of the house. A moment later she was kneeling in the bushes, out of sight, shaking her head. How stupid can you be? she asked herself.

Now what the hell are you going to do?

FORTY-SEVEN

"Did I wake you up?" Eleanor DeWitt asked the next morning, although Monk couldn't see how it could possibly be morning yet. "Sometimes I get a little carried away."

Monk focused on the alarm clock on the nightstand next to the telephone. The red numbers of the LED display said 5:37. He hadn't fallen asleep until almost two. Christ. He covered the phone with his hand and coughed to clear the fatigue from his voice, then struggled to sound semi-intelligent.

"I'm glad you called. What did you come up with?"

"You owe me a ream of paper . . . almost two, as a matter of fact. So far." She paused. "Thomas Franklin is all over the Internet. His art collection, his company—Global Panoptic—and its subsidiaries all over the world."

"Find anything on Evans Medical?"

"Nothing. Global has its fingers in a hundred pies, but none of them is your hospital company."

"What about da Vinci . . . or any mention of a secret art collection?"

"Not yet. I'm going deep on him, Puller, as deep as I've ever been. It takes time, even with the machines I've got here."

Monk hesitated before asking his next question. Years of training made it hard to trust anyone, but that kind of thinking was what was killing the bureau these days. Despite what J. Edgar believed until the day he died, the truth was that oftentimes you had to give up something to get something.

"North Korea," he said. "See anything about a Global tie to Pyongyang?"

"Nothing on that—cyberspace is pretty much a vacuum around Pyongyang—but Seoul's a different story. Global's got money all over South Korea."

"Anything look illegal?"

"Not right off, but you'd have to show my stuff to an AUSA."

Monk frowned. "You didn't call this early to tell me what you haven't found."

She laughed, a very pleasant chuckle. "I think I've nailed your young lady . . . Thomas Franklin's mystery girl, I should say."

Monk felt his body straighten and his mind go instantly clear. "You didn't get pictures," he said. "Tell me you've got pictures."

"Four. I pulled down four pictures."

Monk tried to ask her how she'd done it, but Eleanor beat him to the punch.

"You know Washington society," she said. "Damn near every party in this town has a digital photographer, and these people get off on posting pictures of themselves on the Web."

"So you got Franklin."

"Dozens of times . . . but only four of the parties where his girlfriend was around."

"Now I'm confused."

"FBI agents," she said. "You all spend a lot of time that way, don't you?"

Monk ignored the question. He didn't know about other agents. "She was with him at these parties? Like a date kind of thing?"

"Not like a date, no, . . . but she was there, close to him, but not actually with him." She paused. "Like Monica and Bill, if you remember. Always at the edge of the picture somewhere, never actually in the scene."

Monk nodded. He could still see the president shaking hands over a rope holding back the crowd, Monica in the front row grinning at him, Clinton patting her on the shoulder the way no one but a lover would.

"When were these parties, Eleanor? Any of the pictures recent?" He already knew the answer but had to ask.

"Three years ago was the latest. I spent two hours searching for something more current. There's nothing. She's disappeared from the Web."

"What does she look like? . . . What did she look like?"

"Like a groupie. Long brown hair, sexy hair, dressed to kill, that sort of thing. Striking, I guess I'd call her. A potential marriage killer, for sure."

Monk glanced at the clock again. "Can you e-mail me the pictures?"

"They're not JPEG. Unless you've got the right program in your PC, I don't think you can download them."

"But you can print them."

"Already done, Puller. Waiting for you."

"I need to see someone first thing this morning, but I should be at your place around ten."

"May I help you?" Esther Valenzuela asked, when Sung Kim appeared in the doorway of William Smith's office at ten minutes before seven the next morning.

William's secretary smiled.

"I'm afraid we're not actually open for business today."

"I'm sorry to disturb you," Sung Kim told her. She looked at the metal plaque on the woman's desk, at the name printed on the plaque. "Maybe you can help me, Esther," she said. "I'm looking for an office that's supposed to be in this building."

"Of course."

Sung Kim reached into her purse and pulled out her Beretta, swung the silenced automatic up in one motion and shot Esther Valenzuela just above the left eye. Esther sagged back into her chair, then crashed to the floor. Sung Kim holstered the Beretta and pulled out a second weapon. She turned toward the inner-office door. Before she got there the door opened and William Smith's head stuck out.

"What the hell's going on out . . ."

His voice died when he saw his secretary's body. He tried to close the door, but Sung Kim shot him with the Taser. The darts stuck in his throat just above his collarbone. He went down in a heap, his body jerking in the doorway.

It was two minutes before he could speak.

Sung Kim timed it on her wristwatch.

He looked up at her as his eyes focused. He stared at the Taser in her hand, then directly into the brown contact lenses she'd chosen this morning. He pawed at the wires that ran from his neck back to her Taser. "What are you doing?" He glanced toward the body on the floor. "What did you do to Esther?" He blinked, over and over, as though trying to awaken from a dream. "Why are you here? What is this all . . ."

His voice died, and Sung Kim could see he was putting it together.

So she zapped him again.

William's body elevated slightly. His arms jerked straight outward and he began to spasm. Twitching, writhing, then finally lying still again.

Sung Kim stood over him like a fisherman who'd just flung her still-hooked catch into the boat. Three minutes passed before William began to moan, then opened his eyes again. Now his voice was almost a croak.

"We're both professionals," he managed to say. "We don't have to do this."

"Your floor safe," Sung Kim said. "Open it."

"Floor safe? What are you talk—"

She depressed the switch.

This time his body went completely rigid before the jerking started again.

Five minutes later he came to again.

"What do you want?" he managed to gasp. "Just tell me what you want."

"Open your safe."

He took a breath and pushed it out slowly. He stared at her, then closed his eyes. A moment later he opened them again.

"Open the safe," she repeated, her finger poised above the firing switch.

He seemed to be trying to get enough breath to talk, but when he did, his voice was suddenly stronger.

"Fuck you, Sung Kim. And fuck the people you work for."

Sung Kim shrugged. "There's no rush," she told him. "We have all day."

She pushed the switch. He fell back. His bowel muscles finally let go. Her head recoiled from the sudden acrid stench.

After he hung up with Eleanor, Monk fell back asleep and didn't wake up until nine o'clock. It was half past nine when he backed the Saab out of his parking space in the garage and headed for the exit. At the gate he waited as it rose, then drove up the short ramp and out into the street. He glanced to his left, checking for traffic, then turned right and headed toward William's office. He hadn't heard from him yet, and Monk was tired of waiting. He couldn't help replaying the NSA man's words from the other night. Be careful, William had told him. It might be better to back off whatever you're doing until you talk to me.

Which meant something good, Monk knew.

That he was pushing the right buttons.

Roger Carmody had probably been the last straw. When Carmody told Franklin that Monk was asking about . . .

Lost in thought, he reacted slowly to the delivery truck that had come to a stop ahead.

Monk hit the brake and barely managed to avoid hitting the iron lift gate jutting from the rear of the truck. He nudged the gas pedal, but the Saab's engine died. Damn it, not again. He had too much to do today for this. He turned the key and the engine fired right up, idling fast, too fast now. He tapped on the accelerator to release the automatic choke and the idle returned to normal. Goddamned car. He had to get that choke taken care of.

The light changed and he accelerated with the traffic, but not for long before the line ahead stopped again. Ten seconds later it began to move. This time Monk nursed the gas. The Saab seemed to stumble for a moment before shooting ahead.

Christ!

He had to stomp the brake to get the car back under control. What the hell was the matter with this thing? He better take care of it this morning, right now, before he killed somebody. Barely nudging the pedal, he crept along. Now it was running fine. He came to a stop and smiled when the engine didn't die, when it idled smoothly. In front of him the light changed. He hit the gas and the engine died. "Shit!" he muttered, then turned the key. The driver behind him leaned on the horn, then another one joined in, and another. "Hey!" a voice shouted. "Move it or I'll do it for you!"

In her Volvo wagon two cars behind Monk, Sung Kim scowled. She'd been lucky to get to his loft in time to catch him leaving the garage, but now there was another problem.

His Saab shouldn't be stalling like that. It shouldn't be doing anything but gliding down the street the way a Saab always does. Monk was going to get sick of it, going to leave the damned car in the street and take a cab. She shook her head. You could plan and you could execute, but you couldn't control the equipment.

Then Sung Kim saw what was happening, and sat up straight. The Saab had died again when the light turned green. Now it was a full hundred yards behind the delivery truck ahead. She glanced at the massive black iron lift-gate extending from the rear of the truck, then reached for the transmitter in her lap, pointed it in the direction of the Saab and pushed the switch.

Behind Monk the honking grew even more angry as he restarted the car. He looked up and saw that he was half a block behind the same delivery truck he'd been following. Jesus, no wonder they were yelling at him. Before he could warn himself about the sticky throttle, he mashed the gas. The big turbo roared as the throttle stuck wide open.

The back end of the Saab slewed sideways with the force of acceleration, momentarily out of control before the tires dug into the pavement with an angry squeal. The car shot forward as though fired from a slingshot. Monk's head slapped backward against the padded rest, then bounced forward. The Saab hurtled toward the truck that was now stopped again, directly in front of him.

Monk stood on the brakes, but the Saab accelerated even faster.

Monk kicked at the stuck gas pedal, but it felt welded to the firewall. The engine redlined . . . roaring like a jetliner.

This can't be happening!

He grabbed the ignition key, switched the engine off, and crushed the brake pedal with both feet, but the Saab's momentum was far too great. His head jerked upward. The lift-gate on the rear of the truck filled his vision.

FORTY-EIGHT

"Jesus Christ, mister, are you okay?"

Monk heard the voice as though it came from a long way off, above the tremendous din in his head. Wedged between the passenger seat and the floor of the Saab, he managed to turn onto his back. Now he could see the dirty underside of the truck.

"What happened?" he yelled. "What the hell happened?"

"You went right under the lift gate!" the same voice hollered. A man's voice. "Right underneath the truck!"

"It's a miracle you're alive!" A woman's voice this time.

Now Monk remembered.

Just before impact he'd somehow hurled himself to the floor of the car.

Then he realized the top was gone . . . the entire top half of the Saab was gone. The truck had peeled it away like opening a can of sardines.

But he was alive.

As a matter of fact, he wasn't even scratched.

He pushed himself up and looked to his right, toward the voices.

"What are you doing?" a woman said. "You've got to wait for the paramedics." Now Monk could hear the whoop of an approaching siren. "You could be bleeding inside. You can't move until they check you out."

"I'm not hurt. Help me out of here. Pull the door open and get me the hell out of here."

Monk heard a grinding screech as they jerked the passenger door open. He crawled through it, then out from under the truck. A crowd had gathered, faces staring. Monk turned back to the Saab. Christ, he thought. He'd never heard of anything like this. Even if the automatic choke was completely broken, it should have released long before this happened.

He turned back toward the car, suddenly needing to see for himself.

With the Saab wedged under the truck like that, he couldn't open the hood, so he'd have to go underneath. He bent over and crab-walked under the truck, then dropped to his knees next to the right front tire of the Saab. He could hear a siren getting louder, then stopping somewhere beyond the crowd. The paramedics were here, and they'd grab him before he got a chance to look. He dropped to the ground and scooted under the car, straining to check out the throttle linkage in the semidarkness. His eyes opened wide when he saw what had been done.

It was close, but Monk got away before the paramedics could stop him.

He was around the corner and into a taxi before they knew it.

Now, half a block from the trolley barn, he reached for his cell phone, then stared at it. The phone was turned off. Damn it, when had he done that? He hit the power button and saw that he had voice mail. Good, he thought. Lisa had finally come to her senses.

But it wasn't Lisa.

It was Eleanor DeWitt's voice, and she sounded terrified.

"Christ, Puller!" she whispered, just loudly enough for him to hear. "I think there's someone here! Someone trying to break into my apartment! You've got to help me! Oh God, Puller, how soon can you get here?"

Monk held on to the phone as the cab arrived at the barn, as he threw a twenty-dollar bill at the driver. He didn't wait for his change before sprinting to the door, opening it, and dashing into the garage. He took the Ferrari. Kendall Jefferson would kill him, but Jefferson could get in line. The flaming red Enzo could do two hundred miles an hour, easy. The only thing in his way would be the traffic.

He punched Eleanor's phone number as he waited for the gate to lift out of the way, but there was no answer. He threw the phone aside. Shit. What had he done to her? How could he have let her down this way?

The gate finally rose high enough for the low-slung Ferrari. Monk shot under it and into the street. He turned left toward GW University, his foot dancing on the accelerator pedal as he looked for holes in the traffic.

She was dead when he got there.

The door was standing open, and in her office off the living room, Eleanor was lying on her left side next to her overturned wheelchair. A crusty brown hole bisected her forehead, a single long drip of dried blood extended to her left ear.

Monk backed up through the door and grabbed for his gun before realizing he was being foolish. The killer was long gone. Monk went through the door again and moved directly to her body. "Oh, Eleanor," he said, then looked away. When his eyes returned to her, he felt an icy weight in his stomach. He forced himself to look at her far longer than he wanted to. An image formed in his mind, the face of a billionaire. His gaze swept the room. It was untouched, and that was not good. It meant that Eleanor had put the pictures she'd downloaded for him out in plain sight, that Sung Kim hadn't had to search for them at all.

Monk turned suddenly and left the room, strode directly to the front door and through it. By the time he reached the Ferrari his body was quivering with fury and remorse. There was only one thing he could do for Eleanor now. There was only one thing he could do for himself.

In her home in McLean—in the bedroom she'd converted into a home office—Bethany Randall sat at the desk under the window, staring into the backyard before picking up the phone and dialing quickly.

"FBI," a woman's voice said. "How may I direct your call?"

Bethany told her, and a moment later a second voice came on the line.

"This is Agent Sands."

"It's Bethany Randall." She waited for a response, but there wasn't one. "I think we better talk."

"I've got nothing to say to you, not anymore. Not since Puller made his choice."

"I'm not talking about Monk."

Silence. Sung Kim gave Lisa a few seconds before continuing.

"I have videotape. You thought you were safely hidden in my yard, but the security camera caught your whole act."

"Videotape?" Lisa paused. "Should I have some idea what you're talking about?"

"Another question like that and I hang up. Do you understand me?"

Seconds ticked by.

"What do you want?"

"To talk to you, Lisa, that's all. To try to work this out between ourselves before it gets any worse."

"I told you I have nothing to say."

"Well, I won't keep you any longer then. I'll let you go back to work while I take this up with your boss instead."

This time the silence was twice as long.

"Where?" Lisa finally responded. "Where can we meet?"

Bethany told her, then hung up the phone, sat back and gazed out the window into the backyard she'd grown to love. A few moments later she opened the right-hand desk drawer and pulled out her contact-lens case. She set it on the desk and opened it up, then took her time slipping the brown lenses over her eyes. From a deeper drawer she pulled out her long brown wig. She would put it on in the bathroom, after she'd pinned her hair to the top of her head and fastened the skullcap into place.

Then she opened the middle drawer and pulled it all the way out to the stops. She slid open a narrow compartment hidden in the rear wall of the drawer. Reaching through, she pushed her one-time pad aside to get to the cell phone. She couldn't add Lisa Sands—couldn't add a second FBI agent to her mission—without talking to Pyongyang. It was dangerous to risk another call, but she had no choice.

FORTY-NINE

Lisa didn't respond to her cell phone, so Monk called her office. She wasn't at her desk, either, and he waited for the call to transfer to the squad secretary.

"Sorry, Mr. Monk," Janet Halper told him. "Lisa left a few minutes ago."

"Where'd she go?"

"Didn't say, but she left in a hurry, I can tell you that much. Went by me like a tornado." Janet paused. "You have her cell number?" She laughed. "Dumb question . . . Of course you do."

"I'll try to call her, but if you talk to Lisa before I do, ask her to call me."

He hung up and punched numbers for Lisa's cell phone, but she didn't answer. He left a message on her voice mail, then dialed her pager number and left the same message. Twenty minutes later he still hadn't heard from her, so he did it all again. Still no luck. He threw the phone into the Ferrari's passenger seat, and felt his grip tighten on the steering wheel. He couldn't do anything about finding Lisa if she didn't want to be found.

Then he thought about someone else he hadn't heard from yet. William should have called by now. Monk reached for the phone again, hit the numbers for William's office. It rang twice before an automated voice came on. "The number you have dialed is no longer in service, and there is no new number." Monk frowned. He must have misdialed. He tried again, and discovered he hadn't made a mistake.

Next he tried William's cell phone, but it was the same message, this time from the cellular company he used. Monk stared at the phone for a few seconds before tossing it aside and heading for William's office.

It wasn't there anymore.

When Monk got to the third floor, William's office was gone.

Monk stood in front of the NSA man's door, staring at the empty spot where there should have been the brass-plated POTOMAC ENGINEERING sign. He shook his head as he realized he must have made a mistake, that in his rush to get here, he'd gotten out of the elevator on the wrong floor.

He hurried back to the elevator, but saw when he got there that he wasn't wrong, that he *was* on the third floor. Scowling, he went back to William's door. He tried the knob, but the door was locked. He knocked on it, softly at first, then harder, but there was no response.

"William?" he called. Nothing. "William!" Still no response.

Monk heard a voice to his right, and turned to see a thin short man down the hall, twenty feet away.

"Moved out," the man said. "Last of the movers just left a few minutes ago."

Monk walked down the hall until he was standing in front of the man.

"William?" he said. "William Smith just moved out?"

"I don't know what his name was, but the man in that office is gone."

Monk described William.

"That's the guy," the short man said. "But I never did meet him." He paused. "Had to be a hell of a workaholic, though. Here when I got here in the morning, here when I left at night, but . . ." The short man shook his head. "No wonder he had to move out. The sign on the door said he was a civil engineer, but I never saw any clients."

"You say the movers just left?"

"Not ten minutes ago." The man chuckled. "Now that I think about it, he couldn't have gone broke."

"Why would you say that?"

"Man who's belly-up doesn't hire movers . . . not movers like those guys, anyway."

"Those guys?"

"I've never seen so many, for one thing . . . and I've never seen *any* who looked like they did."

Monk didn't say anything. The man was itching to tell him the rest of it.

"Had to be twenty men," he told Monk. "White coveralls, white shoes. Hell, they were all white, and I don't mean just their clothes." He shook his head. "You know what movers look like these days. About one step from homeless, most of them. Not the drivers . . . the day laborers who do the heavy lifting. But these guys didn't look like that at all. Come to think of it, they looked more like you."

"Twenty? Twenty movers?"

"Took 'em about half an hour, start to finish. I walked down there when they were gone. Never seen an office look so clean after a move." The short man glanced up the hall in the direction of the empty office, then turned back to Monk. "It's a whole lot cleaner in there than it was when your friend moved in." He shook his head. "Matter of fact, it looks like he never moved in at all."

Now Monk had to go to Fort Meade.

He drove to the Beltway and headed toward Maryland. When he hit I-295 he turned north, and half an hour later found an empty space in the immense parking lot outside the equally massive black-glass headquarters of the National Security Agency. Inside at the reception desk, a young man in an earnest blue suit took Monk's credentials and examined them closely before looking up from behind the computer screen on his desk.

"What can I do for you, Special Agent Monk?"

"I'm here to see Director Carter."

"Of course."

The young man typed on his keyboard for a moment, then leaned toward the monitor and examined the screen before looking up again and shaking his head. "I don't see your name here. When did you make the appointment?"

"I don't have an appointment, but call upstairs anyway. I have a hunch he's expecting me."

The young man frowned. "I can't do that . . . You can't just walk in and. . . ."

His voice died as Monk turned and walked away, toward the bank of elevators beyond the reception desk.

"Hey!" the young man shouted. "Get back here! You can't . . ."

Monk didn't bother looking back. The young man would summon the guards without any further help from him. They would show up before he actually reached the elevators. Seconds later they did. Two of them, one on either side of Monk as he slowed to a stop. Big guys in dark blue uniforms. Wide shoulders, no perceptible necks. Large black pistols in the holsters on their hips. The shorter one stood at least six-four and he did the talking.

"What's the problem here?" he wanted to know.

Monk showed his credentials again. "FBI," he said. "Puller Monk. I'm on my way up to see the director."

The guard frowned. "Why would you think you can just walk into the director's office without an appointment?"

"Because I'm here to find out what happened to William Smith. To ask why William and his office have disappeared."

"William Smith?" He glanced at his partner. "Is that name supposed to mean something to us?"

"I'm not here to see you."

Both guards stepped closer to Monk. The bigger one reached out and grabbed his arm above the elbow. "You're not here to see anybody," he growled. The other guard took his free arm. Monk allowed himself to be pulled back toward the big front doors.

"William Smith," Monk repeated before they got halfway there. "William Smith and . . ." He couldn't make himself say any more, not to these guys. "If I don't talk to Philip Carter about Smith, I'll have to go to my own director."

Which was meaningless drivel, but they wouldn't know that. And it worked. Suddenly they stopped. Suddenly they were looking at each other. They didn't exchange a word, but Monk could hear them just as clearly as if they were talking out loud. Like the security guards in Franklin's secret vault, these guys weren't about to proceed without shifting the responsibility to somebody else.

The shorter one let go of Monk's arm and stepped off to the side to use the phone he plucked from his wide black belt. Monk couldn't hear what the guard was saying, but he came back and grabbed Monk's arm again.

"Let's go, pal," he said. "The only place you're going is back to your car."

Monk tried to yank his arm free, but the guard had a grip like a pit bull.

"What are you talking about?" he said. "Did you tell Carter what I said?"

"I told his chief of staff."

Monk shook his head. "Not good enough. Carter himself has to be told I'm here. And why I'm here."

"The chief of staff spoke to the director. I could hear him talking on the other line."

"You heard him tell Carter that I'd go to my own director if Carter doesn't see me?"

"That's what I heard."

"And?"

"And Mr. Carter says he has no idea what you're talking about. He says nobody does . . . and nobody will. He says no matter how many times you come back here, nobody will."

F I F T Y

This was where he was supposed to quit.

Back in the Ferrari, back out on the highway toward the District, Monk realized Philip Carter's message couldn't have been clearer. Go back to your cubbyhole, the NSA director was telling him. Go back to the SOG and forget this whole thing ever happened. Cash in your chips and get out of a game you've got no chance of winning.

Well, fuck that.

Monk stomped on the gas and the Ferrari seemed to come off the ground in its eagerness to run. And he felt the same way. He was tired of losing, and the best way to recover was to throw some more chips on the pile.

He grabbed his cell phone and asked for information, then got himself connected. "Tell him it's the FBI," he told the switchboard operator at the Global Panoptic Building when she answered. "Tell Franklin it's Puller Monk."

"I'm sorry, Mr. Monk," the woman told him. "The chairman's in Gettysburg. He left strict instructions not to be—"

"I don't give a damn what he said. If you have any hope of keeping your job, you'll get him on the phone right now. You'll put him on the line with me . . . or you'll tell him to expect to see me as soon as I can get there."

"One moment, please, Agent Monk. I'm sure he'd like to speak with you."

"I had an idea he might."

Monk's fingers drummed the steering wheel while he waited.

"Monk?"

Franklin's voice was clearly angry. "What the hell is the meaning of this? Do you have any idea what's going on here tod—"

"Shut up, Franklin! I'm coming for Sung Kim."

"For . . . What did you say? You're coming for *what*?"

"Your art thief. Pyongyang's assassin."

"Pyongyang?" Silence. "I have no damned idea what you're talking about, Monk, but I can't see you today. I'm at the farm for the rest of the day."

"And I'm on my way."

A longer silence this time. "I've got people coming. Believe it or not, more important people than you."

"I don't care if the pope himself is on the way. You *will* be available for me when I get there. You'll have the woman there, too. Or you can have your guests watch me drag you away in handcuffs."

"Handcuffs? What the hell are you talking about?"

Monk said nothing, letting his bluff play out. Fifteen long seconds passed without a sound.

"Be at my building in an hour," Franklin said at last. "I'll send my helicopter for you."

Monk spent a half hour calling the Metropolitan P.D. about Eleanor, and trying again without success to get hold of Lisa. When he got to the Global Panoptic Building, the red and white Sikorsky was ready for him. Stepping out of the elevator on the roof, he stiffened his body against the rotor wash from the helicopter sitting on the circular pad, and stiffened his mind against the prospect of yet another flight inside what wasn't much more than a large tin can.

He saw that there was only one pilot this time. The dark blue helmet made it impossible to tell if it was one of the two who'd flown them to Battle Valley Farm the other day. The passenger door was open and the pilot raised a gloved hand without looking at him, motioning for Monk to get in. He did so, then climbed into the nearest of the six seats and forced himself to fasten the shoulder and lap belts, adding even further to his feeling of confinement. Jesus, Monk thought. When this was all over, he had to get some help for his claustrophobia.

The pilot said nothing before they lifted off. The Sikorsky climbed rapidly and Monk stared out the window, down at the District of Columbia as it passed underneath. Just as the other day, the traffic was horrific. The highways were crawling, the surface streets not moving at all. This way he'd be at the farm in twenty-five minutes. Monk glanced at the back of the pilot's helmet, then began to prepare.

It didn't take long.

All he knew for sure was that William Smith's office was gone and that the director of NSA had done just as he promised and was disavowing any knowledge of their agreement. Philip Carter had decided the operation to catch Sung Kim was out of control, and the best thing to do was lay back and wait for another chance. A chance that didn't involve the president's closest buddy and the bureaucratic shit storm that would annihilate Carter should he fail.

Monk glanced at the back of the pilot's helmet, wanting to call out, to urge more speed. Thomas Franklin had the answers. Every minute of delay in getting to him was another minute for the man to cover his tracks.

Meanwhile, he had to try Lisa again.

Maybe she was back in her office.

He reached for the sports jacket he kept in the Saab at all times, that he'd transferred to the Ferrari and then to the helicopter. He fumbled in the pocket for his cell phone, then remembered using it in the Ferrari and leaving it there. Damn it. He stared out the window, then realized there had to be a phone in the chopper.

He looked around, but couldn't see one. He searched for the headset he'd used the other day with Franklin. He could ask the pilot where the phone was kept. He opened the console built into the armrest of his seat and found the headset. Pulling it out, he slipped the headphones over his ears just in time to hear a man's voice.

"When?" the voice asked. It was Thomas Franklin, Monk realized. Franklin talking to the pilot. "And how soon can you get here?" Franklin was saying. "After . . . afterward, I mean."

"I'm ten minutes from the farm," the pilot answered. A woman's voice. Hearing it, Monk frowned. "I'll need about an hour," the pilot said, then hesitated. "It'll take me an hour to get to you."

Monk stared at the back of the pilot's helmet, then unbuckled his shoulder harness and moved up to the copilot's seat. He was still wearing the headset when he got there, the microphone still in place in front of his mouth. Wraparound sunglasses hid the pilot's eyes, but Monk didn't have to see them to know who she was. He tried to keep the puzzlement out of his voice.

"What are you doing here, Bethany? What are you doing in this helicopter?"

Her voice was dead flat. "Sung Kim, Puller. My name is Sung Kim. And all I'm doing is my job."

He stared at her. *Sung Kim? Bethany Randall was Sung Kim?* How could that be? He *knew* this woman. He'd known her five *years* ago. She was engaged to an NSA agent, for Christ's sake. She and William had been about to get . . . Monk's brain paused for an instant before he got it.

"You doubled William," he said, "but now you've killed him." There couldn't be any other explanation for the office that disappeared. "Why would you do that? How often do you get a chance to penetrate NSA?"

"I didn't double him. I realized I'd never be able to turn William."

Monk's mind filled with that night in the hot tub. "You thought you had a better chance with *me?* You thought that fucking me in the hot tub was all it would take?"

"A girl's got to try."

Monk's tongue seemed to thicken in his mouth. He couldn't make himself ask the next question, but she must have seen it in his eyes.

"She's here, Puller. Lisa's here with us."

Monk turned in the seat, his eyes everywhere at the same time, but the chopper was small, hardly more than the six seats and pilot's compartment. There was no room for anyone to be hidden.

"I said here . . . not *in* here." Bethany glanced backward and down.

Following her gaze, Monk's vision blurred as he realized what she was telling him. That Lisa was in the luggage compartment at the rear of the chopper. That Lisa's body was . . . Monk shook his head.

"No way," he said. "No way in hell she'd let you get close enough."

Bethany shrugged. "Have it your way. Doesn't make any difference to me what you think."

Monk looked for a tell, desperate to see that she was lying, but he saw nothing. Lisa's not dead, he told himself. She's not in this chopper. She's back in her office, getting ready to go home to the loft.

"She knows nothing, Bethany. Lisa thinks you and I are having an affair, but that's it. She doesn't have to die."

"I can't help that now."

Monk's hands began to flex as he fought the urge to leap across the seat and kill her. "What about the other night . . . our dinner at your house?" He shook his head. "Why try to seduce me like that? Why bother with a man you knew you were going to kill?"

"Orders. I was given one last chance to make you one of us." She paused. "We could have had a lot more nights like that one in the hot tub."

Monk stared at her. "You and me, Bethany . . . and Thomas Franklin." He shook his head. "Surely you're not that stupid."

"Sung Kim," she said. "I told you my name is Sung Kim."

Monk turned away, his eyes searching out the luggage compartment again, but before he could turn back, he felt the chopper decelerate, then heard the suddenly much louder roar of the rotor blades. He spun around just in time to see Bethany sliding the door open, then reaching for a bright red knob in the control console between the seats, shoving the knob all the way to the firewall.

The engine roar died. The chopper seemed to come to a complete stop.

Bethany swung herself through the open door and dropped onto the landing skid below the door. Now Monk could see the small sport chute strapped to her back. He vaulted across the empty pilot's seat in a futile attempt to grab her, to haul her back inside, but he was too late. He could only watch as Bethany gathered herself to jump from the skid.

Before he could think about what he was doing, Monk leaped after her.

His much heavier body caught her an instant after she hurled herself from the skid. He landed on her back and slid down to her waist as his desperate grip held fast.

As they tumbled together into the sky.

FIFTY-ONE

Over the shriek of wind in his ears, Monk could barely hear the roar of his own voice as they hurtled away from the dying helicopter, as they plummeted toward the forest below. He clung to Bethany, his arms and hands locked around her waist in a grip she'd have to kill him to break.

A moment later her chute exploded directly into his face, then shot past him and opened with a bone-wrenching jerk that seemed to yank the two of them all the way back to the chopper. The sudden deceleration tore his hands away, and he felt himself slipping down her body. His fingers clawed into her, and he stopped sliding just as the helicopter exploded.

Monk's body seemed to flatten as it recoiled from the thunderclap of sound, and his brain stopped dead as the blast hammered them toward the ground.

Bethany began to twist, to buck like a wild horse as she tried to throw him clear, but somehow he managed to hang on.

Now he could hear her screaming.

"Too fast! . . . Too fast! Let go of me! . . . You'll kill us both! . . . We're both going to die!"

Monk tucked his head into the back of her legs and held on even tighter.

He couldn't feel his fingers anymore, and he knew she was right. Her sport chute was designed for one jumper. Together they were too heavy. Without him on her back she was sure to make it . . . and that thought alone strengthened his grip.

Suddenly she was beating on the backs of his hands.

It felt like she had a hammer, but Monk knew exactly what it was.

She had a handgun, of course, and she was using the barrel to smash his fingers until he let go. He slid toward her feet and locked his arms around her legs this time. He waited for the same agonizing blows, but this time a shot rang out instead, and a new pain—a horribly worse pain— tore across his right side.

Monk heard himself screaming as he buried himself even deeper into her legs. It was his only chance. He heard another gunshot, then a third, but now she was afraid. Afraid she'd shoot herself instead.

The gunshots stopped.

But now the hand battering started again.

Somehow it was even worse this time.

More frantic, more desperate.

Monk bellowed as he tried to hang on, but it was no use. He was out of strength . . . he could no longer stand the pain. He felt himself losing consciousness, slipping away now, falling on his own now . . .

His legs struck the tree first as he crashed through the heavy canopy, through the foliage, past limbs and branches, his mind too numb to direct his movements. The world turned to slow motion as he tumbled toward a narrow branch without leaves. He twisted frantically to avoid being impaled, but almost immediately a limb too big to escape rose to meet him.

"*No!*" he roared, an instant before he hit.

FIFTY-TWO

The world tilted and spun as Monk opened his eyes, his brain fighting to make some sense of where he was.

In a tree, he realized . . . in the same tree he'd hit when he'd fallen out of the sky. And then it all came back to him. Bethany's treachery . . . his instinctive leap after her when she left him to die . . . the horrendous explosion . . . Dear God, Monk thought, as he remembered the rest of it, but he shook the thought out of his mind.

Bethany was lying. Lisa wasn't in that chopper when it exploded. He tried to form a mental picture of her sitting at her desk back at WFO, but for some reason he couldn't. It was shock, he realized . . . he was in shock. Lisa was safe, he absolutely refused to believe otherwise. She would be at the loft when he got back, and he could put her out of his mind until then.

He looked over his right shoulder for any sign of Bethany, but didn't see her. He struggled to lift his head and check the other side, then as far below him as he could see through the dense foliage that had slowed his fall enough to save his life. Nothing.

Next he checked his physical condition.

He was battered, bloodied, bruised, and in shock, quivering like a banjo string, with a nose so broken he could hardly use it to breathe. Its steady throbbing matched his heartbeat, and grew even worse when he looked down at the ground that seemed a hundred miles away. He reached up and touched his nose very carefully, tracing its new profile, lumpy now, and pointing a bit sideways. Painful as hell but not enough to disable him. He groaned as he tried to move, then decided he shouldn't until he'd checked for broken bones.

He lifted his shirt first, looked down at his side, relieved to see that the bullet wound was hardly more than a deep scratch. Plenty of blood, but already drying and crusting over. His crash into the tree had done him worse, much worse. Thank God for the thick canopy of foliage, or he'd be dead. He breathed deeply and exhaled. Good. None of the stabbing pain that would indicate a broken rib. Lots of blood on his arms and hands, but bright red, not the kind to worry about. He felt along his face—careful to avoid his nose—and came away with even more blood, again none of it the seriously dark color of blood from somewhere deep inside his body. He wriggled his toes, then his feet, before deciding he was ready to get started.

Unfortunately, that didn't mean much.

Ready or not, he was still stuck in the top of a very tall tree.

A black oak, he realized, as he looked at the serrated edges of the leaves. He was wedged between a massive limb and a smaller branch shooting up and to the left. He used his arms to dislodge himself from the crotch he was stuck in, to pull away slowly, groaning and sweating as he made his way to a limb big enough to hold his weight.

Monk sat for a moment, pushing aside the foliage and staring down, trying to guess how far off the ground he was. Seventy feet, maybe more. This was old growth, the trees as tall as buildings. To fall from here would be nearly as bad as tumbling out of the sky.

He gave himself five minutes to regain enough strength for his descent, then lowered one leg in the direction of the branch below him. Eight or ten feet away, and that was a big problem. In his condition a steep flight of stairs would be a challenge, trying to swing from limb to limb on the way out of this tree was crazy. But so was staying here. Unless he could figure out a way to fly to Battle Valley Farm, he had to get to the ground. Had to use the deeply furrowed bark of the trunk for hand and foot holds, until he was down.

And that's what he did.

Clutching the bark, kicking his feet into the furrows, he shinnied downward, through the leaves, past the branches, until after what felt like an hour he reached the bottom branch, where he sat for a few moments, staring at the ground. Christ. It was still ten feet away. Ten feet didn't sound like much, but right now it looked like a mile. He took a deep breath through his mouth, then lowered himself until he was hanging from the bottom branch for an instant before letting go. The last four feet felt like an endless plunge. Monk rolled as he hit the layer of leaves and soft forest soil, but lay stunned and breathless anyway, gasping like a fish in the bottom of a boat.

A full minute later he rolled onto his back and stared at the dense forest around him, the towering black oaks and sycamores, the sparse undergrowth. He lay there and tried to think, then found himself reaching to his pocket for his cell phone to call Lisa before remembering once again that he'd left it in the Ferrari.

Bethany had to be close.

They'd been falling together until just seconds before he hit the tree. She must be somewhere in this tree with him. Then he realized he was forgetting something . . . that he'd been unconscious, that she could easily be miles away by now. Through the headset in the chopper, he'd heard her telling Franklin to expect her in an hour. It was best to admit that she had a huge head start and that he wasn't going to catch her sitting here.

Monk pulled himself to his knees, then stood, his head spinning for a moment before his equilibrium returned. Gradually his mind began to focus. He had to make his way to the nearest road, then hope to find someone willing to drive him the rest of the way to the farm. He was out in the country. Country people were good about helping out. Then he looked down at himself and realized it might not be that easy.

His slacks were torn—one knee shredded—and there was blood all over them. One shoe was gone, somewhere up in the tree, he guessed, and that made limping around on the other one useless. He kicked it off. His socks wouldn't last long, but they'd be better than nothing until they fell apart. Even worse, his sports jacket was still in what was left of the helicopter, along with his credentials and badge. He was too exhausted to curse. Without his ID and badge, he was just another injured man who looked more like a homeless bum than an FBI agent. No one would pick up a man his size, looking like this. He could claim he'd been in an accident, but they'd insist on taking him to a hospital, not to Battle Valley Farm.

In the next instant, Monk realized he was getting ahead of himself.

He didn't have to worry about hitchhiking until he found a road, and he didn't even know which way to begin looking.

What he did know was that Bethany had none of his problems.

She was expected at Franklin's farm shortly, which meant she had transportation nearby, a vehicle stashed in the woods or a car and driver waiting for her. He'd seen a road from the sky, northwest of their heading, just before he heard Bethany's voice through his headset, and she would have planned to come down near one. She wouldn't have put herself in the position of having to hike for miles to get to her transportation.

He had to get his bearings before doing anything else. The forest was so dense he couldn't see the sun. He tried to remember his Boy Scout training, to recall other ways to determine which way was north. He looked around for moss on the trees, but realized he couldn't remember for sure what that meant.

The sound of a horn brought his head around.

A car horn.

No . . . more like a truck horn . . . one of those air horns the diesel trucks used.

But where? From which direction?

The sound had come from his right, Monk guessed, but he had to hear it again to make sure. He strained to listen, but heard nothing. He remained motionless for two minutes, but still heard nothing. Not good, but at least he now knew the road was nearby. Now all he had to do was find it. He would have to guess, then take his chances. To his right, that's where the sound had come from. That was the first direction he'd try.

He slogged through the underbrush, shoving aside the occasional low-hanging tree limb, trying to keep moving in a straight line. A dozen steps later he tripped and fell, crashing to the ground, but managed to protect his nose from the worst of it. He lay there for a moment, then heard another noise. A car passing, it sounded like . . . a car close by.

He struggled to his feet, staggered a few paces, then fell again when the ground suddenly sloped away sharply. He seemed to shoot through the last of the brush, then downward into a shallow ditch. He lifted himself to his knees and felt a rush of adrenaline as he saw the road.

FIFTY-THREE

This time there was no banter.

As Sung Kim reached the head of a line of cars that stretched at least a quarter mile from Battle Valley Farm's main entrance gate back toward State Highway 15, she could see from the look on Steve Batcholder's face that there would be no kidding around today.

Today Steve's guard shack at the big iron gate was crowded with stern-faced men and women, walkie-talkies in their hands and earpieces in their ears. Watching them closely, Sung Kim pushed the gear lever up into Park, zipped her window down, and smiled as they approached. Steve was in the lead, and he was shaking his head.

"I told you the other day this would happen, Mary Anne," he said. "Not that I don't like seeing you again so soon, but I'm sorry it has to be . . ."

He stopped talking and stared at the bruises on her face.

"My God, what happened to you?" he said. "What happened to your face?"

She smiled. "I fell getting into the van, back at the flower shop. It's nothing. Looks a lot worse than it is."

He shook his head slowly, then turned to the woman at his side, a thirty-something Secret Service agent in a dark blue suit with light gray pinstripes, and a sour look on her square face.

"I know this woman," Steve told the bodyguard. "Her name is Mary Anne White. She delivers flowers to the farm. I see her all the time. Just a couple days ago, as a matter of fact."

The woman took a step closer to Sung Kim's van. "Good afternoon," she said. "Would you mind stepping out of the van please?"

Sung Kim smiled. "Of course not."

She swung the door open and got out. The Secret Service agent moved closer. She was holding a wand in her right hand, a metal-detecting wand that looked a little like a whisk used in the kitchen for beating eggs or sweet cream.

"Extend your arms, please," the agent said.

Sung Kim did so. The agent ran the detector up and down her body, up the inside of each leg, then along the length of both arms, which were just as bruised as her face, although the injuries were hidden by the long sleeves of her blue and white shirt.

"Thank you, ma'am," the agent said when there were no beeps from the detector. "What's in the van?"

"Flowers, lots of flowers . . . and a few plants." Sung Kim smiled. "Mr. Franklin sure loves roses. I brought a load a few days ago, but I got the call today to bring even more."

The agent stepped up close to the van, inspected the driver's compartment, then turned back to Sung Kim. "I need to look in the back."

"It's not locked."

"Please, ma'am, I need you to open the door for me."

"Of course."

Sung Kim led the way to the rear of the van. When she got there, she turned around and saw three more Secret Service agents walk up. One of them—a tall skinny man in a dark blue suit—was leading a gorgeous dog, an immense German shepherd. The bomb dog, of course.

"Open the door, please," the man said.

Sung Kim did so. The man looked at the dog, then uttered a sharp command. The shepherd leaped effortlessly into the back of the van. Sung

Kim watched as the dog zigzagged among the plants and flowers, his big nose darting and sniffing, before he came back and jumped to the ground.

Next, the woman agent stepped up into the van and moved around on the same path as had the dog, her eyes playing over the same plants and flowers. Suddenly she stopped, bent over, and picked up a small unmarked cardboard carton from the floor of the van and brought it back to Sung Kim.

"What's this?"

"Timers," Sung Kim told her. "Watering timers. They run on batteries. I use them to regulate the water lines to the various indoor plants in the house, and around the farm." She reached for the carton. "I can show you what they look like."

But the agent opened the carton herself, picked out one of the timers, a green plastic device about the size of a pack of cigarettes, with a yellow dial on the front, and stubby armlike extensions for the plastic tubing that carried the water.

"It's just a valve," Sung Kim said. "An electrically operated valve, connected to a tiny computer chip that opens and shuts it according to the settings on the dial."

The agent brought the carton up closer to her eyes, inspecting the rest of the timers, then put the one she was holding back into the carton, closed it up, and set it back in the van, next to a pink azalea that Sung Kim could see was already starting to wilt in the heat.

"Can I close up?" she asked the agent. "Are you finished back here? I've really got to get these plants out of the sun."

The agent nodded. "I just have to call the house and make sure you're on their list, then you can go on in."

Sung Kim smiled. She was on the list, all right. One thing she knew for sure was that she was on that list.

FIFTY-FOUR

Monk pulled himself to his feet and stepped into the road.

He looked in both directions but saw no one. He'd been lucky to hear the horns. He might have stumbled around in the woods for hours. He turned to his right. The road ran north. He didn't know how far away from the farm he was, but the road had to run right past it. He could follow the road until he was close enough to see the golf course that he knew from his two previous flights lay south and west of the mansion.

Monk started walking. His nose ached, his whole body hurt. He hadn't walked a quarter mile before he heard a car behind him. Turning, he stuck out his thumb. A pickup truck, Monk saw, slowing down when the young male driver saw him, then pulling over toward the ditch and stopping a dozen yards past him.

"Man," the kid said, when Monk limped around the pickup and stood at the driver's window. "What the hell happened to you?"

Monk tried to look sheepish. "Got a new motorcycle, one of those motocross jobbies. Had to try it out. Just about ended up killing myself."

"Trail-biking?" He stared at the thick woods on both sides of the road. "How can you trail-bike in there? Be hard enough just to walk."

"Tell me about it."

The driver glanced at his feet. "No shoes? You go riding without shoes?"

"I fell. Got into some loose leaves and fell into a ditch . . . I thought it was a ditch, but it turned out to be a gully." He shook his head. "I went in bike and all. Only had one shoe when I crawled out again. I looked around for it, but . . ."

Monk glanced back toward where he'd come out of the trees.

"Christ, I'm lucky I've got any clothes on at all, as hard as I went through that brush. I couldn't walk in one shoe, so I tossed the other one back there by my bike."

The kid stared beyond Monk, toward the woods, as though looking for the bike and the shoe. Monk reached down to massage his knee.

"Bike's all bent up," he said. "Front wheel collapsed on me." He paused. "I think I marked the spot pretty good. I'll come back later and get it . . . look for my shoes at the same time."

The kid shook his head. "You do much riding?"

"First time." Monk glanced back toward the forest. "I'm going to sell the son of a bitch the second I get back to Washington."

"Where you staying here in Gettysburg?"

"Up the road . . . just this side of town. The wife and I rented a place for the weekend." He shook his head. "Christ, she's gonna kill me. I'm an hour late already. Can you take me?"

"Sure, but it's gonna be a while."

Monk stared at him.

"Franklin's farm," the kid said. "Thomas Franklin?" Monk nodded as the kid continued. "There's something going on at Battle Valley Farm." He gestured toward the road ahead. "Got a roadblock up there by the main entrance. A checkpoint. Had to come through it an hour ago, and I've never seen it like that."

"What do you mean?"

"We're used to the Secret Service around here . . . Franklin and the president hanging out and all . . . but this time there were Japanese guys, too. A dozen, at least. Traffic backed up half a mile. Took me an hour to get through."

"Japanese?"

"All over the place."

Monk turned away from the kid to look up the road. Japanese body-guards at Battle Valley Farm. Sung Kim at the farm. Despite the pain in his legs, Monk had to fight an urge to run after her, run her down, and kill her before she . . .

"Look," the kid said. "I can take you, but we've gotta go right now." He gestured toward the bed of the pickup, at the stack of lumber in the back. "My boss is waiting for this stuff at the job site."

Monk nodded, then limped around the back of the pickup to the passenger door, pulled it open and climbed in. "Thanks," he said. "It would have been a hell of a walk." He bent to make a show of looking at the odometer. "How far?" he asked the kid. "How far to Gettysburg. I'll never find my bike if I don't keep a pretty close check."

"I dunno, three miles, a little less maybe."

"What about the checkpoint at the gate? Could I walk to town from there?"

"Be about a two-mile walk, but why bother? Even with the delay at the checkpoint, I'd get to Gettysburg a long time before you could walk there."

Monk nodded. "Have you got a cell phone?"

The kid shook his head. "I'm lucky to have enough money for my lunch," he said, before pulling back onto the road.

A few minutes later they caught up to a car, a red sedan, then another car, and another, until the traffic began to slow.

"Damn," the kid said. "It's even worse going this direction. Gonna take an hour just to get to the gate."

They crept along toward the checkpoint, although the bend in the road ahead kept Monk from seeing the main gate. The golf course was on his left. He couldn't see it through the dense forest, but he knew it was there. With this level of security at the entrances to Battle Valley Farm, getting onto the golf course was his only chance of making it all the way to the mansion.

He craned his neck in an attempt to see the checkpoint, but it was still too far away. From the elevated cab of the kid's truck he could see many of the vehicles ahead of them, but he had no idea what he was looking for.

Bethany could be in any one of those cars or trucks, but Monk had the feeling she wasn't. He had the feeling she was far ahead of him, already inside the property.

He turned to the kid. "Sorry to abandon you," he said, "but I can't just sit here. I'm gonna walk up ahead. I'll catch a ride with somebody up front."

The kid shrugged. "That's what I'd do if I were you. Anybody'll give you a ride to town."

Monk opened the door and slid out of the seat to the ground. He closed the door and gave the kid a wave, then limped toward the car ahead, then past it, limping in the direction of the checkpoint until he was around the bend in the road and out of the kid's sight.

Monk saw the looks on the faces inside the cars and trucks as they reacted to his battered appearance, but nobody met his gaze or said a word to him. He couldn't blame them. The worse you looked, the harder people tried to ignore you, and he was counting on their reaction. It was best if they didn't see him at all. There were enough guards for him to get past already. He walked another hundred yards, turned to his left, and limped between two cars, crossed the road, and disappeared into the trees.

FIFTY-FIVE

The White House press corps didn't know quite what to do.

On his way across the lawn to Marine One, the president had to laugh as he saw the confusion on their faces. Linda Fiegler had done her job perfectly. The White House press secretary had told them of his plan to visit Thomas Franklin's farm this evening—she had no choice about something like that—but they weren't prepared for him to go this early. Even Tom himself didn't know. He and Nakamura would still be on the golf course when the president arrived.

If all went well, the president told himself as he returned the salute of the Marine Corps guard and climbed aboard the big green chopper, he could nail down his deal with Prime Minister Nakamura and still be back at the White House in time for a late dinner with the first lady.

It took Monk ten minutes of hacking with his hands and shoving with his arms through the heavy undergrowth before he came to the fence that surrounded the golf course, and he didn't like what he saw.

The steel chain-link structure was eight feet tall, for starters, but that wasn't the problem. At the top of the fence, a two-foot barbed-wire extension had been added, an extension that slanted out over Monk's head, designed to make the fence next to impossible to penetrate. To get over the barbed wire, he'd have to climb the fence until he could reach up and grab the extension, then pull himself up and crawl over the razor-sharp barbs to get to the other side. There was no way to do that without cutting himself to shreds.

Limping directly to the fence, he reached out and touched the chain links, then stared through them at the golf course. He'd seen it from the air, but up close it was even more impressive.

Rimmed with the same large oaks and sycamores that made up the forest, along with bushy rhododendrons and dogwoods that stretched away in both directions, the course was magnificent. Through the gaps in the foliage Monk could see the fairway and a single bunker filled with white sand, but he couldn't see much more than that. More important, he couldn't see any guards. They had to be around somewhere, probably close by, but they weren't here. He thought about electronic surveillance. The golf course might be covered with cameras. The same security people who'd busted him upstairs at the mansion might be looking at him right now, might have dispatched guards in his direction already.

Maybe it was time to surrender.

To go around to the main gate and tell them who he was, then join the Secret Service to go after Bethany. After Sung Kim.

But even as he thought about doing that, Monk realized he couldn't.

To the presidential detail he would sound just as crazy as he looked.

He had no badge, no credentials, no kind of ID at all. They would listen to his insistence that he was an FBI agent, but they wouldn't believe him. They'd listen to his insistence that a North Korean assassin was on the property, but they wouldn't believe that, either. They would handcuff him instead. And by the time they had made enough phone calls to verify his identity it would be too late.

No, Monk decided. To stop her, he had to get to the mansion, and the Secret Service wouldn't take him there. He'd be sitting in their car when Sung Kim struck.

He looked up again at the barbed wire.

He had to find something to lay over it, something he could use for

protection as he crawled to the other side. He looked down at his clothing. No help there. His cotton shirt was about as useful as Kleenex against
the stiletto-like barbs, his Dockers were not much better, and the already
torn socks on his feet were worse than useless. He turned away from the
fence, looking for a solution in the forest. A piece of tree limb, maybe, or
a chunk of bark big enough and strong enough to use as a shield. He
headed into the foliage, but a couple of minutes later gave up. There was
debris everywhere, branches, bark, a layer of leaves and twigs beneath his
feet, but nothing he could use.

F I F T Y - S I X

This time Sung Kim didn't bother going through the charade of asking
Grace Woods for the keys.

This time she went directly to the skeet house and opened the front
door with her own key, then hurried to the door of the ammunition depot,
opened that door and ran down the concrete tunnel to the short wide
bunker. From behind a stack of cases of dynamite, she retrieved the steel
tube filled with C4 explosive, and ran back to the door of the bunker. She
closed it but didn't bother locking the door again. There was no longer
any point. After today it wouldn't matter.

In the main room of the skeet house, Sung Kim hurried to the wreath
that hung on the two-legged stand leaning against the wall, where she'd
put it the other day. She pulled the stand away from the wall, then attached the steel tube to the other two legs to form the tripod that would
support the wreath once it was taken to Franklin's study. With the tripod
secure, she used her fingers to unscrew the tiny head of a bolt near the top
of the explosive tube, almost completely hidden from view by the ever-
green branches that formed the wreath. She dropped the bolt into the
breast pocket of her blue and white shirt, then pulled a green plastic timer
out of the same pocket, along with a small coil of insulated wire with the

ends bared. She attached one pair of bare ends to the tiny terminals on the green plastic timer, then stuck the other pair through the hole where the bolt had been, embedding them firmly in the plastique. She checked the timer to make sure it was set correctly—so that the electrical charge wouldn't detonate the C4 until she was well clear of the farm—then pulled the wreath into place so that it covered both the timer and the wires.

Sung Kim stepped back and studied her work. It was perfect. Without removing the wreath, there was no trace of what she'd done. She carried the wreath to the van and forced herself to drive slowly toward the mansion. Her body tingled with the need to get inside the big house, to get the wreath into Franklin's study before he and Nakamura got there, but she knew better. Right now the most important thing was to do nothing to call attention to herself along the way.

"Are you all right, Mr. Franklin?"

Franklin looked at his caddie. The caddie stared at the phone in Franklin's hand. "Is there something wrong, sir?"

Franklin handed him the phone. "I'm fine," he said.

But he wasn't.

He stepped to his ball, stared down at the Titleist and realized it must be his turn to hit. "Three-iron," he said to the caddie, then waved at Nakamura to apologize for the delay. He addressed the ball, took the club back and hit a slicing grounder toward the deep rough on the right. On his way to the ball his mind swirled with questions.

Where in the hell was the woman who'd destroyed his life?

What had she done with Puller Monk?

Was he still alive?

Dear God, was *she* still alive?

As Franklin considered the possibility that she wasn't—that Monk had somehow survived and managed to kill her instead—his vision began to blur. Monk could very well be on his way here now. Franklin swallowed hard. He saw again the images that continued to haunt him: Monk and the rest of the FBI agents showing up at the mansion; the handcuffs; the walk to the car.

And the president would see it all.

He was already on his way to the farm.

He'd be standing there watching when Monk hauled him away.

The images grew stronger.

Disgrace.

Prison.

He glanced toward Nakamura, then turned and hurried toward the rough and his ball.

FIFTY-SEVEN

Monk took a few steps along the fence, looking for a flaw, somewhere he could get through without taking on the razor barbs. Maybe the fence wasn't perfect all the way along.

But it was, he discovered, as he checked along the fence a hundred yards in both directions before stopping, breathing through his mouth to minimize the pain in his nose. He looked up at the top of the fence again, but this time noticed something else. Twenty yards down the line in the direction of the mansion—a dozen yards into the golf course side—a huge black oak towered above the fence, but that wasn't what had caught Monk's eye. What made him hurry toward the tree was the matching oak on his side. Another giant whose branches reached toward the fence as well.

A moment later he stood between the two trees and saw that at a point high above his head they came close to touching each other. The last thing he wanted was to go up another tree, but this looked like the only way. He moved to the trunk of the oak on his side, reached up, and got a secure hold in the bark furrows with his right hand, scrabbled with his bleeding left foot until he found a place to hold his weight, then began to climb. Curiously, he felt no pain. His body seemed almost numb, almost beyond feeling anything at all.

Three minutes later he'd battled his way past the heavy branches and through the leaves until he was twenty feet up the tree, standing on a branch that extended straight toward the black oak on the golf course side. Monk stared across. Damn it. From the ground he'd guessed that the tips of the branches were only a couple of feet apart, but it was more than that. Six feet, at least. And they weren't directly across from one another, either. His branch was five feet above the other one. He would have to jump away from his tree and catch the other one on the way down.

He flexed his knees, ready to try, when he heard a groaning sound from the limb he was standing on. Flexed to the breaking point, Monk realized. He looked down at the fence. Christ. If the limb broke, he'd land on top of the fence. If the fall didn't kill him, the barbs just might. He couldn't stay where he was, that much was certain. Life's a gamble, he told himself. Once again it was time to let it ride.

With a quick bend of his knees he propelled himself into the air and grabbed for the opposite branch as he fell . . . but he missed. Arms flailing, he snatched at the branch below that one . . . somehow managed to catch it . . . to clutch it with one hand . . . to feel himself swinging into the tree, hitting hard as he folded himself across it. He held on and edged toward the security of the trunk before pulling himself up and sitting on the branch. He was still sitting there, breathing hard, when he heard the whine of a golf cart approaching, then a voice directly beneath him.

Monk's body stiffened, straining to hear.

"Nothing," the voice said. "I've checked the fence line all the way along. There's no sign of him anywhere."

Monk wasn't surprised. Bethany would have called in an anonymous report of his presence to the Secret Service, just in case he'd survived the fall from the helicopter. Or the kid had seen him go into the woods . . . or someone else had, anyone in the line of cars leading up to the main gate. And Franklin, of course. Sung Kim would have told the traitor immediately that Monk was on his way.

Suddenly he heard a second voice, this one electronic, a voice on the other end of the radio the agent was using. Monk could hear the sound, but he couldn't make out the words of the second agent.

"Yeah," the louder voice responded. "I should be at the corner of the property in a few minutes."

A moment later Monk heard another golf cart approach and stop. Then a new voice. "Follow the fence north when you get to the corner," the voice said. "Matt Williams and Jeff Ruland are starting from the other end. They'll meet you somewhere around the middle."

"I'm on my way."

Both carts drove off. Monk's adrenaline subsided, leaving his legs shaking. He edged around the trunk until he could see the golf carts in the distance. There'd be more, of course. The presidential protective detail would be all over the golf course, all over the rest of the farm, the mansion, and the road going in both directions.

Slowly Monk's breathing normalized enough for him to consider what he was doing. The Secret Service people were the best-trained body-guards in the world. He didn't have a chance in hell of getting past them. They would kill him if he tried. Monk stared at the ground, but before he could make any kind of decision, there were more coming. Two carts this time, two men in the first, a man and a woman in the second. Too far away to see him, but he couldn't stay here. With no time to climb down, Monk dropped straight to the ground, hit with an impact that seemed to shake the fillings in his teeth.

He turned to his right and started to run, keeping low behind the bushy azaleas, grunting with each stride from the pain in his bleeding feet, until suddenly he came to the corner of a building and pulled up short. A maintenance building, he thought at first, then changed his mind when he came to a window, when he looked through and saw a round table covered by a white tablecloth and surrounded by a number of chairs. On the table were plates and silverware, and the obvious remnants of a small meal. A snack shack, at least that's what it would be called on a public golf course. The building was painted forest green to match the trees and shrubbery, with white framed windows, like a little cottage in the woods.

Monk hurried to the door, tried the knob, and wasn't surprised when it opened. With a fence like Franklin had built around the course, it wasn't necessary to lock anything. His eyes darted around the room, looking for a place to hide long enough for the Secret Service to check the cottage, for them to realize it was empty and move on. To give him a chance to make a break for the mansion. He saw nothing suitable. Except for the table and chairs, the room was empty. There wasn't even a broom closet, no doors at all, no . . .

Then he saw it.

A small closed door, maybe three feet high, a couple of feet across, set in the wall beyond the table.

He ran to the door, saw that it could be opened by sliding it upward. He pulled the door open. Now he could see a couple of silver serving dishes inside, and he realized what he was looking at. A dumbwaiter. A delivery system to bring food to the cottage from the kitchen in the mansion.

He dashed to the nearby window, looking for the housing that would cover the conveyor belt as it ran back toward the main house, but he saw nothing. He hurried back to the dumbwaiter, peered into the enclosure. Now he could see how it was built. He looked for a button in the wall next to the doorway and saw it immediately. He pushed the button and the platform holding the serving tray began to descend. He pushed it again and the platform stopped.

There was a tunnel underneath, Monk realized. A subterranean passage that had to go all the way back to the mansion, to the kitchen in the mansion. And the opening was just big enough. He could climb into the dumbwaiter and ride all the way to the kitchen. He stared at the opening and felt a shudder strong enough to buckle his knees. Someone might be able to do that, but not him. Not in a million fucking years.

He turned and ran for the door instead. His hand was turning the knob when he heard the carts again. Shit. They were here. He had no time to get out the door and back to the bushes.

He sprinted to the window, grabbed the bottom and jerked, but the damned thing wouldn't open. Through the glass, he saw a cart approaching. He turned back to the dumbwaiter, his stomach clenching as his mind's eye fixed on the long dark tunnel. He glanced out the window again. The golf cart was closer now. He dashed to the dumbwaiter, grabbed the serving tray and raced to the table to set it there before darting back to the opening. He stared at it.

No way! There's absolutely no way!

And he was still telling himself that as he crawled inside.

He stretched to reach back through the door to push the button. He was barely able to pull the door down into place before the platform began to descend and he was lowered into the blackness.

FIFTY-EIGHT

"What is it, Mary Anne?" Grace Woods said, her voice impatient, as Sung Kim approached Thomas Franklin's housekeeper in the kitchen of the mansion. Grace stared at the wreath and tripod Sung Kim was carrying. "I really don't have a moment to spare right now."

Sung Kim smiled apologetically. "I know you don't, but this wreath needs to go to Mr. Franklin's study before he gets there with the prime minister." She held the wreath up on its tripod so that Grace Woods could see the banner welcoming Nakamura. "Mr. Franklin's going to be very angry if it's not there when he comes in."

Grace Woods frowned. "So why are you standing here showing it to me?"

"I need a favor, Mrs. Woods." Sung Kim glanced downward toward the ID badge on her chest. "My badge won't get me past the agents in Mr. Franklin's study. They'll call you to come and vouch for me. Since you'd have to go to the study anyway, I wonder if you'd take the wreath yourself."

But Grace Woods's frown only deepened. "Are you sure it has to go in there now? I'd like to help, but I've got a hundred things to do before they come in from the golf course." She looked back in the direction of the kitchen. "For one thing, the president's due any minute. And I still haven't—"

"The president?" Sung Kim took a step toward Grace Woods. "What are you talking about? He's not coming till . . ." She stopped as she realized what she was saying. "I mean I heard he might be here, but not until later tonight."

Grace Woods stared at her, and Sung Kim tried to cover her mistake.

"I need this job, ma'am," she said. Tears filled her eyes, tears she'd been trained to summon at will. "Mr. Franklin was real serious about getting this wreath here in time for his guest. It means a lot to me to keep him happy."

"I'm sorry, but I can't. I just can't take the time."

Tears ran down Sung Kim's cheeks.

Grace Woods shook her head, then reached out and took the wreath and tripod out of Sung Kim's hands. "Stop crying, for heaven's sake. I know what it's like trying to keep him happy. I'll take this down to the study right now, before the president gets here. I'll set it up myself. I'll make sure the prime minister can't miss it."

FIFTY-NINE

Jesus Christ, Monk thought, over and over again.

It was unimaginable.

In every sense of the word, it was unimaginable.

On his hands and knees, on a conveyor belt moving underground in the direction of what he hoped would be the mansion, in a darkness so pro\found Monk couldn't even imagine the concept of sight, he hovered on the edge of panic, trying to do nothing more than keep from shrieking.

The pounding of his heart filled his ears. His body was rigid, frozen in place. His hands had turned into claws, his fingers clinging to the hard rubber fabric of the conveyor belt as it bore him farther and farther into the darkness. Although the tunnel had to be lined with concrete, he could almost feel the earth surrounding him. The tunnel wasn't ventilated, either, there was no reason it should be. Humans were never meant to ride this thing. Monk opened his mouth even wider, began to breathe even faster, to pant like a dog, and his brain was on fire.

I'm going to suffocate!

I'll be dead when they find me in here!

Suddenly he was dizzy, hyperventilating now. He had to stop gasping for air. Had to force his mind to think about something else. Had to keep himself from going crazy. He would pretend to be somewhere else. He would pull his mind out of this tomb.

Betty Clement's office.

He would go back to Betty's files.

One file in particular.

The informant report from a source inside the White House, the rumor about Japanese prime minister Ishii Nakamura's visit to Washington.

And what Nakamura would be coming to ask for.

Nakamura had been making headlines with his demands for the bomb he was certain would keep peace in the region. But his people were just as adamant about their revulsion for such an idea. With the prime minister out of the way, it might be decades before another Japanese leader asked for the same thing. Clearly the president was using Franklin to keep Nakamura at Battle Valley Farm—away from the media horde—until they could hammer out some kind of deal. Clearly neither party wanted such a critical meeting to turn into a circus.

And it had worked, Monk realized, so far at least.

He hadn't seen a word about Nakamura's visit in the newspapers, heard a word about it from the talking heads on television. But that would end when the president arrived, of course. Even the most powerful man on earth didn't have that kind of power. When Marine One lifted off the White House lawn, the press would go into action. When the big green chopper landed at the farm, they'd be close behind. They'd be . . . Monk's mind stopped dead.

When the president landed.

His brain processed the next step, but he couldn't accept it. Even the thought was ridiculous. He didn't know the results of his PET scan yet, but to believe he was looking at a presidential assassination would be clear-cut evidence of dementia. Nakamura was a monumental stretch, and the president was way over the top.

But what if it wasn't?

How did Bethany hope to get away with it?

She couldn't possibly escape afterward.

There wasn't a way in hell she could get through the combined security forces of two countries.

And Monk knew one thing for sure. She wasn't here to commit suicide. Sung Kim was a professional assassin. Her service to Kim Jong Il would continue long after this operation was over. Which meant she wouldn't actually be here when it happened. Which meant she was going to use a . . .

A chill enveloped Monk from head to toe.

Suddenly the belt stopped. The hammering in his chest got even worse.

They knew he was in here.

The Secret Service was waiting on the other end for him to come out.

But why did they stop the belt?

He began to crawl forward, his mind leaping closer to panic. He scrambled faster and faster, desperate to get out the tunnel, but hadn't gone more than a dozen yards when the belt started up again.

S I X T Y

After holing out on the last green, Franklin and the prime minister crossed the wide driveway dividing the golf course from the veranda at the southwest corner of the mansion, climbed the short steps to the veranda, and sat together at a large round table under a bright red umbrella. At six-thirty, the sun was low in the sky and the evening unusually cool. One of the assistant housekeepers hurried up. Franklin asked for a gin and tonic. With work still to do tonight, Nakamura wanted a soft drink.

"You have a beautiful home," Nakamura told him in English. Educated at Oxford, the prime minister's accent was decidedly British. "But your golf course is too tough for me."

Franklin forced a laugh. "For both of us today, I'm afraid."

They fell silent as the housekeeper came back with their drinks, but they began to chat when she went away. Golf talk—this shot and that shot, the joy of the good ones. Ten minutes later Franklin glanced at his watch.

"We better change out of our golf shoes," he said. "The president will be here shortly."

Nakamura nodded. They rose and went together to the locker room

off the veranda and changed shoes. On the way back out, Franklin heard
Marine One landing on the roof of the mansion.

"That's him now," he told Nakamura. "We'll wait for him in my study."

He led the way through the veranda to the wide doors leading into
the study, which looked out over the golf course. They moved past a half-
dozen Secret Service agents and Japanese bodyguards standing at the
doors as they went through into the study. Franklin almost bumped into
Grace Woods as she was coming out.

"Sorry, Mr. Franklin," she said. "I was just delivering the wreath."

She glanced back toward the interior of the study. Franklin followed
her eyes to the red and white flowers woven into the wreath hanging on a
tripod near the fireplace, the banner welcoming Nakamura.

"I hope that's where you wanted it," she said.

He looked at her. Where he wanted it? Why was she bothering him
with details he didn't give a damn about? Before he could tell her that,
Nakamura was standing at the wreath, bending to smell the carnations,
turning to Grace and smiling.

"They're beautiful. Thank you so much for bringing them."

Grace smiled as well. "You are most welcome, Mr. Prime Minister." She
turned and left the study.

"Let's sit, shall we?" Franklin said to Nakamura. He motioned toward
the green leather couch and chairs near the fireplace. "Why don't you take
the chair nearest the wreath. The president can sit in the other one when
he gets here."

Nakamura did so. Franklin sat on the couch. He stared at the prime
minister and felt his shoulders tighten. He glanced at his watch. The president would be here in a few minutes. Franklin would be told to disappear
while the two leaders talked. His back teeth began to grind. He wouldn't
even be in the room when the two of them fucked away everything he'd
spent his life to build.

SIXTY-ONE

"Well, that didn't take long, Mary Anne."

Steve Batcholder grinned as he walked over to Sung Kim's van, bent down so his face was looking directly into the window at her. "An awful lot of hassle," he added, "for such a short stay."

"You're telling me." Her smile matched his inch for inch. "But you know how the man is. He wants what he wants . . . and he wants it now."

"Tell me about it." Steve looked like he wanted to say more, but Sung Kim cut him short. "Sorry to rush off," she said, "but I've got another delivery halfway to Washington. Gotta keep moving."

He stepped back and touched his fingers to his forehead in a friendly salute. "Off with you, then." He grinned. "When will I see you again?"

"Soon," she said, then glanced back toward the mansion. "The way he is, could be tomorrow."

She reached for the window button and the window slid up. He gave a little wave, she waved back, then pulled past the gate, past the Secret Service people and the Japanese bodyguards who were still stopping vehicles on the road. In her rearview mirror, she saw Steve smiling as she accelerated away from the farm.

He was a nice guy, Sung Kim told herself. A nothing security guard who went out of his way to make her feel welcome. Steve would be the one who beat himself up the worst when he found out how wrong he'd been.

SIXTY-TWO

And then it was over.

The belt stopped and Monk felt the conveyor lifting him upward. He must be at the kitchen. Now he could hear voices. One much louder than the rest.

"Put your hands on top of your head!" the voice shouted. "Face away from the door while we open it!"

"I'm an FBI agent!" Monk yelled back. "I'm not armed! It's too tight in here to get my hands on my head! I can't turn around, either!"

"Then lie on your stomach! Put your hands out in front of you!"

Monk shouted even louder. "Get me *out* of here! There's a b—" Monk stopped. Not yet, he told himself. "Get me the hell out of here!"

"The door doesn't open until you're on your stomach!"

Monk laid out flat. "Okay, okay! My hands are in plain view! I'm not armed! I'm an FBI agent, for Christ's sake!"

The door slid upward, but only halfway. Monk was aware of eyes staring at him before it slid up the rest of the way. Suddenly there were hands on him, pulling him through the door, shoving him to the floor of the kitchen. The hands moved over his body, up and down his legs, emptying his pockets.

"He's not armed," a second voice said. "And he's not wearing any explosives."

"Where's the prime minister?" Monk asked, his voice muffled against the floor. "Where are Franklin and the president?"

A big hand pressed him harder against the floor. "What are you doing here?" the first voice demanded. "What the hell are you doing inside this dumbwaiter?"

"I'm an FBI agent!" Monk struggled to turn over. "Answer my question! Are they in the house?"

"You really think we'd tell you that? A real FBI agent would know better than to ask."

"God damn it, *answer* me! Where *are* they?"

Silence. Finally he was getting through to them.

But he was wrong.

"Cuff him," the first voice said. "We'll sort out the FBI stuff later."

Shit. Handcuffs. He couldn't allow that. Monk lifted his head as high as he could. *"Franklin!"* he bellowed at the top of his lungs. *"It's Puller Monk! I know you can hear me! I know what she's going to do!"*

Monk took a breath.

"I know you can hear me, Franklin! You can still stop this! It's not too late to stop her!"

The hand holding him to the floor disappeared.

Monk rolled over and stared at the Secret Service agents, half a dozen of them, standing over him with guns in their hands. Their eyes were wide with confusion. Faced with a madman, they had no idea what to do.

SIXTY-THREE

In the study, Franklin bolted straight up in his chair.

Monk was here.

In his house, shouting like a madman!

His eyes darted toward the president and the prime minister, who were both staring at him. She'd failed. Monk had survived.

It was over.

Then he glanced at the door and realized he could be wrong.

Why was Monk shouting?

Why wasn't he standing at the door with his arrest team?

"What's going on, Tom?" the president wanted to know. "What's all the shouting about?"

"It's nothing, Mr. President. Has to be a demonstrator . . . some kook who got past security. Your people will take care of him."

"Franklin!"

Somehow Monk's voice was even louder this time.

"You can't let her do this!"

Franklin rose to his feet. "I better look into it myself. I'm sorry for the intrusion, but I'll take care of this as quickly as possible."

He left the study before they could say anything, went out into the hall, then turned toward the kitchen, toward Monk's voice.

"I'm going to stand up," Monk told the agents in his command voice. Clipped. Brusque. Businesslike. Running the bluff of his life. "I will speak to Thomas Franklin when he gets here."

Now they were even more confused, looking at one another, then back at him as he rose quickly to his feet. He glanced past them, to the kitchen door.

"Goddammit, Franklin," he thundered. "I'm waiting!"

But he'd gone too far.

The largest of the agents stepped forward and grabbed his left arm. A second agent took the other one. They spun him around and jerked both arms behind him. He felt the hard bang of a handcuff against his wrist, but before it could be secured he heard Franklin's angry voice from the kitchen doorway.

"What the hell's going on here?"

The largest agent turned to face him. "Sorry, sir. We had a little problem with this guy. Says he's an FBI agent." The Secret Service man paused. "Sounds like he knows you . . . or thinks he does."

Franklin stared across the kitchen at Monk, made a show of looking him over before shaking his head. "An FBI agent? Anybody can say that. I've met a lot of them over the years, but I don't remember this one."

He turned to leave.

"She was here, Franklin," Monk said. "Sung Kim was here."

Franklin stopped, turned back.

"Sung Kim? Am I supposed to know what that means?"

"She came here to kill you. Pyongyang sent her to kill all of us. The president, the prime minister, all of us . . . everybody in this house."

"Pyongyang?" Franklin looked at the Secret Service people. "Do you have any idea what he's talking about?"

Monk's voice turned flat, as unemotional as he could make it. "She left a bomb, Franklin. She'll be gone by the time it goes off. Sung Kim will be halfway back to Washington when this house disappears."

Now the Secret Service people's eyes began to dart around the room. Suddenly everybody seemed to grow taller.

"Jesus, Mr. Franklin," the largest one said. "You *sure* you don't know this guy?"

"Goddammit, I'm telling you I don't!"

Franklin's voice was hard with authority, but Monk saw his eyes flicker. It was time to push the bluff.

"The helicopter thing didn't work, Franklin. I followed her here. I watched her prepare the bomb. I watched her put it in place." There was no point holding back now. "Take a look around wherever you and Nakamura are going to sit with the president. You'll see something that wasn't there before. Something that belongs, but wasn't there half an hour—"

"Get him out of here!" Franklin snapped. "The man's delusional. He belongs in a hospital."

"Think about it," Monk said. "Think about where Sung Kim would have put her bomb . . . where she would have put it to make sure she got all three of you."

"What are you waiting for?" Franklin shouted at the agents. "I told you to get this guy out of—"

His voice stopped.

He looked back in the direction of his study, and his body seemed to shudder. "Jesus Christ," he said. "Dear God."

He turned toward the kitchen door and bolted through it, shouting as he ran.

"*Get out!*" he roared. "*Get out of the house! Everybody get out of the house!*"

The Secret Service people dashed for the door, Monk close behind.

Everybody in the kitchen followed.

In the corridor, he saw the president and the Japanese prime minister being shoved by their guards toward the veranda. He sprinted harder to catch up as they ran across the veranda and onto the lawn. Now everyone was flailing toward the golf course.

Everyone, Monk noticed, but Franklin.

Monk paused to look back as he hit the edge of the course.

He saw Thomas Franklin standing on the veranda, looking at the rest of them when his house exploded.

SIXTY-FOUR

Suddenly Monk was flying.

The shock wave lifted him off his feet and hurled him forward. He seemed to be swimming through the air until he crashed to the turf and lay stunned in the grass.

A moment later—or maybe it was longer than that—he was able to lift his head.

He saw the president lying a few yards in front of him, a Secret Service agent sprawled next to his boss, one arm across the president's back, still trying to protect him. Monk looked to his right. Prime Minister Nakamura was already struggling to get to his feet, but a huge Japanese bodyguard was holding him down, speaking quietly to him in Japanese. Monk turned his attention back to the president. Now he was trying to get to his feet as well. Two Secret Service men tried to hold him down, but he shoved their arms aside.

Monk rose to his knees and fought off a wave of dizziness, then used his arms to push away from the grass and get on his feet.

Now there were loud voices, shouting, screaming, and people running toward them. He turned back toward the mansion. The veranda was gone.

Most of the south wing was gone. What remained was engulfed in flames fifty feet high.

Damn it, he thought. How many were still in there? His neck tightened with rage as he thought about the woman who'd done this, the woman who for damned sure *hadn't* been in the mansion when it exploded. And that she was getting away as he continued to stand here looking at the remnants of what she'd done.

He needed a car.

Monk saw that the Secret Service cars that had been parked closest to the south wing—only a few feet from the veranda in case of an emergency—had been hammered by the blast and now sat in flames. He looked to his right, toward the front of the mansion. Two of the black Ford sedans sat intact in the driveway. He started toward them, slowly at first, then running, then sprinting. The keys would be in the cars, he knew. It was standard procedure. When seconds counted, cars without keys were useless. A few moments later he was behind the wheel of the first one he came to.

He started the engine and jerked the gear lever into Drive. He couldn't go out the main gate, the Secret Service people out there were too well trained. They'd want to rush to the mansion, toward the explosion, but they wouldn't. They would stay where they were and seal the gate. No one would get in or out for hours. He had to find an alternate route.

The golf course was his best bet.

There had to be a separate service road into the course. A golf course required immense amounts of equipment and material, and there was no way all that stuff would be brought in through the main gate. There would be maintenance sheds as well, probably at the far end of the course, far enough away to keep them out of sight. The service road would lead from the sheds out to the road running past the farm itself, and there would be a gate in the fence to take care of that road.

Monk pulled his car out past the matching black Ford ahead, and as he did so he heard a voice behind him.

"Hey!" a man shouted. "*Hey!*"

In the rearview mirror he saw two men running toward him, guns drawn. He stomped on the accelerator, still watching. They were kneeling on one knee now, lifting their guns. In the next moment his back window exploded, and Monk heard what sounded like angry bees flying past his head. He scrunched down behind the wheel and kept going. He heard more bees, the loud pop-crack of automatic weapons. He turned right, onto the golf course, across the nearest fairway, then right again, in the direction of the fence at the far end of the course.

Hurtling across the turf, he came to a green and couldn't avoid it. A huge sand bunker loomed in front of him but he jerked the wheel hard enough to get past it. He heard a voice on the radio under the dashboard.

"All units," the voice said evenly, well trained to show no emotion. "Suspect on the golf course in one of our automobiles. Heading northwest."

Monk grabbed the microphone. He thought for a moment about identifying himself, telling them who he was and who he was going after, then realized he would just be wasting his time. There'd be another delay while they confirmed his identity, while they questioned him, while they fucked around until Sung Kim was gone forever. So he pushed the button on the mike and kept his voice just as calm as the one he'd heard.

"Suspect sighted," he said. "On the road heading for the main gate. All units respond to the main gate."

"Ten-four," the voice answered, then paused. "Unit calling, please identify yourself."

Monk continued to rocket across the course toward the fence he could now see in the distance. "Repeat," he said into the microphone. "Suspect entering road to main gate. All units, close in on main gate."

But the other voice wasn't buying it.

"All units stand by," it said. "Unit reporting suspect's position *identify* yourself." Then the calm vanished. "Who the hell *is* this?" A pause. "All units, suspect's using our radio! Disregard any voice you don't recognize!"

Monk flipped the microphone into the seat next to him. He hadn't gotten away with it for long, but maybe long enough. He was at the maintenance sheds now, bouncing over the undulating ground between the towering oaks and sycamores, weaving in and out of the bushes as he approached the blacktop service road leading from the sheds to the gate in the fence up ahead.

Swinging the Ford onto the road, he took dead aim at the center of the chain-link gate, then tromped on the gas. The big sedan jumped at the gate, struck with a tremendous crash. Bits and pieces of shattered metal flew toward the windshield as the gate collapsed. Monk recoiled, but the debris flew over the top of the car as he turned up the road toward State 15, heading for Maryland.

SIXTY-FIVE

Sung Kim was careful to obey the speed limit.

Three miles clear of the farm on State 15, she slowed to make the turn into a small road on her right. She drove down the road for a half mile before she saw the gray Lincoln sedan parked off to the side. She passed the Lincoln, pulled the Dodge van over and parked. Opening the door and sliding out, she didn't bother to take anything. There was nothing in the van that could lead anyone to her.

She walked back to the Lincoln. The driver nodded as she approached, then opened the door and got out of the car.

"It's ready?" she asked him.

"Of course," he said. Despite the fact that the man was Japanese, that every aspect of his ID and legend linked him directly to Tokyo, his English was perfect. "The plates are untraceable," he added. "The registration checks out perfectly."

"And the van?"

"By tonight there will be no evidence it ever existed."

Sung Kim nodded, went past him, and got into the Lincoln. She closed the door and watched the man as he walked to the van and climbed in behind the wheel. She started the engine and pulled up to the side of the Dodge, then reached across to the glove compartment and pulled out a small brown leather purse. She got out of the Lincoln and walked around to the driver's door of the van. The driver's eyebrows rose as he lowered his window.

"Did I forget something?" he asked.

Sung Kim moved up close to him, kept the purse down by the side of her leg where he couldn't see it. From the purse she withdrew a Sig Sauer nine-millimeter semiautomatic with an attached silencer. She kept it out of sight as long as possible before swinging it up and shooting him directly above the line of his eyes. The man seemed to stare at her for a moment before he fell to his right across the center console.

Sung Kim threw the gun into the seat next to him, closed the door and went back to the Lincoln. She glanced at her watch on the way, and as she did so she heard a tremendous explosion from the direction of the mansion. The Secret Service and the FBI would be on their way soon. They would find the Japanese man. Later they would find the Japanese fibers in the ammunition bunker.

It wouldn't hold up over time, of course, but it would create doubt. The conspiracy wackos would do the rest. No matter what facts the bureau came up with, the crazies would never believe them. The talk shows would keep the rumors alive for years. It would be decades before the Japanese recovered.

He didn't have long, Monk knew.

Back at the mansion the Secret Service would be dashing around in a state of confusion. They would have verified his identity by now, but they'd be unable to fathom why an FBI agent had broken into the golf course and popped out of the dumbwaiter. They'd be trying to figure out his confrontation with Thomas Franklin—and how his doing so had saved the president and the Japanese prime minister—but that didn't mean they'd stop coming after him.

And he had another problem as well. An even bigger one.

Weapons. He didn't have any.

He'd needed only his mouth with Franklin, but it would take more than words for the rest of this.

Monk reached for the telephone hanging on the dashboard and punched Lisa's cell phone number. He listened to it ring, then her voice asking him to leave a message. Damn it. He checked the clock in the dashboard. Seven-twenty. Could she still be at the office? He tried the phone at her desk. She answered after the first ring.

"Puller?" she asked before he could get a word out.

Hearing her voice, Monk's body sagged. He released a breath he wasn't even aware he was holding. Thank God, he heard himself murmur. Dear God, thank you. He hadn't believed for a moment that she was dead, he told himself, but suddenly he was so weak with relief he thought he might have to pull over to the side of the road.

"Puller?" she repeated. "Is that you?"

"I need you, Lisa. I need your help."

"Christ, Puller, what are you up to? I just came out of the assistant director's office. He wants to know what you're doing at Franklin's—"

"Not now!" Monk snapped. "Just listen!"

A brief pause. "What do you need? Where do you want me?"

SIXTY-SIX

He'd never make it in time.

Monk's leg ached with the pressure of his foot on the gas pedal, but the Ford just wasn't fast enough to make up for the head start Bethany had. And he didn't even know how big a head start that was. Best case, she'd managed to get out of Franklin's farm only a few minutes before the explosion. Worst case, she'd been gone half an hour before he even got there.

And it wasn't like he knew for certain where she was going, either. His best guess was just that, a guess. If he was wrong . . .

Monk told himself to shut up and drive.

He stared through the windshield as he raced south on State 15, thinking about the best way to get to Frederick, Maryland. There were no metropolitan areas between here and the airstrip, just this side of Frederick. At a hundred miles an hour he'd be there in twenty minutes. He thought about calling ahead, but the airstrip was not controlled, or it hadn't been the dozen or so times he'd been there with William and Bethany. There was no tower. Most likely there wouldn't be anyone around at all except the people who ran the gas pumps.

. . .

She couldn't get there without a red light and siren.

It had taken Lisa ten minutes to go to the gun vault on the third floor at WFO, grab a shotgun and a box of rifled slugs, and get down to the basement to her car.

Ten precious minutes.

In the garage, behind the wheel of her Grand Prix, she reached under the front seat and pulled out the magnetic red emergency light, then hopped out of the car and attached it with a heavy "chunk" to the roof. She fed the coiled black cord back through the window and plugged it into the cigarette lighter. She backed out of her parking space and raced to the exit. She pounded on the steering wheel as she waited for the gate to rise, before she zipped up the ramp and out into the street.

Lisa reached to a toggle switch under the dashboard and flipped the siren on, then did the best she could on the surface streets, darting from one lane to another, slipping in and out of traffic. Even so, she was rigid with frustration by the time she managed to get on the Interstate and head north toward Maryland.

He'd made a mistake, Monk realized.

Bethany wasn't coming here.

She wasn't going to use her airplane after all.

Parked at the edge of the airstrip property, hidden by a stand of oaks from the view of anyone near the gray metal hangers, he could see both the hangers and the tarmac taxiway that led out to the runway. There was no sign of her. He chewed on the inside of his cheek. No matter how slowly Bethany had driven, she had to be here by now. Maybe she was using a safe house instead. Maybe she was going to stay in Washington until she could be spirited away.

Monk's stomach began to hurt.

She wouldn't need much hiding, he admitted. She was a chameleon. In a matter of hours she'd be another person, a completely different woman. No one would even know where to start looking for her.

He reached for the cell phone to call Lisa. There was no longer any point in her breaking her neck to get here. But he hadn't punched in her number before he saw a gray Lincoln sedan pull up to one of the hangers, and a moment later Bethany get out of the car. There was no mistaking her long red hair and the way she walked. His muscles tightened. Despite the fact that he was unarmed, it took all his strength to keep from going after her. He finished dialing. Again Lisa answered after the first ring.

"She's here," Monk told her. "I need you . . . I need you right now."

"Ten minutes. Traffic's awful."

"Too long. She'll be gone by then."

"Get off the phone and let me drive."

He hung up and watched.

A few minutes later the big hanger doors swung open, and Monk could see the same blue and white Beechcraft Baron that Bethany used to fly. He saw her come out of the hanger carrying a long metal tool. She attached the tool to the nose of the plane and began to pull. The Baron rolled out of the hangar and when it was completely out on the taxiway, she detached the pulling tool and took it back into the hangar. When she came out, she went directly to the plane, stepped up on the wing, opened the door, and got into the cockpit. She had no luggage, no briefcase, nothing in her hands, as she closed the door behind her.

Monk looked around, hoping somehow that Lisa had been wrong about how long it would take her to get here. That she might show up early. But she didn't. Damn it. He was going to have to ram the plane to keep it on the ground.

Then he shook his head.

Ramming her with his car wouldn't work.

The Baron wouldn't be able to fly, but his Ford might very well be disabled as well. Bethany would climb down and shoot him dead. Then she'd use the Lincoln to escape.

Maybe he should call the cops. He could report her tail number. The police would put out a call to anywhere she might land. But again he shook his head. There was just no point. By the time he got the cops to understand what he was telling them, made them believe what he was telling them, she'd be three hundred miles away. Landing at any one of a hundred dinky private airstrips like this one. Before he could get anybody organized to go after her, she'd be on the ground again, this time in another state and on her way to Canada. She'd have resources across the border. Bethany Randall would cease to exist, but that didn't mean the woman herself would. Sooner or later she'd surface again. A world leader would die, then another, and another.

Monk thought about William's investigation, about what he'd called the *ipyanghan.*

There could be another American-born assassin in Washington already, another sleeper standing by for orders once Sung Kim set up shop elsewhere.

Suddenly he heard the sound of ignition from the Baron and saw the propellers of the starboard engine begin to turn, to spin faster and faster until they were a blurring roar. Then the port engine fired up. Monk's legs began to twitch. The engines would be warm in another minute. Bethany would taxi out to the runway. Monk reached for the phone to call Lisa again, but realized there was no point. She was already coming as fast as she could. The Baron began to taxi toward the head of the runway. Monk started the Ford.

He would have to ram the plane after all.

SIXTY-SEVEN

He'd have to wreck the plane and take his chances afterward.

Bethany was at the top of the runway now. He could hear her running up the engines, testing first one then the other, spinning them to maximum thrust as she checked the oil pressure and vacuum systems. He turned to look for Lisa, saw nothing, then pulled the gear lever into Drive and started toward the Baron. A hundred yards later, he heard the honk of a car horn.

He turned to see Lisa's Grand Prix racing toward him, skidding to a stop next to his car. Monk jumped out and dashed to her. She lowered her window as he arrived.

"Shotgun's in the back seat!" she shouted.

He yanked the door open and grabbed the Remington twelve-gauge from the seat.

"Rifled slugs!" she yelled. "Five in the clip, one in the chamber!"

Shotgun in hand, Monk sprinted to the runway.

Bethany was already on her way, the Baron hurtling toward him.

Damn it!

She was going to take off before he could get a shot at her!

Monk fell to one knee. The Baron's twin engines were screaming as the plane bore down on him. He could see Bethany's face in the cockpit, staring at him, before the plane lifted into the air.

Monk snapped the Remington to his shoulder. As the Baron passed over his head, he aimed at the bottom of the tail assembly and pulled the trigger.

The Remington kicked like a horse, but he held it fast and racked the action to put another rifled slug into the chamber, then tracked the Baron as it continued over his head. He fired again, four more times, racking the action, pulling the trigger. Saving the last round just in case. Making sure that if he needed it, he wouldn't be caught with an empty weapon.

But the Baron just kept going.

Monk stared at it. He couldn't have missed, not five times.

In the next moment it came back down. Bounced once on the tarmac, then bounced a second time before settling to the ground.

He started after it, then realized what he was doing and fell to the tarmac in a prone position, making himself the smallest possible target.

But Bethany wasn't stopping.

He heard the engines revving up again, saw the Baron leap toward the grassy verge at the end of the runway, toward the woods beyond the grass.

He saw instantly what she was trying to do.

She was heading toward the woods. She would leave the Baron and try to escape into the trees.

Monk jumped to his feet, turned toward Lisa, but she was already on her way to him. He turned back toward the Baron. The plane was on the grass already. He saw the cockpit door opening just as Lisa pulled up. He jerked the car door open and threw himself inside as Lisa trampled the accelerator. The Grand Prix shot toward the Baron as Bethany jumped off the wing and ran toward the trees.

Seconds later the Pontiac flew across the grass and skidded to a stop just short of the woods. Monk jumped out, the Remington in his hand. Bethany was twenty yards ahead of him, but he was close enough now.

"Stop!" he bellowed. *"Stop or I'll shoot you!"*

But she didn't stop . . . not for a few more paces at least . . . when she wheeled to face Monk, her arm swinging around in one motion, the pistol in her hand aiming directly at his head.

Monk yanked the Remington to his shoulder and fired.

The recoil rocked him back on his heels. Bethany rose from the ground and hurtled backward into the tree behind her and seemed to hang there for a moment before sliding to the dirt.

A moment later, Lisa was at Monk's side.

Together they walked toward the body.

Bethany lay on the ground at the base of the tree. There was a hole the size of a dinner plate squarely in the center of the long-sleeved blue and white shirt she was wearing, just below the name "Mary Anne," written in black script above her right breast. Her long red hair was flung above her head against the tree, and her luminous green eyes stared at a point somewhere over Monk's left shoulder.

In the distance Monk heard sirens coming their way. Beside him, Lisa's voice sounded just as far off.

"Bethany?" she said. "Bethany Randall?"

She stared at the body before turning back to Monk.

"I don't understand . . ." she began, then stopped for a moment before starting over. "What in the name of God just happened here?" She paused again. "Who *is* this? What . . . ?" She ran out of words.

Monk looked at her, then took Lisa's arm and led her back toward the Baron. The sirens were louder now. The people in those cars would have questions, too, lots of questions he wasn't about to answer until he'd talked with the people who'd be regulating the flow of information about this.

In the meantime, Monk held tighter to Lisa and got ready to lie.

SIXTY-EIGHT

Another funeral, Monk thought.

Although this didn't really look like one.

No church this time. No music. No real mourners.

Just he and Lisa, in this lonely corner of Arlington National Cemetery, and two guys from NSA. Nobody Monk had ever seen or heard of. Blue-suited automatons assigned to see William into the ground. One listening to the preacher, the other's eyes everywhere at once, looking for God knew what. The enemy was dead. Bethany had already been buried, he'd seen it with his own eyes, when he said goodbye to the woman who in the end had been nothing more than a victim herself. An infant ripped away from her parents and brought up to a life of hatred.

"Please take the soul of William Smith," the rail-thin preacher said. "Bear him into your presence, and give him peace."

Peace. At least William had a chance for that now. For the rest of us, Monk thought, well, we know better, don't we? There would never be peace again, not while half the world had no interest in such a thing. Not while the hatred continued to grow, and organizations like Division 39 continued to flourish.

Monk glanced at Lisa and she squeezed his hand. He'd almost lost her,

Monk knew, in a couple of different ways, but now they would repair the damage the last few weeks had done. Her ex-fiancé from Texas had come to his senses and quit stalking her, but that wasn't the only reason to celebrate. Monk patted the breast pocket of his charcoal suit jacket. He would keep the results of his PET scan next to his body until he got completely used to the good news.

The bad news was that the country was in a state of shock. If the terrorists could attack the president of the United States, everyone was saying, then no place in America was safe. The media exploited the hysteria. An outrage . . . another failure of our intelligence agencies . . . heads must roll . . . no stone unturned . . . no rest for anyone until the guilty are brought to justice. That kind of thing.

And the media didn't know the half of it.

As was so often the case, the truth had been carefully hidden away. Even Monk's masters at the Hoover Building didn't know the whole story.

Which was going to be a problem, he knew, and he couldn't help but appreciate the paradox: that by succeeding he'd guaranteed his own failure.

Even though he'd stopped the unthinkable, he'd failed to carry out his bureau assignment. Even though he'd saved the president and the prime minister, unmasked and eliminated North Korea's deadliest sleeper assassin, he'd failed to recover not only the *Madonna*, but the rest of the stolen masterpieces in Franklin's secret vault as well. If the missing paintings had been in the south wing of Franklin's mansion, they'd been reduced to atoms in the explosion. If Bethany had removed them prior to that time, it could be a hundred years before they turned up again. And no matter which scenario proved correct, Monk couldn't tell the Hoover Building even one word about his involvement.

The president had made that pretty damned clear.

For reasons of national security—for the good of the nuclear weapons pact with Japan—the truth about Battle Valley Farm and its billionaire owner would never see the headlines. Thomas Franklin had avoided public disgrace, as had the president for becoming so close to such a man. It wasn't the first time Monk had seen such a trade-off, but he felt no outrage. The president was nothing more than another victim, and even in a democracy the public did not have an unlimited right to know. And the

FBI didn't either. Until the White House was certain there were no leaks at the Hoover Building, no one at Ninth and Pennsylvania would know the whole truth, either.

Monk's gaze dropped to William's grave. The cemetery workers had arrived and were in the process of lowering the casket into the ground. Monk found himself wishing he could say something to William before the man who was once a friend disappeared forever. Bethany was good at her job, he wanted to say, she was a good sleeper in every sense of the word. You never had a chance against her. Franklin didn't, either, and I would have been next. *If I hadn't been walking around lucky, I'd be in the grave right next to yours.*

Again he felt Lisa's hand squeezing his. He looked at her, and as he did so Monk noticed something else.

On the street beyond the headstones, a black limo was approaching. As it slowed, the rear window opened, and Monk saw a face appear. He nodded as he recognized the most important face in Washington. The president inclined his head as well, before the window slid back up and the limo moved on.

EPILOGUE

Could life get any better? Cho Li wondered.

In the long shadows of the late afternoon sun, Rome had never looked more stunning, or the Piazza di Spagna more dramatic. Even the pigeons looked happier in the cozy glow, and the dazzling beauty of the flowers cascading down the Spanish Steps—the reds and yellows, purples and golds—was positively heart-stopping. For a girl who'd just turned eighteen, it was almost too much to bear.

Sitting with her parents at an outdoor table at the Caffè Greco, the girl who'd been born in Denver as Jennifer Browning gazed past the thicket of green umbrellas covering the tables to a young couple stopping at the Fontana di Trevi to add their wishful coins to the countless others. Cho Li smiled at them, then checked out the throng of tourists meandering through the piazza. She listened for a moment to the excited voices, then reached across the table and touched her adopted mother's hand.

"What's wrong, Mom?" Cho Li asked. "Why do you look so sad?"

ACKNOWLEDGMENTS

A novel is conceived in the author's imagination, but it doesn't have a chance to make it to the light of day without lots of help. Listing the names of those who contributed to this one is small payment indeed, but here goes anyway.

Lee Johnson read the earliest version of the story and helped get it started in a better direction, and Gayle Kehrli added her own insight near the end of the project. Thanks to Mike Stafford and Ira Gourvitz, for the gift of unflagging support every writer should enjoy, and Dean Moore, for helping me see Monk's world through different eyes. From the FBI, former Special Agents Clyde Fuller and George Fox, and current Special Agents Gayle Jacobs and Kurt Swann, provided many of the details that found their way into the story. Former Secret Service Presidential Detail Chief Michael Endicott took time from the writing of his own book to help out. Ernie Choi shared his knowledge of the Korean language, and Bill Scott did the same thing with his expertise as both a fixed-wing and helicopter pilot. Pathologist Dr. Bob Keefe knows why people die, and what it takes to kill them.

The insight of Dr. George Pratt, Chairman of the Department of Psychology at Scripps Memorial Hospital, La Jolla, California, was invaluable in the process of deepening and enriching my understanding of Puller Monk, as well as helping me get a better handle on the creative process itself. Thanks also to Dr. Gregory McFadden of the Psychiatric Centers of San Diego for his suggestions that led to new ideas.

From St. Martin's Press, my supurb editor Marc Resnick not only kept the story going in the right direction, but did it far more tactfully than I would have been able to manage. I'm also grateful for the extraordinary amount of attention this project got from St. Martin's publishers Sally Richardson, Matthew Shear, and John Cunningham, and marketing director Matthew Baldacci.

My literary agents, Jean Naggar and Jennifer Weltz, continue to extend my readership into parts of the world I would never have believed possible. Jerry Kalajian, my Hollywood agent, makes sure my work gets into the right hands at the right time, and his former assistant, Bryon Schreckengost, never failed to brighten my day. In San Diego, my great friend and fellow author Ken Kuhlken is always there when the going gets murky.

I would also like to acknowledge my debt to Frederick and Steven Barthelme's *Double Down: Reflections on Gambling and Loss*, a riveting account of two intellectuals and their misadventures in gaming.

My daughter, Brenda Lewis, was a huge part of making this story come to life for me, and my son, Matthew Riehl, is a tireless supporter of my work.

But most of all I thank my wife, Diane Martin Riehl. Her keen eye for the essence of a scene, of a chapter, or indeed the entire novel, helped turn an idea into a full-blown story. I couldn't have done it without her.